JOSEPH CONNOLLY

STYLE

Quercus

First published in Great Britain in 2015 by

Quercus Editions Ltd
55 Baker Street
7th Floor, South Block
London W1U 8EW

A CIP catalogue record for this book is available
from the British Library

HB ISBN 9781848666283
TPB ISBN 9781848666290
EBOOK ISBN 9781848666306

10 9 8 7 6 5 4 3 2 1

Typeset by Hewer Text UK Ltd, Edinburgh

Printed and bound in Great Britain by Clays Ltd, St Ives plc

To Jon Riley

THE OBJECT OF DESIRE

The day I didn't kill a man. But saved a woman. Possibly. Such spare statements may be making my life sound to you to be most sinfully . . . oh, I don't know – exciting, even frightening, or something . . . but it isn't. Either thing. It isn't at all. Wish it were, I suppose. Sometimes. Which is why, oh – so very occasionally, I find myself doing such things. I was on a bus. Of all things. Top deck. For of course had I not been, it never would have happened. Well – it would have happened, because the rest of the cast, the other two, they both were there, of course . . . but just not to me . . . it wouldn't have happened to me, that's all I'm saying: some other wide-eyed unfortunate who just wandered up there instead. Up the winding stair to the top deck of this bloody bus. And that's another rather singular aspect actually, now I come to think about it: the very fact that I was there at all . . . because I honestly can't, you know – I cannot remember the last time I took a bus anywhere. I either drive, or take a taxi. The Tube . . . oh Christ, the Underground, can't even remember when last I was on the Underground. Never did care for it – well, who does? But I don't have to use it any more . . . and so I don't. I daresay, given a choice in the

1

matter, many would behave in precisely the same way. So I'm lucky in some respects.

It was late – rather late. One in the morning – that sort of time. And I had been waiting for a cab to come cruising by me for Jesus, how long? I craved the welcome, the warmth, of that little orange glowing light – a beacon of heaven, in late-night London. The app on my phone, that didn't seem to be working, some damn reason, so that was no good. Wasn't drunk – had a bit, but not too bad. Not cold, it wasn't a cold night, but then it started to rain – and won't it always, times like this? Drizzle at first – not even that, hardly more than a surrounding dampness . . . and then it started putting its back into it all right. Didn't have a coat, or anything. An umbrella – never carry an umbrella. The bus was there, so I got on it. Actually had no idea they ran so late, and certainly not in my direction – but I suppose they would, wouldn't they? Have to, really. Automatically went upstairs – just to be the furthest away from everything I could get, think that was the thinking. If there was thinking. And wishing it was one of the old Routemasters – because all these newer ones, they just don't cut it, do they really? The Routemaster, well – just about perfection that was, so of course it just had to be scrapped. Well naturally – like anything else that's at all decent in this bloody world. Design, you see, it is very important to me – my life, you might say, so I do feel these things most acutely. I didn't look around when I got up to the top deck. You don't, in London. Look about you. First thing you learn. True of everywhere these days, I suppose. But I was struck by the aspect of a woman sitting quite still, and pretty close to the front. She just seemed so incredibly old. Her eyes quite colourless and opaque, the skin like fine and lined translucent paper . . . you felt that if you

2

touched – which, believe me, I was so very far from inclined to – it might just dull and crumble into powder . . . which, yes, one would be horrified to inhale. And I simply thought – what on earth is so ancient a lady doing on the top of a bus at gone one o'clock in the morning? And how ever did she make the stairs, come to that. So that's all I noticed, really. The extent of my observation. There were a few other people further down the bus, that much I was fleetingly aware of – didn't look, though, didn't count . . . but not many, two or three – four, maybe, at the most: the bus was far from full.

I had been to the sort of dinner, black-tie affair, that you agree to months in advance on the grounds that so very distant a date can never actually arrive – though even as you are tapping out your bright acceptance, you just know that the steady, then inexorable approach of the appointed evening will become increasingly lowering, its prospect more and more oppressive . . . until, days before, it looms over just everything you touch or think of, and simply you are dreading it: amazed at your having agreed to go in the first place, and wondering if maybe it's still not too late to back out of it . . .? Flu, or something. Have to be away from London: out of the blue – beyond my control: sorry, so desperately sorry. The thought of being at home instead of having to go through the whole business of bathing, wrestling with the bow tie, fooling with the cummerbund . . . it becomes just so glitteringly alluring: almost glamorous, the sprawling luxury of nothing to do – of just not having to be at the bloody dinner. But I went. Obviously. And while it was by no means as appalling as by now I had built it up to be (the claret was decent, and that always goes a long way to help things out, I find) nor was it the most scintillating. And finally, at the petered-out end of it, I was so very pleased to be

3

away, and baffled as always as to why it is that the dullest evenings always seem to last the longest.

I had been sitting in the bus for, well, hardly any time at all really . . . and then I heard it – just a shift, no more, in the general mumble behind me . . . maybe some physical movement: the merest squeak of consternation, is what I became aware of. And until that moment, I think my mind had been as blank as ever is possible: simply I had been concentrating intently upon the shiver of globular raindrops on the window, lit up momentarily by the glare of a fleeting shopfront, then glumly succumbing to grey. Halfway home, more or less. Or as near to home as the bus was going to get me. But had I been there already – had it been my stop, this one here, the one at which now we appeared to have very briefly paused, engine juddering, the doors downstairs hissing open, hissing shut – then I should have got off. With no curiosity, and nor a moment's hesitation. Would not have looked behind me, would certainly not have given the ancient woman at the front another glance – indeed, already I had forgotten her existence. I just would have got off, and reconnected with the things that concern me. The bus, though, trundled on, and I did nothing. There were more strange shiftings behind me – a young girl's voice, quite muffled, or maybe it was mutely shrill, and then the rumble of a thick and deeper one, which now quite suddenly grew a good deal louder, and was sliced by menace. I had craned my head around in advance of deciding whether or not to do any such thing . . . only two people there then, not three or more as I thought had been possible . . . and instantly I was shocked as my eyes were locked with those of the man staring hard and right back at me . . . my stomach simply fell away, and I felt a rush of cold that made me light-headed and stopped up my throat. For I am no sort of a hero. Why I will avoid situations

4

such as these, if ever I can. And I remembered of course that it was just this sort of thing, or the threat of it, that had led me to abandon for ever any form of public transport: it's the public, you see – that's the bloody trouble with it.

'Everything all right, is it . . .?'

Who said that . . .? Jesus. It was me.

The girl said: 'All right. Yeh. It's all right.'

The man said: 'What the fuck it got to do with you . . .?'

And I tried to smile briefly at the girl – hoping that she might feel considerably more reassured than I did – avoiding the aura of the man completely. The shiny thing she was wearing appeared to be ripped – merest hint of something fairly lacy beneath. Turned back around then quickly. Faced the front. And waited. Because there was going to be more. Wasn't there?

'You hear me, or what? Ay? I say what the fuck it got to do with you . . .?'

Sat there. Just sat there. Willing my neck to swallow my head.

'I got to come over there, do I . . .?'

'Leave it, Nathan. Leave it alone.'

'Shut your fucking mouth, slag. I talking to my friend here. He talk to me first, don't he? So I answers him. But now he don't want to talk to me no more.'

'Fuck's sake, Nathan . . .'

'I won't tell you again, girl. You want a fucking slap, or what?'

And me . . .? Sitting, just sitting. Pretty much decided to get off this bus at the very next stop. Wondering why I hadn't yet gone downstairs. Resolving now that I would. But then the man, his face was hanging there above me. It resembled a pie – glazed and crusty, with occasional slitting.

'Come down the back, mate. Have a little chat, ay? You and me.'

'I'm fine . . .'

'Yeh? You fine, is you? That nice. Come on – get up. Do it. Now.'

'Nathan – just leave him alone, can't you . . .?'

And then he was gone from my sight, and I heard one hell of a crack and she was gasping, the girl, and when I turned around again, she had begun to cry: trying not to though, and biting her lip. Pretty girl, I imagined, beneath all the make-up. And that's when I did this most amazing thing. Feeling quite calm as I was walking towards him . . . the girl, she looked up at me fearfully – fearful for whom, I could not say. Me, presumably – for she, she, poor deluded and stupid little creature, she had been here many times before. Her cheek and jaw were mottled with a spreading redness, her eyes quite glassy and alert.

'Here he come! Here come my mate! All got up in his little dicky bow, look. James fucking Bond, or something. That what you reckon, mate? Nice watch you got there . . .'

'Mm. Cartier Tank. Classic. You like it?'

'I do. And I'll have it off of you, you fucker.'

And I even laughed quite lightly. I felt, now – charged. Really rather excited.

'No. No – I don't think so.'

He was standing now. Taller than me – a thing I hate. It's not that I'm short or anything. Don't have any sort of a complex – nothing like that. Just don't like it, that's all – people being taller than me. Silly thing, but there it is.

'Yeh well I do think so, you cunt. You give it over here, fucker. Else I bloody kill you.'

'*Please*, Nathan . . .! Oh shit. Oh Christ . . .'

'Fuck off out of it, Hayley. Telling you. Now listen, mate – you going to give it me, nice and easy? Or I going to fucking take it off of you?'

'Neither thing, I'm afraid. But look – tell you what: I'll give you this instead . . .'

And then: the golden moment. I had been trying to defer it, I suppose – tease out the sweetness of all that was coming . . . and yet at the same time I was so much yearning to see this cretin's stopped and colourless face. But had I drawn things out for even a moment longer, he was going to put his fist in my face, I simply knew it: you just had to look at the bunch of his fingers – they were getting ready for it. So I slipped it out from the inside of my jacket: this beautiful thing – and then, as his eyes were widening, I pressed the barrel against his forehead. And so here, out in the open and in all its dark and austere glory, was my Luger, my authentic German wartime Luger, complete with a gold embossed swastika to the base of its grip. One of the finest designs ever, in my opinion: it felt so right in my hand . . . and just take one look at its effect, won't you? The man's mouth, it hung wide open and wetly, and the eyes . . . they had died within his skull. He sat down the moment I told him to, and still I was pressing the barrel hard into his brow. The girl was plainly terrified, which I hadn't intended – but it was inevitable really, I suppose. Necessary fallout.

'Apologise to the lady,' I said quite calmly.

He blinked.

'You fucking *what* . . .?'

'You heard me. You were rude to the lady. You hit her. Apologise.'

'No – it all right, mister. Really – all right . . .'

'Well no, it isn't actually – Hayley, is it? Hayley, yes. Far from

7

all right. You don't seem a bad sort of a kid – why do you want to even know such a person as this? He's scum, isn't he? Scum.'

'Who the fuck you calling *scum*, you fucking ponce . . .?!'

'You. Of course you. Now I tell you what's going to happen. At the next stop, you get off. I'm being kind, don't know why. I ought to call the police, but I daresay they're sick of the sight of you by now. And oh look . . . did you hear that? Someone downstairs has just rung the bell. So get up now – because you're leaving.'

'Fuck *off* . . .!'

And then I withdrew the Luger, and struck him hard across the face with it. The resulting and instant spatter of blood was so immensely gratifying, I just can't tell you.

'*Bastard* . . .!'

'Leave him alone! Leave him alone! You're mental, you are . . .!'

'And now you protect him, Hayley. Oh well. I expect you are programmed. Inured. You get off too. Fed up with both of you, now. If you don't leave, I shall shoot you both dead. Please do believe me.'

They got up – he looking what I expect he imagined to be daggers, she just weeping energetically. I waggled the barrel in the direction of the stairs. In addition to the caking blood across his face, I noticed with extreme pleasure a perfect white circle on the bloody oaf's forehead, where the gun had left its mark.

'You wait! You just bloody wait, you cunt! This ain't over . . .!'

'Second-hand dialogue. Fourth-rate moron. Get off the bus. Now.'

And he swore a lot more, and so did she. They clattered downstairs and shouted to the driver that he got a loony up there and he wants calling up the Bill. Then they were gone. I

8

can't remember when last I had felt so just utterly and completely wonderful. I walked to the front of the bus – watched them splattering through the heavy rain – his arms were flailing about as he was dumbly roaring. She would be in for it, poor Hayley: he'd take it out on her, he'd be bound to. So I hadn't saved a woman. Soon, it came to my stop. I realised only as I turned to leave that all this had been happening while I had been standing directly next to the ancient lady, the Luger still in my hand and just inches from her profile. She did not move at all: she registered nothing. I wondered idly whether she might be dead.

There had been no bullets in the Luger: no, it wasn't loaded. So I couldn't have killed a man. I only very recently had come across it, the gun, in the most extraordinary circumstances imaginable – could hardly believe my impossibly good fortune. Because the Luger, here is a landmark design, you see – I have always wanted to own one. I don't really care that it's a gun: to me it is simply a perfect object. Of desire. The only reason I had it on me is that whenever I acquire a new item, well then initially I simply cannot bear to be parted from the thing. I pat it from time to time – whenever I can be on my own, in the lavatory say, I look at it, feel it. Most people, I imagine, will find this quite hard to understand: why long ago I ceased even to try to explain, and now I never even would think to mention it. A couple of weeks earlier it had been a 1950s Parker 51 fountain pen in the rather rare burgundy and gold combination . . . and on this day, it just happened to be my Luger. But it was just as well though, wasn't it, that Nathan the thug had failed to rise to such an audacious challenge. Otherwise, well . . . who knows what might have happened . . .? And afterwards, I was ready for the adrenalin to desert me – I was waiting for my knees to sag, my tongue to go dry, my heart to hurt as it thudded within me . . . but no: nothing. Nothing at all like that. The sensation of pleasure and power, they took a very long time to seep away from me, and I missed it sorely, when eventually it was gone: that feeling.

I have them now, though. Bullets. Three clips. Yes. Because I do like a thing to be complete. Got them on the internet, the dark side, in a very roundabout manner: all a bit of a rigmarole, strung out over how many months. My name is Terence, by the way.

CHAPTER ONE

I MIGHT BE HAPPY

Want to tell you this story, I really think I'd like to. To get your opinion – a brand-new take on the thing. There aren't many people I can really talk to. I'm sure you're going to agree with me immediately, I really am positive you will. And I think you could well be affected by this – it will touch you as a human being, and particularly so if you are a woman, if you are a mother . . . but either way, you are sure to be interested. Because here is something that affects us all . . . it's all about how I came to be happy, quite simply . . . though of course there is one man, there had to be, who tries – still he is trying – to spoil it for everybody. And it has all come about, the blossoming of my happiness, through this huge and very gratifying success which suddenly – after years of his trying so terribly terribly hard – has come to my son. My son, yes – Alexander. Mm – but just exactly as it all was happening for him, on the very day that my boy, he first had the limelight . . . well then my husband Terence, Alexander's father, he called me cruel. His word – his very word. And to my face. He says – he still says it – that I have hurt the boy. Damaged him. Can you believe this? I mean, I know you still are unaware of the ins and outs, the details and intricacies of how all of this has come about – well that's what I'm here to tell you – but even from the little I've so far let you in on, tell me, honestly – can you really believe such a thing? Can you? That I, Alexander's mother – I, who loves him, loves that young man with a passion that sometimes can leave me just perfectly breathless . . . I who loves him, yes, so far and away above and beyond, oh – anyone and anything else on God's green earth . . . that I could ever think of (I can barely bring myself to say it) . . . *damaging* him . . .? That I could find it within myself to be *cruel* to the boy . . .? It is unthinkable – and cruel of my husband, if you want to know what I think: it is he who is cruel, even to say to me such a thing. And he is wrong. Quite wrong. Let that be completely understood right at the outset. Well of course he is wrong. He has it all the other way about. For I have given everything, selflessly devoted all that there was of my life to doing all I could to ensure for Alexander a bright and maybe, yes – even dizzying future. And that is wrong, is it? That is a bad thing for a loving mother to do for her only son, is that what you think? Simply to make sure that the world, the whole wide world will now know of his brilliance. This is *cruel* . . .? This is hurting the boy? *Damaging* him . . .? Please. I hardly think so.

'But Amy . . . you don't understand. It's the long term. Isn't it? You – you're just seeing the here and now. The bright lights. The money.'

This is Terence, of course. The husband. This is how he talks to me. This is how now I am addressed. He sees, he is aware of – he must do, he must be – the gleam of delight so deep within my eyes. He might even perceive my trembling, which is quite beyond all control, aglow with excitement as I am with all that has at long last happened. But there – this is how he talks to me. This is how now I am addressed.

12

'The money is his.' And I say that very drily.

'I know. I didn't mean that you're . . .'

'I don't get any of the money, do I? It's not my money, is it? Is it, Terence? The salary he earns, it's his and his alone. I'm seeing none of it. Not a penny. Don't want it. Wouldn't touch it even if he offered. It's not about the money – it was never about the money. How can you even suggest—?'

'No – I'm not, Amy. Of course I'm not. Nothing like that. Not what I mean at all, is it? It's just that . . .'

'Well what? *What* is it, Terence, actually? Now that you have spoilt simply everything – now that my moment is shattered, shattered completely – well then we might as well hear it from you, mightn't we? Have it out. Once and for all. *What* is it? What exactly is it that you are so convinced is *wrong* . . .?'

'Oh Amy . . . I can't. Can't talk to you when you get like this.'

'You can't? I see. So now you can't talk to me.'

'Can't, no. No point. Is there? Not when you're like this.'

'Happy, you mean? You mean when I'm happy? When finally I have broken through all of the . . . oh God, there are no words for . . . now that I have overcome all of the *worry* . . .? The constant anxiety about the future in this world, this world that has become so very very . . . *hard* . . .? When Alexander now finally has a *life*. A young man with a wonderful life? And all that I've had to live through, all that you've put me through over so many bloody years . . . now that that might just possibly be over, and maybe now I, even I, could enjoy just a tiny bit of contentment, some ease of mind for once in my life? Is that how I am? Is it? Is that why you can't talk to me . . .? Because I might be happy? Is it, Terence? Answer me, please.'

Well no. Not what I mean. She knows it's not what I mean. But there has to be blame, you see – blame for anyone not immediately swept up into her fantasy come true. You yourself might well be the next to suffer, but for now of course, still it's me, just me – well naturally it's me – I'm the one who's lumbered with shouldering it wholly. Look: she's a good woman, a good enough woman, Amy – not saying she isn't. Loves Alexander, course she does – never doubted that for a moment, no one ever would. But she's become obsessed, you see. Is the trouble with it. It's . . . you see, all this, it's taken her over, taken over the whole of the household.

And Alexander – he's no fool, he sees it as well, of course he does. Wouldn't say anything, though. And now, well – now, now after all her work, her striving, if you like . . . her dedication, her completely blinkered and monomaniacal attitude . . . and make no mistake, this has been going on for, God – how long . . .? Well now, she can't be anything but blinded by everything that has just so suddenly occurred. Overnight, more or less. I mean . . . in one way, I'm very pleased for her: she put in the work, and she got what she wanted. More, maybe, than even she could have expected . . . and so she deserves the success, of course she does. As does Alexander. Slogging away all the hours of the day and night, sometimes, it was seeming. CVs, interviews, auditions . . . what I am told by Amy were the right sort of parties. Single-minded, that's how you've got to be. And if ever he was flagging . . . well then Amy, she stepped up and became single-minded on his behalf. So, then . . . success all round. If that's what it is. In any larger sense. But now for Amy, you see – well, there's nothing else. Nothing else at all that she can see any more. The house – well that's gone to buggery. I sometimes push the Hoover around a bit, but I've got my own job to see to, which I think she might have forgotten about, somewhere along the way. Ready meals . . . eat a lot of them.

Because me, well – can't remember the last time she even bothered to enquire how I might be feeling. She maybe doesn't think I have any – feelings. Or Lizzie – even Lizzie, come to that. Sometimes it's as if she's even forgotten she's got a daughter at all – which is just so totally extraordinary, because she's an utter wonder, my Lizzie: truly a beautiful innocent. I hope, anyway, that still she is that, after everything she is put through as a result of all of this ridiculous Alexander business. Love her, always have – I would kill for that child . . . well of course I would. Literally, if needs be. There would be my massive committal of sin, the sin of the father, should anyone ever dream to harm her – if in any sort of afterlife one is truly to be condemned for simply the righting of so terrible a wrong. Not, alas, that such an enormity as that ever could be even approximately righted: merely one would coldly exact the ultimate toll. For one can only ever be the inadequate agency, the bringer of a vengeance, though one that surely must wholly be justifiable in the eyes of any god at all who still can see.

But in Amy's eyes, it's just Alexander – her every waking thought . . . and no doubt she dreams of him as well. Always has been like that, really, since the day he was born. And I love him too, course I do – love the lad, of course I do . . . but I can't help thinking that this, all this . . . at his time of life . . . it just maybe isn't the right thing for him. You know? Well look, let's face it: there's really no 'maybe' about it, is there? It's wrong, this: plain wrong.

And still it gives me quite a shock – still a jolt, I can tell you: I maybe won't ever get used to it. You open a paper, you open a magazine – and there he is. That face, so very familiar to me, and yet it's different, somehow. The lighting, maybe. Make-up. All the women they surround him with. He was on a news

15

programme the other night. No warning – just popped up on the screen right in front of my eyes. That roguish smile he's got (Amy says the camera loves him) . . . because yes, he's a good-looking young man, no doubts on that score. And the clothes he has – all the clothes and things they all, all the big firms, seem to be fighting to shower upon him . . . well, he wears them well, I'm not saying he doesn't. Still and all, though – he's no bloody Cary Grant. Is he? Let's be fair. Even if they are now talking about putting him in a movie, if you can believe it. But you wouldn't know it from the fuss they're making. And yes, okay . . . style . . . he does have a certain style about him, I think that much comes over – something I've always aspired to myself, of course, though I'm not too sure that I have thoroughly achieved it. But to be a model, a model on a catwalk, a model in . . . what do they call them . . .? Photoshoots, or whatever . . . is that really such a wonderful thing? Well in this day and age, it surely does seem to be. Why do they give him so much money? I simply can't understand it. Why, in God's name, do they give him all that money? In just the last month, he's had bookings, Amy was telling me, that are worth more than I've managed to pull in over the last four years. Where's the justifi-cation in that? Hysterical, isn't it? And I don't mean in the funny sense, I don't mean that at all. Although if I weren't involved, I do think I might be laughing my bloody head off, in a bit of a crazy way. But the world, I don't know . . . it does seem to be in the grip of some sort of collective hysteria, and the worst of it is, it's contagious. The trivial . . . it's all people seem to be able to think about, even if they don't understand what is actually happening (and usually it's nothing, nothing at all).

People you wouldn't dream of – suddenly they've fallen for it. Even the couple next door – ordinary people, Sylvia and

Mike, older than us, been here since the year we first arrived, known Alexander all his life, more or less . . . but now, when he comes home (and he's on the road so bloody much all of a sudden, flying here, there and everywhere, it's not nearly as often as it was) you can see in their eyes that they're looking at him differently. They're in awe of him, you can tell it. Of Alexander! In awe of Alexander – can you believe it? Yes well they are – because they open a paper, they open a magazine, and there he is. They probably saw him on the sodding news programme. And now we're on to that – well why was he? Hey? On a news programme? Hey? Yes well – now we come to it, don't we? I think we all know the answer to that one. Well – you maybe don't. You don't, possibly, because you don't yet know the whole of it. But it's you and Amy, you're the only ones left who don't yet see it. And as for Amy, well . . . she genuinely seems to believe that the boy's got some sort of a talent, or something. Star quality. She actually did say that to me, one time not too long ago. 'Our Alexander – it's star quality, that's what he's got. That's what they've seen in him.' Yes – and she said it in all seriousness, you know, no sense of having a bit of a lark. Her eyes . . . oh my God, I don't think I'll ever forget it, that look in her eyes. They were ablaze, is the best way I can . . . can't really explain, it's very hard to quite explain it, exactly what I saw there . . . but it was a sort of . . . evangelism, for want of a better word. Zeal, you might call it. Sometimes . . . well sometimes, she gets close to psychotic, you ask me to be frank with you. But all he really is, when you just stop and look at it, is a model. A pretty boy. A wearer of clothes. Amy, she says I'm jealous. Consumed with it, she says I am. Rubbish. Like so much else she comes out with, these days. Not jealous. Stupid thing to say. But the attention he gets? All the to-do? So much bloody

17

money . . .? The latest freak in the increasingly grotesque freak show that the entire world has now become. So not star quality, is it? No, I wouldn't really put it down to that. More the fact, don't you think, that come next birthday, Alexander is ten years old.

'You heard about Alex, have you? Christ Al-bleeding-mighty . . .'

'Huh . . .?'

'Alex. Alex. You know the latest, does you?'

'What you on about? Alex . . .? Who's Alex, then?'

'Bleeding hell, Damien . . .! What's wrong with you? Ay? Alex. Alexander. Terry and Amy's boy, yeh?'

'Oh yeh, right. With you.'

'Like – them what's supposed to be our bestest friends, I do not think. Their, like – *son* . . .?'

'Yeh yeh, got you. Okay, Dolly. Don't have to go on.'

'Yeh well with you, Damien . . . with you, yeh? I maybe do. Got to. Go on. You know? I don't know if it's you don't hear or you just don't sort of like listen to me, yeh . . .? What it is . . .'

'Yeh well I'm listening now. Aren't I? So what about him?'

'Ay . . .?'

'Alex.'

'Oh yeh.'

'Well what about him, then?'

'Yeh well I don't know if I can even like *say* it, you know? Makes me so fucking sick. And Amy – oh Christ. What she going to be like now? Bad enough before . . .'

'Dolly. Listen to me, girl. What you on about? Only I'm trying to concentrate here, aren't I? You got something to say, bleeding say it. Else let me get on, yeh?'

'Concentrate . . .? That what you said? That is what you said, isn't it, Damien?'

'Oh Christ . . .'

'No but you did. Didn't you? Ay? That you got to, like – concentrate? Concentrate – yeh *right* . . .! What on, Damien? What bloody kid's game you got on the iPhone this time? Ay? What bleeding waste of time you up to now? Go on – tell us.'

'Not, is it? Kid's game. You got to concentrate. Advanced, this is. All I'm saying . . . Christ . . .'

'Yeh well put it down for a minute, can't you? All the time you staring at that thing. Your bleeding thumbs all over it all the bleeding time. Just put it down, can't you, Damien? Once in your life. Listen to what I got to say.'

'Well *say* it then Dolly, Christ's sake. You been going on and on and you ain't bleeding said nothing, have you?'

'Yeh well . . . he only gone and got a part in a bleeding movie. That's all.'

'What? Alex? Alex going to be in a movie? Blimey. That's something, isn't it? I thought it were wossname what he done.'

'Yeh well he do. The modelling. Can't move for seeing his bloody little face all over. But now it's a fucking movie, you believe it. Amy – she'll be on to me. Down the phone. Amazing she ain't already. I got this off of *Heat*, about the movie. Saving it up, I expect she is. Before she, like . . . I don't know – hit me with it. Jammy cow . . .'

'What sort of a movie? What – action movie, is it?'

'How the bloody hell do I know what sort of a movie it is? It never said. And what you mean "action movie" . . .? He ain't going to be in no action bleeding movie, is he? He ain't bloody

19

Arnie, is he? He ain't going to be James fucking Bond, is he? The bleeding little brat – he ten years old . . .!'

'Yeh. Milky Bar Kid, maybe.'

'Don't be so daft, Damien. That's a, like – wossname, ain't it? Ad off of the telly. Not a movie, is it? Milky Bar Kid . . .! Prat . . .'

'So . . . is that it . . .?'

'What you mean – is that it? Enough, ain't it? Christ. How am I supposed to . . .?'

'No I mean – you said what you going to say, have you? Yeh? No more? I can get back now, can I? You done, are you?'

'How can I . . .? No listen to me, Damien . . . it's, like – really important, this is. What I want to know is, how am I supposed to, like . . . keep up with all of this? Can't, can I?'

'Well no you can't. We done this, haven't we? Flogged it to death, this one. They just lucky, Terry and Amy is. That's all. They just lucky people.'

'Don't I bleeding know it. Don't think I can stand it no more . . . I can't, Damien – I mean it. See . . . I never minded when we first, like – met up, sort of thing. That she were posh on account of some sort of flash private school and bit of Daddy's money, shouldn't wonder. I never minded all of that . . .'

'Public school. That's what they called. Not private. Public, yeh.'

'Yeh but it's the same thing, isn't it? Public. Private. It's all the same bloody thing. Yeh but never mind that. What I mean is – it been all, like, different, course it has, since Alex . . . well, since he started being in all the magazines, and that. I mean – look at our Kenny. He ain't never going to be in no magazines, is he?'

'How can it be the same, then . . .? How can it? Can't, can it?'

'What? What, Damien? You mind telling me what you on about now, Gawd's sake?'

'Public and private. Can't be the same, can they? They're wossnames, them two words is.'

'Look. It don't matter about all that. All right? That's not . . . Christ – that's not what I'm talking about, is it? What's *wrong* with you, Damien . . .? Actually?'

'Opposites, yeah. Opposites, they are. Public and private. So they can't be the same. Stands to reason. Not if they're opposites they can't.'

'How many fucking *times* . . .? I'm not talking, am I . . .? I not *talking* about the school what she went to no more. I done that. Said I never minded that. What I talking about is that now she going to have even more money, isn't she? More respect. And me, I'm in hock up to my tits as it is with all I got to do so I can so much as hold up my head whenever I sees her. But now . . . Jesus bleeding Christ. She'll be buying all the real thing now, she will. All them fake Guccis what she got – not going to be good enough for her no more. She and me, we won't be going up the markets no more. That lovely little knock-off Vuitton what she got the last one of – beauty, it is. Yeh well – she won't want that no more. Be going to bleeding Bond Street now. You just watch her. Not Catford. Not no more. Not now. Not Dalston. Not up Petticoat Lane – ooh no, not now, not for Lady Amy. Bleeding Bond Street – that's where she'll be going, sod her.'

'Well maybe she give it you . . .'

'You joking? You, like – having a laugh, are you Damien? Her knock-off Vuitton, you mean? I wouldn't touch it. What you take me for?'

'You always said it were a gem. Wanted to claw her eyes out when she got it, you said. Been trying to find another one . . . ain't that what you was telling me?'

'Yeh but I don't want one *now*, do I? Not *now*. What's wrong with you, Damien? What're men always like this for? You do it on purpose, do you? Or you just bleeding stupid?'

'Christ, Dolly – it's you what wants looking at. You're the bleeding crazy one. You want something – you don't want something. You up – you down. Can't keep on the top of it, I can't. And anyway – our Kenny, he's a good lad, Kenny is . . .'

'I'm not saying . . .'

'Don't have to be no model . . .'

'I know, Damien . . . I know that, but . . .'

'Poncey, being a model. If you a bloke. Don't have to be in no movie neither.'

'Christ, Damien – I know, I know . . .'

'Useful little footballer, Kenny is. Solid defence. Handy in goal. Pretty tasty little all-rounder.'

'Yeh I know . . . I know all that, Damien . . . but he ain't never going to be no *footballer*, is he? Not, like – proper. He ain't never going to be in no premier league, is what I saying. He ain't never going to be the face of this and the face of that and get given a bloody great Rolex. We ain't never going to be looking at Becks and Posh, are we? Ay? Nothing real classy like that. Got to face the facts. Hundred grand a week . . .? Don't hardly think so . . .'

'No well – and nor he ain't going to get hisself nailed by some fucking slapper what's just after his money and flogging the story to the Sunday papers neither. What – you saying you want that for him, do you?'

'No . . . course I don't. Well . . . depends . . .'

'I can't make you out, Dolly. Hand on heart, half the time I don't know what you're about. Why you always caring so much about what *other* people is doing? What other people got. We doing all right. Aren't we? Hey? We ain't doing so bad. Why can't you never be happy with that?'

22

'Because . . . I want more. Course I do. That's not a bad thing, is it? You show me where it says it's a bad thing to want to better yourself. Wanting more. For your family. It's only natural.'

'Nothing to do with the bleeding family, Dolly – and well you know it. What's going into hock for getting them things stuck all over your fingernails got to do with the *family*? Or when you gets seen to downstairs with the wax and that? And that tattoo what you had done – nothing to do with no one else, was it? Hey?'

'No it weren't. That were personal. Whole point of a tatt, isn't it? It's a statement. It's all about who you are *inside* . . .'

'Who you are inside . . .? Who you are inside . . .? You're Dolly – that's who you bleeding are inside. And anyway – it's on the bleeding outside, your tattoo, isn't it? You dozy cow. You ain't Popeye the bleeding Sailorman – you're Dolly. So what you want to go and get a tattoo for?'

'Because it's different, isn't it? It's something what only you got on your body. And it's no big deal – not now it ain't. Everyone's got one, everyone I know. It's beautiful, my tattoo is. Art – that's what it is. Thinking of getting another one, now you come to mention it.'

'You can't see the one you got.'

'I can if I look in the mirror, can't I?'

'What you want to be looking at your arse in a bleeding mirror for? Ay? It's me, Dolly – I'm the only one what ever see it. I'm the one what's got to be looking at it all the time. You go to the bog and what I see is your bum there and then a bloody great vulture on the top of it.'

'What you *talking* about . . .? It's a bleeding dove of peace, you fucking twat . . .!'

'Yeh? Well it look more like a bloody vulture to me, tell you that girl.'

23

'Oh yeh and what do you know? What – you're like all of a sudden an expert, are you? You – you don't know nothing about nothing. Your whole trouble, Damien.'

Yeh well: not his whole trouble, no. Part of it, yeh sure – but if I were going to go into the *whole* of his trouble, Christ . . . be here all night. But don't get me wrong – I ain't saying he a bad person, or anything. He ain't a wrong un, nor nothing like that. He done good by me, I got to say. We been together coming up ten year now. Ten bleeding year: blimey. Ups and downs along the way, of course. Yeh – that's one way of putting it. Was times when I never thought we'd make it, if I'm honest. Were no time before Kenny come along, and we was both a bit gobsmacked, you know? Only been with him, Damien, couple months, not even that. Never thought it would happen, really – never give it no thought at all. Damien, he'd bung on a wossname, course, but sometimes he never bother. Yeh and then I were ever so sick, see, and I get a testing kit off of the internet and it come up positive and he say yeh well that don't mean nothing so I gets another one in Boots and that come up positive and all, and Damien, he go yeh well they just rubbish, them things, ain't they? So I goes to see a doctor up the clinic and he say yeh, you up the duff all right. And Damien, then he say to me, 'Well what you want to do, then, girl?' and I goes to him, 'What you mean what do I want to do?' Yeh – and he's, like 'You *know* . . .' And I'm like 'No I don't bloody *know*, Damien. Actually. As it hap- pens. What you on about?' And he says, 'Well . . . you want to get rid of it, or what . . .?' And I just sort of looks at him, you know? I just stand there and sort of looks at him and I says I Do Not Believe I Am Hearing This, Okay . . .?!' And then he don't say nothing after that.

We wasn't even living together, not then we wasn't. He were

still with his mum, you can believe it, and me, I had that little room up over the bread shop. Liked it there. Cosy, it were. Small, you know? Right small. But I'm small and all, petite is what I am, straight size 10 now . . . 8, if I bleeding starves myself, so that were all right. It were the bread shop what I worked in. I weren't like a baker nor nothing – just like only serving, sort of thing. It were Mr Adams what owns it who says there a room going begging. So I has it. Ever so cheap it were – just as well and all, because Mr Adams, I can tell you – he were ever so free with his Chelsea buns and cottage loaves – his teacakes and his baps, oh yeh. Take an armful come the end of the day. I give them to Damien – he wolf them down like a pig. I didn't want to get to be no fat cow, so I leave him to it. Yeh but Mr Adams, he weren't so keen on paying out too much money though, were he? Oh no. I just had to be on minimum wage. Would've been less, he had anything to do with it. But I had the room – and it were all-in with the electrics and that, and you don't really need that much, do you? Not when you's on your own, you don't. But then out the blue I got a baby on the way, and Damien, well – he weren't doing so good hisself in them days. MOT tests is what he were up to. Yeh but the garage what he work in, well it his now innit? That chuffed, he were. I remember when he sign all the papers, and that – got so bleeding pissed up the Queen's, he come home and I just leaves him on the floor there.

But he work hard for it, my Damien, give him his due. His mum, she sub him quite a few quid, and he save up a good bit (was saving every bleeding penny – we never went nowhere, not never) and then he get a fucking great loan from the bank. Interest and repayment's a right bleeding bugger, but what you going to do? Weren't for the interest and them repayments, I reckon we be millionaires. And the garage – Magic Motors is

25

what he call it, and that's really good, I think – it's up the end of this mews, see, in ever such a posh sort of an area. Damien, he reckons he got it at a knock-down price on account of the old geezer what had it before what was his boss, he let it go something chronic what with the roof and the rot and all and when he die of brain cancer or something it were in bleeding terrible nick, even worse than what he were, and his kids, yeh, they all wanted the money, like – *now*, you know? Seemed a fucking fortune to me though, and it still do, yeh. It the only building in the mews what ain't been all ponced up into a sort of little Buckingham Palace or something, but there's still room over the top of it for the three of us to live, see . . . yeh and that's how we come to be round here. Never afford it otherwise, not round here, not in a million year. Ever so posh it is, round here. Not like where I were brung up round Hackney. My mum, she done her best, poor old cow – dinner lady she were, lollipop lady and all. My dad, he were just a bastard. So then now we's living all right, Damien and me. Not too bad, you know? So I has Kenny up the hospital, and he weren't no trouble nor nothing: shoot out like a bullet from a wossname. Bleeding terror of a nighttime, but I weren't to know nothing about all of that. Never tell you. Do they? All of that side of it. Blimey, months and years of that I had – yeh and Damien, he in bed and snoring his fucking head off. 'I got to work in the morning,' he'd go. Yeh right. Because me in the morning, I were off on a bleeding world cruise, weren't I?

And it never bothered me that Damien and me, we wasn't formally, you know, married and that. Never worried me, God's honest truth. Yeh and then it did. All them other mums, yeh, when I gone and picked up Kenny from his primary . . . they all had a ring on them. So then I had too, yeh . . . but it weren't

26

from Damien. I got it in Argos. Rolled gold, whatever that is. Can't be much, because it were dirt cheap in the sale, if I'm honest. It were them mums, see, what had an effect on me. That were the beginning of it all, really. That what Damien said, yeh, and he were right – he were right, Damien, when he said it. I never see it at the time, but it were true what he were saying – they did, them mums . . . they really, like . . . got to me? Bit by bit, you know? Not just on account of they was married, of course – but I see the cars what they got, and all what they was wearing. So I thought I start dressing up a bit. Couldn't do the car thing – nah, couldn't run to that. Damien, he do up the most amazing motors in his garage – Astons, Beemers, Rollers, Mercs, you name it – but all we got is a beat-up Twingo. So I think to myself: okay then, I'll see what I can do to pimp myself up a bit. Daft I felt, really – getting all dolled up to go and fetch a bleeding kid out of his primary. Yeh . . . but then it hit me, see? I didn't have nothing to get dolled up in, did I? Couple of bits from Primark, this and that out of Topshop and BHS, my Levi's and that. Can't hardly believe it now, way I used to go about. Bag lady weren't in it. But some of them mums . . . bloody hell. Yeh well like Amy, of course. How we first come to talking, matter of fact.

'Like your *bag* . . .'

Yeh – that's the first thing what she ever say to me, Amy. Won't never forget it on account of it were only the second day I been toting it about: shoving it in people's faces, I were – right over the moon when I got it. Yeh cos couple days before that, when I come up the primary I were bringing with me my Waitrose Bag for Life on account of it roomy and I'd seen with all of the mums it were one of the ones it were okay to have slung on your arm, because often as not I stop off at Lidl on my way to pick up Kenny and get in some mince and eggs and Hula Hoops and Kit Kats and beans, all of the basics – and Kenny, he like his Coco Pop Croco Copters which cost a bomb and so does Fruit Shoots, but Cheese Strings, they ain't so bad, and I stuffs all of that in my Waitrose Bag for Life what I got when I gone in there one time for this pack of Essentials bog roll cos it's just as cheap as anywhere else, you know, and so's some of the ready meals if you goes when they're on Sell By date and they mark them down really pretty good and then I get in a couple on account of Damien, he go big on the lasagne and the chicken vindaloo, now they ain't none of them got horse in no more.

But then one day I got to go up Dalston, yeh, because Damien, he wanting this bleeding spanner, wrench or something, and so it muggins here what's traipsing off to what Damien, he say is a like specialist for all them sort of doings and getting it for him because he in the garage, right? And me – like, I got nothing to do never, yeh? You don't got a proper job like working in a shop or a office or something, and men, I dunno . . . they think you got your feet up and swigging down a brew all day long like the Queen of bleeding wossname.

Anyhow, I gets his fucking spanner for him (and he's wrote it all down, what it were, where I were meant to go and that – cos Dalston, ain't never been there before) and I were on my way back to the Twingo when I sees in a market there all of them bananas going ever so cheap and they was banging out a pineapple for fifty pee, and I'd never had none of that, not what didn't come in sort of chunks and syrup, like. So I has one of them – and then I sees these handbags and purses piled up on another stall there. Well – just the two or three of them was out, if I'm honest, but there's like lots of cardboard boxes underneath in them big kind of tartan plastic laundry bags and the two blokes what was running all of the doings, Pakis looked like, needn't of been I suppose, they was ever so edgy, you take my meaning. Sucking on a fag and looking about them, this way and that. Anyway, there were this sort of, I dunno – barrel-shaped, you might call it, sort of a bag thing there what I did like the look of, and it brown and sort of mustardy like, and it got all of this LV all over it – but I knowed nothing back then. Now – these days, yeh? Bleeding expert, I am. Ain't nothing I don't know about all the designers and labels . . . but back then, like I say, I knowed nothing about nothing, really speaking. Well wet behind the wossname, that were me. And I remember thinking it were VL – that's what it looked like to me: never knowed what it stood for, not till later when I Googles it. But I seen them in the magazines – *Take a Break* for starters – and all sorts of women, the really classy ones, the ones what I really do admire, you know? Victoria, Cheryl, Chantal, Tamara – all of them, they got these. Well – they got the lot, of course. I don't grudge them it – they deserve it, I reckon, cos they wonderful, really. But I wouldn't mind it, all they got. But these sort of bags I'd seen on them . . . yeh but not for a bit, though. Even then they wasn't no more the thing – but what did I know? Now, course, wouldn't be seen dead with it: like, so last decade, you know? Bit like Tweeting. I don't never Tweet no more, but I were no good at it anyhow: either too many what-is-it, letters yeh? Or else I got nothing to say about nothing.

So anyway, I says to one of the Paki geezers, I says how much then. He go, 'Yes yes lady, very nice, very pretty, very good price' – you know how they go on in that bloody voice they got. And I'm like – yeh yeh, all right, how much then? And he's like, 'For you, lady – forty pound.' And I'm like, 'Forty *pound* . . .? You just fell out your tree, or what? Do I look like I got "fucking

29

dipstick" wrote all over my face or something . . .? Do us a favour.' And I turn round and he shouting twenty at me and I sort of hang about, then. 'Twenty . . .? Here's a tenner,' I goes to him. Don't know where I got the bollocks, you want me to be honest. I think . . . what I think it were, looking back . . . it come because I weren't too bothered, you know? If I gets it or if I don't. So anyway – bung him fifteen quid in the end: he happy, I'm happy, and that's it. And then – yeh, I remember this – he go to wrap it in a scruffy bit of *Daily Star* and I says, 'Whoa mate, hoy, no – get all muck on it in that, it will.' So he stuff it in a all-creased-up Asda carrier and I bungs that in my Waitrose Bag for Life and I'm hoping that Asda bag, it didn't have no fish in nor nothing.

And when she says it, Amy – 'like your *bag* . . .' – there was a sort of a bit of a laugh going on there, I reckoned. And I weren't having that. I weren't having none of that, was I? She hadn't done what she done next and I would've gone and clocked her, straight I would. Cos I weren't having none of that. But what she done, yeh, she show me her Dior – never knowed that what it were at the time, yeh but after I gone and Googled that and all. Pink sort of shoulder bag it were with the leather tassel on the zipper and all of them gold sort of dangly bits hanging down off of it – and she say to me, 'Dalston . . .? And I really do laugh at that and I says, '*Yeah* . . .!' cos I thought it were really right funny, that, really broke me up it did. And then Amy's like why don't we get a coffee or something and I'm like how can we go and have a coffee if we got to pick up our kids and she go no no no, tomorrow – tomorrow we can both of us get here a little bit early, and then go off to Costa or somewhere. And I says, yeh okay – I'm Dolly, by the way. And she go, Dolly, what a sweet name. Sweet name, yeh that's what she said. And I'm like, yeh well it Dorothy really, but I always been called Dolly, you know? Since I were little. And she go, it sweet, I like it: I'm Amy, Dolly. And I says, yeh? Well all right, then. So yeh – that were the start of it.

And the next day, we done what she say. But blimey, though – I were in a right old state before it, tell you that for nothing. Like – what were I going to put on for this thing then, ay? All the mums that season, see, they was into boots – just below the knee, brown the most of them, some with a cuff at the top and all of them got this what I now know they calling a Cuban heel, right? Amy were – she were wearing boots what were like that when first I talks to her, yeh? And a sort of a drapey coat she had on her and all: Zara, shouldn't wonder. Never heard of Zara back then, of course. Go there quite a bit, now I do – nice if you wanting a more classy sort of a look, a sort of Chanel or a Ferragamo sort of a look, you know? Jaeger – they good and all, but only at the end of the sales, of course. And M&S, they can still do the business – you just got to avoid the patterns, that's all: the patterns, they always a right dead giveaway. Anyway – back to then, yeh? Well the thing was, I didn't have no boots. I had some poxy wellingtons with bleeding daisies all over them (no, don't ask – don't know what come over me) – yeh but brown leather with a little Cuban heel . . .? Puh-*lease*: not hardly likely, is it? And I thought well I know what I can do: I can drop off Kenny real early like, when none of the mums is got there yet (yeh – and especially Amy) and then I can go up Brent Cross maybe and buy myself some boots. Yeh but I never had the money for no boots, did I? So like a bloody sap, the night before I goes to Damien and I says to him – Damien, there something I want, yeh? So can you give me hundred quid? And he's like – hundred quid . . .? Sure that going to be enough, girl? Don't

31

want you going short, do we? What about a grand – that do you? Tell you what, let's not fuck about, ay? Take a million – sweet to be on the safe side.

Yeh well it's not so funny actually, is it? Shouldn't have to be going to him in the first place, should I? Begging. Cap in wossname. Quite miss my little job in the bread shop sometimes I do. It weren't much what Mr Adams give me, but at least it were mine, weren't it? To do what I wanted with.

'No come on Damien – don't be a prat. Give us the money, can't you? I know you got it. Garage is doing good – said so yourself. Ain't often, is it? I'm asking you for something?'

'Hundred quid . . .? It's a lot. What's it for?'

'Don't matter, do it? What it's for. Just need it, that's all. What's wrong with you, Damien? I don't go asking you what you go spending your money on, do I?'

'No well that cos you bloody well sitting in it, aren't you? Ay? This house. What – you think it pay for itself, do you? Ay? There's the mortgage for a start, isn't there?'

'Yeh, Damien. I know about the mortgage. Every day I get told about the bleeding mortgage . . .'

'Yeh well. And that ain't the half of it. Rates – they gone up again. Money what I gives you for the housekeeping. Electrics – all of that.'

'Yeh I know. I know that Damien, don't I? But I need it, see? I wouldn't ask, would I? If I didn't need it.'

'Yeh but need it for what? Ay? What's it for?'

'Bleeding hell, Damien . . .! You going to give it me or what?'

'No I ain't, you put it like that. Not if I don't know what it's for, I ain't.'

'Yeh . . .?'

'Yeh.'

'Well sod you then, Damien . . .!'

'Fine.'

'Right, then. *Fine* . . .!'

Yeh. So that were that fucked, basically.

Don't know what I look like in the end. Well I do – course I do. Won't never forget – but I want to, like . . . blank it out my mind? Go bright red if I thinks of it. And when we was in Costa, Amy and me . . . yeh well it only get a whole lot bleeding worse, don't it? Look – all I can say, yeh, is that it were couple year back, all of this got to of been, and I really come on a lot since then. Different person ain't in it – just so like you wouldn't believe? There a lot of places what you can have a coffee in up our High Street – all the places what ain't selling coffee is selling phones and clothes. We got The Kooples and Mango and French Connection and Gap what I used to go to but I don't never bother with it now and Whistles and Nicole Farhi (I wish . . .!) and then all of them estate agents, course. Someone were telling me they was reading in the local paper, what I don't never see, couldn't even tell you the name of it – well, never see no papers at all, if I being total honest with you. Damien, he buy the *Sun* for the Page 3 tits. He say it for the football, but it ain't: it for the Page 3 tits. I say to him it pathetic, that what it is Damien, it just pathetic, and he say I don't understand nothing on account of I'm a woman. Round and round is what you goes with Damien. What he want to go looking at tits in a paper for? Ay? He don't never look at mine, do he? No he bleeding don't. And they real. Anyway . . . they was saying, whoever it were, that they read in the local paper no one what's like independent can get a shop up the High Street no more because the most of them is owned by the council and whenever one come up they bungs a rent on it what would make you cry, you was the tenant – and them estate agents, they just goes and snaps it up. Or the coffee shops. Or the clothes shops. Or the phone shops – all of them lot, yeh? Amazing, ain't it really though? They must just be selling their coffee and clothes and phones and houses all day bleeding long.

Thing about me back in them days though – and you going to laugh, I just know you going to have a right big fat old laugh about this one – is that I never been in one, not never in my life. Them coffee shops, what I meaning. Tea are what I like. And at home we goes through a ton of PG Tips, no I ain't joking. But even tea, I never had one when I were out, not unless, well – could be I were in Greggs getting us a pasty if I couldn't be arsed preparing no dinner, or maybe up Debenhams or something and my feet was chronic on account of the stupid bloody shoes what I always wearing (fool to myself, yeh – but what you going to do?). And even that – even Debenhams, yeh? I think of it so different, now. Old days, I be there for a couple towels, could be. Got a corkscrew there one time, I remember – dunno why: we never drunk wine nor nothing, but it were ever so cheap in the sales, that corkscrew. Now we does, we drink wine now, yeh, anyone come over, but I still don't never get to use my corkscrew cos it all twisty tops now, ain't it? I don't mind a Chardonnay with bit lemonade; Damien, he'll have Jacob's Creek, but red wine, it go right to my head. Now though, it the designers, ain't it? At Debenhams. You got John Rocha, what look like a girly Eskimo, you ever see him. And Jasper Conran, who do a nice line in smart casual, and I telling you – they bangs them out for nothing in the sales. Most people, they don't know the label, it just what they calling his diffusion line because they don't write Debenhams on it nor nothing so it nice to have one of his coats what you can sling somewhere like if you at a party or you gone over to someone's and if you fold it proper they

34

can all have a look at the label – and that, yeh I ain't denying: it do make me feel good.

I lost my fred. Weren't Debenhams I were on about, were it? No. Amy . . . that's what I were . . . oh yeh! I got it. First time we gone out to that Costa. Yeh – that were what I were going to say: all of them places, they was new to me, see? So we in there, right, and Amy, she walk up the counter and she like going to me, 'So what you having, Dolly?' Well, I weren't so stupid as to say I'll have a nice cup of tea, that all right with you: I weren't so bleeding stupid as that. So I says, 'Coffee, please. Ta.' And she go, 'Yes – but what . . .?' I'm like – oh my God this is just so like *embarrassing* . . .! – I'm like, 'What what? What you mean? Coffee, I said.' And she like, 'Yeh I know but I'm having a macchiato – you okay with that? Or cappuccino? Latte? Americano . . .?' And I go, 'Yeh.' And she go, 'Yeh what?' And I go, 'Yeh, what you said: that first one what you said.' See? Told you. Back then, it make me cry. For myself, really speaking. I knowed nothing about nothing – or not all of the stuff what's important, anyway. Nowadays I be after a skinny frappuccino, no messing about.

And even back in them days, she did talk big, Amy did. Always know what she were about, all what she were wanting. Alex – she talk about Alex before we even gets to sitting down at the bloody table.

'I think it's quite a good school. Don't you? The ratings are reasonably tolerable. Alexander seems to be happy there, anyway. It's hardly my ideal, of course, but it'll do for now. Well it has to – no choice in the matter, just at the moment. But it's later, isn't it? That one really wants somewhere rather, er . . . better. Is Kenny your only child, Dolly? It is Kenny, isn't it? My goodness . . . what a lot of sugar you take . . .'

'Kenny, yeh. Oh God yeh – he's it. Never had another one. Wouldn't go through all that lot again. Not for all the tea in wossname. Never got no kip for best part of three year. Right bleeding terror. Yeh . . . I do got a bit of a sweet, um . . . And what about you? You got more kids, has you? Tooth, yeh. Bit of a sweet tooth, me.'

'Just one more. I have a daughter, Elizabeth. Lizzie, we call her. She's a few years older. But it's Alexander – he, I think, is the one with all the potential. Oh God – please, you must promise me you won't ever tell Lizzie I said that . . .! But he's just so terribly good-looking, Alexander – wouldn't you say so? People often do remark on it.'

Didn't know what to say. What you say – thing like that? I were eating a muffin. Blueberry muffin. Can't hardly believe I'd go and snarf down one of them things – it about five hundred calories, or something. Quarter your daily recommended wossname. Yeh – I gone on like that, I be like a balloon, I would. Size 12 I were in them days – yeh, size 12 going on 14. So I got Amy to thank for it, really. It were her what put me right – about that, yeh, and a whole lot else and all. And she – she were ever so slim. Still are, of course. She say she rather be in agony than go eating. She say she rather die than be fat like some women what you see about. She say how can they stand it? She say how can they do that to their own bodies? She say why don't they all want to just kill theirselves? One time she tell me she go to her doctor, yeh, on account she got this sort of a pain, okay, deep down in her gut, see – and the doc, he go, 'You a drinker? You drink, do you? Have a drink with your lunch, with your dinner . . .?' and she's like, 'Drink with my lunch and my dinner . . .? I don't even *eat* with my lunch and my dinner . . .!' She say it like it were a joke, yeh sure . . . but the truth of it is I don't really never know, not with Amy. You ever gives her a steak, she go and eat the parsley off the top of it. We's ever meeting of a lunchtime, I'm in Greggs half hour before, get myself round a sausage bake so when we in Maison Blanc I can be arsing about with a bit of lettuce and a bit of fish like what she do and say no to all of them lovely cakes, and that. I better now, but couple year back I would of cleared the bloody trolley. She a size 8. Look more like a 10 to me, but Amy, she say she a size 8.

'Can't say I noticed, really speaking. I mean – I ain't being . . . I just maybe only seen him the once, your Alex.'

'Alexander, yes. I think he could one day be a model, you know. That's what we're striving for. That's what he wants. The cheekbones – they're certainly there. My side. I'm very lucky in that department. And he's quite a good height for his age. He has his father to thank for that, at least.'

Her hair, she had it put back loose – like in a scrunchy? And then with a beret on the top of it – yeh what she took off on account of them Costas, they a bit of a sweat pit. A lot of the mums, they has their hair like that of a morning: more sort of done when they come in the afternoon to do the pick-up. Me, mine were back and all, my hair, quite long in them days – but it were right back and tight, you know? In what I now know they all is calling chav: your Croydon facelift. Bloody hell – I well let myself down in them days: I wanted a right good smacking, way I gone on. And the other thing all them mums had was the sort of make-up what don't look like you got it on at all, you know what I meaning. Lip gloss, hardly nothing, and ever so little eyeliner – not like me: blimey, I were going about like bleeding Cleopatra, them days. And shiny cheeks, they got. Never knowed how they all of them has them shiny cheeks.

Know now, course. Clarins. Cost a lot, pot of that. Never be without it, though – not now I wouldn't, not for nothing. Some of the mums, they doing La Prairie, but you got to be a million-aire. L'Oréal – that I do get sometimes: yeh I do, cos I'm fucking worth it.

She did look good though, Amy did. Still do, of course – but what I saying is, that first time what we meet up, we was only having a coffee, wasn't we? Yeh but she look better than if I were getting all done up for a big night out or something. Not that I ever had a big night out, nah. What – with Damien? You having a laugh? He come home knackered of an evening all covered in oil – it even get in his hair, and his fingers is dis-gusting, no other bleeding word for it. He have a bit of a wash but he say there no point in getting cleaned up proper on account of in the morning he back in the garage. Sunday he don't get up till it near on dinner time of a midday, and then he playing his bloody games on the telly with Kenny and them handsets and whooping like a kid and knocking back the Carling. Not Kenny, I don't mean – although I dunno: could explain what happen in Lidl couple days back what I'll tell to you later, you want to be giving me a nudge about it. Yeh and even if I were going to be going out of an evening, like it Valentine Day or something and we might go up a Harvester in Pinner or a Toby Carvery what I like, I never had the gear, did I? Amy, that day in Costa, she were in all sort of creamy colours up top, jumper and scarf, all dead soft: wool what were real soft (cashmere, course – ain't never heard of it then) and she got on a skirt what I don't reckon were polyester nor nothing like that, got to be silk didn't it, and the sort of zig-zaggy colours, they knock your eye out. Brown leather boots with a Cuban heel, course: go without saying. Got a lovely face, Amy, big eyes and lips she got – it her what could be a model no trouble, I telling you.

'Model . . .? What – like Kate Moss, you saying . . .?'

And I were thinking no, we talking about Alex, more like Romeo then – David and Victoria's boy what done that how many years back for Burberry: I first got it off of *Heat*, and I cut out the pictures cos I thought he looked dead lovely actually, Romeo, if you want to know, and real classy like his parents . . . and I also were thinking how I be happy to sell myself on the floor to anyone what come along, I could only be getting my hands on a mac like what he got. Bigger, course – cos Romeo, he were only what? Ten year old, when he done it. Like I suppose what Alex are now.

'Well . . . obviously not quite like . . . I mean: small beginnings, you know? Step by step. But I've sent his portfolio to all the big agencies. Storm, and so on. Just waiting to hear, basically. Proper photographs of course, eight-by-tens, professionally done – because you can't have just, well – you know . . . snaps, or anything. And what about Kenny? What do you think he might incline toward?'

Blimey. Well she had me there, didn't she? Well bang to rights. My Kenny . . . what he *incline* toward . . .? Well let's us have a little bit of a think about that then, will we? He incline toward Big Macs and football and Hula Hoops and Fruit Shoots, Cheese Strings and the same stupid computer games what his father waste all of his bleeding time on. About all I can see in him. And just lately, he incline toward being a right bloody pain in Lidl if ever I got to take him in there. Wanting like everything what he see – and not just all of the crud what they got piled up at the checkouts neither. Just couple days before I having this coffee with Amy – yeh, this is what I were going to tell you – he's went wandering off when I were looking for couple multipacks of Pampers, except they ain't Pampers, not proper, they a cheap sort what they got – yeh cos I still gets a bit of trouble with Kenny like that of a night-time if he having one of his nightmares, you know? Shout the place down and wee something awful . . . yeh and I only finds him in the booze bit with the ring pulled off of a bloody great can of Special Brew and he slurping it away there and I going to him, 'Bleeding hell, Kenny . . .! What the fuck you think you up to? Ay? I got to *pay* for that now . . .' Yeh well. But of course I hadn't never like sort of spoke to Kenny about nothing, about what he like, what he go for, nor nothing (what he *incline* toward) . . . what he, I don't know, might want to be one day, or something like that, what is what I suppose, yeh, Amy must of been sort of getting at. Blimey – he were only nine, just coming up. But yeh – now I come to think of it, never talked to him about nothing at all, really. Wasn't never the hours in the day. And kids, like – well, it ain't never you could have a proper sort of like conversation, is it? Ay? So I sitting there in Costa and I sips this bleeding horrible coffee – tastes like really sort of bitter, you know? Why people want to drink this shit? – and yeh,don't know what come over me, but I turns round and I says to Amy:

'I reckon he could be a presenter.'

Yeh and that come right out the blue. I ain't never – never in my life I so much as like even thought it, you know? That my Kenny, he could be one of them presenters off of the telly. But I had to come out with something, didn't I? Truth is, he not much good at nothing, Kenny. I know a mum ain't meant to go saying stuff like that, but it no good ignoring the facts, not when they staring you straight in the face every time what you look at the kid. How he probably end up is on the dole. Damien, he say he could be a footballer, but that only on account of he so bloody crap at all of them other subjects, and when he playing football all he do is he run about a lot and go shouting to all the other little lads to pass him the ball – yeh but they never. One day he come home and he ever so chuffed cos he gone and scored a goal, and Damien – blimey, you want to of seen him: 'See, Dolly? See? What I tell you? Champion in the making, that our Kenny!' Yeh well. It were only the next day I get it off one of the mums at the gate that all the kids in his team is right down on him now on account of he only gone and boot the ball in the wrong bleeding goal, didn't he? Dear oh dear. Never make no difference to Damien: still he go on. Blind as a bat, Damien, when it come to Kenny.

'A presenter . . .? Really . . .?'

That were Amy. Eyebrows well up in the air. Stop stirring her coffee. And then she go:

'Well yes . . . I suppose so. Why ever not? These days. I mean – they totally go for them now, don't they? Accents. Even the BBC. It's not how it used to be, is it? When you used to have to sound like . . . I don't know – Prince Charles, or somebody.'

'You telling me. Other night just before *EastEnders* come on there were this bloke what talking about the movie what on later, yeh? And I never gets a word of it. Way some people talk – it chronic. Scotch, he could of been. Geordie. Irish. One of them. Sound like he were being frottled. So I reckon if he can do it, no way my Kenny can't. Know what I saying?'

Then we was talking about *EastEnders*, you believe it. Turn out she a fan of *Corrie* and all, Amy. You never would of thought it, not going by the looks of her. She wrote me down her number on the back of a receipt from Accessorize. Pen what she had, black and gold with this white sort of a splodge on the top of it, I did like the look of it, and she say it mong-blong, and I goes, 'Is it . . .?' Yeh – now I knows, course I do, but I never then. And still I ain't never done nothing about getting me a classy sort of pen but I reckon I got to some time because I seen a lot of people with one of them. Course, don't never write nothing, but I ain't so green no more that I don't know that ain't the point of it. You just got to have it, that's all. Like all of the other stuff – just got to have it. That's all. Like your watch. Yeh sure, you can get away with a Swatch a lot of the time, but at the end of the day, you just got to be trading up, ain't you really? Rolex is always favourite, and Cartier or right up there like that, but the day I get one of them is when Damien go and rob a bank. But Omega, that pretty good, and Rotary people don't go laughing at, and some of them others – Seiko and that – they can look well like a Rolex or a Cartier, you squint a bit. And Amy, she had on a Omega that day, silver and gold on a bracelet, ever so smart. She said she had a Limit what she got dead cheap at Argos and it look just like a Cartier Tank (which in them days I must of thought were something like what they drives about in in the bleeding army and shooting out of the gun bit) and she take it all apart because she wanted to paint white on the face where it say Limit and then people might think it a real Cartier but she could never go painting Cartier on it on account she couldn't write that small and it would all go wonky anyway and then she had it all in like pieces and she blank out the Limit bit with Tippex, yeh but then she couldn't get it all put together again so she bin it in the end. And then she say there some markets in London what are banging out fake watches with the name on and everything and maybe we go there some time, what do I say . . .? And I were up for that. And that's how me and Amy, we starts knocking about a bit.

Then she go to me: 'What are your . . . vices, Dolly? Do you have lots of guilty secrets . . .?'

Yeh well: I wish. Can't afford no vices, can I? Still the bleeding same, really. Nothing changes. Not unless you's Amy, it don't. But vices, well . . . I ain't never been much of a drinker. Did a bit of pot, old days, nothing heavy, but all the other girls, they was on the ceiling going all like *woo woo woo*, and me, I'm in the bog, throwing up my guts. So I says that to Amy and she nod and she laugh a bit and she go:

'I still do have the odd cigarette, I have to confess. Now I've got one of these things – electronic. Not sure how it works. The end glows red. I've seen some where it's blue, but that's just plain ridiculous. I won't actually do it now. It is legal, but they still sort of look at you. This vapour kind of stuff comes out of the end – have you seen them? So you sort of think you're smoking. You do feel rather foolish, though. Or I do. And it's nothing remotely like a proper drag on a proper cigarette . . . oh God . . . I'd just die for one now, a proper cigarette . . .'

And then her phone go off with a tune what she later telling to me are called O2 Joy and it the latest iPhone but one and it in a purple case what look like snake and she make a face at me and she say I got to take this.

'Yes . . . well it's in the cupboard, isn't it Terence? Where it always is. Yes? No . . . no . . . the shelf above that. Above where the drawers are. Yes. See it? Do you . . .? Well then you must be just perfectly *blind* . . . what's wrong with you at all? Hm? Terence – listen to me, Terence: are you in the right cupboard? Not the hall cupboard? You're in the right cupboard, are you? Well . . . I just don't know what to say to you, then. It is in there. It's always in there. That's where I keep it. Oh God . . . well leave

43

it. Leave it. Just leave it, Terence, all right? I'll see to it when I get back. Yes. Bye. No well I'm sorry – it's you who can't find it, isn't it? You'll just have to wait till I get home. Yes. No. Can't give you a time. Not long. Soon. Yes. Bye.'

Then she swipe the phone and her mouth go all sort of twisty like she been eating a lemon and she's like, '*Men . . .!*'

'Oh tell me about it . . .! My Damien – useless ain't in it. He just don't get it. They don't, do they? None of them, men. Not never. Like – we was talking about secret, what-you-call-it . . .? Vices, yeh. Well I don't know you call it a vice exactly but I get all of them magazines, yeh, what Damien says is a waste of money. So I brings them in all secret now. Like *Heat* and *Now* and *OK!* and *Take a Break* and all of them really and it do add up, the cost of them, yeh it do, but I'm really dead interested in what they's all doing, the celebrities. Got my favourites, of course. Cut them out, the pictures of them, keep them in a wossname. Yeh so the other night he pick one up and he like flicking through it and he go, "I don't know who the half of these people even is!" You believe it . . .? And I says, "Yeh well that because you pig ignorant, ain't it? Ay? You don't know who they even *is* . . .? What's wrong with you, Damien? They all *famous*. Ain't they? Ay? Whole point about celebrities, ain't it? They all *famous*. What make them celebrities, you prat." And you know what he say? You know what he turn round and say to me and then? Tell you, will I? You won't never believe it. He say to me, "Yeh well . . . if you don't know who they is, right . . . well then, that case, they just ain't nobody at all . . ." Yeh. Honest God's truth. That what I up against. That how stupid he can be.'

And Amy, she were having a good old laugh over that. And then she go to me:

'Oh well. But maybe, at least, he's useful in . . . other departments, yes . . .?'

'Joking. Don't even know where the fuse box is. Can't put a nail in the wall. Give up even asking. It odd, actually – because he ever such a good mechanic. Cars – that what he do. But anything in the house, you can forget it. Like last Mother's Day, yeh? I got a mug off of my Kenny, right? It got on it "Best Mum in the World" . . .'

'Oh how *sweet* . . .!'

'Yeh. Is. Sweet. Well – was. I says to Damien – here, Damien, bung me in a hook over the sink there, yeh? Says it to him every bleeding day for about a month. And then he do. So I sticks my mug on it. Yeh – and the next morning I come down and it only on the floor in bleeding pieces. Hook – come right out. What you going to do . . .?'

'Oh dear. How sad for little Kenny. But I do know what you mean. Terence isn't a great deal better, I do assure you. No, but what I meant was . . . you know . . . *other* departments . . .'

'What like earning, you mean? Well he ain't too bad, I got to say. Can't complain, you know. We do all right, really.'

'No. No . . . I mean . . . oh, you *know* . . .'

Well her eyebrows was waggling like the bleeding clappers, but I never twig what she were on about. And then I does.

'Oh gotcha. You mean all of that, yeh? Yeh. Well . . . can't bloody well *remember*, you want the truth of it . . .'

'Oh I know! I know! I know exactly what you mean . . .! Oh God how funny! But it's awful really, isn't it? The way that that side of it always . . . Mind you, if I'm being perfectly honest myself, I don't actually mind a bit. Rather grateful, really. Truth of the matter is that these days, well . . . I'm just always so crashingly *exhausted* . . .'

45

'Oh leave it out . . .! I could fall asleep right here and now, me. Other night I were stirring in a bit of milk to a tin of soup and I drops the spoon in . . .! I swear I nodded off.'

'Oh I can so completely identify with that. Men . . . you see the trouble with men is that they don't realise, they simply don't realise what it is. All it takes. Being a mother. Running a household. Picking up after them every waking hour of the day. They simply fail to see it. But listen, Dolly . . . I'll tell you, shall I, my absolutely ultimate bedroom fantasy. Shall I? What I'd really adore to get up to in a colossally vast bed with crisp clean sheets and the softest lighting and scented candles and utter peace . . .?'

'Dear me. Yeh all right, then: go on . . .'

'Sleep . . .! *Sleep* . . .! Yes! Yes! Just that – perfectly blissful sleep for simply days and days on end . . .!'

And it were me what were laughing now – cos how many times I thought it? She funny, Amy – that what I were thinking. And yeh, okay – we not the same. Well – plain as day, that is – she all la-di-da in her ways, like, and me the way I is . . . but we women, see? Mums. That it, really. Bond – it's a bond, that is. Sisterhood, yeh. And I looks at her quite fond and I points at her empty cup and I says to her – here, you go another of them, can you? And she nod. So I ups and gets us in another couple. Mine, I never drunk it – God it bleeding horrible, and I still think that: give us a skinny frappuccino any day of the week. But I do remember thinking to myself that I got me a new friend, here.

And she were and all. We done ever such a lot of things together since then, we has. But now, well . . . I ain't too pleased . . . I can't deny it: no point lying, is there? I mean – I were pleased for her, one way . . . but when I start seeing all them pictures of Alex, bloody little Alex, in the magazines, and that . . . well: not the same, is it? Ay? Between the two of us, like. Something got to change – stand to reason. Yeh and now . . . now, he only going to be in a bloody movie, ain't he? A bloody movie, Christ's sake . . .! Well so how I going to keep up with all of that then? Ay? Well I can't, can I? I just can't. No I bleeding can't . . . and I tell you something: ain't joking – already, it bloody well killing me. Mean it.

CHAPTER TWO

DESIGN, STYLE,
CALL IT WHAT YOU LIKE

This dinner-party idea of Amy's, you know . . . well if you were
to ask me frankly, I should have to say I'm not altogether sure
that it's wise. Rather serious doubt about it, you know. Yes
because potentially, a great deal could go very wrong, here.
When first she brought it up – and please don't think it was a
suggestion or a discussion: no no, what we had here was simply
the very starkest announcement – I did try gently to suggest to
her that she might want to exercise just a little bit of caution
before she rushed irrevocably and headlong into such a thing . . .
but of course, and wholly predictably, she simply stood there
and stared at me in that frankly rather unsettling manner that
she very often has about her, lately. Rather as if suddenly she
has been confronted with a small, green and glowing alien
newly dropped out of a starlit sky to land very clumsily and
sprawl at her feet, while speaking robotically in a language
wholly new to her. And then – with her eyes just as wide as they
would go – she took in her breath, highly theatrically, and said
to me (rather witheringly, rather pityingly):

'*Caution*, Terence . . .? *Caution* . . .? Is that what you said? Well how perfectly extraordinary. It's a dinner party we're going to have. Did you mishear me? I did not suggest we all go potholing or climbing mountains in the dark. We are not going to be juggling *sabres* . . . We're simply having a few people over for a bite to eat. That's all. So I don't really think it's anything you have to be terribly frightened about, Terence. Though if it will make you feel a little more secure, I shall hold your hand throughout, I do promise you.'

See? What I mean? Just can't talk to her. Not when she gets like that. And these days, well . . . it's more and more, isn't it? More and more, she gets like that. Can't now actually remember a time when she wasn't, if I'm forced to be scrupulously honest with you. Because it's begun, you see. Everything I warned against, all my fears of how it will be if finally she gets her way (and was either of us ever even for so much as a moment seriously in doubt that of course she would?) . . . well yes: it's begun. It's begun now, yes – and all it can get is very much worse, and maybe unstoppably so. Yes . . . but while one rather is dreading what the future has to hold, still I don't regard it as altogether healthy – on my part, I mean, it's me I'm talking about, now – to dwell unduly upon the past. Holding it up to be mythically idyllic. And particularly at my age, Christ – I'm only forty-five. Hardly old, is it? Shouldn't have said so. Not quite drawing my pension. So I hate to start glorying in 'the old days' because quite apart from making me seem so terribly ancient, starry-eyed and maybe even faintly melancholic, it suggests also that then, in the past, all was perfect, and that now, everything is very poor indeed. Not the case, not the case at all. Much is good, of course it is, of course it is . . . apart from all of the daily awfulness that none of us ever has a hope of escaping: the paucity of elegance . . . the gleeful rapacity of everyday

49

existence . . . of course there is always that, amid so very much more. And that is why, largely, I cannot welcome the changes to come. It's the scale of it, you see – the scale of it. Its proportion. We are in very great danger of toppling over: unbalance is imminent.

Need I really say that Amy, she hasn't always been like this . . .? When first I met her, I was actually rather entranced – and this, apparently, was very evident to all of my friends. None of whom, incidentally – not one – I ever see any more. Well Bob, Bob I do a bit . . . but only because he happens to live just a couple of streets away. I remain unsure as to quite how or why this has happened – the sundering of so many friendships. But the point I am making is that I've generally always been perceived to be . . . I don't know quite how to . . . I think what I want to say is that I was always seen by many to be the eternal bachelor, much to the bile-ridden envy of any married man I should ever encounter. Had lots of girlfriends, of course I have. But before Amy, only two of them ever developed into what I would really call a serious relationship. Well three . . . three, I suppose, if you're going to count Anita, which one rather has to, really – that very stirring Venezuelan who so completely swept me right off my feet before hurtling me high into the sky . . . yes, and from which very eminence she rather astonishingly rapidly dropped me . . . and Christ did I plummet. So like the proverbial stone. To land, needless to say, very badly indeed. Utterly in thrall to her, I was – though apart from the sex, if ever one really can say that (which was so very wonderful it was practically gruelling: I looked forward like hell and a panting animal to the heaven of it . . . though was daunted, nearly crushed, by the looming of so much heavy work) – but apart from that, the sex (which was, let us be clear here, so far beyond a simple man's comprehension and quite sublime in its vileness, this in great part due to the cushions of her lips, though chiefly to her ability and very zesty enthusiasm for seemingly impossible contortion) . . . I'm not sure even now that I quite can understand my utter enslavement to the woman. Which, yes I now see clearly can only appear to be disingenuous in the extreme. But her English was lamentable . . . though maybe, when you're very young, the sex, the sex, that can be more than enough, just on its own: well of course it can, of course it is, with Anita it was, Christ it was – so what am I saying? But any other sort of communication I remember as being always rather a problem . . . and it soon did really become something of a pain, I have to admit, even summoning the energy to try. I'm not sure I ever did learn about her interests, you know – her tastes, or even if she had any. So a wholly sexual liaison, you might easily conclude . . . except for the fact that I was, so far as I could tell, quite utterly in love with her. From within the balmy cocoon of hindsight, it's just as well she ditched me, really (as it turned out, in favour of someone unimaginably rich and very high up in Formula 1, a so-called mate was enjoying to tell me later) because I almost certainly would have made an absolute and total fool of myself with the woman, had she hung around for very much longer. Actually, thinking back, everyone was so very solicitous to me as I lay there broken (after the fling was flung) . . . that I rather think that I must have anyway.

The other two though – they were longer standing, and far more founded in reason. Sally . . . well we were up at Exeter together, so both of us were rather new to the game, and then with the passing of really not much time at all . . . we being a couple, it rather fell into more of a habit than anything. She was a wonderful little . . . well, it used to be called 'homemaker',

51

people used to say that sort of thing then – and that's just what Sally was, that was her forte, unquestionably. Because all we had was a fairly unspeakable little room with a screened-off kitchenette (shared bathroom – shared with most of the university, it often could appear) and at very much the shabbier end of the city – but with a budget of practically zero, you should just have seen what she made of the place. All sorts of printed madras hangings and so on to cover the grubby off-white walls . . . and she did excellent things with odd bits of old furniture and paint: very clever with the lighting too, what little we had of it – the draping of chiffon, orange bulbs from Woolworth's. A very cosy nest she created for us, yes she did – enchanting really, now I look back on it – but then of course she started talking about a rather more permanent arrangement: subtly and in passing at first, then quite directly . . . before finally becoming, well – almost confrontational. She was one of nature's mothers, Sally (well – she mothered me: yes, it was pretty close to it, and I thoroughly enjoyed it all, as any man would, I shouldn't wonder). But you could tell even then that she would never be replete until she had clustered about her person a great and boisterous gang of children, and preferably in a farmhouse somewhere rugged and remote where she would keep them all appallingly well nourished with the fruit of her Aga. She would have looked after me very well indeed, Sally . . . and yes of course I do think about that. And we shared an interest in design and form. It actually appeared to be her primary pursuit, now I come to think of it, although she was actually reading English and was forever trying to force me to get to grips with Virginia Woolf – but Jesus, you have to draw the line somewhere. I, on the other hand, was History of Art and Economics (the latter having been I thought a very unconvincing sop to the authorities in order to secure for me the former, though much to my amazed gratification, it worked like a charm).

God . . . all seems so long ago, now. Well it was, I suppose. More than half my life, after all. Wasn't it? And that was rather the point – or so I saw it at the time. We were both of us only twenty-one . . . and the last thing in the world I had set my heart on was a great and boisterous gang of children in a farmhouse, as you well might understand. I hope though that eventually she got it all, Sally, everything she always wanted. We parted as amicably as ever one can . . . but we didn't keep up. We said we were going to, you know . . . write, and so on . . . and I think we maybe even did do that, once or twice, anyway . . . and then, well . . . you know. How it goes. A very good woman, and still I do think of her fondly. Strange to imagine that now she's forty-five years old, just like me. Doubt she looks any different, though.

Then there were all sorts of different girls after that, I am very pleased to say: back in London by this stage – so you'd meet them in a pub on a Friday evening, have a very jolly weekend, and that was that, more often than not: seemed to suit everyone concerned. At the time I had a very humble job in the Conran Shop, with a view to my becoming I'm not at all sure what . . . but I was in thrall to design by that time, you see, and Sir Terence was something of a hero (very much still is). Years later, when I told all of this to Amy (well – some of it, anyway) she said I only felt about him like that because we shared a Christian name . . . which, I'm afraid, is very much the sort of thing that Amy would say. I don't really know why I was actually working in that shop . . . it just seemed a rather good place at the time for me to be. I didn't want to be behind a counter, obviously, for the rest of my life . . . although I did rather fancy being a buyer at one point, but such a post was never offered to me, and never in those days could I have presumed to ask for it. One girl who also worked there I was seeing for a short while . . . though I can't, isn't it awful, just at the minute actually recall her name, I'm rather ashamed to say . . . that is a bit bad, really, even for me . . . but it was never a remotely serious thing I had going with her (well clearly) but then there was this Christmas party for all the staff – oh yes, I well remember that – in some big nacho joint just off Fulham Road which was terribly 'in' at the time, and everyone was rather pleased to be there – and this girl, whatever her name was, she had brought along her flatmate, who was called Celia. Celia, yes . . . and oh heavens, I took to Celia just about immediately. *Alison . . .!* Yes of course – that was her name, the girl I used to work with at Conran: Alison, yes, yes of course it was. So then within hardly any time at all it was Celia and I who became rather serious about one another – an 'item', as they had just started saying at the time. And do you know . . .? I was with her, Celia, for not much short of four years. Four years – heavens.

And then, well . . . thirty had come and gone . . . which hadn't actually fazed me in the slightest, but I could hardly be unaware that noises were being made – and not just by Celia, but friends, my mother, you know the way it always goes: they just won't ever leave you alone. We weren't actually living together, though . . . and apart from other reasons (we both had mortgages on our own places that we were reluctant to relinquish, rather boring and practical things like that) . . . there did come into it, believe it or not, very much the design thing too, I have to say: it raised its head, and its head was large. Because design, style, call it what you like . . . with me, it had long ago progressed from being merely an interest to an absolute ruling passion – and Celia, who was a bookkeeper for . . . no: no no, not a bookkeeper – she always would go just completely mad if ever I told people she was a bookkeeper. She was an *accountant*, I was firmly instructed – an accountant, yes, that's what she was (though only certified, not chartered) for a small chain of coffee houses (long gone now – swallowed up by the high-street giants, I can only suppose) and although she dressed really fairly presentably, Celia, her ideas about interior decoration – though never would she have called it that, oh no, she would have thought that sounded madly pretentious – well they were frankly simply appalling to me. I mean . . . I know that to some people it's all merely frippery, and that men in particular are just not meant to be bothered about colour and form and decor and lighting and furniture and objects and all the rest of it (unless of course they're professionally involved in their creation and marketing, or else, maybe, are blanketed by some or other cretinous and lazy media umbrella cliché, such as a mincing hairdresser) but I don't at all feel abashed to admit that all of it is vitally important to me, and having around me the things that I love affords me enormous and daily pleasure. This is so strong within me that I have often felt I *ought* to be professionally involved . . . but, alas, I am not. Wish I were. That would be a great deal better than setting up ('designing', very loosely) and maintaining websites, which is the rut in which I currently find myself marooned. I do have some rather big-name clients, it's true (and thank Christ for that) so the money is tolerable . . . but so much of this sort of thing . . . well you see, what is always lurking at the back of my mind (and in the middle of a long and cold black night, it can leap very nimbly to the forefront, unbidden and in seconds) is that more and more, companies are setting up their own in-house departments to deal with all this

55

sort of thing – the only extraordinary aspect being that it all hasn't happened just ages ago – and so Christ alone knows how long it's going to last. And here we have the anxiety about technology in a nutshell, really: it came from nowhere, a bolt from the blue yonder, as if a blessing from God . . . though at any moment it can simply disappear. Yes . . . because of course what none of us can actually quite bear to acknowledge, for it opens up to us the bottomless pit of despair, not to say blind terror and bewilderment – is that none of it actually *exists*, and nor has it ever.

Yes . . . so anyway, where was I, in fact . . .? What was I actually, um . . .? Oh yes – Celia. Celia, yes, and her very ghastly flat. Well the first dreadful thing about it was where it was actually situated – not too much short of Brixton, if you can believe it. Bloody devil to get to, because myself, I've always been a north London man, born here, so you can see the problem. In the early days, in the very early days, when I had to, just had to be with her, sleep with her, every single night (which is, as well we know, all that very early days can ever be for) I used to say to her, 'But listen, Celia I just can't understand it, you know. You've got a pretty decent job, you only need the one bedroom, you could live pretty much anywhere you want. I mean . . . okay, not Belgravia, maybe, or Chelsea or Hampstead or somewhere like that, but pretty much anywhere else . . . so why in Christ's name did you want to go and live over there? Across the river. I mean – it's just absolutely miles from anywhere.' And she'd smile, and then she'd say to me, very patiently, yes, and never without a certain amount of rather knowing and aloof indulgence (which I hated, utterly hated – and either it became acutely more pronounced, this, as time drifted by, or else because her compensating enchantments were wearing bloody thin, I couldn't honestly tell you – but either way, I was increasingly

56

not just aware of, but wildly irritated by it) . . . she'd say to me that 'it isn't in fact, miles from anywhere, Terry – it is simply miles from *you*'. Yes and that's another thing: she had taken to calling me Terry – can't think where it had come from, she never used to – and that, I can tell you, that was driving me pretty crazy as well: I asked her not to – repeatedly I asked her not to do it: Terence, that's my name, I'd say to her – Terence, yes? The way you used to say it – yes? No. Like talking to a wall. But the gist of what she was on about was that you can get anywhere in London from Brixton a damn sight quicker than from Belsize Park – which, yes, is true enough, I suppose, but still . . . apart from the distances, bit of a hellhole. Isn't it? Really. And if I went to her in the evening, well – just had to stay over, didn't I? Which wasn't always the most convenient of arrangements: things to do, you know? But I wasn't going to be wandering around that part of London in the middle of the bloody night, was I? Well – not for long, anyway.

'All it comes down to, Terry, is that really, and you ought to own up to it, you know . . . that really, you're just the teensy-weensiest little bit of a snob. Aren't you, my angel?'

'Teensy-weensiest little bit of a . . .? Oh bloody hell, Celia – what on earth have you actually *become* . . .? Why do you talk like that? You never used to talk like that. Why do you even say these things . . .? And now you're calling me "my angel", are you? I can't believe it! Fucking "Terry" was bad enough – now you've decided to start calling me "my angel" . . .! And what do you mean, a snob . . .? You haven't the first idea what you're talking about, Celia. Honestly. I'm not a snob. What a bloody stupid thing to say. How can you even say that? Do you even know the meaning of the word? Do you? Me – a *snob* . . .? Absolute bloody nonsense. It's simply that – No no, you listen

57

to me now, Celia, you sit still and bloody hear me out: you started this, you started all this with your damned accusations, so you just shut up and bloody well listen to what I've got to say to you. All right . . .? Right. Now . . . now . . .what was I actually going to say . . .? Oh yes – oh yes. Stop laughing – it's no good laughing, is it Celia? Actually. If anything, it's you that's the snob. Inverted, yes. Look – it all comes down to the fact that nice is nicer than nasty. Yes? How many times have I said it? And where you live, let's face it – it's downright bloody nasty. That's all there is to it, really Celia. Not complicated . . .'

'You can be very hurtful, Terry.'

'Hurtful . . . I'm not being hurtful . . .'

'You are. You really are. Very hurtful, you can be, whether you know it or not.'

'I'm not . . . *hurtful* . . .!'

'Look – I should bloody know! I'm the one who's being hurt, aren't I? I know if I hurt or not, don't I? Hey? And I do – I do. You've hurt me, Terry. You do it a lot.'

'Well look . . . I don't . . . *mean* to. I just . . . look, all I'm doing is just . . .'

'All you're doing is hurting me. I don't know why you do it. Maybe you don't either. But you do. You never used to, but now you do. All the time. Sometimes, I think you enjoy it, hurting me. Sometimes I actually do think you get some sort of a, I don't know – kick out of it, or something . . .'

'Oh come on now, Celia – that's just plain ridiculous, and you know it.'

'I'm not sure I do, Terry. I'm not sure I do know that it's ridiculous in the least. All I know is how I feel. And what I feel is . . . hurt, Terry. You hurt me. You do. You really do.'

'Oh look . . . I'm going. I'm going, all right?'

58

'Of course you are. You always do at times like this.'

'What do you mean – "times like this" . . .? What are you on about now . . .?'

'You've eaten. We've made love. You're not enjoying the way the conversation's going. And it's not yet dark, so you won't be frightened walking through dirty nasty Harlem to get a taxi back up to somewhere *nice* . . .'

'Oh *Christ*, Celia . . .! You just drive me crazy – you know that? You just bloody well drive me crazy . . .'

'I'm sorry you feel that way, Terry. I really am.'

'Yeh well . . . And it's *Terence*, for fuck's sake Celia! How many bleeding bloody times . . .?!'

Yeh well. And Brixton – or nearly Brixton, whatever it was called, wherever she was living – it wasn't then even nearly so, Christ, 'bang on trend' as we are eternally told it is these days, but still already it was very much a horribly self-consciously 'cool' part of the city to be in – or at least it was seen to be so by those deluded, white and middle-class incomers (smug in their fatuous 'bravery', their simulated love of the area's – oh Jesus – *edginess* . . .) all of whom so very evidently belonged elsewhere (and probably where they'd just bloody come from). A different story for the natives (in every sense) who were actually born there, grew up there, who still would have surrendered limbs, or even those acquaintances and relatives who regularly are wanted by the police in order to assist them with their inquiries, just for the chance to get out of it . . . but then, cruelly, isn't that usually the way? You just have to look at the newly fashionable holiday destinations in war-torn, barren and abandoned danger zones. The people who go there – the people who by now must be sated with all of the actually lovely places throughout the world, and which, presumably, they have done to death – these people will tell you that such far-flung incarnations of Hades, where the hazard of maiming or death is skulking in any alleyway, the risk of disease constantly perching upon your shoulder, lurking within every water tap and wrap of street food you are rash enough to consume – oh yes they will tell you, these people, for as long as you have the patience to endure them, that all such places are (wait for this) ... *real* ... though it is only the inhabitants, the survivors, the blank-eyed and imprisoned 'local colour' of a thousand iPhone snaps ... it is only they who know this in their hearts to be true.

And now, in London – due to a pervasive slick cynicism that must invade them as a miasma – the underclass, all those with no say, all those with no choice, they can luxuriate in the warmth of such bland assurances as are ceaselessly dinned into them by the satanic alliance of all the snake-eyed journalists and salivating estate agents that every single area of the capital you ever could muster, and so many more you have never even heard of (and particularly those that have been laughingly newly minted and mockingly christened, such heartless nominations generally and unashamedly to incorporate the word 'village') ... that every single one of these areas without exception is currently 'eagerly sought-after', 'fast up-and-coming', 'the next new thing' and – always, always, bloody always – *'vibrant'* ... and therefore in consequence and parallel, of course, now quite ludicrously and wholly disproportionately expensive. The slum that the inveterates, the lifers, the buggered-from-birth recidivists have since their very childhood been desperate to flee from is now become, it is elaborately explained – very much in the manner that Celia herself could well have employed with me – quite unutterably fabulous.

This is what they would have them believe ... but all, barring the gullible incomers thrilled by their own idiotic awareness and gimcrack daring, know it to be nothing but the very blackest lie. And of course each one of these caged and marooned unfortunates is united too in not actually owning whatever shabby rooms in which they worklessly and therefore aimlessly measure out their days in spells of misery and tedium, alternated with those of drugged-up and transitory alleviation . . . oh, if only they did! For there would surely be their only chance of a passport to freedom: hundreds of thousands for an attic at the summit of a derelict staircase – no less for the dank and inky subterranean scullery. But now they must somehow absorb the pain of paying to an unseen landlord ever higher rents for the places they hate to be, these to reflect not just 'market value' but the manufactured desirability of the same old tenement houses, divided and subdivided into a dingy maze of plasterboarded corridors and cubicles, the new and enhanced spurious status made evident on the street only by the wide-eyed and newly arrived middle classes, none of whom lives like this, and each of whom will have not the least compunction in crowing to you over at least a couple of bottles of Sainsbury's Taste The Difference Malbec about how they so very brilliantly sold a two-bedder in St John's Wood at the peak of the market and were thrilled to have discovered the murk of the shadowy badlands, and just how much more 'bang you can get for your buck'. Having had a specialist to restore the badly chipped and crumbling Corinthian capitals surmounting the pillars of their satisfyingly imposing portico (just like Knightsbridge . . .! So like Eaton Square . . .!) they will then have picked out the exterior stucco in Homebase's version of Farrow & Ball Elephant Breath and one of the eleven off-whites (taste the difference) that the range unsmilingly affords, before creating a downlit patch of grass close to the wheelie bins ranked within their newly crafted brick little cottage with a sloped tiled rooflet, mmm, and whose clapboard doors are already off their hinges . . . and highly possibly there will be a glossed and canary big front door with bright lacquered brassware . . . or else dove grey – not quite matt, not quite sheeny – made perfectly spanking by chrome. Even Celia was laughing when she recounted to me that her next-door neighbour had early one Saturday morning driven his 'pre-cherished' Volvo estate (this, yes, is what he was pleased to call it) to Columbia Road Market, where he was overtaken by the dementedly original idea of investing in a pair of lollipop bay trees very conveniently already planted into square white Versailles boxes with acorn finials to each of the corners, these polyresin miracles so very subtly grained as to closely resemble merely carpentered wood. Once he had placed them with care and precision to either side of his raised and fielded front door (aubergine, with black cast-iron furniture and a newly commissioned tinted and acid-etched upper glass panel to echo precisely the one which still remained, following the fallout from the recent riots), he took a series of photographs on his smartphone, these no doubt sent instantly to an agog and eager world – and, as things turned out, it was rather just as well that he had had the wit to secure for himself so lasting a memento (that he had taken the time to pre-cherish the moment) . . . for by morning they were gone.

So there then was Celia, insistent upon living in nearly Brixton – she may even have perceived her presence there as a kindly, certainly unaggressive and possibly even zealously missionary example of beneficial colonisation – though her protestations over how wonderfully vital a melting pot it was, very soon, I detected, were gradually simmering down into no more than a lukewarm and token defence, before hardening into just stubbornness, plain and simple. It got to be so that she would rather have died there (by whatever means – conceivably at the hand of some kaleidoscope-eyed cross-cultural and doubtless throbbingly vibrant neighbour in quest of the where-withal for his latest journey to whatever coloured moon loomed currently the largest in his transcendental cosmos) than ever admit to my face that just possibly there could in fact exist in London some gentler, prettier and altogether more conducive area that did not involve my having to traipse bloody over there, night after fucking night.

Yes but why then, you might reasonably want to know, could she not travel to Belsize Park? Well she could, of course – and did, she did do that, from time to time, of course she did . . . yes but the truth of the matter is . . . that I was torn. Torn, yes – it quickly became a daily dilemma – as to which of these two resolutions affected me less badly . . . which of them would occasion not so much . . . pain. Pain, oh yes make no mistake – and of course I can well understand that that will sound at the very least ridiculous to one who is blissfully untouched by any such aesthetic sensibility . . . but you see, while I loathed, simply shrivelled and cringed away from ever being in Celia's flat (oh God, it was just so appalling – though mercifully she was credu-lous enough to believe that my instant eagerness to turn out all the lights was rooted in a just adorable blend of lust and bashfulness) . . . nor did I care for her to be in mine. Yes because she would touch things. Move things. Or bring me flowers – flowers, yes okay, a perfectly nice gesture, thoughtful of her, loving and generous, of course it was, of course it was . . . but always . . . always they were just the wrong flowers. You see? Quite the wrong flowers, bought from quite the wrong place,

63

and always adorned by not just pale blue damp and semi opaque paper over a crackle of cellophane but a sticker proclaiming a free 25% extra and the extent of time before the wretched things' anticipated demise, with a wet and obscene little sausage of plant food Sellotaped around their horny stems. Dahlias, say. Or carnations. To give her her due, she never actually went to the extreme of gladioli, no – never did she quite go the whole hog (for I really do think that that might truly have signalled the finish) but still let us not forget that once she had flirted with marigolds, so you can see it was a close-run thing. And then she would wilfully misunderstand the purpose of my Starck and Aalto vases: they were not for putting flowers into, even had they been anemones, old roses or gypsophila – well of course they weren't, as would be plain to anyone, you would have thought . . . anyone, anyway, with even an iota of artistic awareness. Rather in the way that she would wonder why none of my Eames chairs or the Florence Knoll sofa would afford her the bounty of scatter cushions (so that then she could joyously plump them). Once she threatened to buy me some. On another occasion – so unimaginably worse – she threatened to *make* me some, and it was all I could do to dissuade her.

All of which, though, is perfectly explicable – I understood the impetus, of course I did. It all came down to her own place, didn't it? Which, she would tell me repeatedly and actually with detectable smugness coating her tongue, was 'cosy'. My flat, she explained, was not 'cosy'. Hers was. She did not go quite so far as to suggest that what clearly was needed here was a woman's touch, but by Jesus – being Celia, she actually did imagine that she would, out of the innate goodness of her heart, be doing me so almighty a favour by gently and in sweet and homely degrees teasing my fine and considered space further and further in the direction of the dementedly configured haven of 'cosiness' as had been attained with such enviable ease and utter and delicate fluency within her own little flounced and spangled oasis in nearly Brixton. Oh dear. Oh dear oh dear oh dear. So I think that by now you must surely understand . . . but just in case you continue to hover, let me tell you as much as I can bear to about Celia's flat, yes? And then just a little about mine.

The building formed the recently truncated corner of . . . yes, I suppose I do have to admit this, one of the more acceptable terraces in the area – although to the right of it, where once had stood the adjoining house, there did lie this shadowy and there-fore always rather worrying little scrap of scrubland permanently strewn with rusting and angrily distorted metal and a protru-sion of gnarled concrete boulders, all of it overrun by a wiry and gritty clambering of windswept weeds. This, proclaimed a bragging and optimistically illustrated hoarding, was soon to be transformed into what amounted to a hideous and vertical swarm of 'loft-style' living, cynically and ruthlessly targeted at biddable and undiscerning morons with millions to burn. For the time being, however, this prime little nugget of real estate was content to play host to a pair of massive and steeply angled girdered buttresses – and we fervently hoped that they would continue to support the visibly bulging flank to Celia's building, roughly trussed and very partially weatherproofed as it was in plastic and tarpaulin. The dumped debris could include any-thing from casually discarded domestic rubbish to – on one rather horribly memorable occasion – the body of a vagrant, frozen rigid. Though always the ground could be depended upon to sport a burnt-out sofa, in addition to a multiplying assortment of yawning and stoved-in fridges (sometimes a

stoved-in stove), the never-ending squelch of discarded prophy-
lactics, and an absolute haystack of hypodermic needles – all of
this an abiding fascination to the tangles of blank-eyed and
unsuspecting children, every one of them seemingly dressed in
the same grey marl, stained and overlarge sportswear teamed
with big and grimy trainers, and every one of them apparently
doomed to be infesting the streets until any parent – or even
some or other quasi-responsible adult who might actually still
feature, if fleetingly, just somewhere in their lives – might maybe
remember where it was they lived, and some time soon make
a token effort to get back there.

To the other side of her was the house with no longer a pair
of bay trees, its tasteful two-tone stucco by this time considerably enlivened in largely the basement area by the staggered
application and constant enthusiastic renewal of an ever-mu-
tating and bright neon spasm of zigzags, tags, and desultory
blagging. In the linoleum entrance corridor to the house stood
a bicycle that no one ever had been seen to ride, budge or even
lay claim to. And then one floor up from the dinge of all that
lay Celia's domain. On the door she had affixed a yellow circular
Smiley sticker, and so as a consequence of that I could normally
be depended upon to be in a reasonably bad mood before I'd
even entered. Then there was what I suppose you would call
the hall: just a piece of the living room sectioned off by battened
blockboard and rendered practically impassable by a great and
hunchbacked slump of coats, this overladen by an impossible
number of the sort of wintry and bobbled tug-on woollen hats
that Celia very plainly adored, and which render anyone who
wears them instantly retarded. In addition to all of that were
three quite sizeable posters which Celia had bought, she had
told me excitedly and repeatedly, for truly next to nothing from

a shop that was closing down – of which, around here, there was seldom a shortage – one of them being *Gone with the Wind* (predictably her favourite film of all time), another being a black-and-white still from *Breakfast at Tiffany's* (predictably her second favourite film of all time), with the very skinny and to my mind quite ridiculously overrated and not remotely sexually alluring Audrey Hepburn in the role of Holly Golightly – in Givenchy, and wearing diamond ear clips and wielding an eti-olated cigarette holder, quite in the manner of every Manhattan whore you will ever lay eyes upon. The third such depiction (predictably, predictably) was of Marilyn Monroe, barefooted, hesitant and vulnerable in a sand-spattered tulle petticoat and very little make-up – so not at all, then, the way that men might prefer her to be (and she was, according to Celia, 'not just a goddess, but a beautiful person'). Also prominent in this very claustrophobic packing case of a so-called hall was strung from the pendant and into each of the corners merely the first of a series of twinkly little bloody fairy lights, this highly unsettling and barely to be supported motif continued with unabated enthusiasm throughout every single one of the rooms – yes including the kitchen, and most especially the bathroom – which lent to the whole place that shimmeringly girly and insinuat-ingly redolent and then quite insistent whiff of those very much grander Uptown apartments eternally and oglingly glorified in all of her favourite American television series, peopled as they are by ditsy, self-consumed and obsessively shoe-buying very thin women, who – and Celia never did quite seem to manage to wholly understand this – were actually, you see Celia, in return for unimaginable amounts of money, only *pretending* to be ditsy (although all those other attributes, they were real enough) while incidentally spawning a universe of

67

empty-headed bleeding female (well of *course* female) gigglingly deluded apostles, each of whom would appear to truly imagine that the only way is sparkle.

Celia then took to spending many whole evenings – and, when I just simply couldn't be bothered any more to make the endless trek, entire weekends – with her furry-muled feet neatly tucked up beside her on the sofa and her hair in an Alice band, while wearing a succession of brushed cotton jim-jams (this is what she called them: she called them jim-jams), these covered in sketchy doodles of anything from adorable sad-eyed pandas to a scattering of open red and pink lipsticks by way of Cath Kidston vintage florals or even 1950s cowboys and spacemen. She would be dipping compulsively into large drums of pop-corn, larger tubs of ice cream, and not just clutching but actually stroking reassuringly her favourite stuffed animal, Mr Fucking Pig (the Fucking is mine) and staring as one transfixed (while mouthing inanely the dialogue which she must, then, have learned by heart) at the rolling show of her apparently unending collection of boxed sets of all these vacuous and indistinguish-able series on a virtually continuous loop, and which – despite my striving endlessly to apprise her of the fact, though never would she permit herself to see it – were themselves collectively and completely responsible for such flagrantly self-conscious and bloody brainless behaviour on her part in the first bloody place . . .! Well . . . well . . . what can I say? That this is how she behaved on a perfectly regular basis should not by now, I think, be really too terribly surprising to anybody at all.

I was going to say more . . . about her flat, I mean. Describe to you some of the rest of the horror . . . but I just don't think I can face it, to be honest with you. Even now, just looking back on it after all this time – and Christ, it's more than a decade ago, all of this, can hardly believe it – though still, you know, it almost quite literally makes my blood boil: I can feel it now – seething in my temples: my hands are clammy, and my head is hot. So certainly she made a considerable impression upon me, Celia, no getting away from that much, at least. Though in the light of all of it, I can see that you might quite reasonably want to ask this of me: how, Terence, if she offended you so terribly gravely, could you possibly have stayed with her for nearly four whole years . . .? Yes well, no very profound answers to that one . . . it's just that you fall into a sort of a habit really, don't you? Convenience, what you're used to, not having to start up the whole of the palaver again, with someone else, someone untried . . . and of course it wasn't always like that with Celia, the way I have been putting it across to you. Oh no – because in the beginning . . . and even for quite a long time after . . . she just didn't behave in that way. All women do this: at some point when your attention is fleetingly elsewhere, they hurriedly slope off to undergo a brain transplant in order to become a completely different person altogether.

But by the stage I've been remembering, she seemed to be . . . I don't know – regressing into some sort of a second childhood, it surely appeared to me. Not in the sense that she was drivelling and incontinent like an ancient person, no of course not. She wasn't gaga, I don't mean – oh no: still sharp, sharp as a pin. But she seemed increasingly to need her toys about her – sometimes quite literally in the form of Mr Fucking Pig (the Fucking is mine) – but certainly she needed her jim-jams, her sofa, her panoply of infantile comforts. I suggested to her that here might well be a reaction to all the violence and ugliness that lurked just beyond her front door: the impulse, if not compulsion, to recede into the nest, gathering the feathers around her – but needless to say she knocked that little tinpot theory very squarely on the head. Rather more of a defence, she argued, against the severity, the wholly uncompromising nature of *you*, Terence: your own ridiculously rigid parameters, within which you are constantly attempting to trap and inveigle me, to force me to conform. Her words – for she was not, of course, unintelligent. And had she said to me such a thing rather earlier on in our relationship (because it was a fairly meaty accusation; I did actually see that), well then I would, I suppose, have taken it reasonably seriously. Yes, I can see myself, a snapshot of myself, lowering my head in what I hoped would come over as a display of penitence, while nodding my head slowly and wisely . . . maybe even patting her hand in a reassuring, though quite possibly thoroughly maddening sort of a way. But by this time, well . . . I was rather beyond caring about or even listening to anything at all she had to say to me, quite frankly. And anyway, by then . . . I was seeing someone else. More than one, actually. I had, in a sense, regressed myself – back to my carefree teens and early twenties. And what then might that have been a reaction to? A defence against? Christ knows. Nothing deep, I shouldn't have said – just easy, wasn't it? Bit of fun. Certainly I remember it being pleasant enough at the time. And then one of the girls I was seeing – and all of them, you know, they were completely random: girls in bars, girls at parties, girls encountered through my work (which by that time had to do with the designing of shopfronts and display areas, so plenty of scope there, you see: no shortage, if you know what I mean) – well one of them, one of the girls, she very quickly rather enchanted me. Yes . . . and that was Amy, of course.

Amy . . . oh, she was lovely, just lovely – and is today, she is today. Many ways. The thing is now, though . . . I'm still rather rattling with all of the Celia stuff, to be perfectly frank with you, so I'm not at all sure now that I can just launch myself into yet another chapter: the history of Amy, the tale of how we met, the way it all developed – blossomed, you could say: yes, it really might be said to have blossomed – and all so extraordinarily quickly. Everyone seemed to be delighted when after really no time at all we announced our engagement – though none more so than all of my married mates (not one of whom I see any more, in common with everybody else). It makes me smile: I honestly don't think they could have borne it for very much longer, you know – the wholly vicarious though shuddering thrills over all I was up to – and certainly not the subsequent agony at the seeping in of the true realisation about my actually quite wonderful existence, and then when it hit them squarely between the eyes: a mortgage so low that I barely perceived it as being even an obligation, the gunmetal Porsche 911, my beautiful flat filled with such a collection of classic twentieth-century furniture and artwork, champagne (Bollinger) always in the fridge, the total freedom to come and go exactly as I pleased, night and day . . . and then of course the women, the girls . . . oh my God. Oh my God. Just thinking of it now: fantastic. A playboy existence, with no strings attached: I hadn't even once become entangled with some vengeful and psycho lunatic, which you would have thought by now the law of averages might have dictated to be a virtual certainty. Yes and all of those married men . . . dear oh dear. It hurt them, viscerally (I witnessed their wincing) – it nearly destroyed them, just to meet and talk to me. And oh yes of course they would regale me with all the things I was missing: the security, the joy of children . . . the security, the joy of children – anything else they could hurriedly, or even quite frenziedly cobble together . . . though it did, I'm afraid, rather tend to peter out after the security, the joy of children. And no one – not them, not I – was ever for a minute even remotely convinced. Because I had it all. Didn't I? You're a man in your early thirties . . .well then, you see what I mean: I had it all. Didn't I? And now, at long last, here I was, poised upon giving all of it up, and becoming one of them. The collective exhalation of relief would have extinguished a thousand candles. I was left in no doubt that they would all band together to do everything within their power to ensure that I was as snug and comfortable as they were, within this new cell, all of my own making – yes and right from the minute I was first sent down.

The odd thing was, though – I was ready for it. Wouldn't have done it otherwise, would I? More than ready, actually – eager, I was eager, totally wanting it, the whole damn thing. I suppose I had known that one day it would happen, but never had marriage been a thing to plan for, though neither to avoid. Fatherhood too – I had never nurtured any paternal desires, partly because I was not at all sure how good at it I'd be. I mean . . . my dad, I thought he was okay – yes but how good is okay, you see? Nothing else to compare it with, is there? We all of us have only the one dad . . . although I suppose that you do know, at least with the twin benefits of hindsight and further experience of other people's families, whether he's just been bloody awful in every way imaginable. But I wasn't against becoming a father, by no means – it was just one of the very many things that I'd never been moved to seriously consider. I suppose you don't, really – until the moment, the stark and very grown-up possibility of such a thing will finally arise. Amy . . . well Amy, she wanted to be married. In the abstract sense, she had long ago decided that that is what she wanted to be. Don't know about motherhood, not too sure what she felt about that . . . but certainly she wanted to be married: that I think I knew very soon after I first met her – in a wine bar, actually it was, but I can't go into all that, not now: take ages, all that. But she was no sort of a career woman, Amy, nothing like that. She had, she told me, tried her hand at one or two things in the past (any details of which she always took scrupulous care to keep defiantly vague) but soon had the wit to see (because many of us don't – just battle on blindly, hoping for the impossible) that she would never amount to more than merely a monthly wage earner . . . and so therefore she wanted to be married, to have someone to take care of all that side of things for her. At first she had been a little ashamed, she laughingly disclosed to me one romantic evening, at how unfeminist, how sweetly old-fashioned her determination, though later she had become rather proud of it. So I suppose that her theoretical ideal would have been a man a great deal richer and more successful than myself . . . though, presumably, this mythical fellow had yet to make an appearance, while I, on the other hand, was standing there before her. But I did not for a moment believe that she was settling: neither of us ever thought that. Because we loved each other, was the point. We simply fell in love, you see, the two of us. And that, really, was all of it.

What, though, was Amy's attitude to design . . .? That all-important thing. Her attitude to the beautiful original furniture and objects that already by the time I met her I had very largely amassed . . .? Well I'll tell you: ambivalence. She did not know what they were – perfectly obviously had never before encountered such things. Didn't like, didn't dislike. Amazing in itself, yes of course it is – because every single one of them, ideally they should sing out to you – though mercifully she had no alternative suggestions to proffer, and nor did she bring with her a warehouse full of tat (as Celia most surely would have done, given half the chance: do you know – Celia, she is the only person I have ever in my life encountered who actually owned antimacassars . . .? Embroidered by her grandmother with roses, and with an edging of lace. Oh stop! I've done with Celia: Celia is out of the story). But Amy – listen to this: she hadn't even heard of Charles Eames. Hadn't even heard of him, for Christ's sake – and he, then as now, is the closest I come to the observation of a formal religion. Now though, very unfortunately . . . well now she appreciates them, says she appreciates them, yes she does, but for all the wrong reasons. She sees them merely as names, the right names . . . she sees them as, oh God . . . just more labels. Yes. To be acquired, and then ticked off the list. Like all her bloody shoes and watches and fucking ridiculous handbags. I try to tell her that it isn't the same: that what we are talking about here is . . . *art*. She doesn't argue. She doesn't care. She just doesn't see it: doesn't see it at all.

K.T did. She – she saw it completely. But no . . . I'm rushing ahead of myself here. Can't yet get on to K.T . . . if ever I do. No – back to Amy: just let me say that after a few years of living in my flat and renting out hers, we finally sold the two of them – more than a wrench for me, yes it was, but it did mean we could buy a rather special though modestly sized coach house in a quiet and nicely tucked-away avenue, and that's where still we are living. Norman Shaw it is, actually – and the classical elements of the architecture (for here he drew more upon eighteenth-century principles, and less upon the rather more high-flown Arts & Crafts for which he is generally rather better known) . . . the panelling, the windows, the proportions (for yes it is only a coach house, but they took their work seriously in

74

those days: please don't get me on to post-war architecture in Britain) . . . they all do work extraordinarily well with the Mies, the Corb, the Aalto . . . and of course the Eames.

So . . . what happened then . . .? Well then Elizabeth came along, of course, dear little Lizzie – such a girl, and I care for her deeply. Yes . . . and it's really just as well that I do, as things have turned out . . . because Amy, now . . . well. Were it not for me, I think that little Lizzie would be feeling decidedly unloved. Sometimes I will glance at her in profile, her eyelids dipped, the peachy skin quite dulled by melancholy: I yearn, at moments such as that, to scoop her up and whisper into her ear all that I would do for her – to feel her grip, to see her eyes ablaze with love for me. Because as I think I've already made clear, everything is just Alexander, with Amy: she simply cannot see beyond him. And yes, very obviously, it is through Alexander that now and finally she has become fulfilled – but at what expense to the boy? In the long term. You see? Yes . . . except that she isn't, of course. Fulfilled. Is she? Never will be. More, is what she wants. More is all she's after. Never used to be like that, Amy. But now she is. She very much is, now. Because she's had a taste of it, you see. More than a taste – a lasciviously dripping mouthful. Alexander's near instant success as a child model, of all things on God's earth – which yes, pretty much took my breath away, if you want the truth. Throughout the whole process, I didn't encourage, and nor did I discourage. From the moment when Amy first brought it all up. This idea of hers. The possibilities. When the two of them were making up his 'book', endlessly sending out résumés, attending all of those auditions. I suppose I thought that nothing would come of it. One mother's dreams . . .? How seldom do they ever come true? Whereas . . . a very great deal has come of it – yes, and

75

alarmingly quickly. And now, if you can believe it (because this is the latest, this is the latest) we are, I am smugly and unremittingly informed, talking Hollywood. Hollywood. Doesn't seem real. And I wish I could talk to K.T about it. She's the only one who could ever understand.

K.T, yes. Who rather seems to have reasserted herself into this narrative (as she does within my mind, and just constantly lately). Because following my marriage to Amy – which, despite its being just as acceptable as I rather thought it might be . . . and still is, in many ways – it didn't take me really very long to fall. A case of old habits dying hard, I can only suppose: scratch a husband, and you'll find a bound and gagged bachelor, hot with sweat and struggling within. Mmm . . . and when I first met her – quite utterly by chance, as ever it is: anything in my life which I have actually scrupulously planned and yearned for has withered on the vine, faded by the wayside, dead before even it has come into bud, let alone blossomed into the thing that I all along had intended it to become. So yes . . . when I first met her, I was engaged in overseeing the installation of something that was a little bit out of the way of the more usual sorts of things I had been working on at the time. Not a shopfront per se, but more a large sort of a fascia affair to be erected behind and above the curvaceous reception desk in the Soho foyer of this film production company, whose name was . . . well I can't at the moment recall it. Which is surprising actually, because I had been juggling for just bloody ages on my Mac so very many permutations of font, colour and the degree of neon (for the most insistent element of the client's brief had been that it must hit you in the eye the second you walk through the door and remain in the mind as an abiding image, that much I do remember). I mean, it wasn't one of the absolute big boys – Fox,

Universal, one of those. British, as a matter of fact, and pretty prominent: they were riding high on a tide of critical acclaim, popular appeal and ultra-fashionable stars, the combination of which had alchemically magicked itself into seemingly permanent box-office gold following an unbroken string of successes which – and the *bien-pensant* seemed to be at one on this – had harnessed, crystallised and exemplified the zeitgeist of the moment. What this broadly translated into was the fact that because the producers had always very judiciously taken the vital decision to cast the sympathetic female lead and the toothy cool nice guy as Americans (the English actors manfully coping with the slurry of cockney whores, salivating shits, lisping perverts and drawlingly upper-class and sadistic crooks) the US of A had bestowed upon these pictures the ultimate accolade of coast-to-coast distribution and big, glitzy weekend openings on the grounds that they were just so typically *Briddish*. Not, then, consigning them to instant and international oblivion, as was the fate of so many other home-grown and infinitely superior movies, on the grounds that they were just so typically *Briddish*.

Anyway . . . the name . . . the name of the company, it hardly matters – though it will come to me, I'll get it, of course I will . . . when I'm thinking of something else entirely, it'll pop into my head – but the name, whatever the company is called . . . of course it's not remotely relevant to the signal fact that it was in the foyer of that building on the corner of Wardour Street and is it Frith, that first I set eyes upon my own K.T. Yes and the first thing I noticed about her was how terribly tall she was – slim, rangy, big green eyes delineated in black, her dark hair stunning in the recently revived Vidal Sassoon/Mary Quant sort of maybe Anna Wintour kind of cut (so swinging in any way you like) – but more than all that, it was her height that struck me: taller than I, which is a thing I don't at all go for in a woman (not over keen on it in a man) . . . although she was, of course, happily aloft in the then quite customary bright red, strappy and fuck-you shoes (not fuck-me – fuck-you) which were, as I say, prevalent at the time in these sorts of professions, if professions they be – and Amy, doubtless, could have told you the brand, their scarcity (for it was Amy who apprised me of the news that shoes could be scarce) and, if still available even in only the sillier sizes, almost certainly the best price that could be obtained online from an 'outlet'. I remember too the dress that she was wearing: short, boxy and geometric – a copy (though highly probably marketed as a 'hommage') of something Yves St Laurent, that shyly clever and elegant thief, had had the gall to come up with back in the nineteen sixties, not too long after he was uniformly and very ridiculously hailed as nothing short of a genius for having taken a traditional gentleman's dinner jacket (or 'tuxedo' as the fashion press would irritatingly have it) and putting it on a woman. I only actually was aware of the history of this dress because the blocking of primary colour severely divided by black was of course a perfectly shameless appropri- ation of Mondrian's quite early exposition of his actually exceedingly complex theories. And very possibly wholly pre- dictably, I have a great deal of time for this artist – though all we had here was a clumsily lumpish interpretation of his vision, wilfully misunderstood and misapplied to a merely gimcrack and laughably overpriced example of nothing more than glori- fied high-street schmutter. Mm . . . but having said all of that, however, I do have to add that she who was so very soon to become my own K.T . . . she did wear it well.

'Hi,' she said to me. 'So you're the designer guy, yeh? Terry – right?'

'Yup. Terence. That's me. And you are . . .?'

'Katie. We've been emailing. You don't look like a Terry . . .'

'Don't I? What do I look like? It's Terence, actually.'

'I don't know . . . Tom, maybe . . . you maybe could look like a Tom . . .'

'Tom? Okay – I'll have it changed immediately. And you're Katie. I couldn't honestly say whether you look like a Katie or you don't. And you say we've been emailing . . .? I don't quite, um . . . Oh wait – you're K.T . . .! I get it. I wondered what the initials stood for. I just assumed some executive or other who couldn't be buggered to sign his full name . . . arrogant sod . . .'

And her fingers – long fingers, long like her legs, and the nails, they were long too and painted bright red, like her shoes, like her lips – they flitted up to those big red lips just at that very moment, and her eyes, green eyes, they squinted into babyish small, and she giggled with not really remotely embarrassment.

'Oh my God I'm so sorry . . .! I didn't know! I had no idea that's what people must think . . .! It's just that everyone here – they all call me K.T, you see. Everybody does. So I suppose I just sort of assume . . .'

'Right. I see. Well now I know. It's fine. Of course it's fine. So let me get it straight: it's K, yes? And then T – right? Like that singer, yes? What's her name again . . .?'

'Yeh. But I was doing it way before she was. Anyway – this sign, this huge thing you've done, yeh? It's going to look great, isn't it? I've seen all the projections. 3D stuff and everything – and now it's actually here! I think it's really great. I just adore design like that. Can't wait to see it when it's up.'

'You do . . .?'

'Oh God yeh. Bit of a design junkie, I'm afraid. Bore for

England about it, my friends say. On at me all the time. They're all going to me: "Jesus K.T . . .! Just shut up about it, can't you . . .?" '

'Really? Well. How very interesting. Look – they're working pretty quickly, aren't they? Contractors. Probably should be done in an hour or so, not much more by the looks of it. So I was actually thinking I might, um . . . I don't suppose you're free to, er . . . well I was just going to get a coffee, or something. If you can get away, maybe . . .?'

'Yeh, I could . . . yeh I could do that, sure. Can't be gone too long, though.'

'Don't have to be gone too long. Just a coffee. No shortage of places round here.'

'Right. Coffee central, round here. And oh my God the restaurants . . .! So . . . Bar Italia, maybe? You know it? Go there quite a lot, actually. Amazing espresso.'

And – while naturally still quite gorgeously awash in all of that design junkie business – I remember thinking two more things: the Bar Italia – yes, I know it: the Soho original, and the very best, that neon façade one of the finest in London. And then I thought: espresso – what a blessing, what a bloody blessing! Not some stupid fucking trendy variation, but just the very thing itself: plain and simple.

'Great,' I said. 'Let's go.'

And just that single half hour in the Bar Italia – and it took just a moment, and years and years and years . . . I remember it as being one of the very most blissful instances of my entire life on earth. Yes . . . and I can't go back there now, to the Bar Italia. No, couldn't possibly. Saw it – saw it, just momentarily glimpsed it really, in a movie on television just the other night . . . and do you know my breath was caught . . .? It was all I could do not to cry out (and had Amy not been there, I just know I would have wailed). Yes. So no – haven't been back there, the Bar Italia, not since K.T and I . . . since we no longer . . . oh well anyway. So that's why I'd never go again. Just too damn painful. Yes but never before or since (well obviously not since, there's been no one since) have I bonded so instantly with a woman – with any human being. We were laughing . . . we were sitting on stools, swigging our double espressi and laughing very nearly hysterically – although nothing was funny, only filled right up to brimming with delight – as we skittered through the insistent and unstoppable cascade of clutter from a cupboard which, until this moment – and I really do believe this – had been jammed tight shut for the both of us: all of our enthusiasms, so very many of them mutual to an almost unbelievable degree. Dizzies me now, even to think of it. And here's a thing: she recognised my battered stone and lived-in trench as being a vintage example of the original Aquascutum made famous by Bogart – not ever a Burberry, as the idiots assume. Eames, she said – I remember this (well of course I do, I remember it all – I remember just everything, everything) – Eames, she said, is a god. And he is, of course: of course he is. Either you know this to be true, or else you are one of them – the outsiders, the flounderers, the stooges, the civilians: all the blind buffoons. She was visibly thrilled when I told her of this amazing house clearance sale upon which I had wholly serendipitously stumbled, oh God – how many years ago must it have been? I was on my way to somewhere else entirely when I caught out of the corner of my eye this roughly scribbled sign nailed on to a tree in a shabby front garden: one of the best and happiest accidents of my life – they simply didn't know what they were selling, the agents:

banging out the stuff for just whatever they could get. Where I got my Eames lounger and ottoman, the Eiffel chairs, an Eileen Gray side table, Vitsoe shelving . . . and then there was that long and low Scandinavian teak sideboard which eventually I sold on for more than I'd paid for just all the rest of it put together . . . though not before discovering, rammed to the back of one of the drawers . . . a Luger. Wrapped and bound in a dark-stained, hardened and sticky sort of oilcloth, and seemingly forgotten for possibly decades. My first instinct was to hand it in to whomever one is expected to hand in such things as a German pistol . . . but then, but then . . . I weighed it in my hand . . . and knew I just had to hold on to it. Always wanted to own one – never thought I would, of course, because how on earth could you? So I kept that, yes, like so much else, simply for the look of it (yes – and only for the look of it). Then K.T and I, we were stumbling over the ends of one another's sentences in a rush to complete them: perfect pitch – harmonic, and making such a melody. While quite in tune with that . . . I was instantly and totally overcome by a boiling and practically violent lust: I could during the very first moments have torn right into her with a breathless force – though yet such ease and sweetness – and there, right there, on the chequered floor of the Bar Italia.

And so it all began. I was not looking for a woman – and had I been, then none would have come. For having married Amy, I had made no vow to myself never to enter into an affair . . . though neither was I aware of the shadow of such a thing skulking deep in sullen corners, a dark intention waiting to be born. Like so much else, I simply didn't think of it. But on that day from God in heaven I had been presented with this, such glorious bounty: so what was I to do? Resist it? Could I ever, seriously, have resisted K.T? Well could I? Stupid question. Isn't it, really? Because of course I couldn't, and nor did it so much as occur to me even to try. K.T and I . . . were meant. Is the simple fact. And still are – still are, of course. For that – that will never change: not for me . . . no, not ever for me: I'll always feel the same, as long as I live. And Jesus . . . oh *Jesus* . . . I miss her so very very badly. Every day . . . every single day, I wake, and then I ache, before bleeding. Oh . . . look . . . look . . . I'm sure I'll come back, return to this, the unimaginably wonderful year that I gloried in her company, and all our loving that was consistently ecstatic (yes because I must, I must return to them, of course I must – I know them by heart, each one of those moments, and it is in that heart that I keep them, as a treasure). But . . . I'm hurting now, I'm hurting quite a lot . . . yes I am, actually . . . and so I cannot linger. Within this reminiscence, I have only the strength for the one more agony, before I'm done for . . . and so now I have to take you to the end: the day that just split me asunder.

'But K.T . . . K.T . . . why are you saying this? How can you say this to me . . .? You're not serious. You can't possibly be serious . . .'

'Oh Christ, Tom . . . why do you even say that? Hm? Why do you even bother? Of course it's . . . Of course I'm . . .! Jesus. . .! What – you think I find this *funny* . . .?'

Tom, yes: having said to me during those first golden seconds of our serendipitous meeting that I looked like a Tom, she had more or less straight away taken to calling me that. Didn't know what to think at the beginning, quite what to make of it . . . then I came to tolerate it, didn't mind it too much . . . and soon – well, gradually, really – I became very fond indeed of the whole idea. It made me . . . separate, you see. Separate from Terence. Because

83

whenever I was with K.T, that is just exactly how I felt – beautifully distanced from just everything that could ever come close to identifying me.

'No . . . no of course not. Of course I don't think you think it's . . . it's just that I . . .! Oh *Jesus*, K.T . . .!'

'I know. I know. I feel the same. I feel exactly the same, Tom. Well of course I do.'

'Well then . . .*why* . . .? How can you . . .? I mean . . . well you can't. You just can't. How would we be able to . . .? How *can* we . . .?!'

'Must. Just have to. Because otherwise, well . . .'

'Well what? Otherwise what? *What* . . .?'

'Because otherwise, Tom . . . nothing will change. Will it?'

'Don't want it to. Why should it? It's perfect. It's perfect. It's just perfect as it is. Why would you want it to change?'

'Perfect for you. Oh look – we've *done* this, haven't we? Been over and over it. You're just never going to . . . *move*. Are you?'

'Move . . .?'

'You know what I mean, Tom. Don't pretend. Please don't do all of that. Not now. You know exactly what I mean.'

'Yes but . . . well I never said I would, did I? I never made you a promise. Did I . . .? I never said that. But I am . . . *committed* . . .'

'Ah but you're not, are you Tom? That's the point, isn't it? That's the whole bloody trouble. And don't you think that our being together, everything we've done, the way we still are . . . and it's a year now Tom. It's a year now we've been like this. Well don't you think that's a promise? Don't you think that's a promise in itself . . .?'

'Eleven months . . .'

'I'm pretty sure it's actually a year, Tom.'

84

'Eleven months . . . and three weeks. It is. If you want to know.'

'You count . . .?'

'I do. Every day. As a blessing. A blessing, K.T. I . . . *love* you . . .! Can't you see that . . .?'

'I know you do. I know that, Tom.'

'And you – you do. You love me. Don't you? Well don't you . . .?'

'Tom . . .'

'Never mind "Tom". You do. Don't you . . .?'

'Course. Of course. You don't have to . . . You know that. You know I do, Tom.'

'Well then . . .!'

'Can't.'

'Can't? Can't what? What can't you do? I'll *help* you . . .'

'You can't help me, Tom. Don't you see? It's you. It's us. It's just me *sitting* here. I need to be with someone . . . *properly* . . . Why do men just never seem to see that? Yeh well – because they never want to, do they . . .?'

'Someone . . .? What do you mean – "someone"? What do you mean you need to be with "someone" . . .? Me . . .! You mean me . . .! It's me you need to be with. Isn't it . . .?'

'Ideally. Yes. Yes of course, you. What do you think I'm doing here in the first place? I'm *offering* myself to you, aren't I? Aren't I, Tom? I'm offering *me* – it's all I have to give you. So if you want me so much – if you really need me the way you say you do . . . well then take me. I'm here. Aren't I? So take me, Tom. What are you waiting for? Hm? Just *take* me. Well why don't you . . .?'

Yes . . . but I couldn't. Face all of that. Thought about it – of course I'd thought about it, Christ: how many endless, sweating

85

and agonised nights . . .? Because with K.T . . . well with K.T, you see, I was alive . . . I was *me*. It was only whenever I was with K.T that I could feel like that. And Amy . . . well now, if ever I was with Amy, well . . . by this stage we were just help-lessly staring at one another across an arid frontier, maybe both of us striving quite desperately to remember just what in God's name it was that we were supposed to be doing. Or maybe we weren't . . . maybe we weren't thinking that at all, nor anything like it. Yes . . . but anyway . . . it wasn't as simple as that, no of course it wasn't – because when, ever, is it? It's never just simply a matter of choice, is it? One thing or the other. No never – because there's always so much else. Just so much. Well I mean for one thing there was little Lizzie, wasn't there? Lizzie, yes – my girl, my little girl. And Alexander, to be considered. The house . . . yes the house as well. And everything in it. So you see – you can see it, can't you? I'm sure that you can – well anyone would. That it was all just . . . too much. Far too much for me to seriously contemplate. So . . . I didn't. I kept everything together. Yes I did. Well . . . not everything. Not everything, no. One factor, only the one, just the one little thing, hardly impor-tant, really neither here nor there . . . fell casualty to a terrible scythe. Because that was the day that just split me asunder.

I thought . . . at first I had thought that I never would – how could I? – be able to absorb the pain, while still being expected to more or less function as at least the simulacrum of a nearly human being: the pain, yes, so very much of it – the slicing pain of being without her. And worse, so very much worse . . . the thought of her with anyone else. Then I would try to contain it, bottle the hurt, bandage its burning, damp it, swaddle it, and maybe unto death . . .? Didn't work. Of course not. It bled, it continued to seep – was oozing through each of the splits in me, before I came eventually to burst. Pleaded with her . . . pleaded with her time and time again . . . abased myself most utterly: promising her anything, if only she'd take me back . . . anything, yes, except the one true thing that always, I suppose, she had been stridently demanding, if only in silence, and which she knew that, out of cowardice, I would never be able to give her – even while I was maddened by needing that very thing for myself, as I continued to tear me to tatters. I would say that I did not take this like a man – though of course I did, and quite completely. She cried, K.T – over the phone I heard her, for her presence, the faint-inducing scent and soft bewitching touch of her, those were cruelly forbidden to me utterly – but she would not bend, she would not see me. And when finally – and after how long? For you surely do realise that I am manfully con-densing the worst of the horror, compressing it, yes, and solely for the sake of my own preservation, as I simply cannot risk the danger of any further implosion, knowing as I do that should I fragment . . . well then I'm done for. But finally, when finally I forced myself to believe that it was over . . . over, yes. Finished. Done. The end of the affair. When finally I forced myself to believe that it was over . . . well then . . . then, I simply could not bring myself to believe it.

So now . . . now I am condemned to yearn within: a constant and nearly smothered whimper of simply eternally missing her. And by some dreadful extension of that . . . me as well. Oh yes: I miss me terribly, every single day, though mostly in the swamp of the middle of the night. And I expected, did I, that life with Amy, with Amy and the children . . . I did expect yes, I suppose I must have, that all would continue, and much as it had before. Yes but then I had never taken seriously, had I, all of Amy's vaulting ambitions. Her soaring aims for Alexander. And now . . . well now . . . everything is different. His success . . . her success . . . it means that everything has changed. Well just take this dinner party as a pertinent example: this dinner party for Friday evening that now she is so very eagerly plotting. Well in the old days, of course, such a thing could never have happened. Simple as that. That is why I was more or less goggling at her, as she breezily was dismissing every one of my heartfelt qualms as no more than torn-up little bits of paper, floating on the wind – and all the while airily referring to the thing as really nothing more than 'a few people over for a bite to eat'. Because, you see, we never have done this. In the past. Had people over. Never. No not once. Well . . . maybe, extremely occasionally, the very odd drink. Christmas, possibly. Though certainly not for a 'bite to eat'.

'Well who's coming, then? Who have you invited to this stupid thing?'

'Oh God's sake, Terence! Why are you constantly making such a bloody big deal of everything? People do *do* this, you know. Have people over. It's not completely freakish.'

'Yes well – people might. But we don't. Do we? Ever.'

'Well now we are. About time, wouldn't you say? We got around to behaving like normal adult people? Have to get used to it. Things are changing fast, I'm very delighted to say. Well aren't they? Although . . . this house . . . it's not really that suited. To entertaining, I mean. Is it? Not on any sort of a *scale*, anyway. Well. Something to think about in the future.'

'I'm not. I'm not going to think about it in the future or any time at all, actually Amy. What – so now you're saying that the house isn't good enough for you, are you? It always was in the past. You loved this house. Or you said you did.'

'I do. I like it. I quite like it. But if I said I "loved" it – which

88

I don't think I ever did, actually – well then that was, as you quite rightly say, Terence, in the past. Wasn't it? And the past is for leaving behind. That's what I think, anyway. It's the next thing – always the next thing. That's where all the excitement lies. Or maybe you've forgotten.'

I haven't forgotten. How could I? I never knew it. And anyway – for me, that very obviously will never be true. Because the past, well – that is exactly where my excitement lies. Yes – that's where it lies, all right: dead and bloody buried.

'Well answer me, Amy. Who's coming? Who have you invited?'

I bet not Bob. Bob, who lives just a couple of streets away. The only one of my old mates that I ever even bump into these days. No – not Bob: he won't be on the list, you can be very sure of that. My friend, you see – not Amy's. And being in insurance, that makes him totally irrelevant – couldn't possibly bring the slightest influence to bear, neither one way nor the other. He is far from a snappy dresser, old Bob, so would hardly grace the table . . . so all in all, let's face it, not even worth impressing with the full and blinding dazzle of glory that is Amy's son and mine, Alexander.

'Well just Dolly and Damien, really. Sylvia and Mike . . . but only for pre-drinks. I don't want them to be at the actual dinner. They're too . . . well – I just don't want them there, that's all. And Portia. Portia is one of the movie people, yes? I've talked about her – though whether you bothered to listen or not . . . Anyway – I think it will further Alexander's cause, let us say. Leave it at that. You'll like her. She's very nice.'

'Just for the "pre-drinks", did you say . . .? Did I actually hear you say that, Amy? What in Christ's name are pre-fucking-drinks . . .?'

'Oh do use your imagination, Terence – honestly! What do you think they are? Drinks before dinner. What else could they be? Jesus . . .'

'Oh I see. Right. Oh yes of course. So Sylvia and Mike, they plod over here from next door and get a drink shoved into their hands – I'm assuming they're not expected to bring their own . . .? And then when you're busy ushering Dolly and Damien and whatever you said the other bitch was called – just as you're showing them all into the dining room, I'm what . . .? Kicking Sylvia and Mike out of the door. That it? That the plan? Well I don't think you can do that actually, Amy. Mike and Sylvia . . . they're old school. You have to understand that. Different generation. In their book, you're either asked over, or you aren't.'

'Oh don't be ridiculous, Terence. I shall explain it all to them beforehand, of course I will. They only want a glimpse of Alexander anyway. Because he'll be here, of course. At the beginning, anyway. Not for the actual dinner – I don't actually think that would be right. But everyone will of course want to meet him, won't they? So I'll have to have him here at the beginning. Because I just know they'd all be awfully disappointed if he didn't even put in an appearance.'

'Oh Christ yes. Absolutely devastated, I'd say. Not to be granted an audience with a ten-year-old kid . . .? Not something you could ever really survive, is it? I'm assuming you'll have a selection of eight-by-tens at the ready, will you? Then everyone can queue up for his fucking autograph . . .'

'Oh Jesus, Terence . . . I do hope you're not going to be like this on the night. Honestly – the bloody fuss you have to make about everything. And rude. You are becoming increasingly rude. Alexander – he is your son, you know. It's almost as if you're ashamed of everything he's achieved, or something. Christ – you'd think you'd show a little *pride* . . .'

'Well what about Lizzie? Hey?'

'What about Lizzie . . .?'

'She invited, is she? Or just for pre-drinks, maybe. Or because she isn't even slightly famous, maybe we ought to dump her altogether. Disown her. What do you think? Christ, Amy – what you're actually doing here is assembling a bunch of droolers – people who are absolutely guaranteed to envy you to hell . . . well, Dolly will anyway, Damien's not quite so much of an idiot – well he is an idiot, of course he is, just not in that particular way, that's all . . . Sylvia and Mike, obviously . . . and then some bitch or other who you think can further the boy's career. Even you have to admit it, Amy – it's all really pretty disgusting, isn't it?'

'Oh nonsense, Terence. You just don't know what you're talking about. And I do wish you would stop referring to Portia as a "bitch". You've never met her, have you? Had you done so, you would know that she is very far indeed from being a "bitch". She is a highly cultivated person in an extremely responsible position.'

'I see. Well thank you for the slapping, Amy. I am properly admonished. And Mr Portia – he coming too, is he? Or doesn't she let him out in the evenings? The bitch.'

'Well – sore point, actually. At the moment they're in the throes of what I gather is a rather nasty divorce. I get the very strong feeling that daggers are drawn.'

'Oh I am so very very sorry to hear that . . .! How perfectly dreadful to learn that there are some desperately unfortunate couples out there against whom fate has conspired to deny the right to the sort of pure domestic joy that it is our happy lot on earth to share in blissful harmony . . .'

'Fool, Terence. I'm not going to talk to you any more. You really are, you know: perfectly ridiculous. And rude.'

'Fine. Stop, then. Stop now.'

'And on Friday evening . . . do try not to look like a tramp, will you?'

And I looked at her. I just looked at her. Because she meant it, you know – oh Christ yes, she meant it all right. And suddenly . . . I was just terribly and utterly exhausted. By the whole damn thing.

'Yes. All right, Amy. I'll try. I will. I'll try my very hardest. Promise.'

Because of course I will: it's all I do. Try. Try to survive. Try not to weep. Try not to be felled even by the thought of another coming day, let alone the battle and pointlessness of the day itself. Yes, oh yes – it's all I do, now. I try and try, I do, I really do . . . but you know . . . just lately, I think I might be failing. Faltering. Not really doing too well, all things being equal. By and fucking large. Though if I do – if I do come to fail, Amy . . . if no longer I am able to keep from crumbling . . . should I fragment, and am done for . . . well then you, my sweet . . . you, my cherished wife . . . you will be the very first to know about it. On that you may depend.

CHAPTER THREE

PURITY OF LINE

'Mortified. Mortified. I just wish to God we'd never gone.'

'Do you? I don't. Quite enjoyed it, really. Seeing the young man again . . .'

'Yes well that was just all of it for you, wasn't it Mike? That's all you've been talking about since they asked us. Looking forward to it, I don't know why. My God – you were like that with The Beatles about fifty bloody years ago. Thought you would have been over it by now. All that sort of thing. *Wrong* with you . . .? Not a child! *Pas un enfant!*'

'Yes but he is really, isn't he? Only ten, after all . . .'

'Not *Alexander* . . .! You! You stupid man. And exactly! Exactly! He's only a little boy. Why were you just so . . . oh – just so all *over* him . . .? Disgusting. Could hardly believe it. Known him all his life . . . only *Alexander*, isn't it . . .?'

'Well I didn't see you *ignoring* him exactly, Sylvia. Telling him how wonderful he was . . .'

'Yes well you've got to, haven't you? Got to do that. Amy there all the time. Hanging around, way she does. Listening in on everything. You've got to. Expected, isn't it? Simple politeness. But you, Mike . . . oh my God! At one point I thought you were going to ask him for his autograph.'

'Oh don't be so silly, Sylvia . . .'

'Lock of his *hair*, or something . . .'

'Goodness' sake. Just taking an interest, wasn't I? Just talking to the boy. Looking very good he was, I thought. Very fit. Quite a colour to him. And those slim blue trousers he had on – and the Chelsea boots . . .! Midnight blue, we used to call that. Did you see them, Sylvia? Lord above, I would've given my bloody eye teeth for clothes like that, back in the sixties. Had to make do with C&A – do you remember? Things I used to wear? Expect you do. Used to quite fancy myself as a bit of a dandy, in those days. Funny to think it now. Dedicated follower of fashion. Remember that song? Kinks. And the way I had my hair? Thought it looked like Paul McCartney. Dear oh dear. Probably more like Worzel Gummidge. And now it's all gone, mostly. Wouldn't mind a head of hair like that again, tell you that. But there's nothing new any more, is there? It all comes round again.'

'All given to him, aren't they? The clothes. Burberry and Paul Smith, Amy was saying. And that stuff on his face . . . did you notice? Amy and him, they were exactly the same colour. Wrong, isn't it? Boy, wearing make-up. Even a girl, that age. And talking of that – where was little Lizzie? Didn't even put in an appearance. Expect she couldn't face it, poor love. Everyone drooling over little brother. What's a girl to think? Your hair never looked a bit like Paul McCartney's. Did you really think that? Did you honestly, Mike? Men – honestly. At least Lizzie, she was spared the sight of you, anyway – behaving as if you were talking to the Queen, or something . . .'

'Hardly, Sylvia. But look – we're not exactly, are we, um

– what do they say . . .? Jet-setters, are we? High-flyers. Movers and whatever it is they are, all these people. Not a lot of excitement in our lives, is there, Sylvia? These days. Face it. And well . . . living next door to a lad who's always in the papers . . . gives you a bit of a lift. No harm in that. Woof – girl in the corner shop, other day – ever so impressed, she was, when old Patel told her I knew him. He was on the cover of something on the counter – buying it, she was, I'm pretty sure. Should've heard her. "What!" she said. Really funny, it was. "What!" she was going. "You mean you actually *know* him . . .? Alexander! You've actually *spoken* to him . . .? Oh wow!" Can't have been more than fourteen, fifteen. Thin little thing. "Oh wow!" she went. Kept on saying it. "Oh wow! . . . Oh wow! . . ." '

'Fifteen, did you say?'

'Could've been fifteen, yes. I would have said so. Fourteen, fifteen . . .'

'Well that's pretty disgusting for a start, isn't it? He – Alexander, he's only ten. Isn't he? Ten years old. What do these teenage girls imagine they're doing? Going all like that over a child . . .? *Dégoûtant.*'

'Well I suppose it's – well, he's in all these . . . what is it . . .? These comics. No – not comics. Don't have comics any more, do they? Whatever these things are that the teenage girls are buying nowadays, I suppose. Whatever he was on the cover of. He's in all of them, apparently, according to Patel. And all over the internet, of course. Quite the little pin-up.'

'Oh yes well I've read about *those*. They're just plain disgusting, those magazines. Can't think how they're allowed. All about . . . well, I won't go into what they're all about.'

'All very harmless, I'm sure.'

'Yes well that just goes to show how very little you know

about the subject, doesn't it, Mike? Doesn't it, really? When's the last time you saw one? And don't say the one on Mr Patel's counter – I mean really saw one. When's the last time you sat down and read a teenage girl's magazine, I should like to know?'

'Yes all right, Sylvia. All right.'

'Well tell me then. Tell me. *S'il te plaît*. You can't, can you? No you can't. Because you haven't. You haven't ever seen one. You wouldn't even know the name of one, would you? And that makes you an authority all of a sudden then, does it? *Harmless . . .!* Not a bit harmless, are they? Whole point. Why that politician, what was her name . . .? Minister, maybe. For something. She tried to get them banned.'

'Banned . . .? Are you sure . . .?'

'Well – maybe not banned . . . but looked into, anyway. Put a stop to the worst of it. It's all just boys boys boys. And not like it was in the old days, I don't mean. It's not like *Fabulous*, or something. It's not like *Bunty*, Mike . . .!'

'Well . . . they are girls, aren't they? Aren't they? Like boys, don't they . . .?'

'Oh . . . shut up, Mike. Just shut up, will you? Don't know anything about it, do you? Want a cup of tea . . .? I'm having one.'

'Ooh – I don't know. On top of all that champagne . . .'

'Yes well you shouldn't have drunk so much of it, should you?'

'Amy – kept filling it up. My glass. She kept on filling it up.'

'You do have a tongue in your head, Mike. Could've said no. Cava, anyway.'

'Hey?'

'Not champagne. It was Cava. Saw the label. Spanish. *Pas*

français. Although I daresay the good stuff has come out by now, of course. Now all the *special* people are there. Now they've got shot of the likes of us – who've only known them since they first came to live in this street, how many years ago. Only known them since before Alexander was even *born* . . .'

'What do you mean? Time to go, wasn't it? Don't want to overstay your welcome, do you? Not when you're just asked round for drinks.'

'Yes but *they* weren't. Were they? That Damien person, and his godawful wife. Dolly. I ask you – what sort of a name is Dolly, for a grown woman? God, they're so common, those two. Can't understand why Amy of all people would even have them in the house, let alone want to . . . oh Jesus, Mike: you really don't see it, do you? You don't see anything, do you? Do you mean to tell me honestly that you really didn't . . .? *See* . . .? What was going on round there? The way we were being edged towards the door and into the hall . . .? The way they were holding back, like that? And so very obviously waiting for who-ever it was who was late? They're having dinner, that's what they're doing. Right now. All sitting round the dinner table, as pleased as you like.'

'Oh I don't think so, Sylvia. Drinks – she just said drinks.'

'Yes – to *us*, she did. They're having dinner, I tell you. Right at this very moment, you mark my words. And if you don't see that, well then I'm sorry but you're an idiot, Mike. That's all I can say. If you can't see what is so plainly in front of your . . . well then you're just a bloody idiot. Mortified. Mortified. I just wish to God we'd never gone . . .'

'Here . . . sit down, Sylvia. Don't get all upset. Making moun-tains, aren't you? What you do. I'm sure it's not what you think.'

'Oh you're sure, are you? Well we'll see, won't we? When

they all wake us up as they're leaving. Slamming car doors. Damien and Dolly and this oh-so-very-important *film* person who didn't even have the manners to turn up on time. I bet she's there now, though. Now we've gone. Now they've got the riff-raff safely out of the way – as soon as we were out of the door they probably rang to tell her the coast was clear. Oh well. Never too old, are you? To learn another of life's little lessons. Well I won't be doing that again in a hurry, I can tell you that much. You didn't answer me, Mike . . .'

'Answer you what . . .?'

'Tea. Do you want a cup of tea . . .? I'm having one.'

'Well yes – I maybe will actually, Sylvia. I can make it, if you like . . .'

'No no. I'll do it. Couple of biscuits. Those canapés – those fishy little things. Went nowhere. Wasn't even offered whatever the puffy ones were supposed to be. Don't suppose they thought they needed too many. Don't need a lot, do you really? Not if you're having dinner directly afterwards.'

'Here, Sylvia – you sit down. I'll make us a nice pot of tea. Do you a sandwich, if you like . . .? Still some of that ham . . .'

'It would stick in my craw. Rude. No Mike I'm sorry, but it was just plain rude. It's downright rude, what Amy's just done to us. I can barely believe it . . . more or less just throwing us out . . .!'

'I'm sure she didn't mean it to be. Rude, or anything. Maybe they've got, I don't know . . . business to discuss, or something. About Alexander. This film of his.'

'What – with Damien and bloody Dolly? Are you serious? He works in a *garage*, Mike . . .! And she . . .! Well God – you've heard her. She can barely *speak* . . .! The noise she makes – you just don't know where to look . . .'

'No I meant with the other person. The person who wasn't there.'

'Yes I know, Mike, but . . . oh . . . oh, let's just leave it, shall we? Let's just leave it . . .'

'I think that's best all round, Sylvia. What I've been saying. Tea, then – yes?'

'Yes, Mike. Thank you. That would be nice. *Une tasse de thé.* Parched. That Amy, though . . . it's not Terence, I don't blame Terence. You could see he was . . . well: didn't care for it, all that was going on. You could see it. You could see it in his face. It's Amy. It's all Amy. Always is. She maybe enjoys it, I don't know. Treating people in that way. Her friends. Her neighbours. And we've been good neighbours, haven't we Mike? You know we have. Always here for them. That time they locked themselves out. Taking Lizzie in after school. How many times have we done that? Lost count. Never expected any thanks. And now this. Well I won't ever forget it, I tell you that. No I won't. And I tell you something else, Mike: I won't ever forgive her either. No. I won't. No no. Never. I never will.'

Terence, still, was idling at the dining table. He was done with marvelling at just how very much debris can quite easily be created by simply a few people – boozing, consuming a bit of food . . . yes, he had done with all that, because really he didn't care about any of it in the slightest. He still was pulling not at all committedly at the final not much more than an inch of a Partagás cigar, his eyes wincing crookedly away from the coil of midnight smoke, his two heavy fingers heated by the give of this increasingly sappy little cushion of Havana, as tentatively he continued to squeeze. The taste had been heady and sweet . . . now was just oily and vile. He ought to put it out. No – not put it out. You did not do that with cigars: simply, you lay them to rest. Yes, that would be the sensible thing to do – because my palate is hot, and my coated tongue . . . that actually is hurting me, now. I shall . . . what shall I do . . .? I know: I shall finish the last of my brandy. Armagnac. Janneau. A good deal less . . . what . . .? Silky than cognac, and that is a good thing, to my mind. Might even have another. Pour a little more. In no hurry at all to take myself to bed, because still I have thinking to do. Thinking to do, yes. Put this evening, this singular evening, into some sort of an order. Perspective, do I mean? In my head. But really, what I really need to do is just to go on clinging to all that remains to me . . . of Portia. To not let the pinprick of sensation yet desert me: I must, I need, still to be troubled by her. Focus on . . . I shall focus on the chair there, that chair just one away from me, and where she had been sitting for the whole of the evening. Her scent, though – dizzy with musk – that is all gone now. I can no longer hear her American laughter. But still I am experiencing a nearly sensation of the essence of the woman . . . and if I stand, you see, or if I leave the room . . . if now I should even so much as think of anything other . . . well then the vapour which is all that remains to me, that will thin, be broken into trails, and then just invisibility.

'Is it actually your intention to sit there for the rest of the night? If so, will you please attend to the lights? And lock up? Before your head actually hits the table.'

I look across at her, standing in the doorway. She is another person, Amy – in appearance, if not at heart – once her denuded face is shining with whatever cream or unction she always so very assiduously applies, the pads of her fingers dipping lavishly into the pot, before adjusting that black and lacy sleep mask, and finally then surrendering herself unto a fitful night. Or so it used to be, anyway, when still we shared a room. I doubt the pattern has altered. Her hair – earlier, glossily tumbling – now is pulled taut, and held by something pink and pleated . . . and those two grotesque and turquoise rollers close to her forehead, always making her seem to me as if she has been forced into costume as some unimagined extraterrestrial, caught in an unnatural blazing of light, as well as unawares.

'Will. Yes.'

'Uh-huh. And that's all you have to say to me, is it? Nothing to add? About the evening? How it all went? Everything? No little word for me? Nothing like – Oh Amy, how very wonderful you are to have prepared for us all such marvellous food, to have made the table so extremely beautiful. For having arranged the whole bloody thing in the first place . . .? No? Nothing? Not at all . . .?'

'It was . . . fine.'

'Fine. I see. It was fine.'

'Different. It was different. What do you want me to say to you . . .?'

Oh please, Amy – just leave me! Don't be Amy – not any more. You've been Amy for, oh – just so many hours. The whole of the house has just been filled up to brimming with you, Amy. Please now go – get your rest, so that in the morning you may rise up anew and be Amy again. But just for the present, oh sweet God . . . just leave me, won't you? Because she is slipping from me now . . . I can sense it very horribly. The last and scintillating traces of Portia . . . I can see them clouding, and slipping into black.

'You are quite beyond belief. Do you know that, Terence? Totally beyond belief.'

I look up. I gaze across at her. I open my mouth. I close it. I simply cannot be bothered to say whatever fatuous thing I had vaguely been intending. I grind out the stub of my cigar. I do not lay it to rest. I glance about me . . . and she is gone. Not Amy. Oh no – not Amy. Amy, she still continues to glare at me from the doorway. But Portia. Quite gone. So . . . I might as well now, I suppose. Get up to bed. Go to my little room. Do the lights. Do the locks. Go to my room, my little room, and get myself to bed, yes I suppose so. Because there is no one down here for me any more. I find myself, once again, quite alone.

Amy looked at him – slumped as he was, and quite without expression – and then just thought oh well to hell with the bloody man. I just can't . . . ! I . . . I'll just never understand . . .! How can he just . . . sit there?! Is he drunk? Is that all it is? Well yes, he did seem so, but that was rather earlier. By the middle of the meal, in point of fact – earlier than I'd expected it. And I've seen him, Terence, when he's late-night drunk, and this isn't it, it's not like this – no it's nothing like this at all. He'll be lumbering about the place, banging into the furniture – swinging around his head a too-full glass of whisky or brandy and telling me he loves me. Then he'll lunge – and I just rush away. Not girlishly – not with the slightest coquettish intent: I simply rush away. And now he's just . . . sitting there. Hunched and sitting there, gaping at me blearily, with eyes of glass. Well to hell with him, that's all. I'm going to bed. I doubt if I'll sleep, though – so much going on in my mind. Think I'll take one of my pills. I have to make the effort, you see – because tomorrow, I have learned so suddenly, is going to be quite a day. Important things to see to, very – the details of which, only as a result of this little dinner party of mine have I been rather shockingly made aware. But at least now it's all in the open: at least now it's very clear to me, everything that has to be done. So I can't, can I? Turn up looking like a washed-out rag. I have to appear at my very best . . . and without sleep, well . . . not only do I look absolutely dreadful, but I just can't function. I am very jealous of those who can. Those who have the ability to catnap. Churchill, wasn't it? He was rather famous for being one of those. And Thatcher – she got by with what was it . . .? Three hours a night? Something. Well yes – but then she was a very wonderful woman in every way imaginable, as any sensible person will tell you. I am in total awe of that woman, and always will be: an example to all of us, if it's my opinion you're after. But I – I, alas, am not of their number. Can't doze. On a plane, on a train – just can't do it. Terence, he can be in a virtual coma the moment his backside hits the seat: I stare at him coldly with loathing and envy for the duration of the journey. I think it must be because he so very rarely has anything on his mind. Anything pressing, at least. For he has no aim. No dedicated goal – nothing even approaching a vocation. Those websites or whatever it is he designs, well – he goes through the motions, and then they pay him. They actually pay him, those clients of his, whoever they are, really quite astonishingly well, I do have to say that. Otherwise how would I have been able to devote myself so utterly and completely to establishing Alexander? So there's that to thank him for, Terence, at least. That and nothing else.

Anyway – whatever he may think . . . and who can honestly care, actually? Any more. About what he thinks of anything. But despite his saying the evening was merely 'fine', in my opinion it was – with the huge and glaring exception of the obvious – an absolute triumph, and in more ways than one. Alexander . . . he of course was perfectly charming to everyone, just as I knew he would be. Making sure they all had a little piece of his individual attention – working the room, quite the little professional; it made my heart glow, just to be watching him. And it's all quite instinctive, you know: he's had no sort of special training – no, not yet he hasn't, although I daresay all that is to come: already we are discussing voice projection. I didn't let him stay too long – just enough time to give everyone a taste: first rule, isn't it? Always leave them wanting more. Yes and he made up for that extremely moody and ill-tempered sister of his who completely refused so much as even to show her face, and after I'd practically pleaded with her to for once in her life make at least some sort of an effort on her brother's behalf. Wouldn't hear of it. Stomped off to Annabel's for a sleepover – said she couldn't bear even to be in the house when all of it was going on. Can't understand what gets into her – and more and more she's behaving like this, you know, and it can't all be down to her bloody hormones. Well there it is – that's what you get. That's what parents are expected to put up with, these days. Like it or lump it.

Oh but Alexander . . . he looked, oh – just so darling . . . they all remarked on it. Well beautiful, actually: perfectly beautiful, is how he looked. I had only just had time to fetch him back from the hairdressers (and they give us a tremendous discount now: it won't be long before they are paying me to take him there – and no, I am not exaggerating) and so then I had to set the table rather more hurriedly than I would have chosen. The food, I must say, was sublime, just divine – that deli, my God they do know how to charge, but I must say they did everything quite superbly from the charming little amuse-bouche, right down to the cheese; the main course was very special indeed . . . and at nearly three hundred pounds all in, it rather ought to have been. The flowers were late in arriving, of course, so they had to be dealt with at the very last minute. I really think I'm going to have to find another florist, you know, because it's not by any means the first time that this sort of thing has happened. And I must have – I need it, I need it – dependability in my life.

Mike from next door – he was terribly taken with Alexander; you could see that very plainly. Sylvia was too, but she was damned if she would show it. I really don't know what's happened to her, just lately: she always used to be so terribly friendly, but now she can be awfully sour. Envy, I suppose. Understandable. Well – you have to strive to see it from the other person's point of view. Or maybe it's just her age, I wouldn't know. Anyway, we got rid of them pretty seamlessly, I think. Damien and Dolly had been given very firm instructions to go into the back room and stay there till they'd gone. Because I'd known from the beginning, from when I first was planning the whole event, that those two were essential to the thing, Damien and Dolly. Well it's all a question of contrast, isn't it? Light and shade. And dear Mike and Sylvia – it won't so much as even have glanced across their consciousness, this little sleight of hand on my part. Because yes, I had been intending to explain it all to them beforehand, but then when it came to it I just thought oh well why bother, actually? Terribly annoying that Portia still hadn't got here by the time they left, though – I'm sure they would have been most awfully impressed by her. Well who wouldn't be? I was. I freely admit that. I had only met her on that one occasion for breakfast in The Wolseley (never been there before, and I certainly do want to again – so my sort of place) and though of course I remembered that she was an attractive woman who was completely on top of her game, I maybe hadn't fully taken in how terribly young and more or less beautiful she was – and, being a New Yorker, how impossibly well groomed. It wasn't that I was put to shame, or anything – obviously I had been to enormous effort with my clothes, my make-up, my hair, well of course I had – but goodness . . . how utterly immaculate Portia was. She made Dolly look like no more than a slattern, quite frankly, in that rather vulgar little green dress of hers – and green, as I have told and told her, just isn't, and never will be her colour: so very few can carry it off. Shiny it was, and in quite the wrong way: Primark, I'm guessing. Possibly BHS. But then Dolly, love her dearly as I do, she can rather look like that sometimes, and never more so than when she strives so terribly hard for the opposite effect entirely. She still has a very great deal to learn, as at times like this I am reminded. Well what can I say? I've done what I can for her – but well . . . there is a limit, isn't there? Silk purses, sow's ears . . .? Can't honestly tell you quite what she and Damien can have made of the occasion: he was wholly oblivious to the overtones, the undertones, and even the tone itself – but being Damien you'd expect that, wouldn't you really? Well quite. Dolly, however, was not oblivious, oh no, quite the reverse, which rather was the point. And both were unremittingly gauche – well of course they were, they always are – but I think that served to reflect rather well on me. Always a risk, though – the mix of people around a dinner table: you simply have to take measures to ensure that you emerge on top.

And Portia . . .? Prada. Chanel bag and shoes. The Rolex with all the little diamonds around the bezel: authentic, obviously, the gold of the deliberately quite loosely hanging bracelet just divine against the honey of her skin, those tiny little platinum hairs twinkling so very prettily in the candlelight. And those candles I had set at a very low level, along with the three little bowls of ranunculus and gypsophila – globular glass, their bases clustered with bright marble pebbles in the palest blue and pink. In a way . . . in many ways, actually, it was good for me to see her. To be so forcefully confronted. To be reminded of just how excellent everything can and should be. And in my own particular case, I am quite determined, very soon will. Everything in my life, just everything, and before too long at all, will be just utterly perfect. I shall have my own Rolex with little diamonds around the bezel. Chanel bag and shoes. Not fakes – oh God no, not fakes any more. Not even approxima- tions. I'm having no more truck with any of that. Leave it all to Dolly, poor thing. Because honestly – the money that Alexander is now commanding: the contracts, the appearance fees, the photoshoots, the openings . . . soon, I'm sure, the endorsements, and then there's this film, of course . . . well it surprises even me, though naturally I'd never say so. And it is important, of course it is, that I look, well – yes, perfect, whenever I am by his side. Well isn't it? It is key to his continued success. I must be taken seriously. So call it a business expense, if you want to: all money-making enterprises, they have to incur overheads, don't they? Well there you are then. Or an investment: yes, I like to think of it more as an investment.

I do hope that she enjoyed herself, Portia. She seemed to. And I hope too that Terence's general idiocy, the way he was talking, the way he was looking, I hope it didn't too much embarrass her: because I had rather forgotten just how very ghastly he can be in company, it's been that long. She said quite wonderful things about Alexander, but I would have expected that – she is his number one fan, after all. Well – after his mother, of course, ho ho. But she had something else to say too . . . something, I confess, I had not at all been bargaining for. Not seen coming. A bombshell . . . it really wouldn't be too much overstating the

107

matter to say that it came to me as a complete and utter bomb-shell. I had suspected nothing of the sort – nothing like that had even been hinted at when we were having breakfast in The Wolseley, for all her insisting over dinner that I knew everything about it. Was it sly, the way she insinuated this very great thing into the run of conversation? Or had she really assumed that I already knew? That all this procedure was quite the normal thing. Hard to say – I haven't yet decided. Though anyway I do hope that I covered my amazement with a modicum of grace: I was not stunned into silence – no one saw me gaping. And my anger, I hope that too was well disguised – because I was, still am, quite infuriated over this. I consider it high-handed. A reminder that I need an agent, a very highly placed sort of, what is it . . .? Business manager – yes, and sooner than I thought. But . . . it simply makes me that much more determined. I have already decided what now must be done. And immediately too – first thing in the morning, if I have any say. Because nothing . . . nothing ever now will stand in the way of Alexander's progress. That, after all, is what has got him so far: my absolute determination. And now, quite clearly, it is to be tested again. Well fine – bring it on, as they say: I am more than ready to deal with it.

She didn't come out with it immediately, Portia, fairly naturally. In fact, for much of the first course, she hardly spoke at all. Terence and Dolly, they seemed right at the beginning to be holding the floor . . . yes, so you can imagine. At one point rather early on though, I was absolutely forced to haul him up short:

'Yes but there's no need to go *on*, is there Terence . . .?'

'Well I wasn't, in fact, um – going *on*, actually Amy. It's just that Dolly here passed a remark about the table, how much she liked it, yes? And I was just, as it were, filling her in on it. She said it was a lovely table, didn't she, and I was simply seeking to apprise her of the fact that it was by Saarinen – no listen – by Saarinen, circa 1957, and a revolutionary manufacturing process of that time due to the seamless fusion of oval marble top and aluminium base – which can't actually at the moment be readily appreciated as we all are clustered around it, but it is very sinuous – practically liquid, you might say. It was, in Saarinen's own words, intended to "clear up the slum of legs" to which he so very much objected . . .'

'Oh God – now you're saying it all over *again* . . .! Honestly, Terence – I'm perfectly sure that nobody is in the slightest bit interested in a dining table. I myself would prefer something very much more straightforwardly rectangular, so that I could actually put a cloth on to it – but Terence, oh dear me no . . . he simply won't hear of anything so normal as a tablecloth. Will you, Terence? Mention a cloth or a cushion, and he will start boring for England about . . . what is it, my sweet? Oh yes – "purity of line", yes, that's it. I absolutely had to put my foot down about curtains, if you can believe it, otherwise we'd be living in a goldfish bowl. So I really am most awfully sorry about Terence, everyone – it's just that the furniture, the whole "design" thing . . . it's just that with him it's become a leeetle bit of a hobby horse, you see . . . and I'm afraid that once the bee is in his bonnet . . .'

Amy grinned, and very contentedly, at that. 'Hobby horse' . . . 'bee in bonnet': that will be more than enough to make him absolutely livid, I should have thought. Yes oh look . . . his lips are white and tightly compressed – he glares, and he's gone quite red. Excellent.

'Actually, I were just meaning, like – all of the flowers and glasses and that. Ever so nice. You done it really nice, Amy. All look lovely.'

'Why thank you, Dolly. How terribly sweet of you. So you see, Terence – it wasn't the actual *table* that Dolly was complimenting so much as all the things upon it. Can I give anyone a few more prawns . . .? Another scallop, maybe? Portia – you'll manage a little more, I'm quite sure.'

'I'm good, Amy, thank you. The soup cappuccino? That I did like.'

'Ah – my little amuse bouche. So pleased. It's amazing just how many ingredients it takes to make such a tiny frothy thing. All the things you have to put into it. Smoked haddock and cauliflower, rather bizarrely – they were the key. I hope everyone else enjoyed it too . . .'

'Were lovely, Amy. How you get in all them little bubbles . . .?'

'I don't mind couple prawns, they going . . .'

'Of course, Damien – plenty. Terence – could you pass the bowl to Damien, please? Yes . . .? Thank you. A little hand whisker, Dolly – that's the secret. And more of the salad, Damien? Eight sorts of leaves, believe it or not. You can just get everything these days, can't you? We're all so terribly spoilt. What about you, Portia? Little more salad?'

'Thanks, Amy – but I'm good. I did notice the table actually, Terence. It's awesome. They have one just like it in the Condé Nast building? The chairs, though – not the same designer, am I right?'

'Ah no – well spotted, um – Portia. You see, Amy? *Someone* is interested in the table. But no you're right, Portia – the chairs, they're Jacobsen. Same sort of period, though – all late fifties. Golden age, many ways. One designer is Swedish, the other Danish. Pretty sure that's right. God, you know – I used to know all this sort of stuff backwards. Bit more Chablis, Portia . . . yes?'

'It a real nice name what you got. I think so.'

'Why thank you, Dolly. I won't have any more, thanks Terence. Yeah – my pop. Shakespeare nut, you know? Brought up on the Bard.'

Terence smiled. He ought not to like her accent: it ought to have him spitting – but actually, he found it exhilarating, and increasingly so with each successive sentence that she uttered. Even when she said 'Bard' just then, and made it sound like 'bored' . . . still he didn't mind. Her nose, it is small, dead straight . . . and yet when she talks, it moves. Really very seductively. Sometimes her hair will fall over an eye, and then she'll shake it back.

'Oh blimey – don't talk to me about bleeding Shakespeare! I hate all that. Done him at school, but I never take to it. Yeh . . . I expect that make me sound really stupid, or something . . .'

'Yeh me and all, Dolly. Couldn't be doing with none of that. All of the "thee" and the "thine" and the kingdom for a wossname. Couldn't make head nor tail.'

'Yeh, Damien – that what we all thought and all. Well I dunno – just how they talk in them days, I suppose. But your dad, yeh – he really like, what – really go for all of the Shakespeare lark then, do he? What I don't get – what that got to do with your name though, ay? I mean – I know they never had no cars nor nothing back then . . . not that stupid . . .'

And that brought the table to silence: Amy's fork was hovering just before her lips; Terence's eyes were twisted into puzzlement.

'Sorry, Dolly . . . don't quite, um . . .'

'Well what I mean to say, like, is why he go and call you Porsche . . .?'

'Well . . . you know. Character in the play . . .'

'Yeh? Really? All them years ago? Gaw that's funny, really. But there were a model one time what were called Mercedes, so there you go. She were big. Not big like as in big, of course – dead skinny like what they all of them is . . . but real famous, yeh? Don't know what happened to her. Got knocked up by a boxer, that I do remember. Last thing what I read, she were battling her demons.'

'Them prawns was really good. Like prawns. And then there's Mini, ain't there?'

'That Damien all over. Always stuffing his face. You let him near a packet of Kenny's Cheese Strings and they gone. Minnie who? Who's Minnie? Can't remember what the name of the boxer were though . . .'

'Never a fan of the pugilistic arts, I must confess . . .'

'Really, Terence? You do amaze me.'

'Well no I don't amaze you actually, Amy, because you are horribly aware of all my tastes, prejudices and sundry peccadilloes: such is the fruit of, what is it . . . fifteen years of marriage. Christ.'

'Just coming up to fourteen actually, Terence my sweet . . .'

'Fourteen? Really? Seems longer. But anyway – talking of boxers, it always did amuse me whenever they appeared in the ring and they take off their gowns and are wearing these absurd sort of satin shorts, or whatever they are – can't be called boxers, surely? That would be really too good – simply in order to get beaten black and blue before the baying horde . . . does anyone know what I mean?'

'Well if you tell us, Terence, then maybe we might . . .'

'Don't mind a good fight, me. Bit of the old one-two. Ali, he were a god. No, Dolly – I never meant Minnie like in Minnie. I never meant that. I were like saying Mini, yeh? Like the car?'

'What you on about . . .?'

'Yes well never mind that for the moment, Damien – but do you know what I'm talking about? The boxers' shorts, yes? The way they always used to have Everlast written across them, yes? Maybe they still do – I wouldn't know.'

'Yeh. Oh yeh. Everlast, yeh.'

'Mm. Right. Well I always took it to mean that they would lose. Do you see? That no matter how many rounds, bouts, whatever they call them . . .that the fighter concerned would ever . . . be last. See . . .?'

'Right. Nah . . . don't reckon it mean that . . .'

'No. Well no I know it doesn't mean that actually, Damien. Else it wouldn't have taken on, would it really? Portia – are you really sure you won't take a drop more? I've got a rather good red in store for the mains. Bordeaux. Youngish, but quite forward.'

'Red wine, I don't use it. Intolerant, you know? Plus it stains the teeth. And calories, oh man – don't even go there. Amy – I guess you know all about that.'

'Oh God absolutely! Tell me about it! Well it's quite all right – plenty more white, plenty of champagne. Isn't there Terence?'

'Vats. Though you'll be cleaving to your customary bottle or two of red, I'm assuming, Amy my love . . .?'

'What I think it mean, yeh . . . is that it like . . . last for ever . . .? Yeh. That what I think it mean.'

'Thank you, Damien, yes. I'm absolutely sure you're right.'

'Tell me, Portia . . . do you actually, you know, um – *count* all the calories, then? With every sort of meal, and everything? I mean – oh God, do please tell me if I'm being totally out of line here . . . if I'm being far too personal – but do you actually, um – diet, at all . . .?'

113

'Well . . . I have a dietician, Amy, yeh sure. Wheat, gluten, carbs – they're a no-no. All the basics, you know? Regular detox. Then my personal trainer – he's like so into seeing I'm burning it up! Man, can he be one tough mother . . .!'

'You don't look as if you need to do any of all that sort of thing . . .'

'Well thanks, Terence . . . for the compliment. But hey, if I didn't – oh wow! Guys – am I right, Amy? Am I right, Dolly? – they just don't get it. Listen up: you really don't want to know, guys, all the stuff we girls got to do!'

'No – I expect you're right about that, Portia. A woman – she should always preserve her secrets . . . have about her an air of mystery. I've always thought that. Are you clearing away now, Amy? Next course coming, yes?'

'My Dolly – she ain't got no mystery, have you love?'

'Not really. Suppose not. What you see is like what you get. Yeh.'

'Nothing wrong with that, Dolly. Rather refreshing, this day and age – wouldn't you say so, Portia? Now then – everyone had enough? Yes? All done? Well in that case I shall take up my husband's suggestion and clear away for the second course. I hope we're all, um . . . I mean – should've asked earlier, I suppose – but there aren't any vegetarians, are there?'

'Eat a bleeding horse . . .'

'Ha ha! Yes – well I'm awfully sorry to have to disappoint you, Damien, but horse, I'm afraid isn't on the menu tonight. I can however offer all of you beef, in the form of what I am hoping will be a rather nice Wellington.'

'Not that sort of a wellington, she don't mean Damien . . .'

'Yeh right – thanks a lot, Dolly. I think I do know that. Bloody hell . . .'

'What will your personal trainer and dietician have to say about that little lot then, Portia?'

'I do *eat*, Terence . . .! It's just like you got to be aware, you know? And I am perfectly positive it will be just totally delicious, Amy.'

'Well – let us hope. Terence – do the wine, would you? While I'm gone. Shan't be a minute, everyone.'

'Reckon I don't do enough. Well I don't do none. Exercise, and that.'

'Hey! You look great, Dolly! You're in real good shape.'

'Yeh? Well thanks, Porsche. Thanks a lot. But that because I bloody well starving, most the time. I heard of an exercise though, what meant to be good. Pilots. That it . . .?'

'Pilates, I think you'll find it is, Dolly . . .'

'That how you say it? Yeh well you'd know I suppose, Tel.'

'That's how you say it. Unless of course you actually meant that you were going to take up flying. Can't quite see you as a Biggles though, if I'm honest.'

'As a what? What's them?'

'Nothing. Nothing, Dolly. Go on. And it's Terence, by the way.'

'Ay . . .?'

'Terence. Not Tel. My name. Okay?'

'Oh right. Sorry. Touchy, aren't we? Blimey. Well that's it, really. I don't have nothing more to, er . . . just thinking of doing it, that's all.'

'In New York, you don't hear so much of it. Not now.'

'Yeh? What they do in New York, then?'

'Coke.'

'Oh come on, Terence! Don't you be such a naughty boy!'

Which made me smile. A 'nardy buoy', is how she said it.

115

Her eyes ablaze, and her little nose moving, the way it does. Hm: I'd quite like to be. A 'nardy buoy'. Very much, actually. Very much.

'Well it's true, isn't it? The diet aid to end them all, I'm told.'

'In the movies, maybe . . .'

'Shitload of sugar . . .'

'Sorry, Damien . . .?'

'Coke. Bout twenty spoonfuls in every can of it, what I heard.'

'Oh *Jesus*, Damien . . .! Sorry, Tel. Sorry Porsche. Terence, I mean. Terence, yeh? That my Damien all over . . .!'

'Oh . . . right – I just gotcha. Right. Right . . .'

'Well *duh* . . .! If it ain't to do with motors, he just don't know nothing. But I mean that nice though, Damien. Kissy-kissy, yeh?'

'What – you're saying it doesn't happen, Portia? Naïve, aren't you . . .?'

'Oh sure it goes on. But that's the talent, Terence . . . or else the nobodies. The "hey you" guys, yeah? People like me who are, like – working the thing, yeah? We're clean. No I mean it, Terence – honest to God. We're the guys who got to make sure the picture comes in on time and on budget. And that you cannot do if you're high, you know what I'm saying?'

'I see. Well wine – that's always been my drug of choice. Scotch, obviously. Brandy, time to time. Talking of which – who can I top up? Amy'll kill me if I haven't "done the wine" as she calls it.'

'Must be ever so exciting, Porsche, working in the movie business. I'd love it. I'd just love that. You get to meet all the stars, yeh? I'd love that. Just love it. Me, I never met no one. No one, like – famous, you know? Ant and Dec, once I seen. They was opening a Tesco's.'

'I don't mind a drop, you asking . . .'

116

'One drop coming your way, Damien. Sticking with the white . . .?'

'Whatever . . .'

'Well you know, Dolly – it's not as fantastic as everybody thinks. I mean – I love my job, don't get me wrong – and sure, there are great times. Parties, you know? When it's a wrap. When we got a deal for a big new picture. And yeh, I've been introduced to some guys and you're just like "oh wow!", you know? But hey – it's a business. Yeah? We work. We work real hard for that paycheck. Nobody believes it, but that's what we do. You can be in London, you can be in New York, Hollywood, wherever – but still you got to work your butt off. Hollywood, they're all just hustling, you know? Chasing the next dollar. You let up for just one second, and man – you just get blown away. You are so over. Bus boy. Pumping gas. Valet parking. And still trying to sell that screenplay. Hey Mr de Niro, hey Mr Spielberg, hey Mr Cruise – you just gotta read my screenplay . . .! Yeh – like they could even get that far. One guy I know, he was busted from Fox. What did he do? Day one, he gets high. Then, he like became – reborn? Like – totally reinvented himself, you know? I just have so much respect for that.'

'And what does he do now, Portia? Jehovah's Witness . . .?'

'Funny, Terence. No – actually now, he's an eyewear designer.'

'He's a *what* . . .?'

'You know? Eyewear? He's doing good.'

'Eyewear . . .? What – as in spectacles, do you mean? That what you mean? Bloody hell. What – two bits of glass in a frame? Is that really what you're saying? How many ways are there to design a bloody pair of glasses, Christ's sake . . .?'

'You'd actually be very surprised, Terence. It's real big business. Wayne – that's his name, this guy I'm talking about, yeah?

His name is Wayne – he hasn't yet made the big bucks, but he has a presence in Bloomingdale's and he's doing real good. Moved in with a new guy, new condo uptown. He's one happy mother . . .!'

'A new guy. Yes I see. Mandatory in Los Angeles, is it?'

'Ha! Sometimes it sure does seem so! Where have all the real guys gone? That's what all the girls are saying. Where's Clint Eastwood when you need him? But he isn't gay, Wayne. Not really. More like – bi-curious . . .?'

'Bi-curious, I see. And that's what, in fact? Maybe some sort of code, is it, for a particularly strange pair of spectacles of his own manufacture . . .? Ah – Amy . . .! Look, everyone: food's here!'

'Oh it look real lovely, Amy. Don't it look lovely, Damien? You been to ever so much trouble . . .'

'Oh it's nothing, Dolly. Just hope everybody likes it, that's all. Now what I think is best is if you give everyone a plate, yes Terence? They're on the warmer, look . . . and I'll sort of cut this, yes? And if you all can then help yourselves to vegetables, which I'll just bring in in a minute. Can you see to the red now, Terence?'

'I certainly can, Amy my sweet – just as soon as I've seen to the plates . . . which are, just as you say, on the warmer, look. Now Portia – I am aware that you are reluctant to have crimson teeth and put on twenty pounds of unsightly flab . . . but everyone else is all right with a bit of claret, yes? Don't have to ask you, Amy . . .'

'Bit go to my head, red do.'

'Not this one, Dolly. Rotgut, yes. Rotgut will. But not this one, I can assure you. Try some? Yes?'

'Yeh well – go on, then. Oh – look at that beef! You see it,

Damien? It all pink inside all of that sort of pie thing. Enormous ... must of cost a fortune. How you do that then, Amy?'

'Oh you just hope and pray, really. A nice big slice for you, I'm guessing, Damien?'

'Prime. Yeh. Ta. Lovely jubbly.'

'And Portia . . .?'

'Not near as big as that, Amy.'

'Well you can just eat as much of it as you want, yes? I'll just quickly get the vegetables. Oh and the gravy! Mustn't forget the gravy . . .'

'Dolly . . . what are you, er . . . doing?'

'Pardon, Tel?'

'Terence. What are you actually, um . . .?'

'Oh – I'm like taking a picture of the food, yeh? Bung it on Instagram. Do that, time to time. Did it in McDonald's the other day, didn't I Damien? Because sometimes it just what you wanting, ain't it? Big Mac and a shake. I wrote under "I'm lovin' it". Yeh. What I do, time to time. So go on then: tell us, Porsche – who you met, then? You met Nicole Kidman? Really like her.'

'No – Nicole I have not met. But I so totally agree with you, Dolly – she's great.'

'What about George Clooney? You seen him? Reckon I'd die, I saw him.'

'Not George either, I'm afraid, Dolly. Sorry – reckon I'm a pretty big disappointment. I guess maybe the biggest star I ever met is like – Brad Pitt?'

'Oh – Brad! Love Brad. Brangelina, they just such a real and lovely couple what just loves to give back. Were he nice? Bet he were lovely . . . Jew remember when he were, like – face of

119

Chanel number wossname, five? Yeh? Well me, okay – I like totally bought into that. Got myself some in Debenhams – never had it before. Normally I'm like into Poison? But Brad, he really done it for me. And you met him, yeh? Amazing. Were he nice? Bet he were lovely . . .'

'Beautiful woman, Angelina Jolie . . .'

'Yeah, Terence – all guys, they're totally into her.'

'Hold that thought. But all these bloody so-called movie stars – obscene, isn't it? Money they earn. Well – I say "earn" . . . I mean, what? Ten million a time? More? And they seem to bang out about three films a year, some of them, and they're mostly just completely useless. How can they justify it? How can they? Well they can't. Just obscene . . .'

'They worth every bloody penny, you ask me. They stars, ain't they? They like royalty. Worth every bloody penny . . . more than bleeding royalty, anyway.'

'Really, Dolly? Do you really believe that? Don't you mind just a bit? I mean – you and Damien, you don't earn ten million, do you?'

'Joke . . .'

'Well why should they and not you? Why don't you care?'

'That just stupid, Tel, what you saying. They stars, ain't they? They stars! And what's more, they really nice people. Porsche'll tell you – they nice, ain't they Porsche?'

'Some are, sure. Better than rock stars. Some of those guys, they can be real badass, you know? I guess they're like that because they're rock stars.'

I look at her as she says it. Now that the habitual effluence from the moron Dolly is temporarily in abeyance, I can glory in the sound that Portia is making, and the movement of her nose as she does it. 'Rack stores' . . . that's how she pronounced it.

'Bedder than rack stores'. Lovely. Enchanting, really. Shouldn't be, but it is.

'Oh look: here she is – the vegetable queen! Well done, Amy. You have just missed the most riveting conversation about absolutely bugger all, this to include the glittering rebirth of an eyewear designer by the name of Wayne. It was Wayne, wasn't it, Portia? Oh and it's Terence, Dolly: Terence, yes? Now then – can everyone reach? Otherwise I can pass. Broccoli looks rather good, I must say. Quite partial to broccoli, actually. Is there hollandaise . . .?'

'Not too al dente, I hope. The hollandaise is right in front of your nose, Terence. Oh God – don't talk to me about Wayne. There's a Wayne in Alexander's class at school. Has Kenny ever mentioned him, Dolly? Beastly boy – complete and utter bully. One of the troubles with that school – we're just going to have to find something a great deal better. And there's a Shane, a Blaine – Kane, Zane . . . Duane, pretty sure . . . oh God, it's just ghastly. That's it, everyone – pile in. There are two boats of gravy – do you see? So you don't have to, uh . . . Now, Portia – what can I get for you . . .?'

'Couple beans . . . the broccoli, yeah sure. Looks awful good. No potatoes for me, Amy. You English – you really get off on your potatoes. I see that all over.'

'Mm . . . because America is a total stranger to French fries, yes . . .?'

'That, Terence, is different. You can't have a burger without fries and ketchup. That's sacred. Like a hot dog, and heavy on the mustard. Like . . . I don't know . . . popcorn and a cold one when you're at a baseball game!'

'Baseball . . . bloody girl's game, baseball. Like wossname – rounders . . .'

121

'Don't pay him no attention, Porsche. That were rude, Damien. Rude. Their national game, ain't it? Wouldn't like it, would you, someone come over and start knocking West Ham.'

'Football's a proper game. Everyone know that.'

'Yeh well just shut up about it, can't you? So listen, Porsche – who else you met, yeh? What about Al Pacino? Really like him – but in *The Godfather*, not in, like, *Scarface*.'

'Oh honestly, Dolly – let Portia enjoy her meal in peace, won't you? She doesn't want to be talking about film stars for the whole of the evening, I'm perfectly sure of that. Maybe we could, though, talk just a little bit about *our* film . . . that's just *so* exciting. Is everything all right for everyone . . .?'

'I can't tell you how good, Amy. To die. The meat – it just so melts. Just like so divine. Real good. And you want to talk about our movie? Well what can I tell you about our movie . . .? I guess you know what I know. Once we got the final screen test out the way, we're smokin'. And I'm sure Alexander is just going to really, like – blow us away?'

'Screen test? We've done the screen test, Portia. We did that.'

'First round, sure. I explained that – you remember? Say – is there any more water?'

'Water, Terence. Still, is it? Sparkling . . .? Oh – sparkling. Sparkling, Terence. Explained what? What did you explain to me, Portia . . .?'

'About all how . . . you know . . . how if Alexander wins through against the other little guy – which I am so sure he will. Well then we just set the date for principal photography, and . . .'

'"Other little guy" . . .? What – another boy, you mean? Another boy of Alexander's age? Are you hearing this, Terence? Is that what you're saying to me, Portia? What – you're not saying . . . you don't mean they're up for the same part . . .?'

122

'I explained this, Amy. Didn't I . . .? Sure I did.'

'Not to me you didn't, I can assure you of that. Not the sort of thing I'd forget. Is it? You may have discussed it with the casting people and the director and the writer and whoever else you might talk to, but I tell you this, Portia: you most certainly have not discussed this with me. So let's get this straight . . .'

'More wine for anybody . . .?'

'Be quiet, Terence. And listen. This is your son we are talking about. So let's please just get this straight, shall we Portia? You now tell me there are *two* boys . . .'

'Two, yeah. We got it down to two. Like from how many. And Alexander is one of them. It's looking real good for him, Amy – they all love that he's in these like papers and the teen mags and all. You know . . . I'm sure I already told you all of this . . .'

'Well you didn't. Can we please just now accept that as an indisputable fact? You didn't. This is news to me, I assure you. And by no means welcome, I have to say . . .'

'Gee, Amy . . . I thought you knew. But hey – it's no big deal . . .'

'It may be "no big deal" to you, Portia . . .'

And that's when Terence knew it was coming. He had smelt the beginning of seething in her earlier – just the first hit of a whiffy vapour, and hence his gormless and doomed interjection over wine. But now her eyes were gripped, she was clipping her words, and the easy grace of her hostess's blandishments was just this close to disappearance.

'Steady, Amy . . .'

'Oh do fuck off, Terence – just be quiet. Sorry, everybody. As I say, it may well be "no big deal" to you – you, Portia, you are dealing with movies every day of the week. That's your job. But I can assure you that it is a very big deal to me. A very big deal

123

indeed. I am Alexander's mother. And it matters to me, you see? It matters to me very much.'

'Look, Amy . . . I'm sure that Portia knows the process . . .'

'Yes well let's hear it then, shall we? I wasn't aware, as I say, that there was any longer a "process" to be gone through. So what is this "process", then, Portia . . .? Do please enlighten me.'

'Gee, Amy – it'll be fine. Sure it will. It'll be fine. Trust me.'

'Any more spuds going, is there . . .?'

'Terence – pass the potatoes to Damien, will you? Well I hope, Portia, that you are right. I very much do hope so.'

'Wish I could cook like this – I really do, Amy. You's ever so good. It ever so tasty. Ain't it, Damien? Real tasty.'

'Yeh. Right good. I wish you could cook like this and all.'

'Oh honestly, Dolly – there's really nothing to it. A knack, that's all it is. If you can cook an omelette, you can basically cook anything.'

'Which is a complete load of nonsense, of course, but we'll let it lie, will we . . .?'

'Why is it nonsense, please, Terence? Why now am I speaking nonsense?'

'Well because I can, you see – I can cook an omelette fairly decently, but that's all I can cook. Grill a steak, maybe. And that's it. So it doesn't at all follow, is all I'm meaning, Amy. That if you can cook an omelette, that suddenly you are a three-star Michelin chef . . .'

'I can do a omelette. What you put in yours, Tel . . .?'

'Um . . . well . . . eggs, Dolly. Fundamentally. And I'm not going to tell you my name again. Just can't bear it . . .'

'Yeh all right, then – *Terence*. No but like I mean like ham, and that. Go for ham, I do.'

'Egg whites only for me . . .'

'Yes well, Portia – why does that fail to surprise me?'

I don't know why I keep being rude to the woman. Why do I keep on doing that? Maybe because everyone else is around me, could be. Possibly because I am now a bit drunk. But I must stop doing it. Because I don't want to make an enemy of her, Portia. I want her to be my friend. She's stunning. She's absolutely stunning. The most thoroughly attractive and alluring woman I have encountered since . . . well . . . in a very long time. Her voice I could listen to for ever. And watch the way her nose is moving. The body . . . well, hardly bears thinking about. Clearly magnificent. No idea whether or not she likes me . . . what she might be thinking of me. If she thinks of me at all. Maybe she hates me; it's rather hard to tell. Maybe she'll be laughing . . . once she gets back to talking among her spectacularly cool, young and sophisticated circle, this little dinner party will be no more than the most absolute hoot, and of all the inadequates present I may well be singled out as particularly crepuscular and vile. Who knows? Who can ever tell? For she gives nothing away, this woman – I have received no sign. But for my part, well . . . I want her, you see, to be my friend. I want that, yes. I really, really do.

'I'll just see how the desserts are faring. Terence – I think we have a Sauternes or something or other of that sort, don't we? Wasn't that what you were saying? Do you people like the cheese before? The way the French do it? Or after? Up to you. Makes no difference at all to me.'

'No cheese for me, ta Amy. Make me have nightmares. And that red wine – it gone right to my head. Don't mind afters, though. Sweet tooth, me. Oughtn't to, I know – but fuck it, really. Sorry . . .'

'Right, Dolly. Damien? Cheese?'

'Nah. Stuffed.'

'And you won't presumably, Portia . . .?'

'Uh-uh. Dairy. But hey, Amy – I just got to say, okay: don't let this thing like eat you all up, yeah? It'll be cool. And maybe I didn't tell you – Willy Ouch, he is so totally on our side.'

'Willy *what* . . .? Willy *Ouch*, did you say . . .?'

'Yeh Terence – I know! Crazy name, huh? He's the producer. With Arabella Gernstein . . .?'

'That a funny name too . . .'

'Oh? Why, Dolly . . .?'

'Well: Gernstein. Jew, right? And her first name, it got Arab in it.'

'Right. Yeah. I never thought of it.'

'That's another strange thing about Hollywood . . .'

'Oh God: now Terence is an expert on Hollywood, all of a sudden. Back in a jiff, everyone.'

'What, Terence? What about Hollywood?'

'Well you see, Portia . . . all these producers, all the people with power, they do seem mostly to be Jewish, don't they? I mean to say . . . Ouch. That won't be his real name, will it? Though why, if you want to anglicise your name you go for something like Ouch is completely beyond me. An expostulation from a comic strip. But anyway, what I'm meaning to say is, all these Jews, still they're bashing out all these films about the war, about the Nazis. Aren't they? That's how it seems. Seventy years on, and they just can't get enough of it. Odd. Still – in one way, of course, the Third Reich has been really very good to them, wouldn't you say . . .? I mean for myself, I have nothing but contempt for them, the Nazis, of course I do. No denying, though that they did have the most exquisite uniforms. Well – officers, anyway. Particularly the SS. The black, you know? Boots. Leather greatcoats. And then there were the flags . . .! Those amazing red streamers with the swastika in black on a circle of white. Seen them in how many movies? Perfect design – perfect. Such a shame really that it's just so completely taboo, these days. Look wonderful on the wall. Oddly, the other absolutely perfect design to my mind is the Star of David. Superb. Funny really, isn't it? Will anyone want a cigar, later on . . .? Anyone here a smoker? Not you Portia, I'm guessing. Only I've got these Cubans – Partagás. Wonderful, actually. Damien? You up for that?'

'So Terence . . . you got a what? Problem with Jewish people . . .?'

'No, Portia – no no. None at all. I thought I had made that clear.'

'Nah – you know me, Tel. Smoke roll-ups, I do. Reckon a cigar be wasted on me . . .'

'Fine, Damien. Up to you.'

'No you didn't, actually Terence. Make that clear at all. All I got was that the SS, they look like, oh just so real cool, you know? And American Jews made a whole shitload of money on it. What about the Gestapo – they're okay because maybe you like their fedoras . . .?'

'Ah. I clearly would appear to have offended you. You're, um – Jewish, right . . .?'

'Right. You got it.'

'Yes well look I'm most terribly sorry if in any way I . . . look, obviously, I had no idea – but I didn't actually, you know, say anything against the, ah . . . I mean to say – I was only talking about *stuff*, wasn't I? The paraphernalia. But I think that's half the trouble, actually – with everything, these days. You can't even so much as *mention*—'

'It's the whole package, Terence. The whole deal. Some guy walks in here right now, starts waving a gun about the place, threatening to kill us, all of us, even Alexander – you're going to what? Compliment him on his *shoes* . . .? Guy's a killer, Terence.'

'Well no I . . . obviously I . . . but yes, point taken. I'm sorry, Portia. Truly sorry. I meant absolutely no, um . . .'

'I know you didn't, Terence. I do know that. But still: you got to go careful.'

'Everybody all right . . .? Now look, I've brought the cheese and the desserts, so you can all just choose what you want. Both, of course, if you'd like. Terence – you haven't done the Sauternes . . .!'

'Forgive me, treasure – I'll do it right this minute. Monbazillac, as a matter of fact.'

Yes and oh God – forgive me, Portia . . .! I mean – I haven't actually done anything wrong, said anything remotely out of order, as ought to be perfectly plain to any even vaguely sane sort of person . . . but everyone's just so fucking sensitive about absolutely bloody everything, these days: can't so much as open your mouth. But never mind all that – because it's you . . .! You, that I'm actually concerned with, here. Your reaction. Because I was worried before that you might dislike me, might regard me as little more than a laughing stock . . . but now, oh dear God: now I can see that in your eyes I'm shallow, boorish, utterly seduced by the wholly superficial, a racist and a bigot to boot. Oh Christ. I cannot remember the last time I so very much needed to impress a woman, make her see how fine and in tune the two of us are, and yet all I seem to be doing is . . .

'That look amazing, Amy . . .!'

'Bit of fun, isn't it Dolly? Trifle, basically – but the glazed fruit

128

on the top, yes . . .? Not usual, of course, but it does rather add something, don't we all think . . .? Do please all help yourselves, won't you? Cream over there, look. And cheese . . . but it rather seems as if it's just for Terence, the cheese. Because I won't. Oh do go on, Dolly – take some trifle. Do.'

'Yeh. Right. I will, then. But no – I do know what Terence were on about, what he were meaning, like. See, Terence . . .? I call you Terence. All right? Happy now? Terence, Amy – he don't like it when I calls him Tel. Nark him something awful, don't know why. But what he were saying, Amy, when you was out, like, were about the way what things look like. And I totally gets it, course I do. Like your watch as a sort of for instance, Porsche, yeh? Can't take my eyes off of it. Lovely. It really lovely . . .'

'It's okay, yeah? I got to admit I totally love it. But oh dear . . . you guys are all just so going to hate me when I tell you about this watch! You sure you wanna know . . .? I'll go straight to coffee, Amy, that's okay with you. Decaff . . .?'

'Nespresso, actually. I've written out all the different pods we've got – do you see? Little list there of all of them. Though I do have various tisanes, if that's more . . .'

'Peppermint tea, maybe . . .?'

'Yes, I . . . yes, I'm fairly sure we have some of that. Twinings. Anyone else care for some of that? While I'm up?'

'Got any, like – ordinary tea, have you?'

'What do you mean, Damien? English breakfast, do you mean?'

'Yeh. Builder's.'

'Right. I'm sure that can be arranged. You certainly seem to be enjoying the trifle anyway, Damien. There's fresh fruit salad there as well, look. Portia – maybe I can help you to just a little of that . . .?'

129

'S'lovely. Reckon I go a bit more . . .'

'Goodness me – and your plate is still quite full. Terence – do pass the trifle back to Damien, won't you?'

'Well what about it, Porsche? Your watch. What about it?'

'Oh yeah . . . well actually, people – well here it is: it came from a gifting bag, I am totally embarrassed to say. From after the Golden Globes . . .?'

'Here's the trifle, Damien . . . spade on its way . . .'

'Oh ta, Tel.'

'Yes. Pleasure. Terence, actually. Remember? You seem to have contracted your wife's disease, now – and just as she appears to be recovering quite nicely. And if you could just pause for a moment in your enthusiastic consumption, you might find that this pudding wine will go rather well with it . . .'

'Just have me tea, ta.'

'Oh just shut up about your bloody tea, can't you Damien . . .! Porsche here, she going to tell us about her watch. A "gifting bag" . . .? That what you said . . .?'

'And what more-ghastly-than-usual Hollywood thing might a "gifting bag" be, then, Portia? Pray do tell. We are agog.'

'Well you see, Terence . . . it's like, when all the big movie stars are at the Awards? Afterward, they each get a goody bag, right? A thank you from the sponsors. To take home.'

'What . . . and you're telling me there was a bloody gold Rolex in a goody bag . . .?! Christ-al-bloody-mighty . . . I can't believe it . . .'

'Oh sure. And a whole load else besides. Tickets for, like – a cruise? Designer bags, designer pens, designer eyewear . . .'

'Wayne's, by any chance . . .?'

'Not Wayne's, no. Not yet. But one day he'll be up there!'

'Wow. How utterly inspiring. To know that on some golden

horizon of the future, Wayne will be there, and able to scale such Olympian heights . . .! To have a pair of his glasses given to a pack of spoilt and vacuous film stars as a thank you . . .! And a thank you for what, that's what I'd like to know. A thank you for turning up? A thank you for being rich and bloody fabulous? A thank you for just fucking well *existing* . . .? Christ – as if they didn't get paid enough . . . Um – you all right, Dolly . . .? Gone rather quiet . . .'

'Something wrong, Dolly? You do look rather pale. Something I can get you . . .?'

'No . . . no I fine honestly, Amy. It just that . . . I can't really get over all of that. Like, what . . . like, they just, I don't know . . . they just, like – give all of this stuff away for free, is it . . .?'

'Obscene. I said it was obscene.'

'Well sure – in one way it is, Terence. And only the real A-list can get it.'

'Oh yes of course. Naturally. The people on ten million a movie.'

'Some of them get a whole load more than that, I can tell you. Ten million . . .? I know agents, they wouldn't even put through the call, ten million on the table. So yeah. What're you gonna do? That's the system. That's the way it is. Yeah so on this occasion, there was this one bag left over, you know? We were like – *excuse me* . . .? Never happened before. Some guy, he just couldn't be bothered to take his bag. We make some calls, and zero, zilch. So what we did, what we decided to do, all of us in the office, we auction it all off for a, like – charity? Except . . . the watch. We all so wanted that watch. So . . . we draw up lots, and . . .'

'You pulled the winning straw. Well congratulations, Portia. And I must say it suits you very well. Oh dear – poor Dolly! Seems in a state of shock . . .'

'I can't . . . I can't . . . I just can't get my head around it. Coleen and Alexa, they got exactly the same model: I seen it in *Heat*. Blimey . . . I dunno . . . I had a watch like that, I just be the happiest person in the whole of the bleeding world: end of.'

Well . . . what really can you say about Dolly . . .? *'End of. . .'?* Oh dear oh dear. Though it very nearly was, of course, by that time – the end of. The end of, yes, our wonderful and Amy-masterminded little dinner party. And as she so very deftly fielded the rolling bouquet of richly coloured compliments, the mandatory female marvelling over all of her culinary brilliance . . . was I tempted to oh so casually, and with just the barest little twist of lemon, let slip the name of the wildly expensive local delicatessen who had in fact been responsible for just every single little bit of it . . .? Well it crossed my mind, as such things will . . . though then I do rather remember performing a sort of a mental shrug of pretty much indifference to the entire shebang; and anyway – why ever would I do such a thing? Why would I? I am not the saboteur. Yes and from that point onward, nothing much else was forthcoming – nothing I can really recall. Damien seemed wholly absorbed in the drinking of claret and tea alternately, these to accompany his third great bowlful of trifle. Amy brought along a plate of petits fours, some point, and he ate those too. Dolly, still apparently shellshocked, did seem slightly to recover herself – enough, anyway, to regale the careless company with even one more of her extraordinary pronouncements, this one all to do with whom she alluded to as 'her little Kenny', the charmless and lumpen offspring. He had, we were raucously informed, squawked out loudly in some or other hellhole supermarket, 'Look at that bloody horrible woman, Mum!' – and Dolly, keen as ever to observe the proprieties, had duly admonished him in the following fashion: 'Here!

132

Woss your game? Don't you go saying nothing like that, Kenny! You apologise to the lady. She not horrible, is she? You don't know nothing about her. I think she probably a very nice lady. You say sorry, all right? Else I give you ever such a thumping. Say sorry to the nice lady, Kenny. Go on. Do like I tells you. She just old and ugly, that's all – don't mean she horrible, do it?' Dear Christ. You do wonder if she ever actually listens to herself, don't you? Still: can be amusing, I suppose – in very small doses.

I was by this time smoking my Partagás cigar. Sublime, but of course I was hardly concentrating upon the insinuation of its essence, of its aroma – well was I? No, naturally not. And nor on the Armagnac. For . . . well . . . it was Portia. Portia, yes. I had Portia on my mind. And still I am dizzied by everything she has somehow come to mean to me. How can this be possible . . .? There is no rapport, of that much I just have to be sure. She hates me. Maybe. More likely utter and complete indifference, this highly probably tinged with contempt. It's that indifference, it's that which will be difficult. Hate, this I have encountered before: hate, you can turn it around. Erode its foundations, play upon its passion. Barely polite carelessness, however . . . there is truly a mountain. She had told me in passing, Portia – while in the midst of frowning and very ostentatiously batting away my smoke . . . but I wasn't about to put it out, not even for her – that it is illegal for an American to puff on or even own a Havana cigar, even if he isn't in America. What a country, I don't know. I told her in return that I happened to know that just before Kennedy announced the total ban on Cuban imports, back in nineteen sixty whatever it was, he had his aides buy up every single decent cigar in the whole of the United States, so that he would be free to enjoy them in the White House in perpetuity. Not knowing, obviously, that in his

133

particular case, this was not really destined to be terribly long. What a man. What a country. And even to this day, America is said to account for more than thirty per cent of Havana imports, legal or not. Joke, really. Well there it is. What a country. Yes . . . and even as I was hearing myself droning on and on with such impenetrably dull nonsense, still I simply could not believe that I was doing so. I *burned* for the woman, even as I was pushing her ever further away from me.

And then Portia . . . her device began to bleep, and she quickly quelled it amid a flurry of apology. Her car had come, was the upshot. And she left. She was gone. One moment, the aura of the woman was filling up the room, along with simply all of my emptiness, and then she simply went. Much hugging with Amy amid repeated reassurances, a little bit of whooping from Dolly, rather as though she had been encouraged to do this by a perspiring and desperate game-show host – then came more babble and the swoop of nearly kissing. She didn't ignore me, exactly . . . though nor did she say anything that even I in my chilled and yearning fascination could construe as even in the slightest way significant. Or even committal, one way or the other. Which is rather more than a pity, actually: for it would be good to know where I truly stand. Then Damien and Dolly . . . they pushed off. Well they must have done, because certainly they were no longer here. 'You're not driving, are you . . .?' I remember saying that to one or both of them, not remotely giving a flying fuck in either direction.

And now . . . I would surely appear to be quite alone. Amy, her pointed appearance in the doorway, which quite annihilated the few and lingering traces of Portia . . . that too now is over. Amy has gone, her sourness having been duly dispensed to me. And I have said to her, assured her, that I will do the locks, do

134

the lights. Do the locks, do the lights. And her face, Amy's face . . . was taut. Only word for it. Not with her more or less customary displeasure at the sight of me, not through fatigue, and certainly it was nothing whatever to do with drink. Because despite what I say, she doesn't really drink too much at all, Amy. Simply she sullies the rim of her glass with the slur of lipstick. No – the tautness in her features (for it is the only word) this all relates to the mind beyond. For that mind, now . . . it has travelled further. She is roaming among the more distant tracts of all that she is even more determined than ever finally to achieve. She will soon be taking us ever further, more deeply into her projected and envisioned future. She now wants . . . oh, everything. But specifically, and most immediately, she wants a new school for Alexander. She wants a new house, so that we may not just continue to, oh God – 'entertain', but do so on a scale of her own imagining, and certainly one that she will see as befitting what she genuinely perceives as our just and coming status. Oh yes, there will be that. I saw it so clearly when the barely controlled explosion of 'the other boy' very suddenly was detonated – this anonymous second candidate for all that Amy had assumed was already tightly within her fist, a prize that was Alexander's alone. I glimpsed it once again during all of that perfectly infuriating chatter about the 'gifting bag': I smell her mind, hear it working, trace like a blind man the thrumming of her every jagged thought. One day . . . one day . . . it is Alexander who will be invited to the awards. Is how she is thinking now. Alexander will be the deserving recipient of not just a 'gifting bag', but a Golden Globe as well. Next stop an Oscar. But of course: and then the moon. In one sort of a way, I even can understand this compulsion of hers, so utter a commitment. The necessity of exacting for your child at the very least its due. As seen with your own eyes. As I would do, yes – this very thing, though in so impossibly different a manner: silently, yes, and in secret. For Lizzie. My Lizzie. Upon her behalf. But let me instead consider something altogether unimportant . . . what, say, of Dolly . . .? Oh she wants much less, much less than Amy. She wants a gold Rolex watch with diamonds around the bezel . . . but you see Dolly's problem is that she is just so *sick* with wanting it, you see. She will not forget this evening: it will have made its mark on her. None of us will, I think, though for very different reasons. Well hardly Damien, of course – he will have forgotten it already, I should have thought. For all that Damien wants is a good night's sleep – and he said so (because he's in the garage in the morning).

And for myself . . .? Well . . . I want . . . I want to finish this cigar. I want another Armagnac. And . . . well . . . you know the rest. You know all about this new and great big thing. That continues to consume me. Of course you do. Because yes, very bafflingly, what I want above all else . . . and look: if I could rationally explain it you, don't you think that that is what now I would be doing? So that I could hear it for myself? I have been sitting here, just sitting here . . . willing it to be no more than the drink. The drink, the lateness of the hour, the hole within me and my rebounding loneliness – a useless rush of lust for the only woman in the room who did not actually repel me. Didn't work, though: knew it wouldn't, but I just had to try it for size. And it didn't fit, not even where it touched. And so now . . . all I want above everything else is that which merely hours before I had not known existed. Yes: because it is her that I want. Need her, really. And if she is coldly indifferent, if she blinks with surprise and maybe even a gauzily veiled irritation at the very next sight of me . . . then it will really be so very hard. I want so

136

much to ignite within her a parallel, if not identical craving, for now she has come to personify all that I have been for so very long lacking, and only just now have I come to see it. So therefore . . . well – I've got to have her. See? Somehow. Must. Just must. You do see, don't you? I want her to be my friend. Because she's stunning. She's absolutely stunning. The most thoroughly attractive and alluring woman I've encountered since . . . well . . . in a very long time. Her voice I could listen to for ever. And watch the way her nose is moving. The body . . . well, hardly bears thinking about. Clearly magnificent. And so Portia . . . one day – and here now comes my own determination – one day soon, I will have her as my friend . . . yes and then, she is going to fill me right up. Because from Portia . . . I need love.

CHAPTER FOUR

BEAUTIFUL DREAMERS

Yeh well that just about gone and done it for me, that did. I mean – I weren't, like . . . happy before, no I bleeding weren't . . . but still I were just about sort of like coping, you know? Holding my head up, sort of thing. Yeh well – but that bleeding dinner, I telling you – that done it for me. That really done it, and I ain't joking neither. I could of lost it, there and then. All what were going on, all what I were thinking inside. Could like just of gone apeshit. But still I just were sitting there. Taking it. Because what you going to do? All of this fancy fucking food stuck in front my face – and Damien, he eat the most of it: amazing he ain't the size of his fucking garage, stuff he put away. Me, I were only picking, really. Felt all like tight and sick inside of me? With all what were going on? Had a bit of Tel's red wine what he were on about: gone right to my head that did, like what I said it would. *Terence*, I should be saying – else he start up again about it, about his bloody name, stupid prick. I only take his poxy bloody wine because I thought it might make me go all sort of floaty or something – but nah: just give me bleeding headache.

And Amy – she going on about this movie, and all. All

moaning about it because her darling ickle Alexander ain't already right up there in lights with, I don't know – Matt Damon or something. Jesus – like life ain't good enough for her already. I swap with her. I would. I swap with her any day of the week. Yeh but it weren't even that. Nah – course it weren't. Were Porsche, weren't it? What really got to me. She like . . . really bring it home? Make me see it sort of proper? Because I'm playing. Aren't I? All I doing. Just messing about. There's people out there what really got it. What got it all. Looks – well yeh, you got to have that for starters, else you's nowhere, everybody know that. Well I reckon I ain't too bad – never had no complaints, you know what I saying? Yeh but it more than that, course it is. Money. The know-how. The what they call it . . .? When you just ain't taking no crap off of nobody. Attitude. Yeh. Attitude, that's it. And style. Real style. And that Porsche, she got it, she got all of that – yeh and in buckets, she got it from birth. Her dad, who I bet were a rich old Yank geezer, pots of money, oil billionaire or something – not like my dad, who were a bastard drunk, basically. Her dad, he will of give her everything right from the off, so she know what she doing. He read all of that Shakespeare shit to her when she just a baby, know what I saying? And he name her after a motor – which yeh, bit funny that, I ain't denying. Still: could of been worse, at least it a posh car – he could of called her Twingo. Yeh but although I gone on about the watch, that beautiful watch what she got . . . it weren't just that I were meaning – although yeh, I loves it. Loves it to bits. But what I getting at . . . on me, it ain't going to look so good, is it? Ay? Got to be faced. I mean – I ain't never going to get one, that I do know . . . I ain't so stupid I reckon I going to get one . . . but just for the sake of wossname, just say like I did, okay? See what I saying? Just say one of them watches, it drop out the sky, like. Land at my feet. Well – I bungs it on, right? I goes Oh Wow. And I looks at me in the mirror – look at the Rolex on my wrist there, all gold and with them little diamonds all round, and that . . . and it won't do nothing. For me, I mean. I only just got that. That I never seed before. That it won't do nothing for me. Still want it, course. But I got to do other things first. Because what I ain't got – never mind the bleeding watch, let's just leave the sodding watch out of it for the minute – because what I ain't got . . . well what I ain't got . . . I ain't got 'it'. See? That's the thing. I want it, but I just ain't got it. This sort of . . . style, what all them posh rich other women got. Like in the magazines what I get. Like if you a model or a presenter or in *EastEnders* or whatever. Skin all sort of glowy and shiny . . . hair – that glowy and shiny and all. Teeth what'd knock you out they's that bleeding bright, like advert for Dulux. Then there the way what they talk and walk and move and sit and that. All what they does with their hands, so it don't look like you got a couple bunches of bleeding bananas hanging down off of the ends of your arms.

All start with money, though. That I do know. Well everything do, don't it? Start with money. So what I reckon is, that where I got to start and all. Start small, course. Ain't going to get no job in the movie business like what Porsche got, yeh I do know that. But a job, a job of some sort, nothing too shitty – that I do got to get. Don't know why I never think of it before. Not just the money neither: it be nice when someone say well what you do, then . . . be nice I got an answer. Ain't going to be easy, what with Kenny and that – but other women can do it, so I don't see why I can't. Good as they is any day. Because I can't always be having my hand out. Can't always be asking Damien, can I? And he a right tight little bastard, best of times. I mean I know

140

he got . . . what is it . . . commitments, and that. Bleeding mortgage. All of the rest of it. Yeh I think I do know that: he won't
hardly let me forget it, will he? But he should give me more.
Should want to, really – but even if he don't, even if he don't
want to, he got to see I need more than what he give me. Bloody
hell – I am his wife. Ain't I? Ay? Not his bleeding skivvy, though
you never know it – all the fetching and carrying what I does
for him.

Yeh. So . . . that what I doing here. Been sitting in here for
near hour and twenty minutes. Bleeding awful place. All mucky
white walls and all these bits of like sort of orange all over it.
Get you down. Job Centre is what they used to call it. Something
else, now. Labour Exchange in my dad's day. Him, he used to
have a bit of a kip in there, once he come out the pub. Then he
go back down the pub again. Same thing though, ain't it? Name,
I mean. Call it what you want, it the same bleeding thing. It
where people come when they got nowhere else to go. There a
drop-in centre just next door to it, bloke here were telling me.
He go in, they says to him wotcher, want a cup of tea and he
say yeh all right go on then. And then after a bit they goes to
him – fancy another cup of tea do you, mate? And he's like yeh
all right go on then. And after that, they don't say nothing, and
you out on your ear, son. Rain or no rain. So you got to have
money. Got to. So you signs on. Whatever. And all the time you's
hoping for a job. Job of your dreams – the job what you always
wanted. Yeh. And then when that don't come along you going
to settle for something not quite so glitzy, ain't you? And after
that, when all them months gone by and still you hanging
about . . .you takes anything. Any job at all, shouldn't wonder.
Poor buggers. Yeh and I one of them, now. Close on hour and
half, I been stuck here. I goes up to a window, time to time. Fat

141

bitch in there, she say we experiencing a high volume of demand and we aware that you waiting and it shouldn't be too long now: please take a seat and we thank you for your patience. Yeh well I took a seat, I says to her. Took a seat near hour and half back, and I can't feel nothing in me arse no more.

Got this number. Hundred thirty-six. You walks in, see, and you talk to this geezer what want to see all of your doings like passport and that and then you answers like where you live and all the rest of the bleeding palaver and when he typing it all up on his screen he give me the eye like either he fancy me something chronic or else he looking at me like I just a piece of shit what the dog drag in, I couldn't work it out. Then he give you this number, and then when it come up on the screen there, look . . . then they ready to see you, bloke were telling me. Not the bloke what give me the number but the bloke what go in the drop-in centre: all pale he were, now I thinks of it – like he ain't got no blood left in him. Don't know why I got hundred thirty-six. No more than dozen people in here, shouldn't think, so Christ know where they get hundred thirty-six from. Oh Gawd . . . I could bleeding die in here. Old age. Wouldn't mind a fag, as it happens. Help pass the time. Don't even smoke. Messes with your mind, this place. Ain't kidding. Just as well I brung couple magazines with me, because the ones what they got in here, oh blimey. Them out the Sunday papers, all seem to be. Old, and real like tatty? One there about computers. One for women, one with some old slag and a cake on the front of it. So I got *People* and *Hello!* here. Victoria's on the cover of one of them. Usually are. Other's got the wedding of that one out of *I'm A Celebrity*. Kate Winslet is taking a well-earned break on Necker Island with friends and family and Justin Bieber, he there and all and he been seen wining and dining Eva Longoria

142

off of *Desperate Wossname* though romance is strongly denied by both parties. Yeh well they would, wouldn't they? Mind you, she old enough to be his mum, Eva is, but then who ain't? Be Amy's bleeding Alex what out there next, on Necker bleeding Island. I got that, what were it – not Maybelline, other one, what Eva were the face of and yeh it do give you longer fuller lashes like what it say, but still it a bugger to get it off of a night-time. And Coleen, she got a new condo in LA with all of these toilets what is heated and they gives you a great big whoosh of like pong after they cleans you up all nice, sort of thing. Don't knows I care for that. Bit funny. Shouldn't of read it, you want the truth: made me want to go to the lavvy, now. I do that, they going to be calling hundred thirty-six, you can bet on it. What they call that? Sod's something – law, is it? Yeh – that's it. Sod's bleeding law. Then I got to start all over from the very beginning again, shouldn't wonder. Dolce & Gabbana . . . oh look: Dolce & Gabbana, they got this new perfume out what's just for babies. Ahh – reckon that ever so sweet.

What she . . .? What she up to, then . . .? Fat bitch in the window, look. Waving her arm about, and it all, eurgh – horrible and wobbly. Oh blimey . . .! I just twig: hundred thirty-six, can't hardly believe it! Right then: about bleeding time. Let's get this done and sorted, will we?

'Thank you for your patience.'

'Yeh well . . . you said that.'

'Now then . . . let's just see . . . right . . . right . . . oh right. Well I seem to have your basic details on the screen here, Mrs, um . . . But if you wouldn't mind just answering a few more questions, yes? And then we can get you properly on to the system.'

'Yeh – okay then. Right. What sort of, er . . .?'

'Well first a little bit about your past employment. Have you brought a CV at all . . .? Reference from your previous employers?'

'No, I . . . no. Reckon I might be able to get one – reference. Off of Mr Adams. Could be dead now, though. Half dead then. Were a while back.'

'I see. And this is your last employer we're talking about, is it? How long ago was it, in fact?'

'Oooh . . . got to be . . . how old little Kenny now . . .? Yeh, must be – ten year? Eleven, maybe?'

'You haven't worked for ten years . . .?'

'Yeh – got to be that, easy. Eleven, maybe. Well – I have *worked*, course I *worked*. Work like a bleeding skivvy, don't I? I married, sort of. I a mother. So course I work. But I ain't had no job in a like sort of office nor a shop or something, that what you meaning. Not for ten year, anyway. Ten, eleven year. Yeh.'

'Right. I see. And you are returning to the workplace . . .?'

'Yeh.'

'No – what I mean to say is: *why* are you returning to the workplace . . .?'

'Oh right. Well like anyone else, I suppose. Want the money. Yeh but look – I ain't expecting nothing too wonderful. Like Queen, or something. Job taken, right? But no look – I know I ain't got none of the, uh – all of the wossname, and that . . .'

'Qualifications . . .?'

'Yeh them. I got none of all of that. But I don't mind putting in the hours, know what I saying to you? Ain't no shirker.'

'I see. Well that's good. And what sort of job are you thinking in terms of? Let's start with that, shall we?'

'Well . . . ain't really gave it no like thought, to be honest with you. It only just come into my head. Shop, maybe . . .? I done that before. I were in a baker's. Don't really want a baker's,

144

though. What about a little clothes shop, maybe? Something nice up the high street?'

'Rather thin on the ground, I'm afraid. The whole of the job market is very very tight at the moment, as I am sure you are aware. But we won't be negative. Maybe you have undiscovered talents, yes? Now let's see . . . do you speak a language, maybe . . .?'

'Yeh.'

'Oh well that's very good. And what language would that be . . .?'

'English.'

'English . . .'

'Yeh. Thought that were obvious. What's wrong with you . . .?'

'Ah. I was actually meaning . . . another language. A different language.'

'Oh right, I get you – like foreign, you mean.'

'Ideally, yes.'

'Nah. You want my Kenny. He only eleven, just coming up, but he doing French at his school. He not great at it, if I'm honest. I mean – he ain't fluid. Nothing like that.'

'I see. Right. Well . . . I think I've got the picture. Right then . . . let's just have a quick little scroll down the, um . . . just see if there's anything at all here that might suit you. Let's see . . . let's see . . . let's see, let's see . . . Ah. What about this, I wonder? Marriott Hotel? Swiss Cottage?'

'Oh yeh – I knows it. Opposite the swimming pool what I takes Kenny to of a Saturday, sometimes. Hotel, ay . . .? Could be good. What's the job? Sort of receptionist kind of thing, is it? Saying hello to people what come in, and that?'

'No. Not receptionist. Chambermaid. Stand-in for maternity leave. About six months it would be for, it says here, if you're interested at all . . .'

'Hey . . .?'

'Six months. The period of employment would extend to approximately . . .'

'Chambermaid, you saying? Chambermaid? Making the bleeding beds?'

'Well . . . largely, yes. Cleaning, you know. Bathrooms . . .'

'Yeh well you can forget that for a start. Joking. I got all that at home. You got to have something better than that, surely to Christ . . .'

'Well you do have to appreciate, Mrs um . . . you're not exactly a qualified person. I wouldn't be so hasty in turning it down, if I were you. Jobs, any sort of jobs these days, they're really so very hard to come by. I could make a call immediately, if you'd like me to. You would be doing shifts, of course. Some early morning, some late nights . . . they are offering eight pounds an hour, which these days . . .'

'Eight quid. That what you telling me? Eight quid an hour. *Cleaning* . . .? Right. I'm out of here . . .'

'Are you sure . . .?'

'Yeh. I am. Stuff it. No disrespect to you, I don't mean. But no. Just stuff it. Know what I saying? I'm gone. Jesus – they want to pay you eight quid an hour for sitting in this poxy place and wasting your bleeding time . . .'

'If that is your attitude, Mrs um . . . then I think it is better that you do leave. Clearly we are unable to be of service to you.'

Yeh. Too right. So I gets up and I walks out the door. Just as I going, a light come up on the screen there and it say hundred thirty-seven. Some gel, she give a nudge to this poor old slapper what look like she can hardly get herself up and on to her feet. They'll have her making beds and cleaning the bleeding bathrooms till she go and drop dead on the floor.

Went home, and I were right upset, you know? Because it getting worse and worse, all of this – and I saw it wrote, plain as day: I just ain't never going to get out from under. Not possible, is it? People like me. Cleaning – that all I good for, then. Blimey – my old mum, she done all sorts, her. Yeh but she never done no charring, she never go that low. How'd she feel? Ay? If I gone charring. Wouldn't of known where to put her face. Bloody hell – I got a husband what got his own bleeding business in a right smart part of town and I ain't got no money for the things what I needing. How's that right, then? Ay? Not right, is it? I want a pair of shoes, or something – what Amy, she can just get whenever she like on account of her son a bleeding superstar and my son a fucking dweeb what ain't never going to do nothing with his life, got to face it, he just go on playing his bleeding computer games with his sodding father . . . and Porsche, oh bloody hell – don't get me on to bleeding Porsche: she got shoes coming out her ears. But say for the sake of wossname that I want that, okay? Pair of shoes. Not talking the moon, am I? Ay? Only a pair of bleeding shoes – and I ain't talking Louboutins nor nothing: they don't got to be Manolos, though I wouldn't mind, course I wouldn't bleeding mind. But just something nice – like say Kurt Geiger or even Office, I don't care. Yeh – and for that I got to go skivvying after someone I don't even know who he is, for Gawd know how many bleeding hours . . .? Not fair. Not fair – is it? And I says it to Damien:

'Went up the wossname centre today.'

'Yeh? What's that then?'

'The – you know. Wossname. Job thing. What they call it?'

'What? Job Centre, you mean?'

'Yeh. Except it ain't. Call it something else now.'

'What you do that for?'

'What I do that for? What I do that for, Damien? What you bleeding well think I done that for? Want a bleeding job, don't I?'

'A job? You having me on? What you want a job for? You got a job. Ain't you? Ay? This here your job.'

'Well I don't, do I? Don't want a bleeding job . . .'

'Bloody hell, Dolly – you just gone and told me you do . . .'

'Yeh I do – I do! But I don't *really* . . .! I just don't got no money, do I Damien? Ay? What you gives me – just go nowhere. Ain't nothing never left over for me. You give me more money, and I don't have to be taking no poxy little job.'

'Gives you what I can, Dolly. I got commitments . . .'

'Oh bleeding hell . . .!'

'Well it true, Dolly. Young business, ain't it? Got to grow. Be better one day. Maybe ten year down the line . . .'

'Ten year . . .? Ten bloody year . . .? And what I supposed to do in the meantime then, Damien? Ay? Go begging, or something? What – I got to go and stand on a street corner, do I? Offer some geezer a real nice time? That it, Damien?'

'Don't, Dolly. Don't. Don't even say that . . .'

'Yeh well. Can't see you even noticing.'

'Don't, Dolly. Please . . . don't . . .'

'Well you don't want it, does you? Ay? A real nice time? When we done it last? You remember? Do you? Because I bleeding don't, I telling you that.'

'Got a lot on my mind, Dolly. You know how it is.'

'Oh yeh. Yeh I do, Damien. I know exactly how it bleeding is . . .'

'So, what . . . you get a job then, did you . . .?'

'Nah. Wasn't nothing going, was there? Waste of bleeding time.'

'Well look . . . maybe you could help out down the garage, like. How that sound? I could pay you. Business expense then, see?'

'Yeh . . .? Like doing what? Don't know nothing about cars, do I?'

'Nah – not that side of it. Trev and me, we got all of that, no problem. But some of the motors what we get in – top end, like . . . well you could do a real nice inside valet job. And a waxing. And then all of the chrome, and that. Be a real service, that would. Charge a lot for that, I reckon we could.'

'Yeh . . .? How much, then? How much is a lot?'

'Well . . . have to go into it, wouldn't I? But ball park – off the top of my head, like . . . I reckon you could be looking at a tenner a time. For yourself, like.'

'A tenner? A tenner a time . . .? What – for cleaning a whole bloody limo inside and out? You having a laugh, Damien? Ay? Are you? Do I look like I got "twat" wrote all across my fore- head? A tenner! A fucking tenner . . .! Take bleeding hours, that would, do it proper.'

'Yeh well. Difficult times, ain't it? Market forces. Well there it is, gel. Only trying to help you out, aren't I? You takes it or you leaves it.'

Yeh well. So I leaves it, don't I? Course I bloody do. That were my husband talking – you believe it, do you? Tight-arsed little toerag. And then I thinks to myself – well all right then, Dolly: cards on the table, what you going to do? And I tell you, will I? Tell you what I decided? Tell you what I done? I only gone back up the bleeding Job wossname and I sits there another fucking hour and half and I gets this big black bloke this time round and I says to him listen mate, I were down here yesterday, right, and there were this chambermaiding job going up the Marriott

149

and he say to me oh yeh, that one, I know that one, that still on, pretty sure, you want to try for it. And I says to him yeh well go on then: I don't want it – crap job, right? But I tries for it. I tries for it. And he nod, and he get down to type out all the doings. And then he look at me, don't he? With them big old sad and soupy eyes what he got. And he go to me – real quiet, like – he go to me: you reckon that a crap job, innit . . .? You want to try this one some time, lady.

I slept, when I slept at all, perfectly atrociously. The brandy, of course – that hadn't helped, and when ever does it? But it was everything else as well. That true . . .? Not really. I feel I rather have to own up to being just a tad disingenuous, here. Wasn't . . . 'everything'. Was it? One thing – it was one thing, and one thing alone. Banging away at me. Though why would I do that? Lie to myself. Well simple: because I don't want the answers, do I? Don't think frankly I am even close to the beginning of dealing with just any of all that. Well – I say I don't want answers. There aren't any answers – or not one, anyway, that immediately is appearing to present itself. An answer, actually, would be completely refreshing. Something cut and dried. But what I really do not wish for, even as I am alive to its imminence . . . what I sigh with weariness at just the trailing odour of its coming, is the irresistible allure of this meandering avenue of unconsidered possibilities . . . this beguiling trail whose every curve is unknowable, and initially lined with coloured clumps of wild and vivid wayside flowers . . . but there exists no option to squat at the verge, you know: for quite without pity, it beckons you on . . . and yet already I am rather terribly aware that my easy ambling must soon step up to a doggedly determined pace, before it then will harden into a punishing route march . . . and, finally, the dizzied sleepwalking through the thousand-mile trek . . . and at the end of that I shall be blinded by a light while at the same time all then will be so very bewilderingly dark, as I drop to my knees, a parched and beaten rattle of bones amid nothing but dust and bracken.

And still this bombardment of appalling and yet incomprehensibly thrilling questions that my mind, my very troubled mind, apparently refuses blankly to pack in putting to me. Because I could not forget her. You see. Wanted to. Sort of. Did I . . .? Well yes I did. Want to. Sort of. Yearned to rouse myself from a sleep so dreadful that it felt as if I had in desperation been attempting to grapple with a mocking giant not just so very gallingly slippery but even filled with rage and always unflaggingly vigorous, the cliff of whose shoulders I had no hope of scaling and never mind pinning to the ground . . . it felt, as I tossed – bruised, in a gloss of sweat and wild-eyed to the point of derangement – it actually did feel as if I were fighting for my very life . . . and Jesus, all I'm bloody trying to do is get a bit of sleep, here . . .! Yes . . . but when eventually I had more or less come to, what I yearned for then was the ugly pad of hungover thickness within my head . . . for this, almost comfortingly, would presage no more than only a bad afternoon of gloom, inertia and bilious acidity, with maybe – flung my way, and glimpsed in a mirror – just a wry and self-loving little twisting of the mouth, an affectionate acknowledgement of my own enduring folly. In simple words, for me to see now plainly that all that had occurred here was that my head had been momentarily turned by an attractive woman, I had drunk a little more than had been altogether circumspect, and here now is the lovely potential of a bright and new clear day when I can rinse away all of my nonsenses, along with the sleep from my eyes.

But . . . no. She clings to me, you see. No . . . no, not clings – far more than that: I am wrapped up in her. Wrapped up in her, yes: I know now what that means. You see, what it is . . . on a fundamental level . . . mm, how quite can I put this . . .? Well look . . . examples: I can see before me now the dazzle of her eyes . . . and wonderful though that is, a vision to revel in, it isn't that that I am meaning. Hear her strange inflection . . . I can hear it, yes, but not that either – it's not that either that I am trying to get across to you. Remember . . . remember how the candlelight touched that hair that would sometimes fall forward, and then she would shrug it back . . . the candlelight that delineated with a strong white bar the dead straight nose that wriggled in time to the music of her speaking . . . ? Yes but these, all these, are hardly more than the successive elements in a slideshow. It is maybe . . . yes – this might get us fractionally closer, I think: it is more, much more to do with her form, the slipping of the silk that contained her limbs, to the very curve of her. That, yes, and the scent of the woman that was truly of her very essence. And then – much deeper still – the quite unglimpsed entity within, that now I just have to know, you see – touch, be part of, and therefore quite thoroughly invade. Does all this amount to this thing they call 'smitten', would you say . . .? Well you might – but I hardly can think so. That to me will suggest only the merest little spasm of giddiness following some glancing and inconsequential blow. But what I feel is . . . devoured. Swallowed whole. Still I am me – still me, yes (and rational – I hope that's clear) . . . but not any longer disparate. I now am encased quite wholly within something else entirely.

152

And how could the host be unaware? You see? Here is the establishment of a seed that only can burgeon. She had me, really, at the mention of my Saarinen table. Her sincere appreciation. It was only then that I began really to see her.

But the practical looms – as it will, and never more frequently than in the lives of the romantics and beautiful dreamers who least are inclined or able to cope with it. Simply I must – and more or less immediately – get in touch with this woman: and then the rest will follow, I just know, with swift and I admit rather frightening inevitability. But in the meantime: do I even know her surname . . .? I maybe once did – Amy, she must at some point have mentioned it to me, but if so it's gone – and all I have at my fingertips . . . is Portia. And this company, this film company she works for . . . did its name arise at any stage of the conversation . . .? Damned if I know. Since the deal first was mooted, Amy, she will have said it to me countless times, talked about nothing else . . . but who can be listening to any of that? But certainly I don't know it now. Well fine: here is not a problem. Not remotely difficult, any of this. It just means that now I have to go up to Amy's room. The children are at school, Amy herself – no doubt on some wholly determined mission upon Alexander's behalf – left the house quite incredibly early this morning (while, in sleep, the unforgiving Titan and I still were locked in furious combat) . . . so I just have to walk up the stairs and into Amy's room. Which I do very rarely. I have never especially cared for its atmosphere: it is so utterly of her, and not just the aroma. I have no interest at all in whatever it is she gets up to in there, this little room of hers. Office, she calls it. Always locked, of course. I have a key. Naturally.

And although I am in no doubt whatever that the house is empty – Mrs Mullins, she comes in only every other morning

153

to be rather horribly confronted with all of the tasks which Amy tells me constantly she simply cannot bear even to so much as contemplate (so I can only assume that the considerable debris from last night's delicatessen dinner will be left until tomorrow to coagulate and fester) . . . even though I know I am perfectly alone in the house, still I am padding up the staircase in the manner of a sneak thief. And so very aware of my own quite inexplicable furtiveness, I bend to the business of the key in the lock, and it's as if I hardly am daring to breathe. There's a closeness inside, is the only way I can describe it – and it's not at all a good description, it doesn't really nail it. It is closeted, and covered in fitted carpet. Any better? Not really. Yes because we were never admirers of the hard wooden floor, Amy and myself. And how perfectly extraordinary that there could indeed have existed a time when the two of us – over a bite to eat, maybe . . . or conceivably sitting with a drink in front of the fire – could actually and possibly even animatedly have discussed such a thing. She has filing cabinets over by the window: Bisley, a classic design – one red, the other that two-tone sort of fudgy donkey colour, same as an old GPO telephone, from way back when. They look to me rather quaint, these days, filing cabinets. Though still they are, I have to admit, solid and rather reassuring: I do quite understand why many people still should be wary of wholly committing to the vagaries of ether. Amy is computer literate, naturally – my God, you'd be dead if you weren't, face it – but I think she would agree that it's fair to say that she has never thoroughly taken to the medium. It used to amuse me (it used rather to delight me) when in the early days of owning a laptop she would affect such alarm at some really very simple little glitch. Ironing it out was the closest I ever came to masterful. Sometimes I could have set everything to rights with the stabbing of a single key, but would deliberately prolong the whole business . . . I suppose by way of a rather pitiful demonstration that all I do is not so wholly mindless and simple as sometimes she has suggested. I think she divined this. Anyway . . . soon after, she ceased to consult me on any detail at all. Which is when she reverted to all the filing cabinets, folders and ledgers: then she was free of the need for my expertise. Levels were restored.

Piles of paper all around. Nothing strewn, however – hardly Amy's way – everything neatly stacked . . . though not, or so it would immediately appear, labelled, alas. The filing cabinets . . . those little slots where the handles are, they're empty: no names, no code, no alphabet. And these cabinets, I wonder . . . are they locked . . .? Well well – they are indeed. Locked cabinets within a locked office: anyone but myself might even, I don't know . . . care, or something. So . . . the desk then, I think. For all this is very much current affairs, no? There will probably be . . . yes – one of those Manila folders, I should imagine: one of those, yes, that should tell me everything I need to know. But what . . . what is all this . . .? On the floor, there . . . looks like loads of, loads of . . . what . . .? Letters. Letters in envelopes – coloured, a lot of them: pink, yellow . . . look at them all. Bound by rubber bands in neat little bundles. And oh my Lord . . . I'm not really too sure quite what I was expecting, but I rather feel sure I wasn't expecting this . . . they are all of them addressed to Alexander. The handwriting is rounded and rather carefully formed – at least it is on this top one, anyway. And there is a little rainbow of glittering stars arching away from his name. There must be about . . . how many? How many letters in this little bale? Six? Six or eight, I'd say. Each of them neatly slit open. And there's a Post-it, look – Amy's hand. She has written 2nd

155

April. And the stack beneath . . . 9th April. Then the 16th. On and on. Once a week, then. She rations them. Good God. The thought she puts into it all. I had no idea that he received . . . mail. But then I don't tend to think of any of all of this, do I really? No I don't. No I don't. But . . . oh good Lord: I cannot believe I have only just noticed . . . to the side of the filing cabinets, there are . . . sacks. Gunmetal – a sort of a nylon weave, looks like. And what might we have within the sacks, do we think . . .? Do we think . . . coal . . .? No – we don't really, do we? Christ . . . it's letters. More letters. Bloody hundreds of them, could be a thousand – envelopes covered in hearts and messages, flowers and little stickers . . . bloody hundreds of them, could be a thousand, more than a thousand. All very tidily cut open . . . and oh look: a cross. A red cross. Someone – Amy, I can only assume – has marked each envelope just beneath the franking with a bright red cross. Well. And so from the topmost envelope, this one that spills from the mouth of the gaping sack, this one that is nearest to my hand – it is green, and after Alexander's name there are five exclamation marks, each progressively larger than the last – I slide out the sheet of paper, and as I do, a photograph flutters from the fold to the floor. As I flap out the letter, I stoop to retrieve the picture . . . and . . . am confronted by an extraordinarily lovely face, the face of a rather young girl, jail bait sort of age – as all such radiant angels really have to be – with straight and long fairish hair, a great deal of eyeliner, and the most pert and cuppable little breasts you ever have seen in your life: nipples like the sweetest rosebuds.

And, you know . . . I rather think I have to sit down now. Think about this for just a little bit. These, then . . . are the letters that Amy . . . Amy, who opens and reads, evidently, each and every one of them . . . has deemed unsuitable for Alexander's eyes. And rightly. Good God – not sure they're even suitable for mine. Because I'm never, am I, going to get rid of that image in my mind? Not now I'm not. And she signed the picture. Added two kisses. Linda, she's called – the jail bait with the straight and long fairish hair. A glorious innocent, and yet the expression smeared across her face is that of the purest filth. No bloke would say no to her, you see. The ensuing prison sentence endured not just in solitary but beneath the lowering cloud of abiding fear at the hourly possibility of excruciating death at the hands of slippery and endlessly vigorous giants . . . well yes, that could well take the edge off the thing, there's no denying the truth of it . . . but here is the sort of retribution that will cause a man to rue his sin and stupidity, wring his hands in anguish, howl out to his God above . . . but only afterwards: before, it is solely his lusty impatience that is boilingly compelling. And here's another one, look . . . from Scarlet. *Scarlet* . . . ! Good Christ. Scarlet says that Alexander's picture is above her bed and she looks at it before she goes to sleep each night. She wears nothing in bed . . . and I only know this because Scarlet, she's just told me: it's here in black and white. Or, well . . . red and white, actually – red ink, yes . . . scarlet, I suppose. And then she describes in reasonable detail exactly what she would like Alexander to do to her when it is dark and they are quite alone, this involving the Burberry umbrella which he apparently was holding in a fashion shoot in a recent edition of *Stella*. And there are sackloads of these. Sackloads. While the factor here that really I have to address now is that Alexander . . . my little boy . . . he's, um . . . ten years old. Which I'd forgotten, rather. And I maybe look at Amy now in quite a new light: she is not merely the reckless promoter. She is taking much more care here than ever I had imagined. Well. Well well. On the other hand, of course – it's all because of her . . . this, all this, it's wholly due to her perfectly ludicrous and obsessive ambitions on the boy's behalf. Isn't it? That's why each of us, here we now find ourselves.

But this is not the reason I am here. Why, though . . . why did she never mention to me that the boy receives letters . . .? All these letters. She hasn't ever said so – and yes I admit that it never, not once, has occurred to me that he might. Thoroughly obtuse on my part, maybe. I dare say. But still: it's odd. Is it? Odd? That she's never said so . . .? Don't know. I don't know. Can't really . . . rationally think about it. Not just at the moment. And anyway . . . this is not the reason I am here. There is someone other who is on my mind. Someone I must get to – and somewhere, in this room, there will be the means. So I open the topmost folder – flip aside the cover with rather a forced and self-conscious insouciance, I suddenly am aware. Quite as if wishing to convey to the scrutiny of an imaginary audience that here is a man completely careless of whatever he might find here . . . and even just that . . . well just even that, it very much strikes me, is really rather odd in itself. Though still, for some mildly surprising and quite unanticipated reason, my heart . . . I can feel it thudding, and my fingertips, which now are hovering above this Manila folder, they are almost tremulous – alive with girlish nerves and an alien uncertainty. And . . . it's bills. Household bills. How very terribly dull. I've always thought that: why Amy deals with it all. Never could be doing with any of that. So: press on – what's in the next one, then . . .? And why, actually, is none of them marked? Why can't she label them? Write something on the front? How can she know where to put her hand on a thing? And those cabinets too – all anonymous. It's not even as if she is protecting herself from prying eyes: the

158

room is locked – she is expecting no one. And . . . there's nothing of consequence in this folder either . . . just a collection of correspondence from what the letterheads suggest would appear to be an accountant of some or other hellish sort, so absolutely no interest there. Well I don't know. What to do. Can't be going through all of these folders. Can I? Go mad. And I can't really decently break into her bloody filing cabinets either. So . . . I don't, um . . . at the moment . . . really know quite what to do. Feel, actually, a bit of a fool. Just being in here. And rootling about.

What was that . . .? Hear something? Did I . . .? In the house? On the stairs? Don't know. Not sure. Keep still. It could well have been no more than the shifting of my feet – the creak of the chair I am sitting on (ugly object – a cheap and swivelling secretary's chair from Staples, or somewhere: charcoal plastic and royal blue ersatz tweed . . . I myself could never contemplate such a thing). Might even have been, what I thought I heard, my own subconscious clearing of a throat that has, actually, just lately been raspy. Well hush – keep still. That's what to do. And listen. Listen. Just listen. Right. Well. Done that. And I can't hear a thing. Nothing. I'm straining – straining hard . . . and no: nothing. Can't hear a single thing. Not sure now I can recall even the nature of the sound I had imagined. Did I lock the door though, is what I'm thinking now . . .? Behind me. When I came in – did I lock the door, or did I just leave it? I think I'll lock it now. If I didn't before, then I'll lock it now. No point, of course – no real point. Amy, she's gone. She won't be back for a very long time. She really does pack in the day, you know: once she's out, she's out. But still – better to be safe, yes? So I'll get up now and go and lock the . . . wait a minute, wait just a minute, though . . . hang on . . . hang on . . . what was that? Hear it? Hear that? I'm sure that was something. This time I'm sure it was. So I'm frozen. No longer sitting down, though not quite up. Don't want to make a noise. Want to be still so that I can hear if I'm hearing. So hush. Not a sound. Don't move. Just stay exactly where you are . . . and listen. Right. Okay. I'm very horribly bent, hunched up and in rather a strange position all round – the backs of my calves are killing me, frankly . . . but I'm still, quite still, and I'm listening. I'm listening. I'm straining – straining really hard . . . and I can't hear a thing. Not now. Nothing. Not a single thing. And this now, it occurs to me, is becoming ridiculous.

It is not right of Amy to make me feel as if I am an intruder. If she only would speak to me – if she just wouldn't feel she had to conceal . . . if she didn't fucking well go and lock everything up . . .! Christ Almighty – all I'm after is a name: an address, that's all I'm needing. And here I am – look at me! – padding about like a burglar. Oh dear dear dear . . . where the hell can I find what I want . . .? Maybe . . . well maybe it is on her computer after all. No harm looking. The tablet, she'll have that with her – uses it as a diary, a phone, and for buying things, of course – but the laptop, that's here. And naturally I know the password. Well naturally – and you do too: because it's 'Alexander', isn't it? Of course it bloody is. So . . . let's see . . . log on . . . tap tap . . . and enter, yes. So what am I looking for? Where should I be looking? Film? Movie? Portia . . .? Oh heavens, what a name – too divine, and so perfectly right for her. Let's see . . . let's see . . . no: that draws a blank. Film, then . . .? Film Deal . . .? Movie . . .? Movie Part? Part In Movie? Christ. Oh Christ. Ah . . . wait a minute . . . Hollywood! That will be . . . yes! Yes! Here it is – Hollywood, yes. Well that wasn't too difficult. Pasadena Pictures, apparently. Well okay – if you say so. It's a decent, old-fashioned sort of a name for a film company, isn't it really? Not one of the stupid and meaningless modern ones like, I don't know – Thumbnail, say . . . or Shoe Soles or Zip Bloody Fastener, or something. Pasadena Pictures – okay, got it. And that's all I need – the rest I can get. Oh yes – it's all here, look: Willy Ouch . . .! Jesus. How can a man in all sincerity go under a name like that? Well – gets him noticed, I suppose. And that's what it's all about, isn't it? Hollywood. Getting noticed, just getting noticed: there, that is what passes for style. But never mind this man: let's just pass him over – for it's not Willy Ouch that I'm interested in. It's Portia, isn't it? It's Portia, yes – for she is very heaven.

But hang on, though . . . what's this? What's this, now? Let me see . . . money, figures, sums . . . is it really? Yes – there's money talk here. Big money too – frighteningly and quite incredibly so, God curse it: never been offered such a sum in my life, nor even a fraction of it, and never will be either. But a fairly spirited and lengthy exchange has been taking place over quite a few weeks now – or so anyway it would appear, at a simple glance. Well how can that be, then? Last night we discovered that the part, Alexander's part in this film (and what film, actually? No idea. Nobody's said, nobody's mentioned it – or not, at least, to me) – and however starry or fleeting it's going to be, this part, this part of Alexander's, it's not quite clinched, not yet wholly in the bag. And goodness – you should just have seen Amy's face, the clouding in the eyes, the greying and sag of both of her cheeks, when that particular bombshell was detonated. She was testy for a moment – visibly thrown and anxious, though possibly this was apparent to no one but myself – but then she rallied, and really so terribly well: soon she was smooth, and a hostess again. But maybe . . . she has a point. If money, a fee, has already been discussed or – who knows? – even agreed upon, then how could the part not yet be Alexander's? Portia . . . Portia the divine . . . was she prevaricating, do we think? Because . . . mulling it over, tossing it all around again now . . . it seems to me . . . well look, just look at it this way: if Amy truly had already been made aware that some other boy was still in contention for this role, would she really be likely to have forgotten it? Are we actually to believe that this little fact, this so pivotal and potent a variable, would have, um – slipped her *mind* . . .? I hardly think so. And therefore, on balance . . . I do consider it reasonable to assume that last evening, at our sour and singular delicatessen dinner – over the Wellington, over the gravy – was indeed truly the very first that Amy knew of it. Which leads me to ask this, then: was Portia in turn genuinely believing that she had already spoken to Amy of this uncertain situation – as why would she not? And do we further assume then that it is Portia the divine who is actually the absent-minded one? That prior to all of this she certainly had fully intended to tell Amy . . . though in fact forgot to do so, while remaining completely convinced that she had . . .? Or was she quite cleverly just covering her omission? Smothering all traces of her considerable culpability. Or could here be a very recent turn of events, a new and sudden element thrust into the situation (some unheralded upshot), the gall of which she was seeking to sugar? Or was it no more than a tactic? A twist in the negotiation? Or, Christ . . . something bloody else, the nature and purpose of which I simply cannot imagine – because I honestly have not a clue on earth where I am supposed to be going with this . . . for all these sorts of thing, these sorts of people, well . . . I simply don't understand. And look at me – just look at me: I'm thinking, behaving like a spy, now: floundering in the murk, and not knowing whom or what to believe, what even to think, and nor even what I am actually doing here in the first place. Caught up amongst it all. Because I'm telling you . . . this world . . . the world into which Amy long ago deemed it wise to dip our collective toes, and now we find ourselves waist-deep in, and wading, like it or no . . . I so much do not care for it, you know. And if we continue – and surely we are committed to continuing: you just had to witness the tightening of Amy's expression, the iron in the eye, to be in no doubt whatever of that – well then this, all this, it can only become denser, can't it? Denser, darker – the marshy ooze continuing to suck at our feet, teasing us ever down deeper. We just must, I suppose, strive ever harder to keep all our heads above water.

Jesus. What was that . . .? Noise – hear it? Think so. Can't be sure. On the landing, maybe. Or was it outside the window? Don't know. Can't be sure. Sort of a, what . . .? Creaking, was it? Like a footstep? Could have been. Could have been me. Could have been this machine that I'm fooling with. Stay still. Don't move. Just listen. Hear it . . .? Hear anything? Can't. Can't now. Quiet as the grave. Right, then. Nothing there. You're jumpy – you're just jumpy, that's all it is. Unfamiliar territory. Every sense of the word. So get a grip, that's what to do. Yes, that's the idea – and just you carry on scrolling, scrolling down . . . yes . . . until we arrive at . . . until eventually we come to . . . can't be long, must be here somewhere . . . yes: here we are, here she is. Portia Hazelstein. Hazelstein, good grief. If only I'd known that before: now she probably thinks I'm Heinrich bloody Himmler, or something – and yet I didn't really say anything that was, er . . . I mean, it's not that I personally am in any way, um – you know. Or anything. Oh well: can't be helped.

Not now. Can it? Done. Isn't it? The thing is next to try and build bridges. Build bridges, yes. Oh fuck building bloody bridges – meet her, that's all: I've just got to meet her, see her again, get myself close to her. The rest will follow. She'll see it – she'll feel it. Quite convinced about that. Right . . . okay, then. Got her name, got her email address and the company she works for. All I need. All I wanted. So get out, will I? Well I will, yes – soon I will. In just a minute. But I first might take just a little look at all of this correspondence. See if there is anything here that might, I don't know . . . help me in some way.

It's all rather elaborately informal. 'Hi . . .!'. Yes: 'Hi . . .!' – that comes up quite a fair bit on either side. Which is odd on Amy's part, I must say. I mean – you expect it, don't you really, from an American. Hi. Or hay. They know no better. Yes, hay – they do say hay quite a lot, I've no idea why. But Amy – I've never heard her use either of these expressions. Hello, is what she says. And even 'how do you do'. Not hi, though. And certainly not bloody hay. 'Exciting' – that's another word that seems to occur quite regularly . . . then there are projected meeting times . . . an obscene amount of flannel concerning Alexander . . . and here is a suggestion of breakfast. Nothing much at all. So Portia would appear to be maybe rather less central to all of this than she might have wanted to imply. More the PR, possibly. Well – nothing wrong with that. Known a few of those in my time – usually assured, generally good to look at, very rarely stupid. Right: nothing for me here. So I'll go. Yes – I'll go now, get back to my study. Email her. Establish a link with Portia. Get the ball rolling – then settle back into the thrill of its gathering momentum.

Christ. Oh yes – that was something, that was something: that was definitely something – a noise from outside, oh yes

164

that was something all right. Oh no – I'm not imagining it this time. This time, I'm absolutely sure I heard it. Bloody hell – someone's out there, and no mistake about it. Oh crap. But who in hell can it be? Who can actually be there at this time of day? Oh crap. Could it be that I've got Mrs Mullins's days wrong? No – she's like clockwork, Mrs Mullins: the sole unwavering constant in a life of unremitting flux. Children . . . they're both at school – unless one of them is ill, or something. Been sent home by the teachers, or something. No – I would've heard. Phone hasn't rung. Landline or mobile. Can't be that. Oh crap. Amy, then. Got to be. Amy back early, God curse it. Oh crappy crap. This could be tricky. This could be very tricky indeed. If she decides to just cruise on into her office. If she just turns the key in the lock . . . and oh Christ did I, actually? Get up and lock it eventually? Did I? If I hadn't already locked it when first I came in here. Did I? Is it open . . .? Is it locked . . .? Don't know. Can't remember. And is she still there? Still out there? Is anyone there? Oh crap crap. Be still. Listen. Be quiet. And just listen. Concentrate hard. Can't hear. Can't hear anything now. Don't know quite what to do. Oh crappy crappy crap. Wish I were somewhere else. Wish to God I wasn't in here. Well look . . . what I'll do is, I'll just quickly scribble down Portia's details on any old scrap of something around, shut down the computer . . . and wait. Just wait, I suppose. Wait until I'm sure it's quiet again. Wait until whoever was there has gone away. What else can I do? Should be working out a plan, of course. A plan for what I am going to say, how I shall react, which way I shall be playing this, should Amy just suddenly walk into the room and confront me. Can't, of course. Too terrifying even to contemplate. If Amy just walks into the room and confronts me, I shall maybe just hurl myself through the transoms and glazing bars

165

of the window in a splintered explosion of timber and glass that will shear me to ribbons before I crack open awkwardly on the York stone driveway two floors below, there to sprawl . . . broken, bleeding and – with a bit of luck – dead. Or else if Amy walks into the room and confronts me, I shall just stand precisely where I am standing and say hay. But if no one's in the passage any more . . . well then I should be all right. My study, it's more or less opposite, you see – so I could easily sprint across and into there in next to no time. Yes . . . but I've just got to be sure, that's all. That there is no danger whatever of what would be, let's face it, an extremely unfortunate collision in the corridor.

I'm standing right next to the door now – standing right in front of it. My ear is pressed that close to the panel I can sense in the pinkness of my lobe a rasp of tiny abrasions in the not remotely flawless, then, gloss of the paint. The booming din of my silence is coming near to deafening me. And nothing. I can hear nothing at all. So I now, and with stealth, am trying the handle. No give. Quite firm. So I did lock it, then – I must automatically have done that as soon as I walked into the room. So I fumble in my trousers for the key – and a spasm of fear of what in blue blazes I am supposed to do next if I somehow have managed to lose the bloody thing . . . oh yes that thought does, I freely admit it, just fleetingly flit across my mind – and then it starts to loiter about for a bit, before completely going for broke and looming large: nothing for it then, I suppose, but the crashing myself through the sodding window scheme again . . . but no, it's all right, it's okay in fact, for I have it now in my hand, the little brass key. Which I insert, and next am turning, as softly as I can possibly manage. Then I force myself to be still again, and am listening hard, which for some reason is making

166

my eyes feel like a couple of ping pong balls. But what if – and why oh why, sweet Lord above, do these awful possibilities just keep on occurring to me? – what if Amy should be standing directly to the other side of the door, her ear too pressed close to the panel . . .? Will we hear each other's breathing . . .? Will our palpitations be strictly in tune? And then when swiftly I barge open the door and make a blessed bid for safety and the sanctity of home, as actively I am preparing to do – would the door in turn simply bash her brains out and on to the floor and then send the mangled rest of her cartwheeling all the way down the bloody staircase? Oh Jesus. So many immeasurables, you see. But anyway – the time has surely come: I'm now going to go for it. And I do that – I'm doing it, yes: I've done it now, and wildly I look about me in the passage outside before I flee like a fugitive and into my study – the very air just so very chock-full of crime – where then I just throw myself into a chair and sit there bug-eyed, shivering and icy – yet in a welter of sweat and panting like a fucking carthorse as if from the exertion of not having simply hopped across the breadth of a corridor, but the entire extent of the Kalahari, without the benefit of a canteen and topi.

Still can't hear anything . . . anyone. Doesn't matter now. Safe. Home ground. I'll go down soon, downstairs – go down and have a look around in a minute . . . but I'm sure it wasn't my imagination. My paranoia. Guilt, if you like. Wasn't any of those. So now I can exhale, and spread myself a bit – just transfer Portia's address to the iPad and . . . oh look, look at this: well well. The thing I quickly jotted it down on. Back of that picture. Photograph of the child, the jail bait with straight and long fairish hair: face of a cherub, leer of a slut. Linda, yes that's it: written on it, see? And I seem also to have pocketed a letter – not

167

Linda's letter, I don't mean, no not that one . . . but the other one, the one I just happened to glance at. From, um . . . now who was it from again . . .? The one who wears nothing in bed. Oh yes: Scarlet. *Scarlet . . .!* Good Christ.

Right – okay, then: well I'm back. I'm back from that . . . that bit, it's over, over for now at least . . . sort of got all of it out of the way, think it's looking good, far as I can tell. Can't see that anything at all could, well . . . go wrong now – no, couldn't, no not now, not after all my . . . Jesus . . . all that very significant *effort* I've just been putting in . . . and what I think I need, all I want to do right at this moment is just have a cup of coffee . . . yes, coffee, pretty sure . . . sit down somewhere quiet, office possibly, and then just go over it. Go over it all. In my mind. Try to get completely straight exactly where we are standing now. Alexander . . . and myself, the sacrificial mother. Amid what had begun very worryingly to be seeming to be a wholly impen-etrable tangle . . . though now, surely, I must have slashed my way through the bulk of it. Broken the back of it: that's the phrase. Very nearly literally, if the beastly noises that emerged from that on the whole, you know, really rather disgraceful man were anything to go by. Oh God, what a time. Sons . . . if only they ever were aware of even a fraction of the sheer endeavour a mother is not just prepared but eager to offer up on their behalf. Rather best they don't. Coffee, yes – and maybe have a cigarette. That would be nice. It's actually rather a relief, you know, just to be at home. Because Soho . . . it was really quite a shock to me, just even my being there – because I haven't, you see – well, for simply ages. I used to go with the girls. I used to go with the girls all the time because that in those days is what the girls used to do, and I'm sure still will. Caroline, Andrea, Zoe, Belinda . . . Anna occasionally, but she just would keep on having babies, and so rather dropped out of the thing . . . and then there was me – Amy, making up the half dozen. Don't see them any more, any of the girls. Hardly miss it. And anyway I can't, can I? Isn't the time. Not now.

Zoe, she phoned me, actually – just only the other week: Amy, she said – I'm having a little bit of a get-together, rather like we used to, yes? Everyone was saying that they haven't seen you in simply aeons – we miss you, darling! Where have you *been*? So me and the girls, we were wondering whether you might like to . . .?

Yes, that's what Zoe said . . . but I can't. Can I? Isn't the time. Not now. Sweet of her – sweet of all of them to think of me. If that's truly how it went. Or could it be not remotely anything to do with me, but all about Alexander . . .? Likely, isn't it? Human nature. To want to get close. To the source of the light. Because I haven't really seen them, not one of them, since first it all began to happen for Alexander. So why now then, all of a sudden? Hmm? This sudden revival of interest in me. You have to ask yourself. They all will have seen the pictures, of course they will. Covers. Features. When he was mentioned on that news programme, that time. Probably hate me, they probably must. Which I can't say I mind, particularly. Because it was always them, you see – they were the ones who had the fashionable careers. That, or a wealthy husband. I was nothing, really. Why they maybe had me along in the first place: because you need that, don't you? To make the dynamic work. A nobody, somewhere in the company, smiling to order. I've learned that myself, of course, so I completely understand. Well: you only

169

have to look at Dolly. We'd go to the Groucho, sometimes, the girls and I – I took some time to persuade myself that I did actually like it. Just a bar, really – friendly enough, but I couldn't ever see what all the fuss was supposed to be about. The only famous person I ever saw in there had to be pointed out to me: never heard of him. I think he was a novelist, they told me, something like that – but novels, well . . . never a huge thing with me, I have to admit, apart from Joanna Trollope occasionally, and Jilly Cooper on holiday . . . but I don't really read them at all any more. Well I can't, can I? Isn't the time. Not now. Zoe – she was the member. I always thought it was meant to be for creatives, that club – television people, stars, writers, whatever. But Zoe though – successful, oh yes very, but hardly one of those: something to do with designer bathrooms, far as I could ever make out. We'd have a bottle of Pinot Grigio. Sometimes champagne. And then always another, at the very least: it's why girls got together – it's what girls did: whooping occasionally, to make absolutely sure that no one could be missing any of the spectacle. But it was pleasant enough. Well it always will be, won't it? This sort of nonsense. When you've nothing to do. But just lately, well – couldn't contemplate it. So I said no to Zoe. Well I can't, can I? Isn't the time. Not now.

I did think of it all, though – this morning, when I found myself back after how long among all those familiar little streets. Used to love it, Soho . . . though I can't remember why. One of the things one said: Soho . . .? Oh, I love it, just love it . . . though I can't remember why. Pasadena Pictures . . . well I had expected them to be in Wardour Street: as soon as I heard that they had offices in Soho, I thought oh well then – that'll be in Wardour Street, that's where they all are . . . but they weren't. Actually Walker's Court, which is no more than a

170

rather tacky little alleyway where that ghastly Raymond place used to be, what was it called? It links the rather lovely Berwick Street market – Revuebar, yes that was it, beastly-looking place – it links the market, Walker's Court, the sweet little market where I always used to buy the most unbelievably cheap avocados, and on one occasion I do remember a fake Chanel purse, before they started clamping down on all that sort of thing around here . . . links it with that road, that other road – what is it? Can't remember. Oh God I'm hopeless – used to know the whole of this area like the back of my . . . not the road that has all the homosexuals in it (can't say gay, I refuse to say gay – the word, it depresses me unutterably) but the one, the other one, that connects with . . . don't know. Not Dean – I know it isn't Dean, because that's where the Groucho is, remember that much at least, and that isn't here. Not far, obviously, but not exactly here. Anyway – it doesn't matter. But at first, when I got to Walker's Court, I actually did think Oh no – this can't be right: this can't be right, surely? They can't possibly be here. There was this place called Girls Girls Girls – shuttered, of course, because it was morning, though God alone knows what it must look like once the evenings here are well under way . . . and some sort of coffee and cake bar, café kind of thing, and then a little crack of a shop selling all these . . . I don't know – Chinese-type things, really. Lanterns, and vile little gaudy cats that very annoyingly wave a paw at you and statuettes that I am sure are not made out of jade, though they did have a sort of a jadeish look about them. Anyway – there was the doorway, I found the entrance, and yes I was having my doubts, I don't at all mind telling you (they don't make *those* sorts of films, do they . . .?) – but when I stepped in, once I actually got through the door and had a bit of a look around

171

me, I must admit I did feel, oh – a great deal better. The reception area was very surprisingly spacious – it actually appeared to be a great deal larger than the whole of the street I had just walked in from. Carpet, very deep and comforting – which you don't often encounter now, do you? All marble, isn't it? Marble simply everywhere you go, these days. The girl at the desk, a serpentine and wilfully glossy sort of affair – the desk, I mean, but her as well, I suppose . . . looked just like that actress, you know – what is her name? Dark hair, dark eyes – she was in that series of films about, oh . . . something really rather mindless, I can't even remember. With that actor I do rather like, Keanu Reeves. Anyway – lovely-looking girl, she was. Hair just so. Perfect make-up – just perfect. Pale long fingers, and the brightest red nails. It's not Sandra Bullock I'm thinking of, I'm fairly sure – but it's someone rather like her.

'Good morning. I am here to see Mr Ouch.'

She looked up at me with extreme and open suspicion. Her fringe was just pricking the thickish arch of her eyebrows – a look, actually, that I have always found to be enormously attractive, but if you've got hair like mine, well then a fringe of any sort at all is just completely out of the question. The whisper of an attempted smile of greeting that barely was hovering now became completely obliterated by the sheer din of consternation that was dancing all across her face.

'I don't, um – think that Mr Ouch is actually, um . . . expecting . . .?'

'No. No no. But he'll see me, I'm sure. I am Alexander's mother, you see.'

She blinked. The girl – who suddenly was seeming so terribly young, beneath the make-up, beneath the grown-up patina of her glorious disguise.

'I'm sorry . . .? Mother? Alexander who? I'm not quite sure, um – who, er, is Alexander . . .?'

Well, I thought: we're not off to an altogether good start now, are we?

'It seems that you haven't been doing your homework. Alexander is an extremely famous male model who now is to star in a major Pasadena Pictures production, as I should have thought you employees might actually be aware. Is it up this staircase? Upper floor, is he?'

'Oh! Alexander! Yes – I know Alexander, of course I do . . . but still I'm terribly sorry but I can't possibly let you up there without an appointment. I can ring through to Mr Ouch's PA, if you'd like, and . . .'

'Yes – that's a very good idea. You ring through to his PA. And in the meantime, I shall just quickly pop upstairs and speak to him.'

Not Sandra Bullock, no. More like Rebecca Hall, although that's still not actually the one I was thinking of. Not with nearly so beautiful a voice as Rebecca Hall, of course, because underneath it all . . . this girl, you know . . . she's really rather common.

As I went up the staircase – which I did straight away, couldn't waste any more time talking to someone who clearly knew nothing – I was aware of a little bit of a flurry behind me: I imagine that she had emerged from behind her glittering little counter acting rashly upon some sort of impulse to head me off, or something – though then evidently she had very wisely thought better of that, and made for the phone instead. The corridor, landing, wherever it was I came out on to, was actually quite shockingly long and broad, within such a sliver of a building: I think what we must have had here is one of those things that is called a 'lateral conversion'. Think that's it: pretty sure it is. Read it somewhere. Quite proud of myself for having remembered the term, actually. Maybe Pasadena Pictures occupied the upper floors of the whole of Walker's Court, who knew? I would have been momentarily flummoxed, I admit, by the avenues of doors to the left and right of me, had not the very one opposite been displaying a too large silver plaque, chrome I suppose, that proclaimed in somehow rather stupidly bold black letters: W. OUCH. Went straight in. Didn't knock – didn't bother with it. I thought that to do so now would be rather silly. Went straight in.

'Amy. Well well. I guessed from what Jocasta has been saying to me that it might have been you. Surprise . . .'

'Mr Ouch. How are you? So nice to meet you, finally. I'll sit down, shall I?'

This office, I think – just glancing about me – initially had been designed to impress. You know the sort of thing – quite large, rosewood panelling, what Terence would eagerly rush to tell you are chairs by probably that bloody Eames person who he is forever very tediously banging on about – and of course the great big curvy fuck-off desk . . . but now, the whole of the room, it's just so shockingly cluttered: boxes, carrier bags, papers, books . . . scripts, I suppose they must be. Screenplays. And all of the framed posters that are covering the walls – and there really are quite a few of them, along with a couple of gold discs and sort of diploma things – but every single one of the posters has got that Burt person in them . . . who is he again? Man with the moustache. And in that one over there there's that woman with all the big hair: I think she was a Charlie's Angel. Dead now, pretty sure – as may easily be the Burt person. Odd – because they're absolutely ancient, all these films . . . and I know they've had much more recent hits than those. Well of

174

course I know: I researched Pasadena Pictures, didn't I? Quite extensively. Wouldn't have allowed Alexander to be involved in the first place if for a moment I had considered the company not to be up to scratch. Well maybe . . . I don't know . . . maybe Mr Ouch is simply an enormous fan of Burt, whatever his name is, that actor with the moustache: used to be all over the place. I do hope, however, that it doesn't mean that our Mr Ouch here is a homosexual. Because they like them, don't they? Men with moustaches – aren't they supposed to like them? Well I very much hope that it doesn't mean that.

'Sit – yes of course, sit. Do please. Forgive me. Although I have to say, um . . . Amy – I don't wish in any way to appear, um . . . I do hope you see that . . . but in a very short while I am actually expecting a, er . . .'

'Someone. Yes. I quite understand. I did come unannounced. Perfectly understand. But do you know what, Mr Ouch? It's really rather funny because I am actually feeling rather . . . well, confused is putting it a bit too strongly – but, well, ever so slightly thrown, maybe . . .? No I am. Because for some strange reason or another I had it firmly in my head that you were going be an American person.'

'Oh really? Ah. I wonder why. Well – as you may see . . . I'm, um – not.'

'No. It might have been Portia. It might have been that. I may simply have made the assumption.'

'Indeed. Yes I can see that it could well have been that. I suppose. And well of course in LA – the business end, as it were – they all are. All of them. Americans, I mean. Well they would be, wouldn't they? If you think about it. But Portia, well . . . she's actually the only one in London, so far as I am aware. Maybe a plant. To keep an eye on us all.'

'Really? You think so?'

'No. No no. Joke. Just a little bit of, um . . . humour. M'kay?'

'Yes. Oh well yes of course. Well now look, Mr Ouch – I know that you don't have a great deal of time, so . . .'

'Willy.'

'Mm?'

'Willy. Please.'

'Oh yes. Right. Of course. Well, Willy – obvious why I'm here, I expect.'

'Not, I confess, to me, Amy. I thought it was all . . . that we all were, um . . . I was led to believe that . . . well I rather assumed that everything was all, er . . .'

'Yes well so did I, of course. And that's rather the whole point. Isn't it? But just last evening – well Portia, no idea if she's mentioned it to you at all, but I had a little supper thing. Of no consequence – dinner sort of a thing, nothing remotely special – though you would yourself, of course, have been hugely welcome, if only I had, um . . .'

'Ah no I couldn't have. Not last night.'

'No. Well that's good then, isn't it? So anyway . . . Portia, during the – you know: course of it . . . she dropped something of a, well – bombshell, really. About Alexander. Well of course about Alexander. That there were two of them . . .?'

'Two of them . . .?'

'Mm. Up for the part? I did not know this.'

'Ah.'

'I was not told that.'

'Mm. I see. Yes I see. But now . . . you have been . . .'

'Yes but why, Mr Ouch, did you fail to make me aware? Before this. I find that quite baffling, to be perfectly honest with you. In all our correspondence, in not a single one of your emails was there ever so much as even the merest hint of anything at all like that. Nothing of that sort was ever even mentioned. Willy. Was it?'

'No. Well. I'm sorry if you, uh . . . I maybe ought to have explained to you, Amy, that here is a, well . . . it's a completely normal procedure. M'kay . . .? Gradual selection. This is how it generally happens. And then eventually, of course, we, er . . . make our choice.'

'Yes well this is precisely what I've been saying to you, isn't it? I was firmly of the understanding that a choice had been made.'

'Well . . . no. Not yet. Not quite.'

'Well no. Clearly. So I really would love to know what on earth it is we have all been talking about, for so terribly long. Anyway – all right: that's done. So what I want to know now then, Mr Ouch, is quite what we are both going to do about this situation. Resolve it, yes? Willy.'

'Sorry, Amy . . . *do* about it? Not quite sure what you, um . . .?'

And now, as I intake my breath, perfectly steadily, for all now that very clearly I just have to come out with next, I am regarding him, quite levelly. For of course I have been actively assimilating the man throughout all of this rather inconsequential and frankly very deeply disappointing chatter – evaluating the man, do you know . . .? Trying to quite decide upon his nature. For I have to be sure that what I say next, quite how finally I come to frame the thing, will in no way jar . . . be heard to be out of kilter: I just must feel utterly confident, wholly sure of achieving the end. Yes . . . yes, that's all very well, but there's something else. Isn't there? There is, there is – and from my point of view, it is a decided complication. Stumbling block, if you like. Because while I was speaking the truth when I told him that I had been expecting him to be American (well the name alone – you really would have thought so, well wouldn't you?) still I find myself very much disconcerted by a whole lot more than that. His manners, so very English, they seem to be hardly less than flawless . . . so all of that is so much to the good . . . but . . . but . . . well Jesus, it's the *look* of him . . .! Isn't it? Well of course it is . . . it really is the look of him, you see. It is that which, just for the moment, and I freely admit it, is giving me considerable pause. I mean to say . . . how *can* he . . .? How can a senior executive of a prestigious movie company actually, you know – *look* like that . . .? I mean for one thing – and this is maybe the main thing, because there's just no ignoring it . . . he is quite unbelievably small . . .! I don't mean short – it isn't just that he's on the shorter side of what ideally one might prefer . . . he's simply unimaginably tiny! Like some sort of a malnourished prepubescent . . . though at the same time, rather worryingly old. I didn't quite notice it at first – not when he was still sitting behind his desk . . . but as I continued my sweep into the room, he of course had bobbed up briefly (those manners, you see – exquisite, in one way . . . as well as, one cannot help but think, really quite tragically wasted) . . . and well at that point – honestly! I am telling you . . .! His eyes – alert, though I suppose quite inevitably, piggy – were on a level with my breasts. The underside of them, though – not much north of the navel. And yes okay, I'm wearing heels (Louboutins – finally I have them: these are the blue) but still, but still . . . Then there is the matter of his hair. None. There's none. Well there is just a little bit, scruffily about his ears – large ears, Plasticine lobes, and a fair amount of hair going on in there, all right – and this little there is of it, it seems to be smarmed down shinily with some or other unguent that I just simply know in my gut is going to smell quite vile – conceivably send me reeling. His neck . . . I cannot work out, to be perfectly honest, whether it truly is as mottled and thin, as meagre as that of a chicken, or whether this utterly farcically overlarge and floating circle of the collar of his shirt simply serves to cruelly exaggerate its redly razored and total scrawniness. The nose is comically, parodically big. Latticed by an explosion of angered veins, and with a decided curve to it. Lips . . . his lips are quite utterly mismatched . . .! The upper is thin and has those close-together and vertical striations as seen always on the mouth of any inveterate smoker of a certain age . . . while the lower is indecently plump and really rather horribly yielding, not to say occasionally wet. Never – hand on my heart – never have I seen anything remotely like it. And from this perfectly bizarre great head of his, balancing very gamely atop so absolutely teeny a frame, there emanates a deep and mellifluous, perfectly enun-ciated and utterly calming voice . . . so very velvet, and completely beautiful: had you but spoken to Mr Willy Ouch on the telephone, you would surely have envisioned an Adonis.

'Would you care for a cigarette, maybe? Willy . . .?'

'No no – I, uh . . . I don't, um . . . look, Amy – I hate to be, er . . . m'kay? But . . .'

'Do you mind if I do, then? Would you mind, awfully . . .?'

'Mm? Well – strictly speaking, in this building we do actually operate a, er . . .'

'Well I've lit it now, I'm afraid. So it's rather too late. No going back on the thing – not now, Willy. See? Smoking. And you don't mind my sitting here, I hope. Just on the corner of your desk, like this? Not taking up too very much room, am I? None at all. And I promise I shan't disturb any of these frightfully impor-tant-looking papers, and things. It's just that . . . that chair, well . . . it's just so terribly far away from you.'

179

And I suppose that he couldn't any longer. Ignore it. Just couldn't any more. Well could he, really?

'Amy . . . what are you . . .? What exactly do you think you are doing . . .?'

I touched his head. Just to the side. The skin was soft, and surprisingly warm. I could feel the whole of him becoming tense quite immediately – a spasm of rigidity, it seized and then bolted just straight through the man. His eyes were flicking up at me, though he was not actually recoiling – and I simply can't tell you how I was almost tearfully grateful even for that much. For had he leapt up out of his chair – appalled, open-mouthed and trembling quite badly . . . had he stood there, drawing himself up to the full extent of his stature and looked me straight in the tits with accusation and outrage, well then I would confess to finding myself completely out of strategy – I would have no false trail to lay, nor the comfort of even so much as a vestige of face-saving camouflage. But no: still he was sitting there. The tussock of hair to which then the teasing of my fingernails had rather deftly progressed . . . well it was wholly as greasy and perfectly disgusting as I simply knew it had to be, and the utterly extraordinary odour that rose up from it would have you quite literally staggering, your eyes not just smarting, but widened by its sheer impossibility.

'Why . . . are you doing this, Amy . . .?'

'Power . . .'

'I beg your pardon . . .?'

'Yours. Not mine. No listen – I know now what you are thinking, I know just what you're thinking: but honestly – you really are quite wrong about that. Not my way. You have to believe me. That is not the sort of woman I am. If I could have controlled this – oh well then please do believe me: I would

180

have. You think I enjoy appearing weak like this, in front of you . . .? But it is power, you see. Your power. And I am powerless, quite powerless, when confronted by power. It is thoroughly enslaving. I sensed it . . . even as I walked into the room. This . . . aura. It surrounds you. It oozes from your every, uh – pore. It is, quite frankly, Willy . . . utterly devastating. Oh but come on . . .! Don't play games with me – you must have been told that how many millions of times before . . .? Every woman you have ever come into contact with simply must have said all that to you . . . and if they didn't, well . . . well then they were all just so much stronger than I am. That . . . that's all, Willy . . .'

He turned up his head then and looked at me quite expressively. Yes but just what it was that that face appeared actually so eager to express . . . well . . . it is quite wholly beyond me. There was a trace of amusement there, I think, in the brightness of the eyes – actually, his sole redeeming aspect, despite that undeniable pigginess – this also suggested by the crinkles that surrounded them . . . that, and possibly a degree of just mildly affronted toleration. What was horribly clear, though . . . the thing that was made quite perfectly plain to me was the absolute certainty that I had failed to take him in: no, hadn't done it, and not for a moment. So quite how things were now to progress . . . well honestly I hadn't a clue: just not as I had so unthinkingly assumed. That's all. For I am quite unused to appearing resistible. But whatever he said to me next, I decided quickly to wilfully misunderstand – yes, or else to quite stubbornly ignore it: I just had to continue with this now rather risible, oh God – seduction . . . because it was all that was left to me. You think I was relishing this . . .? The prospect of it . . .? No. But here was this woman's already rumbled but solitary weapon, which

181

somehow just had to be wielded. That's all there was to it. And I couldn't give in. Just couldn't. Because what is at stake, here . . . well it's only everything. No more than that. Just simply everything in the whole wide world.

'No, Amy . . . no one has. Ever said that to me. Or anything remotely like it. Nor, I am quite sure, has it ever so much as occurred to them. What do you think I am . . .? I am under no illusions. And nor, Amy, you should know, am I stupid. I am old. I am old, and I am ugly. You think I don't know this? Men do know this, you know. Men are . . . aware. I was ugly even when I was young, and now . . . well, it's simply worse. And all this other nonsense you're giving me . . . I'm surprised, very frankly, Amy. I'm surprised at you. Because I have no "power". No "power". Not in any real sort of . . . simply a little influence, is all I . . . if even that. So listen to me, Amy – no, listen, just listen to me, before you say another single word. Can you truly imagine that I take it for granted that a woman as beautiful as yourself, Amy – and you are, I have to say, quite remarkably beautiful, and you of course *do* know that – you think I do not find it just a leeedle bit strange that one such as you should behave like this? To me? No. I know quite well what is going on here, and I am sorry to have to tell you it is not the way I do things. Do producers, still . . .? Maybe some – I really wouldn't know. Maybe in the old days. But I, Amy . . . I am not one of them. Best to have all these things out in the open, don't you think? Because do please understand – I don't want to spoil, er . . . relations between us, Amy. Don't want anything of that sort. M'kay? So now look . . . as I hope now it is perfectly clear to you that I am well aware as to exactly what you're, uh . . . oh listen to me, Amy . . .! Don't you think it would be altogether better, better for all concerned, were you just to say no more,

182

not another syllable, and leave now, yes . . .? M'kay . . .? Yes, Amy? Yes?'

'No, Willy. Frankly I don't. But don't *you* think it would be altogether better, better for all concerned – heavens, what phrases you do come out with! – were you just to say no more, not another syllable, and lock the door now, yes? And buzz through to Jocasta – oh my God! *Jocasta!* – and tell her that you unexpectedly find yourself caught up in a dreadfully, dreadfully urgent meeting, and would she therefore terribly mind rescheduling your eleven o'clock . . .?'

There was talk then, of course – more talk, more talk. Men will. It's the only time they ever do – talk, when actually they should be doing things. The only time they'll ever say a word: anything, anything, to save them from the slightest semblance of commitment. But it was getting to the point now where I could hardly, if I am honest, actually tolerate it any longer: cajoling a man into an action, that's nothing, not to any woman who is used to taking care of business – ah, but one which you yourself were actually shying away from . . . that, well that . . . that can never be easy. And if soon he didn't break (or crumble – that would do) . . . if soon I couldn't slice into and through this really rather strange and ultimately thoroughly irritating little man's seemingly limitless pomposity, this tiresomely portentous defence of his, I think then I might either lose all that is left of my fraying nerve, or else this physical, this visceral, repugnance that is welling (I smelt it, and it was green; I sensed that – yes, and boiling) in the face of, oh . . . just the absolute *whole* of him . . . this could gather muscle, reassert itself in the form of a poisonous tsunami – mm, and altogether disastrously. And all this I was thinking as he continued to talk at me – I wasn't listening to it any more: for I knew that all it could be

183

now was just more of the same. But the real point was, of course – and this had hardly escaped me, for how could it? – that still he was sitting there. He hadn't got up. Had he? Shown me the door. He did not tremble with indignation, either righteous or illusory. Nor was he summoning the quite idiotic Jocasta. No: within this room there was hanging no air of finality: a curtain had not been janglingly rung down. Because if a man really, really doesn't want a thing . . . well: of course he will make it clear. Very quickly. We all do, I suppose, one way or another. And I sort of understood the pain of this dilemma with which I had suddenly and so very starkly confronted him. Well what am I saying . . .? Of course I did, of course: I understood it wholly. He *wanted* me – of course he *wanted* me: what man doesn't? But it was the consequence of his actions – it was the fright of that, simply that, which had clouded and now was thickly muddying the clarity of his lust (while a much younger man, I just knew, would have been possessed of no such fore-sight, nor hesitation . . . or else would have throttled either, at the first squeak of doubt). For consequences surely there will be. Why I was there, after all: what I was doing there in the first place. One thing, you see . . . has to follow the other. Has to. Just must. It is the essential nature of the thing.

I closed my eyes. I stooped, to kiss him. Full on the mouth – and that mouth, it was not so wholly repulsive as I had gin-gerly anticipated: not *pleasant*, oh Christ no, there was no way at all it could ever be said to be even so much as approaching *pleasant*, not by a very long way indeed . . . but still, though, not so wholly repulsive as I had gingerly anticipated. And he nei-ther responded, nor retracted. I could not see whether he had closed his eyes to the touch of my lips, for, as I say, I had closed my own at the thought of his. And then I touched him. There was nothing else to be done. He might, you see, have been poised just upon the very pivot of immediate decision: he might have been about to stand up abruptly – call a halt, and rudely, while still he imagined there might still be time. So I touched him. There was nothing else to be done. My eyes, they were shut even tighter than ever by now – for the next few moments, I was frighteningly aware, must surely be revelatory. And . . . he groaned. A sigh, maybe, that grew darker and guttural towards its deadened end. Yes and I can't tell you how good . . . and bad . . . that was making me feel: as now I would have to go through with the thing. My intention, of course my intention all along – the wholly necessary and big black deed, yes yes yes, but of course I did completely understand that . . . but still, but still . . . there could no longer be evasion on either of our parts: now I would have to go through with the thing.

As I drew slightly away, I saw that they were, his eyes, closed – really quite screwed down, as if he were dreading and in awe of any sight whatever that might be a lurking menace, beyond those empurpled lids. His breathing seemed even and shallow as he took my hand and guided it lower, and under, to where he most wanted it to be. His suiting, though sheeny, was rather coarser to the touch than ever I could have foreseen. I almost laughed with gratitude: all he seemingly needed me to do was to touch him, to feel him, further and deeper. My own sweet body, then, was to be spared all degradation . . . and nor was I to be put to the clumsy humiliation of tugged-at and ugly, partial undressing. Only at one point was I momentarily thrown: I am not at all sure, you know, that ever previously have I actually encountered a buttoned fly. Only then did I glance back anxiously at the door . . . not knowing, not remembering, whether or not it was locked, supposing not, and hardly

185

relishing the entrance of the wide-eyed infant that is Jocasta . . . this brief spasm of anxiety causing my fingers maybe to stutter and flickeringly contract . . . though I relaxed them immediately as I sensed in his composure an instant spike of concern, a quietly rumbling tremor of unease. This strange sort of undulating sigh continued to come from his loose, now, and ragged lips . . . then it would approach a sort of gurgle, before dying back down. I was beginning to feel quite proud, which few, I can see, might want to comprehend. But soon it would be done, you see, whereupon only the future can gaudily beckon.

It was then, though, that I first felt his hand upon me. Well I had expected that – a little of that I had expected before: because men, at times such as these, they will like to cling. Soon though I was aware of the weight of this mitt at the back of my head, and it was that which he was urging quite roughly downwards, the pressure becoming insistent. Instinctively I resisted . . . and as I did so, felt the return of his tension, hesitation, the beginning of withdrawal . . . and so consciously I unbunched the muscles at the base of my neck, and leant my body obligingly forward. There was nothing else to be done: now I would have to go through with it. And please do not misunderstand me when I say that as I willed my nostrils into numbness and exercised fluidly my lips and fingers . . . I thought – not, as a joke might have it – of England, no no, not at all . . . but of Alexander.

And now, following all of that (and there wasn't really much, no not really, not when it actually came to it) I am safely back at home. The essential manoeuvre, this most necessary sacrifice . . . done now, and offered up. Women will do this, for the things that they believe in, as men look on, in wonder. Tess. Tess of the whatever-it-was . . . she was, wasn't she? Sacrificial in some sort of a way, I very distantly recall. Anyway – detail doesn't matter: let us simply presume that the gods (or devils – their appetites really very comparably voracious) are now appeased. Yes. So . . . I am safely back at home. In my office: the calm and secret place. Which I know, just know, has been invaded. Sense it. Was aware, just as soon as I entered. And by whom else, do we suppose, but Terence . . .? How did he get in here? Why did he get in here? What was he looking at? What was he looking for? And what did he find . . .? Is there something missing? I feel sure that there is something missing. And so therefore I must ask myself: what else, what more, has he taken from me now . . .?

CHAPTER FIVE

THEY JUST DON'T SEE IT

And suddenly, there seemed to be this, well – avalanche might be going it a bit, but certainly a whole load of emails, which hadn't been the intention at all. None of them meaningful, it goes without saying – many, actually, precariously verging upon the really most abysmally trite, and even quite close to deranged (mine, naturally). Because the whole thing was . . . well yes – my fault, I suppose. Clearly, I had taken her completely unawares, Portia, my Portia. And on the face of it, it truly would appear – wholly incomprehensibly – as if even so slight an advance as I had ventured had been in some way actually unwelcome. While all I had wanted was to . . . I don't know . . . alert her? Alert her, yes, to my coming, you see. Perfectly simple, no? Because it had quickly become my absolute intention to go over and see her (had to, just had to) – because I mean . . . well, you don't really like to, do you? Just sort of *present* yourself. Unannounced. Particularly as all along it has been Amy and Amy alone who Portia's been dealing with. And I was thinking, well – might have considered it odd, mightn't she, if I'd simply pitched up at Pasadena Pictures without any sort of a warning. Well what am I saying . . .? *Would . . . would* have considered it odd, of course she would. Strange in the extreme. I understood that. Saw it clearly. Which is the only reason, Jesus Christ, that I emailed her in the first fucking place.

Hello, Portia. Do hope you got home safely last evening. And that you didn't have too bad a time . . .! Just was wondering whether you would care for a coffee some time. Very best – Terence (Alexander's dad).

Jesus. Jesus Jesus oh Jesus. I actually did send that, you know. Those, out of all the others at my happy disposal, were the very words I selected. Didn't check it over, you see – was in such a bloody tearing hurry for her to be reading it, of course. And as I clicked to send, I actually did find myself thrilling even to this ethereal, and therefore by definition quite utterly intangible communion. It was only as I was tip-tapping away on the side of the machine with a pathological ballpoint that it finally occurred to me to read the thing through. Only then did I fully realise what a litany of idiocy it very truly was. I mean to say: 'Do hope you got home safely last evening'. . .! Well Christ Almighty: she had previously texted her personal driver who had texted in return immediately upon his arrival. We watched her – Amy and I, we stood at the door, waving inanely, and watched her get into the car, a black and large, glossy Mercedes. And her personal driver, we may safely assume, was perfectly aware of her address, don't we think so? Yes – so short of the bloody car turning the corner and exploding into a carnival fireball, I really do believe that we may take it as read that yes indeed, home safely is exactly how and where she must soon have arrived. Then there was that so very forced and jokey teeth-clenching irony and self-deprecation all balled-up tackily in that 'not too bad a time' little throwaway jeu d'esprit of mine. How could that not come across as just mere and pathetic angling for multiple thanks and compliments? Then I continue blithely to wonder whether she'd care for coffee. When I know, of course I know, that she doesn't ever drink the stuff, though I can't remember why. The caffeine, was it? A command from her personal trainer? Something. And 'some time'! Why did I suggest that this should be 'some time'? That thoroughly nebulous moment in some mythical and airy-fairy future dimension that is never ever to arrive. *Now* is what I meant: *now*, right this bloody minute. So . . . was all that enough, do we imagine? Well no, not quite. Because then I just had to make clear that of all the Terences with whom last night she had been dining, I was the one who a decade ago was responsible for fathering that glittering prodigy, Alexander. Christ. I don't know. Went through then a very brief period of simply dreading her response. Very brief indeed: soon I was yearning quite madly for it. When the machine was finally pinging, I nearly fell on the floor.

Hi Terence! Good to meet with you. Had a great time. Hang in there! P.

What . . .? *What* . . .? Well what in God's name is that all about, then? Hey? What on earth is that supposed to mean? How is it that Americans have so very many completely ridiculous ways of saying absolutely bloody nothing at all? And what about the coffee, then? She didn't mention the coffee. Because I was wondering, wasn't I? I said that in the email: 'just wondering whether you would care for . . .' And yes I know she wouldn't care for, I know that, I know that, because she doesn't bloody drink the stuff, right? But, what – I was supposed to lay out some sort of a bloody *menu* for her, was I? Peppermint tea, herb infusion, green oriental bleeding *tisane* . . .? Why must women be so eternally literal? Hey? You tell me that. I mean, Christ

– when did 'coffee' last mean 'coffee'? So: back to the sodding keyboard:

Yes – I enjoyed talking to you as well, Portia. Very much. Was wondering, actually, if we couldn't continue with that just a little bit? When I said 'coffee', of course, I didn't mean it actually had to be 'coffee'. Maybe we could just meet for anything you like? Possibly I could just pop in to your office very briefly? I realise you must be terribly busy, but I wouldn't take up too much of your time, I promise. Best, Terence.

Well this one, though prolix, was a little bit more grounded in sanity, anyway – and surely as clear as day? Even, I should have thought, to an American. Took an age for a reply to come through, though.

That would be great – but at work it's real crazy at the moment. Can I get a raincheck? P.

Well I won't go into it: it's just how they go on. But 'raincheck', I don't know . . . always makes me think of Alexander's Burberry trench. And did I stop, then? Throw in the towel? Bow out like a gentleman, and generously concede? Did I buggery. Sent off another whingeing little plea – tried to make it light, but the smarming of sheer and dripping desperation I just knew must have been staining the thing. And when, after nearly a whole bloody hour, there still was no response . . . I sent her off another. As any man would. And there were no bones about this one: it was both abject and useless, plain and simple. And after it became perfectly plain that there was to be not one iota of reaction to that one either, I actually did become really quite angry. I mean to say – what is *wrong* with her at all? Why is she being so wholly obtuse? We're *soulmates*, aren't we? So why isn't she bloody behaving like it? Yes well. So I just had to come to a decision, no matter how painful. Because that's that then, really.

Isn't it? Got to be faced. Can't do it any more. Can't, can I? Send yet another email. No. That would be just too ridiculous. Because even I have my limits. Yes. So I rang her up.

'Hi. Portia Hazelstein.'

'Yes – hello, Portia. It's, um . . .'

'Hallo . . .? Portia Hazelstein . . .?'

'Yes – it's, er . . . can't you, um . . . hear me? I'll just . . . there – is that any better? It's me, in fact. Terence.'

'Oh. Terence. Right. Hi. I'm like really late for a meeting . . .?'

'Oh I see. Well sorry, but . . .'

'Uh-huh. One hell of a day. Was up before dawn . . .!'

'Oh really? Who's Don . . .?'

'Huh . . .? Who's Don . . .?'

'Yes – that's what I said. Who's Don? You were up before Don . . .?'

'Oh no! I didn't say . . .! Oh, okay, okay – I'll do it in *English*. I was up before *daaawwwn* . . . okay?'

'Oh yes I see: got you. Up before . . . right. Right. So who's Dawn . . .?'

'Terence, I gotta go. You know . . .?'

'Right-o. So how about some other time then, Portia? Some other time . . . soon.'

'Sure. Call you.'

'Well you don't actually have to do that in fact, Portia – because I called you, you see. We're actually speaking . . . as we speak, as it were. So to speak.'

'Uh-huh. But really I just gotta go. So call me. Kay?'

She just put the phone down, then. So I didn't ask her who Kay was, or anything: because I had only now just understood the whole of the 'dawn' rigmarole, you can believe it or not. Jangled, you see: very. But the inrush of embarrassment was

192

mingling oilily with the bile of hurt, and hot disappointment: all I could do now was leave them all to it and wait to be filled up right to the brim with whatever resultant and toxic bubbling mixture of slime that would gleefully meld, shortly prior to coagulation. Had a glass of whisky, to help it along. And after that, my course was clear: I'd go straight over and see her. Had to, you see. Had to.

Even then, though – I didn't just dash. Because there was my appearance, wasn't there? To be considered. Well look: had to make on her some sort of an impression. Good one, I mean. Good impression. Must be seen to be, well . . . taken seriously. No? Because thus far into the game . . . it is, I have to admit it, rather beginning to seem as if thus far into the game (game . . .? Game . . .? Is it a game? Doesn't feel like a game. Feels quite desperate. To me, anyway. It does. Feels quite desperate. Doubt whether she sees if like that either, Portia, my Portia, a game. Not playing, anyway. Is she? Not really on the team. Hardly picking up the ball and running with it, I think it's fair to say. So not a game, no. Not for either one of us). Yes. And so . . . what was I actually, um . . .? Thinking, now . . .? What was my train of, er . . .? Oh yes: way I look. Because my love of design, it does indeed stretch to clothes, as a matter of fact. Doesn't for most men, as I am very aware, *GQ* or no.

Always rather amuses me, actually (or else it makes me angry). In the house magazines, the home magazines, the design-driven pieces that are padding out the supplements. Some pair of architects, say. Husband and wife. Or husband and husband, could be – whatever these types care to call them- selves, these days. One of them a wife, is he? Two wives? Both husbands? Who knows? Can't keep up. Don't want to. Because actually: who bloody cares? Or industrial designers, commercial designers, textile designers, whatever the hell they might be. Eyewear designers. And there they are, pictured looking arrogant, smug or just plain clumsy in their bright white would-be Lloyd-Wright, light and possibly even cantilevered space. Poured rubber floors, shouldn't wonder. Polished concrete, conceivably. The total check-list of architectural furniture, present and correct. The usual keynote and definitive objects, the spatter of name-check rip-off having-a-laugh 'artists', yes, and this entire demonstration of quite palpable desperation will be spiked by just the merest odd flourish of pop frivolity (this in order to demonstrate that the child within them, he or she of wide-eyed wonder, is alive and frolicsome yet . . . yes and also to underline the presence within the muscles and hard delineation of their utter and cold professionalism, a lighter side, a warm ray of sunshine, a streak of sweetness, a fucking sense of humour). So a Coca-Cola sign, could be. Tinware robot. Pedal car, rocking horse. Shop mannequin. Or maybe some or other gaudy throw-out from a derelict circus or fairground that will have cost them simply thousands. Anything immediate and gaudy to sock you in the eye and once belonging just anywhere at all bar a domestic living room. Maybe no more than an ironic row of Campbell's soup cans, ho bloody ho. Or a garden urn, sick with lichen. Yes . . . yes, but what always they plainly refuse to see is themselves. See? Amid all of this. The thinning hair, pot belly, scrubby bristles, the bloody Levi's 501s and grey marl sweat or T-shirt. And that's just the women. They sit there, oh-so proudly in their chair by, oh . . . I don't know – Corb, Aalto, Mies, Eames, Jacobsen, Saarinen, you name any one of them . . . thereby, ruining it. Destroying the purity of line. Their very hideous presence, indeed, rendering the whole of their practice and achievement quite utterly void and contemptible, not to

194

say perfectly ridiculous. And they just don't see it. They cannot see themselves, you see? But how could they fail to, you might well wonder. Yes well, there it is: 'go figure', as Portia, my Portia, could so very easily come out with.

But me – I do. I do, oh yes. I do see myself: I see myself quite perfectly clearly. Because I look. See? So I like my clothes to fit. Be tailored. Colours to coordinate. Not strange, is it? Shouldn't really have said that in one who constantly is visually aware that such a thing is so terribly strange. I mean to say: would I throw a clashing, ready-made and ill-suited loose cover over my light oak Rietveld zigzag . . .? I can't really see it, can you? And I rather like still to wear a tie. Useful. Touch of colour – yes, and the glamour of thick, hand-woven silk, pulling the whole outfit together. Can't remember the last time I saw a man of my age wearing a tie. The only people who seem to, have to. Office workers, middle management, estate agents, loss adjusters – you know them: the whole grey sea. And at the end of the day, you will glimpse them, these beaten-down and uncompre-hending soldiers in a ragged and bankrupt army waging so hopeless and unceasing a war against quite the wrong enemy – oh yes, you've seen them, come six o'clock, come the pub, come the wine bar, come that sunken-eyed and clutched-at moment that drips and screams with 'Christ, oh Christ, just put a big drink into both of my hands, for the love of bleeding God, before I dissolve, or die of fury!' – dragging those carefully non-descript and greasily fingered tie knots down and out of the collars with such deliberation and almost delight, sometimes even to the extent of giving off a purposely audible sigh of what is evidently intended to be both seen and heard as relief, and from deep within the heart. So silly. As if . . . a blacksmith had just riven their fetters, the liberated drone so very gleeful as the great iron ball just is rolling away from him. As if . . . for each of us men, there is nothing more than a tie, a ribbon of fabric, that is repressing us all, binding us all, damping every one of us down, and down, and down. Mm. But why can't they see that it's people – it's people that kill us, not . . . *ties*. Well anyway. Though me – I'm not like that. No. Not me. Uh-uh. Not a bit. To me, this is just a foreign country.

And I left quite hurriedly, after all of that. Suddenly aware that somehow, while I hadn't been looking, it had become rather late. Odd, really – because I had, hadn't I, been so very eager to be gone. But it's because I get involved, you see – too involved, and the time, well . . . just flies by. Putting the clothes together. Assembling the whole. Rejecting this or that actually perfectly acceptable article, adding it to the crumpled pile – turning away from the easy convenience of any tried and tested combinations out of sheer and utter boredom (disappointment too with my own quite shocking desertion of imagination). Then to the stage of being, yes – more or less satisfied, so far as ever I can be . . . but still unable to stop myself wondering whether in fact the other boots, the very dark brown ones, the ones I had had on in the first place, the ones with gussets and the subtly punched toe, whether they might not really, when all is said and done, actually be far more the thing . . .? Knowing that a certain cashmere scarf would be perfect in completing the entire ensemble, and knowing too with a lowering clarity that you just had to take one look out of the window to see that it was far too hot to be wearing anything at all of that nature . . . while still remaining very reluctant indeed to altogether abandon the idea. And all these clothes, they don't come cheap. Nothing decent ever does. And we're not all Alexander, are we? We don't all have the manufacturers of the world's very finest queuing round the block in order to plead with us to wear the bloody things. No.

Anyway – finally did get myself out of the house (hoping that she, Portia, my Portia, might look upon this eventual choice of tie out of how many dozens of possibilities as no more than bright and engaging, as I surely did, and not in any way too overt, or even garish). Was thinking taxi, a taxi, that's what I'm needing now (there'll be nowhere to park, never is, and the Tube, it's just too filthy) and just as I was locking the front door – first one key in this one, then the other key in that one, and all the time thrilling to, as well as shying away, nearly flinching, from the unimaginable truth that soon I would be with her, Portia, my Portia, actually within her presence, gazing once more upon the truly awesome wonder of that face, that face, quite dizzied by the scent of her . . . yes and though quite thoroughly consumed by all of that, still I was suddenly then aware of her, Sylvia, in that shamingly neat, though one has to say altogether far too prim and primped-up little front garden of hers (because Amy, she is the nominated gardener in our household, so I think I hardly need to say another word on that particular subject, need I?). Big thick gloves she had on . . . of course those glasses she habitually sports, Sylvia, rendering her expression hardly ever more really than a glint. Greenish sort of quilted thing I have no doubt she has forever referred to as the 'gardening coat', and pruning assiduously some or other thorny thing . . . Sylvia, she raised up a hand as she put down carefully into a trug – proper trug, split wood and hand-made affair – the pair of secateurs, wafting back a flop of hair and away from her forehead . . . now was coming over – yes yes, here she came, and clearly quite determined to talk to me.

'Off out, are you Terence?'

197

'It would seem so, Sylvia, yes . . . Very nice, uh – to see you last evening. Hope you and Mike were, uh . . .'

'It was lovely, wasn't it? Short and sweet, but very lovely. And the rest of your evening – all went well, did it? Dinner, and so on . . .?'

'Oh yes. Thank you. Well – that is to say, uh . . .'

'It's not that that I wanted to talk to you about actually, Terence. Pleased I've run into you, though – because I've been meaning to have a little word with you for quite some while.'

'Oh. Really . . .?'

'Mm. About Lizzie.'

'Lizzie . . .? What – my Lizzie, do you mean?'

'Well . . . yes . . . of course your Lizzie.'

'Oh. Well what about her? Everything all right, is it?'

'Well that's just it, Terence. I'm not actually sure that it is . . .'

'What . . .? Well what's, uh . . .?'

'Oh look I don't think it's anything *ghastly*, or anything – and I suppose that really it's absolutely none of my business, but . . .'

'But what? What, Sylvia? What's wrong? What's going on?'

'Well it's probably nothing. But it's just that . . . well – have you *talked* to her lately, Terence? Lizzie. Have you, Terence? Spoken to her?'

'Spoken to her . . .? Well of course I've . . . I don't really know what you mean. I mean – naturally, we *speak* . . . well of course we do. She's my daughter, isn't she?'

'Yes, but I mean recently, Terence. Specifically.'

And Terence then found himself thinking just this: recently? Specifically? I just can't understand, Sylvia – if, indeed, you are saying anything at all – just, well . . . *what*, exactly. And the other thing I am thinking is this: Portia, my Portia – I've got to go to her now, do you see? Got to. Just got to.

'It's only that . . . well, Terence – do please tell me to keep my nose out of other people's business if you want to, but . . . well . . . I don't think she's very happy, that's all. In fact I know it. I know she's not. It's really rather sad. Don't you think so . . .?'

'Not happy? Lizzie? Really? What – she's said something to you, has she? Have you talked to Amy about any of this? But what do you mean, "not happy"? What sort of "not happy"? I don't really understand what you're getting at, Sylvia . . .'

'I haven't, no. Spoken to Amy. She always seems to be so terribly busy. Well you know that, Terence. Always concerned with, well . . . other things.'

I suppose, Terence was immediately thinking, she means Alexander.

'You mean Alexander, I suppose . . .'

'Well, Terence . . . I suppose I do. But all I'm really saying is – and believe me, I have no wish to pry, you know, into matters that do not, em . . . concern me . . . but all I really wanted to say to you is just . . . well . . . have a word with her, won't you? I feel that, well – with you, she might . . . I don't know . . . open up a bit . . .? You know? Because I really do believe she ought to be talking to someone.'

And Sylvia just watched him as he assured her that he would. As he thanked her for the information. As he promised her once again that he would, he would, of course he would, at the very earliest opportunity, talk to her, Lizzie: find out what was wrong. She watched him then as he cantered into the street and around the corner: with so very clearly something altogether more pressing at the forefront of his mind. And she decided then and on an impulse that she had had more than enough of gardening for one day.

So what I shall do now, I think, is gather up all my bits and pieces, give my hands a little bit of a rinse, yes . . . and then I'll make myself a nice cup of tea.

Selfish . . . so very terribly selfish, Terence and Amy, always have been – Amy particularly, of course. And does she truly believe that it's all about Alexander? Can she? All this . . .thing she does? Everything she's now just so terribly involved in. I can't really believe it. Because whatever Amy might be, she's not a stupid person. Calculating, yes. Vain beyond all reason – oh yes, most assuredly: the treatments she quite regularly undergoes, beauty things, whatever they are – oh my goodness, you just wouldn't believe. Nails and hair colouring, obviously ('Titian' she calls it, if you please: yes well), but also – and she told me all this at extremely tedious length – some other awful things that I can barely imagine. I mean to say: eyelash extensions . . .! Not even just the hair, oh no – but eyelashes! And then something else called 'eyebrow threading', I think that's it, I can't even think about that. Martyr on the cross of fashion, did she but see it: she ought maybe to be taken to one side and have explained to her very gently that what appears to be so very wonderful in the magazines and so on need not always . . . well – translate, shall we say. And she is rather of an age, wouldn't you think, where all the latest 'trends', or whatever they're supposed to be . . . well what I mean to say is, they're much more for the very young, aren't they really? What we always used to call the Carnaby Street crowd. The King's Road set. But after a certain time, I really do think that all that sort of nonsense ought quietly to be put away in favour of one's very own idiosyncratic and unique sort of personal style. Don't you think? Well Amy very evidently doesn't. More handbags than you could possibly imagine, most of them unwieldy and verging upon the absurd – oh well yes but that's Amy for you, you see.

And she's rude, of course . . . uncaring – a rather, on the whole, *shoddy* sort of a mother, if the truth be told: her ridiculous exploitation of little Alexander – for what else is it, actually? How else would you describe it? – and plainly she cannot see the degree to which her own daughter is suffering . . . yes, and increasingly, so far as I am any judge. Appalling wife as well – in that respect, I have to admit, my heart goes out to Terence. Well yes – she's all of those, quite clearly: it would be ridiculous to attempt to deny it. Pushy . . . deeply insecure at base, I rather fancy – and, although she is nowhere near so beautiful or alluring as she genuinely seems to imagine herself, still quite embarrassingly flirtatious, she can be, whenever she senses that something can be turned to her advantage: I've seen her – and honestly, what an exhibition . . .! You just don't know where to put your face. Traffic wardens . . . the man from Ocado was the last one I witnessed: quite shameless. Arrogant . . . domineering . . . indolent in any of the matters that truly may be said to be important – and, I can even think . . . quite pitiless. Yes yes – Amy, she's all of that and more, much more: oh I'm telling you, we could be here all night. Though one thing she isn't is stupid, it has to be said. To be fair to the woman.

She wasn't always like that, of course. Terence too – he was really quite different, when they first came to live here. Before they had the children. Such a nice young couple – and I'd said that to Mike: such a nice young couple, yes, and we took to them immediately. Though of course you do have to remember that between Mike and myself and Terence and Amy there's, what – there must be twenty or more years between us, I should say – even twenty-five, it could be – but that gap, I don't know . . . it didn't seem so terribly pronounced in those days. Hardly was aware. Now though, well . . . Amy, when she deigns even to so much as recognise my presence in the first place, all she seems to treat me as is, I don't know – some sort of a gaga old granny, or something. Toothless hag from *Macbeth* – someone deaf and stupid. Which I rather resent. Because I don't think I'm quite yet for the scrapyard, shouldn't have said so, anyway. Still presentable – always have taken pride in my appearance, though I do say it myself. Still in possession of all of my, um . . . oh, you know: when you're thoroughly compos mentis and firing on all cylinders, thank you very much. What is that word that I'm searching for . . .? Anyway.

Of course, in the beginning, apart from being literally neighbours, we all four of us shared this quite literally single state of childlessness. We were just two couples, alone. Faculties: that's the word I was . . . but obviously the two of them had plans for the future, Terence and Amy. In terms of children, I mean. And it would have been a crime, in one way, if they hadn't gone ahead and had a family. Good-looking pair – always did look well together. Amy . . . well as I've said, she was no model, no great beauty, whatever illusion she may have been labouring under, and continues so to do – but a trim little figure, and altogether really quite nicely turned out. Terence too – smart, clean-cut, which I always do admire in a young man. But for Mike and me, of course . . . well, the die had long been cast by that time. Children . . . mm . . . well alas no, they were not to be. Ironic, I suppose, how things were eventually to turn out – because in the early days, back at the height of the sixties, I had really been pretty adamant: very happy to just continue being me, and free. It wasn't that I was a hippy, or anything . . . well obviously I never could have been one of those . . . but there was . . . this sort of a feeling in the air then, you know? Well you will know, of course you will – you'll know exactly what I'm meaning if you happened to be young at the time – or else, I suppose, you will have read and heard endlessly about what really was a genuinely exciting spirit of the age. But to me it all seemed to be about the simple joy of just being alive. And young, of course – no good at all if you weren't that: my generation, we seem to have invented youth, quite singlehandedly. Mike, he was wedded to The Beatles, of course. Still is. And I was more than happy with all my Quant and Biba miniskirts (in truth never either thing – British Home Stores, mostly) – but I did have rather a good pair of legs in those days – not too shaming even now, I have to say – so where was the harm in showing them off? And then – oh my Lord, did I really . . .? Those perfectly ludicrous eyelashes I used to so very painstakingly apply each and every morning, quite religiously, and heavens they were fiddly – Miners? Rimmel? Max Factor? Can't remember . . . and I came to feel quite naked without them. Then all of that mascara – huge fan of Dusty, you see. Oh dear me: so long ago. And so I had said to him quite frankly, Mike, that I didn't want them, kids, not on any account. Couldn't see the point. Couldn't bear the thought of them cluttering up my life, interfering with my eternal girlhood, my fabulous freedom, I suppose – that, or something like it, I'm pretty positive, must surely have been the thinking. It was, looking back – though nobody, of course thought like that at the time – a very self-centred era. Not just me: everyone. And Mike, dear Mike . . . well you could see he was unhappy. With my decision, I mean. Might even have been more, much more than that: it's something, if I'm honest, that I've never really cared to dwell upon. But he wouldn't have said anything, of course: Mike, he never does – not really.

And then the years, well – just skittered by (and heavens, it gets so very much worse, you know, the speed of passing time, the older you become – oh yes, I am constantly and increasingly aware of that) . . . and I don't at all know if it was that 'biological clock' thing that people keep on talking about . . . maybe it was that, but more, I think, just seeing, looking at all the other women's children in their prams and stripy pushchairs. In the park. At Tesco. And so I said to Mike that I'd changed my mind about all of that – and oh, the look in his eyes! Won't ever forget it: never seen him so happy – not since the days when we first were married. So I threw out the Pill (never that happy about taking it, if I'm honest) and we did then become really quite systematic about the whole business. It wasn't at all about passion . . . well, hadn't been for quite some time. But I knew, I'd been reading about cycles and so on – times of the month, the juggling of likelihoods – and so we found ourselves sticking to a fairly rigid regime: I was really quite stern about the regularity of his performances. And although by that time I had utterly convinced myself that there was nothing on this earth I now more desired than a baby of my own, so utterly and unshakeably convinced was I by now of my supreme potential as the mother to end them all . . . nothing happened. Not at first, no, and then not for a very long time after. Consulted a doctor. Consulted another. Mike – he went first: I told him to. It's quite common, I remember saying to him – and really so very breezily: low sperm count, quite common, nothing remotely to be ashamed of: I'm sure they'll be able to fix it, sort it out in no time. But . . . and maybe all along I knew this, did I? . . . it wasn't him at all. Me. Oh yes. All sorts of simple yet incomprehensibly complicated and extremely saddening reasons. Just not possible, apparently. Well – there we are. Nothing to be done. Grin and bear it, basically: just take a deep breath and get on with things. Very down, though ... I was really so very down – within myself, you know? – for quite a good long time after all of that: couldn't go out – didn't want to face the world. I just felt myself to be such a failure. As a woman. And that everyone would have seen it, commented upon it, this terrible failure of mine. Should really have spoken to someone, I suppose – someone, you know, qualified in all these sorts of things. Nowadays you would, of course – nowadays it would be quite the automatic thing ... but you didn't, you simply didn't, not back then. Hadn't occurred to me – wouldn't anyway have had even the first idea of where to go, who to turn to. Mike though, he couldn't have been kinder. No hint of recrimination, not even the merest mention of his deep disappointment, which of course I just knew he must have been feeling. Me, oh dear – crying all the time. Couldn't stop. Kept on saying in between the tears that I was no sort of a wife to him ... and he told me not to be silly. Made me tea. Forever doing that, he was: making me tea. And throughout all my idiotic and impossible behaviour, heaven only knows what he himself had been going through. So yes ... now I look back on it, Mike ... he could hardly have been kinder. As for Amy, well ... she was quite ... solicitous, I suppose – at first she had been, anyway. Then some time after that she had Elizabeth – Lizzie, they immediately started to call her – and then later on came Alexander. Yes ... and now just look at how all that's turned out. Amy thinks quite miraculously, of course, but I really do have to wonder. And heaven only knows what Terence is thinking: always seems to have his mind on something else entirely – never quite, I don't know ... attuned. Ah ... it's all so funny, really. Isn't it? Life. All that happens to you. It can be really quite bewildering. Some people, in the grip of eternal frustrations and uncooperation, they call life Kafkaesque, I think. Don't they do that? Not maybe in the context I'm talking about, but they do, don't they? Call it Kafkaesque? Not though, is it? Kafkaesque. No – all it is is just normal.

'Garden's looking nice . . .'

'Oh Mike. Didn't hear you come in. Miles away . . .'

'Looks very nice.'

'I stopped. Didn't really do anything in the end . . .'

'Well – looks very nice anyway.'

'Oh God's sake . . .'

'Just saying it looks nice . . . that's all I'm saying. Put the kettle on, will I?'

'What have you got there? What have you brought back this time? I was going to make tea. Why I came in, actually . . . but I don't know: just didn't. What on earth is that thing . . .?'

'Cost me next to nothing. Total bargain. I can only think they didn't know what it was. What they had here, what they were selling.'

'Well I'm rather in sympathy with them, Mike, if I'm being honest. So what in fact is it? Looks like . . . I don't know – a coffin for an animal, or something . . .'

'Well that's a very funny thing to say. No no – it's a knife box. Mid Victorian, I think. Could be later. Coffin for an animal . . .? Where on earth did you get that from . . .?'

'A what? A *knife* box? What sort of knife? Why would you want a box to keep a knife in? And what's wrong with the lid? Why is the lid like that?'

'Not just one knife, Sylvia. See? Velvet slots inside. Whole set. It would have gone on the sideboard. With a wine cooler, maybe, and those silver serving dishes. And tureens.'

'Yes well it's not going to go on my sideboard, I can tell you that right now. Shabby thing. And the piping, the edging – that's all come away, look . . .'

'Yeh it's like that now, maybe – but a bit of beeswax and I'm telling you: you'll be amazed. Mahogany, it is – lovely bit of wood. Beautiful graining. Very fine workmanship. This is a quality piece – see it a mile off. And it's inlaid beading, that's what that's called – no trouble to glue it back in. Although there is a piece of it missing at the back, but I'm pretty sure I can knock up a short length that'll match it. Set up the lathe. Take no time.'

'Oh . . . make the tea, Mike. There's a good man. And what about the lid, though?'

'Hinge, that's all. Broken. Probably got a spare. Right – I'll put the kettle on.'

'Yes well don't just leave the thing on the table. Take it away, will you? Honestly – I don't know. I despair. All this stuff you keep on bringing home. Does it ever occur to you that we don't know where they've been? Could be alive with God knows what. And we've no space. We've no more space. Keep telling you.'

I do keep telling him, yes – though I don't any more ask him why he actually does these things, because now I understand it. Still don't particularly approve (still think it remarkably silly of him) but at least I do now appreciate the curious little thought processes behind it all. Never used to. Said he was demented. Everything he bought, it was never quite obvious what it actually was. Always obscure. And always defective in some way, or with a part of it missing. I used to say to him Oh for the love of God, Mike . . .! If you're going to keep on buying these stupid old things, then at least can't you for once bring back something beautiful and practical that isn't actually falling to pieces . . .?! It was quite a time before I saw it: he buys them because they are broken. He always used to love to repair things, you see. Hobby, you could say – though more for the feeling of being useful, I would have said. That, and the small satisfaction of seeing a given object functioning again. Big hands, Mike has got – large thick fingers, though he can be really quite surprisingly adept, you know – almost dainty, and even with the tiniest and most fiddly little things: it truly is a pleasure, sometimes, just to watch him working. His hair, what there is of it, will fall across his brow when he is deep in concentration: he intensifies the narrowness of his eyes behind his glasses and gestures to me with considerable irritation if ever I move to smooth it back. It's good, really, that he's latched on to something he can do while sitting down, because his joints just lately, they're not so good: knees, mainly – hips just a bit, and one of his ankles now – but apart from that and of course the constant bowel thing, he still is in reasonably good shape, I would have said, for a man of his age. Yes but the point is – what I was really meaning – is that there's a limit, isn't there, to how many things in a house can be in need of repair at any one time. You see? That's what he must have come to realise. And so I suppose I ought to be grateful that instead of actually going around smashing things that were perfectly all right in order to restore them, he took to garnering from elsewhere the damaged and the strange, the fractured and discarded, all the outcasts, the misfits, so that he could lovingly nurse them back to ruddy good health and demonstrate to anyone rash enough to linger, their inherent functionality and charm. He can, Mike, at times, be really quite overwhelmingly tender, you know – far more so than I. There was maybe always something of the square peg about him. Retired now, of course, but in insurance all his working life, and yet always and forever yearning to be a Beatle – or, failing that (he told me early on) needing to work with his hands.

In truth, many of his salvaged little oddments do eventually find their allocated places, dotted here and there. Mike, to give him his due, he does restore them properly – taking his time, not really ever wanting the process to come to an end – and some of them can really be quite decorative. They tend to fit in, I suppose, because we have always favoured the more traditional sort of home, the two of us. Not fuddy-duddy, I hope – it's not without colour, it's not all beige and brown or anything, though still it's quite restrained. Tasteful, but at the same time with a lived-in quality, if you see what I mean – yes, so the whole thing I think of as being rather . . . well . . . I don't know – *cosy*, I suppose is how in a word I would best describe it. And that word, it's probably seen to be perfectly filthy, these days. Certainly it would be to Terence, anyway. Oh, how we did use to laugh, Mike and me, when he really started to become so very terribly serious about all this extraordinary furniture and so on that seems to continue to consume him. Hardly any *wood* – that was always Mike's observation, and I saw what he meant, of course I did. There's marble – that funny sort of egg-shaped dining table they've got that Terence seems to love so much – and chrome and iron and glass and bronze and heaven knows what. The only wood, though, is on the floor, and that's the very place I simply can't abide it: give me carpet any day – and rugs as well: rugs on top of fitted carpets, utterly lovely. Because why would anyone want a hard floor in their living room? In the hall, well maybe – but not in the living room, surely. And in the olden days, I'm quite convinced, they all had planking simply because they couldn't afford anything to cover it up. Not that I suppose there can have been too much around: the odd drugget, I suppose, or a dead animal pelt, rather obscenely splayed out. But just you try offering a Tudor some wall-to-wall broadloom and I'm telling you – he would leap at it with both hands you may be quite sure of that. Terence, he calls it 'style', all his ideas about interiors. Well maybe – but I always want to get hold of the man and give him a damn good shaking and say right into his face but *look*, Terence: you're not living in a *showroom*, are you? It's not some sort of a shop *window*, is it? Home – that's what it's meant to be: home. So why do these people never want anything homely in it, then? It's a mystery to me, it really is. Oh but look – back in the sixties, I would have loved it all: op art, pop art, psychedelia, swivel chairs, blobby lighting, sag bags, you name it – oh yes, loved it, loved it all. Never actually had any of it, of course – just saw it in Habitat and the supplements and so on. But it's a bit like Amy's attitude to fashion, isn't it? There must come a time when you want to lay all that aside. I mean: not still playing with toys on the nursery floor, are we? Well then. But in the case of those two next door . . . apparently not. And I don't envy them. Truly I don't. And certainly not Amy, though clearly I'm meant to. Except, possibly . . . in just the one regard.

'Oh Mike, you are a treasure. I do so need a cuppa now . . .'

'Piping hot. Put it down here, will I? Or are we going in the back?'

'Oh no it's fine here, I think. Have to get the fire going other-wise. Did you bring . . .?'

'They're here. Both sorts. I know how you like to alternate them when you're dunking.'

'Lovely. And the . . .?'

'Already in.'

'I'm going to try to cut down to just the one spoon.'

Lucky, aren't I? So very lucky. And don't you think I don't

know it. Every day I thank whoever is up there for granting me this life of peace. I'm not saying it's perfect, Lord knows – what life is? Tell me that – because of course there have been the setbacks and the pitfalls, the pain and then the heartache. But still, though – we're really so terribly fortunate, Mike and me. Just to be here like this. To have one another to be here for. And so I really do not envy Amy, not one bit. Well . . . except for just in the one regard.

'Bumped into Terence earlier.'

'Oh yes?'

'He was just leaving the house. I was, you know – in the front.'

'Uh-huh. And what did he have to say for himself? All right, was he? Thank him for last evening, did you? I was thinking of emailing, and then I thought . . .'

'It was just as I said, you know. They did have all the others to stay for dinner.'

'Really? Well. What – he said that, did he?'

'Well no of course he didn't actually *say* it. Tried to cover it up, not very successfully. But it happened all right. Saw it in his face. Plain as day.'

'Oh well. Expect they had their reasons. Business, like I said.'

'Oh yes – *business*. . .! What – with Dolly and Damien . . .?'

'Mm. That bit's odd, I grant you. Top up?'

'Lovely. But I'm not going to have another . . .'

'What? Digestive? Oh heaven's sake, Sylvia – take it! You know you like two.'

'Easy for you to say – you never put on any weight. Me, it goes straight to my hips.'

'Nonsense. You're as slim today as the day I first set eyes on you.'

211

Oh – so far from being true, alas, but lovely of him to say it. Don't you think so? And so what, actually, if he brings back bits of useless splintered odds and ends? Godsend, isn't he? My Mike. Where would I be without him? And that's why I don't, I couldn't, remotely envy Amy . . . except just in this one single regard: through Alexander, she has carefully nurtured and engendered her own rebirth – for her, a new and fruitful flowering is both large, and looming. But as far as nearly everybody else is concerned, well . . . we just are never going to get that chance. At my age – and I fully recognise this – what is done is done: all we now can do is look back over our accomplishments, or lack of them – the little satisfactions . . . triumphs . . . even the thrills, if you are lucky. I had one of those, a thrill one time, yes – and his name, his name was Fabio. The only real boyfriend I ever had, apart from Mike . . . and even now – rather horrifyingly, not really that much short of fifty years on – I'm hardly sure it was real at all. We were engaged, Mike and I – far too young, I suppose – though I was already booked up to take that one last holiday as a single girl. With Carole, who I used to work with. Classic sort of 'dolly bird', she was, that's what people used to call them – long, dead-straight hair, big kohl eyes, pale pink – nearly white – lipstick, and quite the thinnest legs imaginable, drove me crazy. Harrington & Farr, that's where we were working – a solicitor's in Mayfair. Not me – I wasn't a solicitor, I don't mean, oh heavens no. Wasn't even a secretary – PA they call them now, someone was telling me recently, though I can't think why they do, because a secretary is all they are. I daresay I would have become such a thing, had I stuck at it, but at that time I was just a shorthand typist who made the tea. Anyway, we went to Amalfi, Carole and me, and there, on the very first afternoon – against the glitter of the sea, the dizzying and deep blue sky, the wonderful warmth of the Italian sun – was Fabio. He stood on the hot white sand wearing just the tiniest trunks, and his fingers were pushing back the weight of his long and drenched, thick black hair. A thin gold necklace was glinting against the deep soft brown of his skin, alive with all these shimmering little globules of the sea. And when he smiled that smile, I was just close to devastated.

We spent the whole of the week together – that trattoria, all the wine, the heat of his touch. He had a bright red motorbike. I never could have imagined a man in white trousers – even in Carnaby Street, that might have been seen to be going it a bit. His were tight, and he looked just simply wonderful. And at night . . . he took me over. I was frightened by my feelings – my body scared me in its intensity, and dangerous reaction. He told me he loved me . . . *Ti amo, Sylvia* . . . Seeeel-via, is how he sounded my name: I had never before noticed how beautiful it was. And I held him and kissed him and said to him: Fabio . . . I love you . . . I will always love you . . . until my dying day . . . and beyond, beyond . . . long into eternity. And even as I said it, I knew it was a lie. But oh dear God, I did so want it – to love him, to be possessed by him . . . to be young and with him in this eternal summer, in the sun, in bed, in the trattoria and on the back of his bright red motorbike . . . yes, and for ever. When I left, his eyes were dancing as I clung to him and told him through the tears that I was going to save up all my money and come out again to Amalfi as soon as I possibly could and that then we could be together again, and never be parted. Pulling away from his arms, such unwilling extrication, was so very peculiar an agony. Carole, she was beastly to me – and I suppose with reason. I had abandoned her utterly – didn't know or care how she had spent a single minute in Amalfi. On the bus back

213

from Gatwick she told me that Fabio by now would have found some other stupid English girl straight off the plane: to touch, to smile at, to eat with in the trattoria, to take on his bright red motorbike, and then to bed. I *screamed* at her to stop, called her every sort of liar, and knew that it was true. Quite soon after, I married Mike.

My memories, now . . . they keep me warm, but I know they are all that's left me. And here then is the sole regard in which I envy Amy – this is it, this is the point: for me, there can be no thought or idea of renaissance – there will surely now be nothing new. I shall not be born again . . . I shall simply continue to age, and then, eventually, I shall die. Somewhere, and in some or other manner. Quite as people do. And I really have lived such an uneventful life, you know . . . it often makes me wonder where on earth the time can have gone to. Always I have taken a very great pride in the house – you'll not find a thing out of place, and I dust every morning, with a good and proper clean and polish reserved for first thing on a Friday. But that, all that . . . well: doesn't account for a lot of time, does it? So where, please tell me, does all the rest of it simply vanish to? And not just the hours, but all the years, and then the decades? It takes me twenty-eight minutes to hoover from top to bottom, including the stairs and landings (although it's a Dyson we've got now, quite new, bagless, good suction, so I shouldn't really be saying it, should I? Hoover? Using the word). I shop every day, just as I always have done: not really a determination for freshness in all things as I'm constantly telling Mike . . . more a way of filling in the time. Gives me a reason to get dressed, and out of the house. Because I never did have a job, not really – Boots Library for a very short while indeed, though how was I to know that soon they were going to close down all the

214

branches? I still do read a great deal, though – why I had taken the job in the first place, and always something of a passion of mine. Mike gave me a Kindle just ages ago, birthday or anniversary, can't quite remember, and I still can't really decide whether or not I like it. I used to be quite wedded to Jane Austen, read her continually, but I find her really such a terrible bore, nowadays. Isn't that an awful thing to say? The Janeites would skin me alive. But reading and rereading the same six and silly books . . . waste of time, isn't it? P. D. James I think is very good indeed, and not too gory – I can't bear those, can't stand to read them, all the very gory ones. I'll look at Mike's *Telegraph*, sometimes try to fill in the gaps he's left in the crossword, though I seldom get too far with it: I'm not sure I've ever fully grasped the concept of cryptic. I used to play my LPs such a lot in the old days – boxed sets of all the operas as well as Rachmaninov, Debussy . . . Strauss I like very much: leave The Beatles to Mike. But it tends more and more just to be Classic FM these days: easier, less bother.

So – Fabio aside – hardly a life that has been packed with incident, I think it's fair to say. And up until very lately, I have been completely content with all that, expecting nothing else – as how could one, actually? But . . . I maybe shy away from thinking now the way I have been thinking – I maybe do not care to recognise deep down within myself all of which I believe I truly might be capable. I am feeling more and more that if this one life, so soon over and done with, is our general allocation, ours to exploit or fritter as we please – or as much as God wills it . . . well then Amy cannot really be deserving a new and second lease, and one which plainly is destined to be altogether magnificent. Why should that be hers? Why? She has not earned this. There ought – in fairness, and really very soon – to be the

215

looming of some unanticipated mishap, the suggestion, and then appalling surprise of sudden anguish . . . even the advent of a cataclysmic downfall . . . and although I quite see that as matters presently are standing, any such occurrence is, oh – so completely unlikely . . . still though, something of the sort might happen. It just might, you see. Well mightn't it? Things do. Happen. That's all I'm saying. Because look: you just never really know, do you?

I were stunned, you want the God's honest truth, when they turn round and tell me I got it, this bleeding job up the hotel. Damien, he were and all – see it in his face. Reckon he thought I were just messing with his mind first time I gone and said about it. But even when that black bloke down the Job place, when he say to me I were on, like – I still never quite believe it. Because I were thinking yeh you says that to me now, but when the geezer at the hotel – and he give me his name, man what I got to go and see, Mr Mumtaz what he called – well then this here Mr Mumtaz, when he like go into all of whatever they got to do, yeh? And then he twig I ain't never had no job nor nothing, not since the baker's what were yonks back, and even a crap job like chambermaiding, well he just going to tell me to sling it, ain't he? Course he bloody is. But nah – he never. Must of been, I dunno – desperate, or something.

Got to be there bleeding early. I make a bit of a noise when I getting up – banging about in the bathroom, and that . . . but he never wake up, Damien. Kenny and all – just like his bleeding father: just as well it ain't a school day – don't know what I going to do if it a school day. Peeing down outside, just typical.

216

Not even proper light, yet. All right for Damien – he just got to stick on his overalls, walk down the stairs and bang – he in the garage. Radio 1, and then he bung the kettle on. Yeh well – very nice. Me, I got to schlep down the Finchley bloody Road – get a bus I see one – but still I going to look like a drowned bleeding rat once I get there, ain't I? Yeh and I don't know what I gonna put on. I wear my good stuff, it going to get soaked. I turn up any old how and they going to think I a right little scrubber. Yeh well – chambermaiding, innit? They ain't hardly going to be expecting no Kate Moss or Angelina Jolie to come rolling up, I don't think. Yeh so I just got jeans and a mac and them old boots what lets in the water – which yeh I know it's fucking stupid, I do know that, but my good ones – new ones, yeh? I don't want them spoilt. Still – I got my fake Fendi bag what's really nice and all like plaited strips, and I got my black Chanel watch, you don't look too close. I calls out to Damien before I out the door that he got to get Kenny his Cheerios – egg, he want it – and still he just lying there like he bloody dead, or something. I dunno what it is about men.

Bleeding awful wind and all – yeh and my hair . . . I got a sort of a beret on me, yeh, but still – my hair, all over the bloody place and flying about, it is . . . can't think what I gonna look like. And there ain't no bus, course there bloody ain't – waiting at the stop like a right bleeding mug, no shelter, and then I thought oh fuck this for a game of silly buggers – I'll walk it. Yeh and when I can see the place – when I see the hotel there, just round the corner – then the bloody bus come, don't it? Yeh well: too late now. Shoves open this bleeding great glass door what they got there and it hiss open all on its own and I nearly going arse over tit. Go up the reception – and I dripping all over the marble floor there, then I dripping all over the carpet. She

217

all smiles, gel there – lots of teeth, and a bow she wearing. Then I says to her what I'm about, and she more or less tell me to fuck off down the stairs where they keeping the bins. Door I goes through – it don't look no more like it done in the reception. All concrete steps it is, chunks coming out the plaster. Down and down I going, and still the steps they keeps on and on. I pulling off my beret and I trying to flatten down my hair and it just drenched and it gone all frizzy, look. Then there a lot of clatter and a right lovely smell of bacon and that, and I starving. I says to some bloke what's having a fag, I says to him where this Mr Mumtaz then? And he say to me Mr who? And I go Mumtaz, Mr Mumtaz – here to see him about a job. And he drag on his fag and he go Mumtaz . . .? Nah – never heard of him: why don't you go and ask Brenda? And I says to him because I don't know who bleeding Brenda is, do I? Ain't never been here before. And then some fat old slapper, she come up to me and she don't smile nor nothing and she say to me Mr Mumtaz, is it? And I go yeh, and then I follows her where she going – yeh and all the time I thinking blimey, what I got myself into here, then? Ay? Right old bloody do, this is.

He in a cubby hole, couldn't never call it no office. The old dyke what brung me there, she say my name what I give her, then she fuck off and he just sit there, this Mumtaz. He just sit there looking at his computer like I not even about. Hello . . .? Hello . . .? Mr Mumtaz . . .? Anyone at home . . .? He stick a finger up in the air, and he go on looking at his bleeding computer. Might be all my doings from the Job Wossname – could be porn, what do I know? Still he just staring at it. So I'm thinking fine, okay then, all right . . . so either I just goes on standing here till I like dies of old age, or else I picks up this computer, right, and smash it down on the top of this Mr

218

Mumtaz's fucking head. Know what I saying? Yeh and then he turn and he look at me: telling you – don't know how close he come.

'Done job like this before, yes?'

All sort of sing-song, it is – like all of them Pakis. Stupid moustache he got.

'Nah.'

'Maria – she tell you all you need know, you see.'

'Yeh?'

Nodding away he is now, look at him: like a bleeding puppet.

'I take you see her.'

'All right.'

'Honest, mind. I want you be honest, isn't it? You honest lady?'

'Yeh – course I am. Bleeding cheek . . .'

'Okay well then. I take you see Maria.'

'Brilliant.'

And Maria, she turn out to be really nice. Originally, she were telling me, she come from somewhere, don't know, can't remember. Small, she is – real tiny, and ever so sweet. Sorting me out a uniform. Blimey: like joining the bloody army. Lovely big eyes she got – dark eyelashes, and it don't even look like she wearing any slap: some people, they lucky like that. Good tits and all – yeh, quite a looker, our little Maria. Never thought I be undressing, or nothing – never give it no mind. Bit embarrassed, I'm honest – not on account of my body I don't mean, nah, feel all right about my body, I think. Just wouldn't of had on a apricot bra when my pants is crimson. Dress is all stiff and a bit scratchy, thin pink stripe it got, and Maria, she faffing about with this little white collar what clip on round the back. Then we got a pinny, and these bloody awful shoes, I telling you

219

– look like a bloke's. Black and a dead round toe and they feels all springy when you walks in them, and Maria says it what you wanting, knocking about all day. She says tights, they got to be beige but mine is black and she say it okay for today, but next time they got to be beige. There this elastic belt and you got a key chain on that – and the keys, telling you, weigh a bleeding ton. I says here Maria, I thought it were all plastic and techno and that these days, and Maria go yeh a lot of it is, but these is for store cupboards and fire escapes and that.

She stick my hair back in a scrunchy, and she say to me it nice – nice hair you got Dolly, is what she say to me. Ever so sweet. Yeh and I looks at myself in the mirror there and I thinks oh blimey, oh bleeding hell, I wouldn't of recognised me: look like in them telly shows about all nurses in the nineteen fucking fifties. And then I thinks, bugger – what Amy think, she see me now? Yeh – and what she go round saying to everybody? Have a field day, she would: just hear her voice. And it then I get all of these doubts going about in my head: who the fuck I think I kidding? Ay? I mean to say: here's me, after a few quid, out to better myself, want to have a bit of style, once in my life . . . and I all dickied up like a bloody Victorian skivvy. Yeh well: what you going to do? Then Maria, she take me up in a manky old lift with a mop and bucket in the corner what pong of disin-fectant and then we down this really long corridor and the carpet, it proper thick, and Maria and me in these bouncy bloke's shoes we got, we ain't making no noise at all: like we a couple of ghosts, all like sort of floating. She open up a room what's been made up already like, and she say to me okay then Dolly: this is how it all got to be, yeh?

'Hokay – so, bedroom first. See counterpane?'

'See what . . .?'

'This is counterpane. On top of bed, yes?'

'Oh yeh right. Counterpane – that what they call it?'

'Is counterpane, yes. Hokay. So – straight on edges, see? Touch floor. Smooth tight, yes? In evening, knock on door for turn-down. Fold back, see? Like this. In triangle. See? Then two chocolate. One each pillow. Want one? Jes? Mint. Very tasty.'

'No, ta. Ain't had no breakfast . . .'

'No breakfast? We get you. After. If clothes on bed or chair or floor, you pick up and fold. Dust everywhere. Do curtain and tieback. Is tassel here, see? Sure no mark on mirror. Then big hoover. In minibar – see here in cupboard? Check on list – list in pocket with keys – and see what taken. Chew tick off and replace. Yes?'

'Ever have a quick one, do you?'

'Oh jes. But not from minibar. Other way to do that. Tell you later. Now bathroom, jes? See how look now? Is how has to be. Bathroom big job. Often big mess in bathroom. So: toilet – clean spotless, must be. Anything inside, chew take out.'

'Do what . . .?'

'Not crap, I mean. Crap is flush. Tampon, condom . . .'

'Oh lovely . . .'

'Not lovely – just to be done. Clean bath, really shiny – taps and shower, jes? New towels. Then new soaps or any bottle they use. And shower cap. Even if yust open, you replace. Hokay? Then toilet roll – chew fold like this, see? Triangle. Like bed.'

'Joking . . .'

'No yoking. Just like this. See? You want try?'

'What the fuck's that for . . .?'

'Is stupid, I know. Just got be done. Hokay?'

'I suppose . . . if they want to wipe their arses on a triangle . . .'

'Hokay. Now I take chew to room where people gone out, jes? And you make up. Hokay? Then I come check and see. Hokay?'

'Oh Gawd . . . I dunno about all of this . . .'

'Not worry so much, Dolly. Me too – big worry at first. But easy. Soon chew do it no time.'

'Yeh. Yeh I know. Not really what I were meaning, Maria . . . but yeh, okay. Give it a go, will we?'

So we goes right up the top floor then – and it's a bigger room, this one, bigger thing altogether. Got a settee in it for starters, what the other one never had, and the telly, that just massive – bed and all. Damien, he be happy spending the rest of his bleeding life in here, no trouble at all. Telly, sleep, necking down the minibar, noshing all the minty bloody chocolates and wiping his bum on a triangle. Maria, she fuck off now, and I alone with it all. Hell of a bleeding mess. People live like this at home, you reckon? Or they just do all of it on account of they knows some poor old bloody loser like myself is going to come in and clear it all up for them? Bastards. Real high up here . . . but there nothing to see out the window. Glass all grey, and it still pissing down. You way up here, people say you got a great view, but it rubbish that, because you ain't. Not a great view, is it? Look at it. Just the same old shit from higher up, that's all it is: instead of looking at shit, you looking down on it. That's all it is.

So . . . what we got here . . .? Don't know how long Maria she going to give me to get all of this done, she never said – so I better make a start on it, yeh? Men and women's stuff all about. Couple. Lucky sods. Stay in a swish hotel, have theirselves a bloody good dinner, nice bottle of wine, then they maybe think they want to fuck each other's brains out in this here bleeding bed what I just about to see to – and before you go off swanning

222

about London all day, why don't you just leave all of your doings anyhow and all over the bleeding floor, yeh? Because there's muggins here to sort it out for you. Nice. And I ain't even copped a sight of the bathroom yet. Telling you: I'm in the wrong game. Yeh – and it not even a game. That's the bloody trouble.

Yeh and blimey – just take a look at this dress then, will you? Georgina Von Etzdorf, classic wrapover style, silk jersey it is, blue and this real bright yellow, lovely to the touch. I seen all the knock-offs, but I never seen the real thing. Lovely, it is. And all screwed up and chucked over in the corner. You believe it? Stockings . . . what's laddered . . . black, and real sheer, like. Something on the side, then, this has got to be. Obvious. Wives, they don't never wear stockings. Know I don't. Amy, she maybe do. And that Porsche, oh yeh: all Agent Provocateur, shouldn't wonder, lucky cow. And the bloke too, look – ever such a smart shirt and tie. I like a man in a tie. Don't reckon Damien even got a tie – can't remember the last time I seen him in one. Jermyn Street, these is – what I heard of, course I have. Yeh and I got to look in the wardrobe, have a rummage in the drawers, course I do. Yeh well I wish I never, now: blimey, she got ever such lovely stuff, this bitch, whoever she is. Burberry, Pringle, Donna Karan . . . a bit of M&S too, mind – cashmere V-neck. How long she staying, then? Enough clothes for a bloody month, here. Oh and look at this . . . only a bleeding Prada bag, that's all . . .! Midnight blue and sort of lizard, or something. Feel fantastic. Fuck me – got to be looking at not much off of two grand on that alone. Make my fake Fendi look like a turd. Oh Christ, it ain't fair . . . just ain't fair. Drive me bloody mental, all of this . . .

Yeh and here something funny: I were hoping . . . yeh, and I were dreading it and all, that the bed, it smell of sex . . . can't explain it . . . but nah, it never. Smell of perfume, real nice. Don't know what it is – not cheap, though. So I strips off all of the sheets and the duvet, and Maria, she left me the new gear, didn't she? So I get stuck into that – and blimey, that mattress, telling you, I never knowed anything like it: near done my back in just tucking in the bleeding sheet: weight of a bloody elephant. And then – don't laugh – the fucking what is it . . .? Counter something – counterpane, yeh that's it. Tight, straight, whatever she said. On the dressing table, there's these earrings . . . look like pearl, don't know if they real. Trusting sort of type, is she? This woman? What with this and the Prada bag, all just left hanging about? Or plain bloody stupid? Maybe they been left there on purpose, yeh? By Maria and that bleeding Mumtaz – see if I goes and nicks them. Yeh well: not my style. Too mumsy for me, these earrings is. Wouldn't mind the bloody bag, though, kill for that, I would. Right . . . so . . . I done the curtains and all of them tassel things, which was bleeding fiddly . . . and I pick up the clothes, pile up the mags on the table, plump up all the cushions – about a hundred bloody cushions – which Maria never said for me to do, but I done it anyway . . . now what else? Oh yeh – dust about. Hoover. Don't look like it need no hoover, but I hoovers it anyway – in case they outside maybe, Maria and that bleeding Mumtaz, waiting for the noise of it. Mirror all right, so sod the mirror. Bathroom now. See what we got in there.

Lovely bathroom it is . . . wish I had one like it. Pretty poky, ours is. Up in the rafters, so you not careful you banging your head on the bloody ceiling. This all shiny grey marble with white and black in it – all the walls as well as the floor. Wet towels all about. And in the bath, there still all these little like bubbles what's making a popping noise and they smelling the same as what the bed was. Coco Mademoiselle is what it is – she got it all lined up, look. Whole range of it. Chanel lipstick and nail varnish and all – dark red, and what they calling nude, what I know because I seen it in Debenhams. YSL Touche Éclat . . . Floris soap . . . and the gear what the hotel's laying on, that Molton Brown, so we not talking rubbish – but nah, she ain't even so much as gone near none of that: got her own, ain't she? Whole range. And that's the way to do it, ain't it really? Ay? Style, that is. That's real style. What I want. That's what I want. And it ain't just that, but it's everything . . . everything here, you can just tell – you just know it: they got 'it'. Bloke's washbag – all soft leather, it is: Dunhill. Even the toothbrush, look – it black and electronic, ever so smart. Not too much of a mess they made, though . . . there's hairs in the sink there, but I'm used to that from Damien. I don't never say nothing, but I reckon he be bald before he forty. And down the bog, thank Gawd, there ain't nothing what oughtn't to be there. So I actually does it all in no time, just like what Maria says to me. And when it all lovely like this – all of that chrome and marble and mirror and that – it just look brilliant when you done it. I could spend a week cleaning in the bathroom back at home, and when I finished with it, all it is is poky, and the grouting coming out the tiles, and you not careful you banging your head on the bloody ceiling.

And then Maria come in – just like she been watching me or something, and somehow she knowed that right at that minute I just got it all done. Maybe she were – secret camera they got rigged up, could be: just as well I never nicked the Prada bag. Nah – kidding: I never would of done that. Only get caught, anyway. And it stupid of me, yeh I know it is, but still – when she look about her, Maria, once she had a real good nose about the place and she say to me very good, Dolly, chew done it really nice – I felt all good inside and right proper proud of myself, you know? Really pleased I done it right. Only thing she have to say is I got the body lotion next to the shower gel when it wants to be next to the shampoo. I know – anal, or what? Like anyone'd give a shit – and they ain't going to be using none of it anyway. Then she say she going to take me down the staff kitchen and give me a bit of grub (and thank Gawd for that – bloody starving, telling you) and then I got to do nine more rooms . . .! Nine of the bleeders! Bloody hell. Yeh, and then she say to me oh no Dolly, that nothing – she going easy on me, she says, on account of it only my first day – hokay? Next shift, which are down for tomorrow, I be doing hell of a lot more – and she laughing, Maria, when she say it to me, so you got to love her really, aintcha? Telling you though: not used to all of this, I am not joking – reckon it going to kill me, on top of all what I got to do at home. And just as we come out the door, we walks right into this geezer what's sticking his plastic card in the lock – and he don't look at all like how I picture him, bloke what's got the room. I thought he be like Brad or Matt or Leonardo or something, but he really quite old – sixty, I reckon, could be even more, but ever so handsome with it. Lovely smile he give me, real nice smart suit and tie on him, and his hair all grey and shiny. Look loaded. Which he is, course – just got to look at all of the gear. He got 'it', all right. 'It' . . . ? He got it wrote all over him.

Yeh and I back at home now, and it look a right old tip. Damien, he ain't lifted a finger, as per bloody usual. Half a bowl of Cheerios stuck in the sink there, look – mugs all over, old T-shirt on the floor. Yeh well I done my chambermaiding for the day, thank you very much Damien – you can bloody well clear

226

it all up yourself, else you can leave it there to rot, all I care. I sure as hell ain't doing it though – that I do know. My back – Jesus effing Christ. Can't hardly stand – it's them bleeding mattresses, telling you: weigh a bloody ton, I ain't kidding. Have a good long bath, I reckon – bit of Radox, that'll set me up: was going to nick some shower gel, but I forget all about it in the end. Yeh – a bath in my scuzzy old bathroom, that's what I'll do – and I'll be careful not to go banging my head on the bloody ceiling. Fifty-four quid I earn today. Fifty-four quid. Not even enough for a couple YSL Touche Éclats. And then end of the week, the tax is coming off of that. Slave your bloody guts out for a couple pennies, and then the fucking government come along and nick the half of it off of you. Not right, is it? Can't be right, that. It don't bother them two in that first room what I done. Probably drinking champagne now, could be. Having a laugh. Maybe fucking each other's brains out in the bed what I done. Another world. Ain't got a clue what it really like outside. What it all about. Yeh and that's where I want to be. In that other world. Fed up with just looking at it, I am. Want to be there. Won't never do it – I ain't stupid. I do know I won't never get there, but still I ain't never going to stop trying. Because it's what I want – so I got to try, don't I? Got to. Because I really want . . . it. And style, and all. Yeh: style: I want style more than anything else in the whole bleeding world.

CHAPTER SIX

ANY DARK DESIGN MUST BE
DELIBERATELY QUELLED

And now Amy and I – it grieves me to say, or even realise it – we surely would appear to be conducting another, yet one more, yes indeed, yes indeed, of what I am sure she would perfectly happily term our 'conversations'. Not though, are they? Never are. Conversations? I hardly think so. She talks, I nod. Sometimes even go so far as to listen to the odd little smidgen, not often: only if ever she employs an intriguing terminology, or else starts shrieking. But today . . . today – what with all that I'm feeling and have been through . . . all that, yes, and even an unfamiliar and therefore rather deeply shaming tug of conscience on the top of it all – today I really do think that things just must be different. Oh look – I'm in turmoil, no two ways about it. Because I went there, didn't I? To see her – Portia, my Portia . . . yes and something just so terribly extraordinary happened, unbelievable, still I'm just reeling from it, completely knocked to pieces . . . and although, very obviously, that of course is not at all what I'm now wanting to talk about, still it is so terribly brutally within, and clambering just all over me.

Yes and at first and for a good long time after that I didn't think that I was even going to be able to – see her, I mean: get to her, Portia. All sorts of obstructive men and women. Like turning up at, I don't know . . . Buckingham Palace, or something, and demanding to see the Queen. Jesus, though – these film people: who the hell do they actually think they are? Not so much delusions of grandeur we are coping with here – more a collective and seemingly unshakeable belief in their personal and inalienable divinity. Anyway, eventually – and after a whole load of . . . I . . . oh look: can't go into it. Can't – not now. I'm in turmoil, I tell you – turmoil. So first, what I have to do now, before I stir up all the muck of that, I've just got to talk to Amy about something else entirely. Because despite my anguish, still it has been preying on my mind: all that Sylvia said to me about Lizzie. Didn't even know I'd been listening to her, not at the time, but I must have been, I suppose. On some level of consciousness – and maybe even that of a father. So before she just goes thundering on, Amy, like a bloody runaway express train, mashing and obliterating anything on the track, I just have to get things said.

We're sitting in the dining room – can't actually think why we are, because it's not as if we're actually dining, or anything. I like to touch the beautiful Saarinen table from time to time, feel its silkiness beneath my fingertips: I like to be in contact with beauty – things that I know will never let me down. Amy has a cup of coffee. I have a Glenmorangie, touch of water (Christ – way I'm feeling, I could neck the whole bloody bottle in one, and Jesus alone knows how much in God's name I have put away already today; amazing I'm even capable of thinking straight, or even at all, let's face it). But Amy, she's got coffee – yes, and just a minute ago, after she had been stirring into it a slug of cream, she had rather carelessly replaced the spoon in

229

the saucer – yes and in so slapdash a manner that it clattered on to the table. She replaced it, oh yes, but still there is a beige and sticky stain there. She maybe hasn't noticed it. She maybe did the whole thing deliberately. I don't know – I can't know, can I? – whether she's noticed it or whether she hasn't, but I have, I have, oh yes I have all right – and I can't take my bloody eyes off the thing now, that mark, that stain. I know it will come off – I'm not upset because something perfect has been scarred for ever . . . but still, that little blotch in all its defiance, it's actually ruining for me being in touch with the table at all.

'The thing is, Amy – before you utter another word – I really do think we have to talk about the *girl*, for once. Not the boy – the *girl*.'

'Yes well I quite agree. And it was "girl", but it's not just "girl" now, is it? Yesterday it was, but this morning, when you were out . . . well. Couldn't believe it. How on earth did they . . .? That's what I can't understand. I've always been so careful. Well yes anyway: that's why things have got to change. It's gone beyond now: we've got to do something.'

Thrown, of course. Completely knocked off balance. Because she can do this, Amy. You think, like a fool, that you know where you're going with a thing – imagine like a pie-eyed and deluded little fuckwit that you have finally got a grip. You demand your say, you momentarily even believe yourself to be in control, command, of the high ground – and then *bang!* She sideswipes you – just like this, just like she has done now. Never see it coming – and nor can you fathom even the bloody nature of what she is actually on about this time. So you've got to ask, haven't you? If you can't face the thought of just standing there, blinking into a void, you have to wade around, gummed into her brand-new mire: tentatively seek some sort of clarification. Yes – and then

Amy, suddenly once more she is in the ascendancy, God curse it. Yeah – as if she ever left it: she never somehow does.

'Girl . . .? What on earth are you on about?'

'Well the same thing that you were, I imagined. For once, I thought, you had perceived a given situation and were prepared to actually be active about it. But no, apparently. I ought to have known better, really . . .'

'But . . . but . . .'

'Yes I see, Terence. Very well put, on the whole. Succinct. Right then – I'll just have to fill you in then, shall I? Bring you up to speed on this. This thing that should be perfectly plain to you. I mean – you do *live* here, don't you? You do have *eyes* . . .? What on earth's *wrong* with you, at all?'

See how she does it? Piles it on, buries you up to the neck in it. Insult, scorn – the flagrant parade before absent witnesses of my very apparent incomprehension and palpable stupidity. Yes, but still she gives no hint, you see? Still there is nothing I can strike out for, leap on to – nothing to clutch at: just a shred of *anything* . . .

So I sighed. I heard the sigh, and it surprised me: sounded like it was coming directly from the heart.

'I thought . . . I thought we were talking about Lizzie . . .'

She looked at me, Amy: openly amazed.

'*Lizzie* . . .? What on earth has *Lizzie* got to do with any of this?'

'Well rather a lot, I'd say. We've maybe lost sight of that.'

'Why? What has she been saying to you?'

'To me? Nothing. She never says anything to me. We used to talk, Lizzie and me. Pals, once. Don't seem to be, though – not any more. I just thought, I don't know . . . well I thought she might have said something to *you* . . .'

231

'What about? Is there something wrong with her? She looks fine – she seems okay.'

'Well I don't know . . .! How should I know? That's why I'm asking *you*. Supposed to be her mother . . .'

Yes well – I don't really require to be told, thank you, that this was a bad move, very. Just look at her: cheeks have coloured, and she's glaring at me hard. The hardness of Amy's glare, it can wither a dazzle of flowers . . . cause masonry to tumble.

'How *dare* you . . .! *Supposed* to be . . .? I'm *supposed* to be her mother . . .? I *am* her mother. I'm mother to you *all* – that's the whole bloody trouble Terence, you idle and absolutely useless . . .! Oh God honestly . . . I just can't . . .!'

'Look . . . I didn't mean . . . it's just that Sylvia, she was saying . . .'

'*Sylvia* . . .? Sylvia next door, you mean?'

'Well of course Sylvia next door. How many Sylvias do we know?'

'Well what has *she* got to do with it? To do with anything! Nosy bloody bitch. What's she been saying? Be all down the street. Jealous – that's all Sylvia is. Always has been.'

'She didn't actually say anything. Just that she thought Lizzie might be, I don't know . . . unhappy . . .'

'What's she got to be unhappy about? She gets everything, Lizzie. God, it was only last weekend I gave her the money for that awful thing she's been plaguing me about for just ever. What was it . . .? Some sort of red leather, I don't know . . . jacket affair – totally unsuitable, but there you are: that's Lizzie. So I can't imagine what she's got to be unhappy about.'

'Well I don't know. I don't know. Maybe she isn't unhappy. Maybe she's very happy indeed. I don't know. I just don't know . . .'

'Well – I'm absolutely sure that she's completely fine. Just Sylvia trying to make trouble. Eaten alive – that's the trouble with Sylvia: dead inside. Anyway – I'll speak to her, Lizzie. See if there's anything. Not today, I can't. Absolutely up to my eyes with all of this other thing, now. And anyway – she just shuts herself away in her room – never get a chance to talk even if I want to. And I can't remember the last time we all sat round a table and ate as a family. Not my fault – got a freezer full of food. But listen, Terence – I have to go out very soon to put all sorts of things into motion, so may we please get back to the important issue?'

'Lizzie *is* important . . .'

'Don't please try to score points, Terence. You're absolutely no good at it at all. And I simply can't be bothered to say to you "yes I *know* that Lizzie is important", so may we please now just address the problem?'

'The problem being . . .?'

'Alexander's safety. Actually.'

'Alexander's in danger . . .?'

'Daily. And increasingly so. I've been talking to various people about it.'

'Uh-huh. You haven't, however, been talking to me about it, have you Amy?'

'No well I'm talking to you now. Aren't I? Or trying to, anyway. It's girls, Terence. Fans. One yesterday. Three this morning. They somehow have found out where we live. Can you believe it? Before it was just letters to this whatever they call it that I had set up, oh – just ages ago: PO box sort of thing. Letters I can cope with. But this, now . . . this is different altogether. And with all the social networking, this is going to get a whole lot worse, and extremely quickly. What am I saying?

233

It's instant. By the morning, the whole front garden could be full of the little beasts. They could be out there now, for all I know. And it –'

'Oh Amy – I really can't see that a couple of young girls . . .'

'May I finish? May I, Terence? What I was attempting to say was that this, this very much brings to a head all the factors that I have been considering now for simply ages. And it's not just a *couple* of girls, is it? Have you not understood what I have just told you? This will go like wildfire . . .'

'Which are . . .?'

'I beg your pardon . . .?'

'The factors. The factors you have been considering for simply ages. They are . . .?'

'Well first and foremost, Alexander must, just must now attend a private school.'

'A private school. You mean a public school.'

'Well of course I mean a public school – what do you suppose I mean? I have my eye on Highgate. It's close, but it's just enough out of the way. And he must be escorted there.'

'You mean you want me to drop him off. Well I always used to do that. Highgate, though . . . bloody expensive, I should think . . .'

'No I don't mean that – you dropping him off. That is simply not good enough. Alexander, he needs a bodyguard. I've known it for quite some time. Not just to get him to school, of course – but at all the shoots, personal appearances, all of those things: be invaluable. And yes of course it's expensive – what do you think? One of the oldest schools in England, isn't it Terence? So it's hardly going to be cheap. They do have the most wonderful grounds – the headmaster, he was showing me around. Nice man. Seemed to understand the situation. Not the first time he's encountered it, I imagine – a pupil in the public eye. But the money, that's all taken care of. I was speaking to the solicitors, and it's perfectly fine for a proportion of Alexander's earnings to be put towards his education. Terence . . . why are you just *staring* like that . . .? Nothing to say . . .? Oh – I despair. Truly – I despair of you. Looking even more gormless than usual . . .'

Well I did have something to say, yes I did. And so I bloody well said it:

'A . . . *bodyguard* . . .?! A . . .?! Oh now look: you – even you, Amy – you simply can't be serious . . .!'

'Rhetoric as well . . . ah well. Oh of *course* I'm serious, Terence – when have I not been? And until we've got the school all sorted out, he'll have to have a tutor. At home. Full time. I just can't have him roaming the streets. God, Terence – you just have to understand: when all's said and done, Alexander, he's only ten years old . . .!'

'I know he is. I never forget that. That's why this, all of this, it's just so . . . sometimes, though, it feels as if he's older than I am . . .'

'There are occasions, Terence, when I think that everybody on this planet is older than you are. Most men, well – they just never grow up, of course they don't – but particularly you, Christ knows.'

Didn't argue with that one: think she's right. I like to think of myself as a fairly sophisticated sort of a fellow, all round – but sometimes I think I could maybe be retarded. I mean . . . just look at the pathetic way – pathetic, oh yes, pathetic: believe me, it's the only word for it – the absolutely pathetic manner in which I was conducting myself in Pasadena Pictures, when I went to see Portia, my Portia . . . and then, Christ, all of that other thing happening afterwards. Jesus, I'm telling you . . . it was . . . oh but no: still not the time to be digging up all of that, thank Christ – because Amy, look: she's not yet finished:

'And there's another thing, Terence. Something rather more fundamental.'

'What would that be, Amy . . .? You've been talking to people about having me publicly executed . . .? Lesser sentence? Pelted in the stocks as the village idiot? Oh but Christ though, Amy – a *bodyguard* . . .! I just can't believe you're . . .'

'I'll go on, will I Terence? I'll just keep talking, saying what I have to say, and just assume, yes, that some of it is penetrating? I shall? Yes? Very well, then. So that other thing, you see, is the house.'

'The house. This house?'

'This house, yes. Not the House of Commons, not the White House in Washington, no no no – this house, yes Terence, the very one in which we are sitting. It's on the market.'

I regarded the stain on the table: no longer seemed to be sticky, now. It had hardened.

'Ah. So this would be the house that I pay all the expenses on, then – that the one you mean, Amy? My house, in fact. Which now you are telling me is going to be . . .?'

'What do you mean *your* house? By what extraordinary and tortuous thought process have you arrived at the conclusion that this is *your* house, Terence? It's *our* house, isn't it? *Our* house. Joint names. Remember?'

'Joint names, yes. One mug who pays for everything, though. Me.'

'Oh God please don't now add meanness to the tally of your perfectly horrible defects. You were never mean, Terence. This is unworthy of you.'

'I'm not being—! Look: if it is "our" house, then why haven't

236

"we" discussed its possible sale? I like this house. Why should we sell it?'

'I just don't frankly believe you, Terence. Have you actually taken in a single word I have said? It is *known*. Do you understand? The security aspect – it's simply untenable.'

'The *security* aspect . . .? It's not bloody Heathrow airport! We're not talking about ten bloody Downing Street . . .!'

'Don't be hysterical. And because it obviously won't sell immediately, Alexander and I will be renting somewhere in the meantime. I have it all arranged. While we're looking for somewhere new. Something . . . suitable. You can stay here until it's sold, of course. Once word gets about that Alexander isn't here any more, I shouldn't think you'll be bothered. And you can show people round, and so on.'

'Jesus . . . Christ . . . Almighty . . .'

'Oh God – is that the time? I have to go. I should have been out of here half an hour ago. Got to go. Got to go. Have to pick up Alexander from kendo.'

'Kendo? I thought it was origami he did . . . or maybe ikebana . . .?'

'. . . be so stupid, Terence. It's kendo, as well you know. He's becoming impossibly good. And tae kwon do. Really good at that as well. Got to go – so late . . .'

'Jesus . . . he's supposed to model *clothes*. Sounds more like we're training him to be a bloody Ninja assassin. And what about Lizzie? You haven't said a single word about Lizzie. What about Lizzie?'

'What about her?'

'Christ, Amy – that's what you keep on saying. That's all you ever say.'

'Well she can stay here with you, I suppose. Haven't really

thought about it. She won't want to come with Alexander and me, I'm perfectly sure of that. Never a word for either of us . . . never seems to open her mouth.'

'Well that's what I mean – that's exactly what I was meaning in the first place, isn't it? Maybe there is something wrong . . .'

'Well I said I'd talk to her. Didn't I?'

'Yes but will you?'

'I said so. I said I would.'

'Well when, then?'

'Oh honestly, Terence – now you're sounding like a *policeman*. Look: I'm late. I'm really late. I have to go. Why did you go into my office?'

Didn't see that one coming: wasn't meant to, of course.

'What . . .?'

'You heard me, Terence. My office. Why were you in my office?'

'Your office . . .? Don't know what you're talking about.'

'So you deny it.'

'Certainly I deny it. What would I want to go into your office for?'

'Exactly what I am trying to determine.'

'Haven't been near your bloody office. Anyway – it's locked, isn't it? You always keep it locked, for some unfathomable reason. What have you got in there, Amy? Crown jewels?'

'I know I keep it locked. That's why I want to know why you were in there, and just how you managed to gain access.'

'Managed to gain *access* . . .? Oh Jesus, Amy – who's sounding like a policeman now? I didn't gain *access*. Wasn't there. Have no interest whatever in your poxy little office. Why would I?'

'You're lying.'

'Not lying. Why would I lie? You're paranoid.'

'Not paranoid. You're lying.'

'Oh Christ's sake, Amy . . .'

'You're lying. Anyway – it'll keep. I'm late.'

'So you keep saying. Go, if you're late. If you're late, just go, why don't you?'

'Take out the cups and things, will you?'

'No.'

No. Sad and puny gesture, I suppose – but I never forget that it is the little acts of selfishness just such as this that help keep a marriage stale. She doesn't know I was in her office. She's guessing. I just must have knocked something awry, that's all. If she knew, if she absolutely knew for certain that I'd been in there, she wouldn't simply have accused me of it, she would have hit me with a chair. Mm. And probably one of which I am inordinately fond. And then she did. Go. Went – gone in a flash. I stood up and licked a Kleenex I had in my pocket and wiped over the stain on the table. It dragged on the tissue, though. It's going to need a cloth, yes – and maybe just a touch of Fairy Liquid. Think I'll do that now, then – and I will take out Amy's cup and saucer, the little cream jug, of course I will. They don't look nice on the table. Get myself another drink while I'm about it . . . and all of this wilful and brazen displacement activity will serve very well to do everything that displacement activity is famed for . . . it will put off for just a few moments longer my having to plough through . . . to try to make some sort of sense of . . . all the . . . oh, just everything, every bloody bit of what I have been forced to undergo this day. Christ, I'm telling you – feel like I've been put through a mangle. Can't even think straight. And she was right, Amy – I didn't really tune in to a lot of all that she was saying. Zoned in and out, you know. Tried to focus, but didn't honestly do terribly well. Well look: after all

239

I've been through, not to say the booze, I'm amazed I'm even vertical.

It all had started with the very purest of motives: it was to be fine – a coming together, you see . . . one that I had considered to be simply pre-ordained, and really so very sweetly inevitable. Yes well. Not quite how it went, I think it's fair to say. Got there – that was no trouble: took a taxi. As soon as I'd shrugged away Sylvia, I shot round the corner and leapt right into one, more or less immediately. And Lizzie . . .? Did she still linger, even at the perimeter . . .? No, she did not. Lizzie, alas, had come and gone, and really so terribly fleetingly – Lizzie no longer was within my consciousness, nor, I am ashamed to confess, even identifiably upon the face of this earth. Poor, dear, sweet little Lizzie . . . how has it come to this? And what am I going to . . .? What are we going to do about her . . .? Because without being able to so much as hazard a blindfolded fling in the uncertain direction of what exactly or even approximately the poor girl's problem might conceivably be, I do feel sure that she does indeed harbour one, am deep down convinced that something is almost certainly awry – have known it instinctively, I think, even before Sylvia had so tentatively intimated the possibility of any so troubling a thing. All down to maybe just something about the set of Lizzie's shoulders as she walks out of the room – taut, and yet at once they seem slumped into a sort of resig-nation. Yes but what was I, of all people, supposed to do with even such slight awareness – insight, intelligence of that sort? Not equipped, am I? Can only gape at it in abject wonder. But Lizzie herself, though: what can she be thinking? Little Lizzie. About us. Does she actually think of us at all, can I truly sup-pose . . .? Amy and me. As people, I mean. Humans. Because, you know . . . for Lizzie, maybe, there isn't even contempt there

240

any longer – maybe she just strives her damnedest to simply blank us out . . . and Jesus, who could possibly blame her for that? Dear dear dear. Oh dear me.

Yes but look: it's Alexander, isn't it? He's at the root of it – got to be. Hasn't he? Has he? Or possibly not. Maybe it's nothing to do with Alexander at all. The thing is, you see – I don't *know*, do I? Of course I don't. Don't know the first thing. Haven't even the vaguest idea what young girls can be thinking – well how could I? How they see things. And not just Lizzie, I don't mean – but all the others, the hundreds of them, could be thousands, who write those extraordinary letters, do those drawings, enclose those photos . . . these very girls who now apparently are set at any moment to be ten deep and choking our front garden, simply in order to . . . what, exactly? Stand there, I suppose. Collectively thrilled. Young, so very alive, scintillated, and excitedly yearning for even the flickered shadow on an upstairs curtain, the merest suggestion of my ten-year-old son – or, failing that, hugging to themselves the warmth and shocking kick of knowing that at least he is close to them. Lord in heaven above. Why in the devil's name would they want to do such a thing . . .? How could they even be bothered? Well I don't know. Do I? Couldn't begin to understand it. And I can hardly think that I am the only male out there who would be similarly confounded. Not our area, is it? Our specialist field. That's what mothers are for, surely. But Lizzie's mother, well . . . wholly consumed by the boy. To my total exclusion. Because Alexander, he doesn't need me, not remotely, that much has been completely clear for, oh . . . just ages, now. And if ever I found myself in the slightest doubt about that, Amy, she soon set me right, you can depend on that. So it is I who would appear to be the useless parent, then – the one so very demonstrably lacking in

241

any sort of a role at all. But just supposing then that I did . . . what if I did approach Lizzie . . .? Because Amy, she says she will, she says she's going to talk to her, but she won't, she won't, of course she bloody won't. She'll just . . . what will she do . . .? She'll just say to her, 'Everything all right then, yes? Everything at school? Feeling okay, are you?' Much as I might myself, I suppose. And Lizzie, from deep beneath that protective fringe that pricks her very eyes, she will flatten her lips in the way she has taken to lately, while deliberately willing her eyes to deaden . . . and then she will shrug. If pressed – should Amy be troubled to persist with it for a moment, should she seek final confirmation and an end to the bloody matter by way of simple iteration: 'Sure? Sure you're okay?' . . . Lizzie, then – she'll either shake her head in a practised, theatrical, though still no doubt deeply heartfelt manner, before leaving the room . . . or else say something along the lines of 'Shit-I've-said-I'm-okay-so-for-Christ's-sake-just-leave-me-alone-can't-you-why-do-you-keep-going-on-and-on-and-on-about-it-Jesus?' And then leave the room. Conceivably she'll do neither of these things: at the first sign of Amy striking up one of her dread 'conversations', she'll just – simply in order to save time, if nothing else – turn around and leave the room. But whatever happens, if anything does . . . well then certainly Lizzie will end up leaving the room. Because that, recently – and more and more so – is most of what Lizzie does: I've seen her. Yes . . . but then if I do it . . . if I approach Lizzie myself . . . well I have to ask myself honestly: would the consequence be in the least bit different? It wouldn't, would it? No. It wouldn't. No. And so that's that then, really.

And it's now, it's only now that I'm mulling over all of this – uselessly and idly. At the time – when I'd just more or less run away like a madman from the maybe thoughtfulness of Sylvia, and bounded into that gloriously joyous taxi . . . well then on the blood-hot sands of the desert of my mind, Lizzie no longer was anywhere to be glimpsed. The sole mirage that shimmered amid that thick and hovering heat, and so utterly beguilingly in the alluring distance . . . was Portia, my Portia . . . and Portia alone. The taxi fare was twenty-two quid. Had no change on me, of course, no coins at all – my change, any spare coins, I throw all that into an ashtray, Orrefors crystal, cubic, big and handsome brute it is, it's next to my bed, but of course I hadn't been thinking about scooping up any of that, not in the state I was in, could hardly be concentrating upon any nonsenses of that sort, I think – so I just thrust at the cabbie a couple of twenties and Jesus, he was fumbling about there and it was drizzling just a little bit by this time – which has nothing to do with any of this, perfectly naturally, but I'm just simply recalling it, that's all, it's no more than that – and now I was staring hard at the square brass plaque just to the side of the entrance, and amidst its gleam it had 'Pasadena Pictures', black and deeply incised in Albertus typeface, one of my absolute favourites – and the rush now, the sudden sheer and twanging urge within me to just get myself in there, to absolutely reach her now – Portia, my Portia – it was practically beyond all control, and so I said gruffly and tersely to that cabbie that he should keep it, just keep it (and in my voice I hardly could recognise the lacquered depth, nor that gritty set of determination that so coarsely was cemented around it) and he looked up from all of his ferreting about, this now suddenly vexing and accursed cabbie, and he said to me, here – you sure, mate? And me, I said nothing at all – just left him, turned my back on the whole of the other and outside world, and made in gangling bounds for the golden door. And even as I pushed it open, even while still my fingers

243

were smarming all over the thick plate glass of it, I was thinking Jesus Christ, you maniac – what the bloody hell did you go and do that for . . .? Eighteen quid tip . . .? Fuck.

'Hello. I'm here to see Miss, um . . .'

I said that to the girl there – girl behind the desk affair. Sexy thing, in a vacuous sort of a way, as I suppose they all have to be, these receptionist people: in the old days, I already would have been oozing all over her. Looking up at me, smiling quite tentatively . . . but the pause, yes, it's stretched out just that little bit too long now, you see, and still I can't for the life of me remember her surname – isn't that awful? To me she is just Portia, my Portia . . . because angels, they don't need them, do they? Surplus to requirements, surnames.

'Miss, uh . . . Lichtenstein. Brandenburg . . .?'

'I'm sorry . . . we don't, um . . . have anyone of, um . . .'

Her voice was neutral, yet at the same time quite feather-weight and brainless. Still, in the old days, I would have been oozing all over her, knowing that we would never be acquainted for nearly so long that this voice of hers could begin to grate, let alone come close to deranging me.

'Portia. It's Portia. I'm here to see.'

'Ah – Miss Hazelstein, oh yes. You have an appointment?'

'Yes. Hazelstein, that's it. Couldn't for a moment remember her, uh . . . Hazelstein, yes of course.'

'You do have an appointment . . .?'

'Yes. Do, yes.'

'And you are . . .?'

'Terence.'

'It's just that there's nothing down here for, er . . .'

'No well I've just spoken to her. On the phone. Emailed her. I've emailed her, you see. And I've spoken to her on the phone.'

'Right . . . it's just that there's nothing down here for, er . . .'

'No well she's expecting to see me. If you could just tell me where to go, maybe . . .?'

'I'll ring through, okay? Care to take a seat?'

'Okay. Fine. You ring through. Stand, thank you.'

She messed around with her damned machine. Barcelona chairs, they had there. Chocolate brown. Lovely in themselves, of course, but oh . . . such a cliché, really. Designed about ninety years ago, and all these corporate numbskulls – the twelve-year-old little ponces who purport to 'design' such spaces as these, either they are terminally lazy or else they actually do imagine such pieces to be 'modern', or something. In that they are demonstrably not Elizabethan or Louis XV. Ignorant pigs.

'Miss Hazelstein is in a meeting, I'm afraid sir.'

'Yes I daresay. But I'm sure she'll see me. If you could just point the way . . .?'

'I'm very sorry, sir, but she's in a meeting. If you'd like to phone and make an appointment . . .?'

'Yes well I've done that, you see. Already done that. As I told you. I phoned, I emailed. I emailed and I phoned.'

And then a man, stupid-looking sort of a man, he came up to me then. Not quite sure where he had sprung from – maybe a concealed trapdoor. Conceivably one of Portia's personal protection squad.

'Everything all right here, is it?'

'This gentleman . . .'

'No it's not all right, actually. Everything isn't. I'm here to see Portia Hazelstein, and this young person here is being exceedingly obstructive.'

'I phoned through to Miss Hazelstein, Harry. She's in a

245

meeting. I did explain to this gentleman. He hasn't got an appointment.'

'I see. Well sir – if you would care to phone and make an appointment, then I'm sure that –'

'Yes but I've done that, you see. As I was explaining to the child. I've phoned. I've emailed. I've emailed and I've phoned. And now I am here. In person. As you can see. And I insist, I absolutely insist upon seeing Miss Hazelstein without a moment's more delay. I do hope that is clear.'

'I hear what you are saying, sir, but without an appointment . . .'

'Can I just stop you there . . .?'

His face was filled with blurred expectation.

'Oh I've nothing more to add: just wanted to stop you there.'

The man who is apparently Harry – appalling suit, I just can't tell you, and you could see the twin strands of black elastic to either side of his tie knot – he looked at me blankly, then uncertainly, and his eyes blinked once. He went round the desk to the idiot girl's side and tapped a few numbers into the phone there.

'Hallo . . .? Hallo . . .? Yes – so sorry to trouble you. Harry here. Yeah – Harry. There's this gentleman in reception who . . . yes . . . yes . . . yes, I see. Right . . . right . . . it's just that he's . . . yes . . . well yeah, exactly . . .'

And while still cradling the receiver, he was looking at me now. The simple infant, she wasn't, no – she was regarding her long, red and glossy nails at the ends of stiff fingers, rather as if considering whether or not to buy them. But Harry was, he was looking at me – eyeing me, wondering whether or not this very evident loony and all-round nasty piece of work was at that instant intending to detonate his suicide vest which could

246

be jam-packed with sufficient explosive power to take out the whole of Soho, and maybe even right up as far as Oxford Street.

'Uh-huh . . . right . . . yes . . . yes, right then. Okay. Got it. Okay. Fine, then. Yup. If you say so. Okay. Okay. Fine.'

Then he replaced the receiver and glared at me.

'Miss Hazelstein will be down directly. If you'd care to take a seat . . .'

'Good. Thank you both so much. So that was all a great waste of time then, wasn't it? Stand, thank you.'

And how foolish he had been, the loathsome Harry, to have suspected me of wilful suicide (as now, amid my highly possibly profoundly skewed manner of reasoning, I am thoroughly convinced he did) – and this to entail the incidental obliteration of Portia, my Portia. Good God – what can he have been thinking, the ridiculous man? Last thing I need: I want to live again. Don't I? Why I'm here.

And so, time . . . I suppose not very much . . . it passed away in silence. Had there been a clock, I should certainly have heard it ticking. The great wall of Harry had dissolved into vapour as instantly and mystifyingly as his large and initial looming – while the girl could not possibly have been so very pointedly not looking at me than she so very concentratedly was doing already (and you just had to look at her to know it). Her machine would occasionally mutedly warble, when she would raise her eyebrows as if in wonder at its singular impudence, then idly jab at a subversive key, this immediately arresting all such nonsense, putting paid to any of that. I had been standing for a good long while now, and was actively considering whether a Barcelona could indeed be about to receive me – while actively quelling even the whiff of conjecture, and certainly suffocating all anticipation. There was a flurry then – somewhere to the side of me, couldn't place or detect quite where it might be coming from . . . and . . . oh . . .! Oh . . .! Of a terrible sudden, there she was before me: Portia, my Portia . . . Portia, my Portia . . . and I shivered in the shadow of her presence, so hot yet bloodless, and in a weak and quivering near paroxysm I could never have put a name to, and only just barely could contain. A flush oak door was open to the left of her, and with her face set hard, she beckoned – and then with an irritated rush of an arm, urged me quickly to arrive, to get there, to just go through it. So I did that, I did that, yes – stumbled on into the room beyond . . . and before I could speak, before even I could say to her a single word of greeting, let alone unleash such ripe and vast effusions of a passion so gorgeously great, she was talking and talking at me . . . her lips, so divine, were taut, yet they were moving so fast – faster and then faster still until I thought surely by now she must nearly be through with it . . . though still I had yet to hear, absorb, assimilate a word. I moved to close the door behind us, but by means of the merest gesture, she somehow made it perfectly clear to me that she was not for a moment standing for any of that. Her hands were on her hips, legs just slightly apart – and this, just this, I found it more exciting, viscerally thrilling, than I could possibly even begin to explain. Her expression, though – it was hardly encouraging: several notches down from expansively warm and inviting, I think it's fair to say. But I had to speak now, say something – for momentarily, it appeared to be quiet. It suddenly did seem as though a slot had been provided for me: comment, I felt, was somehow now required.

'Portia . . .!'

'Yeh so listen, Terence: you got me, yeah? You got it? All I been saying?'

'Got you . . .? *Get* it . . .?'

Because I didn't, of course. Either thing.

'Look, Terence – listen to me, okay? One last time. This just is not the way we do business. Okay? I'm trying to be nice here, but you're making it real hard, and you just got to see it. Willy, I got to tell you – he's like, oh man – apeshit over all of this, you know?'

'Like apeshit? Really? Willy? Is he? But listen, Portia . . .'

'He's real mad. And Willy, believe me, you don't want to make him mad – you see what I'm saying? First it's Amy, and now it's you – just, like, turning up, you know? How crazy is that? Huh? I told you – didn't I tell you both over dinner? It's looking real good for Alexander, okay – but we can't have this, like . . . *pressure*. You know? When I spoke with you on the phone, Terence, I thought I made it like totally clear that I couldn't see you today? And yet you're here. What can I tell you? We'll let you know real soon what we decide about the part. Okay? And now I got to ask you to leave.'

And I just gaped at her. Didn't know what she was on about, you see. I had just been staring at the loveliness of her face – the twinkling hairs on her forearm where the gold Rolex was just hanging there so terribly elegantly . . . because even in the appalling lighting of this utilitarian and decidedly dingy little antechamber into which I had been so very discourteously siphoned – they were gleaming quite magically. Wincing away from her extraordinary syntax, yes I might well have been – but even so, I was drinking it all down deeply. Still, though – didn't know what she was on about, you see. So better try to say something else, then – and quickly too, because these almost subliminal messages that this divine creation could apparently effortlessly give off by means of the tiniest movement, the merest shift in the air around her, they decidedly did not bear the complexion of ruddy good health, nor even the pinkness of neutrality – no, here was far more the pallor of a wasting malaise. At the frigid core, there was exit written all over it.

'What . . . do you mean . . .? *Amy* . . .? *Alexander* . . .? What on earth have they got to do with any of this . . .?'

And it was she now who was looking . . . well, I wouldn't say flustered, but certainly confused – her composure, the clear upper hand, just momentarily knocked: so whatever it was we had here, quite plainly it could hardly be termed communication.

'Look, Terence – I really need for you to go now. Okay? I'm sorry – I'm real sorry. But what you got to know, Terence, okay, is that if Pasadena do gift Alexander with the part, it'll be on account of he's the top guy. See? Nothing Amy or you say to us is going to mean squat, you want it straight. I don't want to be mean, okay – but so long as you, like . . . *understand*. Yeah?'

And then I sort of saw it. A pale and misty glimmer, just at first . . . but then it did loom large: something was decidedly taking shape. And already it was making me ill.

'The . . . *part* . . .? What – this film, you mean? Alexander in this film? Christ – I'd forgotten all about any of that. Nothing like that was even on my mind. Jesus, Portia – you think I'm here about *Alexander* . . .? Oh . . . *fuck* Alexander – sick to death of hearing about *Alexander*! Couldn't give a bugger in blue bloody blazes about anything to do with that – if he gets the fucking part or he doesn't. Christ – what do I care? He's already got money and all these gorgeous little girls coming out of his sodding ears. Oh no – Christ no, Portia . . .! Forget all of that. This isn't about any of that. I'm here to see . . . *you*! All this . . . all this . . . it's all about . . . *you* . . .! I thought you knew that. You do know that – don't you? I felt sure that you knew that . . .'

And that now, oh goodness – all I had just that moment come out with, that really had apparently amounted to quite some punch: knockout, right between the eyes. But still the eyes, those fabulous great and captivating eyes of hers, they were not shut, black or bloodied by the blow – simply they were made huge . . . huge, yes, and, I am surmising, through an electric combination of shock . . . a whiteout of amazement . . . and maybe even a little bit of greenish and incredulous, even quite piteous scorn. Not, I just have to hope to Jesus, absolute revulsion – but whichever way you try to cut this, here was by no means the consummation devoutly to be wished for. The eyes of a woman – always, but always, it is the eyes of a woman: in there, there is everything you yearn for and shy away from. The body, they can make that do anything they want . . . ah yes but the eyes . . . the eyes . . . they give you the lot, ready or not. And it hurt me now to see this – it hurt me, yes, and very, very deeply: the slicing went straight to the bone. Don't really know if I can drag myself back up from the floor, now. Should I try – do I want? Is it still now within me? – to clamber back up and face a further beating? Or shall I just lie here, sprawled and deadened by the bitter and weighty luxury of unequivocal defeat . . .?

It was Portia who spoke first. Just as well, because I never could have.

'Terence . . . I . . . look: I don't know what to say, okay? This is just so . . . I never, never gave to you the slightest indication . . . I don't know how you could think I . . . oh look: please, I need for you to just go now, okay? We'll say like all of this, it never happened. Yes? Like you were never here. We zip it. Okay . . .? Okay, Terence . . .?'

I nodded. I nodded very slowly. Yes but then I shook my head.

'Can't.'

'Ex . . . *cuse* me . . .?'

'Can't do it. Just go. Not now. Can't. Just can't do it. Zip it . . .? No. Took me so long even to get this far, you see.'

'Terence . . . please. You're making this real difficult for me, you know? I don't want to have to call security . . .'

'Security . . .? There is none. Never is. You learn that. Oh – Harry, you mean? Yes: you don't mean that – you mean Harry.'

'*Please*, Terence . . . this is just so . . .'

'Is it? Yes. I suppose it is. All right then, Portia. I'm sorry if I've been . . . well I *have* been – *have* been, obviously. Yes – and I'm sorry for that. You don't have to call Harry. Poor Harry. Sick of the sight of me, shouldn't wonder. As, apparently, are you . . . Oh well. Right then. Okay. I'll leave.'

And I traipsed back into the hall thing, entrance, foyer, whatever they called the bloody place – and feeling a hundred years old, oh yes, and weighing many tons. And Harry, he was there anyway, old Harry: looking at me the way he does.

'Everything all right is it, Miss Hazelstein . . .?'

'Oh sure – we're good, Harry. Terence is just leaving now. So – goodbye, Terence. Are you needing a, uh . . . I don't know . . . cab or anything?'

'Yes. No. Yeh, but I'll get one. I'm fine. "Good", as you say . . .'

And I would have: smiled weakly, and just once more at her, before trailing away, thrashed and solitary, back into the chill of the street outside. I nodded to Harry, before he could think to lay a finger on me. Even gave a nod to the infant moron behind the desk, there – and she was just goggling at me now: openly, though fearfully too, as if I might easily be not just quite horribly disfigured, but also very highly contagious. So yes, you see . . . I was meek, bowed, resigned to it, and truly all set to – as

252

they used to say – go quietly. But then . . . well then . . . then, I just did what I did. I'm perfectly amazed now even to recall it, cringing away from the memory: I just can't imagine what on earth can have come over me . . .

'Terence for Chrissake what in hell do you think you are *doing* . . .?! Get off of me! Get off of me, will you . . .?! *Jesus* . . .!'

'But *Portia* . . .! Ow . . .! Get off me, Harry! Get your bloody hands off me, you bastard! Ow! Jesus. *Ow* . . .! That's my *arm* . . .!'

'Terence! Get *off* of me – you're a *crazy* person . . .!'

'I won't tell you again, Harry! This is personal business between Portia and me. Ow . . .! Christ. This is your absolutely final warning, Harry. Ow! Oh look just fuck *off*, can't you . . .! Hey . . . wait a minute . . .! Do you smell *gas* . . .?'

That made him hesitate for just long enough for me to squirm away from beneath his tenacious grasp, and biff him briefly in the stomach.

'What in *God's* name is going on here . . .?'

A new voice – something new – and it chopped into the scene like an axe. And just as well – because Christ knew where all this had been heading: blood and prison, I should have said. But my arms now, they simply left off from the welter of argy-bargy, this rough and grappling invasion of all of Portia's person, and just dropped to my sides as if every source of power had been suddenly cut.

'Oh God I am *real* sorry about all of this . . .! This guy, I really do think he might be crazy . . .! Mussed up all of my hair . . . See, Terence! You see what you did? Are you *leaving* – or do we need to call the police . . .?'

But now I am just standing there, oblivious to any of Portia's clamour, my eyes as wide as wide – and staring at this new woman before me. And she too, just take one long and lingering look at her, will you? She is staring right back at me. Tall, taller than I – even taller, in the fuck-you shoes. Slim, rangy, with bright and clear green eyes . . . and now, at the corners of her mouth . . . just the beginnings of the beautiful smile that I so well remember . . . and oh God, how it lights me right up. Oh yes – oh my Lord yes: because here – standing before me, and seemingly glowing, practically radiant . . . is K.T. My K.T. After all this endless time. The love of my life: she is come to save me.

'Hello, Tom . . .'

And then we were sitting in the Bar Italia . . . the Bar Italia, where I'd had neither the heart nor courage to set foot again, not since. Too painful, you see – just too painful. And God, though . . . can I believe that this now can actually be happening to me . . .? Of all the ways this day might have gone, how could I ever in twenty lifetimes have come close to imagining just anything approaching this . . .? And oh yes, back at Pasadena Pictures there had been a good bit more to-ing and fro-ing, but you'd expect that, wouldn't you really? In the singular circum-stances. But K.T, she quickly quelled all of the nonsense: she said to a frankly disbelieving Portia that everything was fine, that all was all right, and that she would handle it, take care of things from here. Although there was the flame of rebellion alive in Portia's eyes, she did not protest, she did not even demur. She simply – and very much not so much as glancing in my direction, even to glare – went across to the lift, jabbed a button, and turned her back to the sliding doors. K.T then quite brusquely instructed the blighted Harry to be about his busi-ness: he more or less scuttled. The imbecile girl behind the desk had ducked right down and now was earnestly engaged in her laughable best to appear to be actively pursuing some or other vital endeavour that might serve to portray her as at least rather higher than detritus. So. All was serene. Well well. My my: K.T . . . she ruled the roost.

'Well Christ, K.T . . . how long has it—?'

'A while. It's been a while.'

'A while, yes. It has been a while. You're looking . . .'

'And you too.'

'Yes but I mean – you're *really* looking . . .'

She laughed. She laughed that laugh. It shattered the ancient dam of my own quite painstaking creation: all of her, now – it flooded out and tumbled all over me: I was thrilled to be drowning in not simply the complete and thorough, oh . . . just sheer splendidness of all of her, but the heat, the heat of us was once more and instantly throbbing, as if already we were entwined . . . and my love, my true love, it was filling me to overflowing. And when I said that she was *really* looking . . . here was no mere glib and chuckaway compliment – oh yes, this just has to be believed: truly, she looked even finer than I remembered – and I did remember, oh God . . . I remembered and remembered her, all the bloody time. The tremendous change was in the hair: no longer that so terribly chic and sexy little Sassoon sort of a bob affair – now it was long, with the tossed and casual suggestion of loosened and just barely high-lighted ringlets . . . even sexier, actually – but then this woman, oh . . . she could still be quite sexually devastating even if bald, and trussed up in rags. Not that it was rags she was wearing: what – K.T . . .? Joking. No no – the jacket, that was Chanel, real thing, no arguments there, spot that a mile off (so they're paying her properly at Pasadena, then – because Chanel, that used to be no more than a long-held aspiration for K.T in the old days) – and a brooch, dull gold cluster, just at the shoulder in the traditional manner, though obviously not all the garlands of pearls, and so on: she was never a literalist. The skirt was a very dark wine colour – good, very good with the deep dusty pink and charcoal fleck of that jacket. Glossy black tights . . . yes, had to be tights – skirt was way too short to allow for stockings and all the attendant splendid paraphernalia, although I recall with both warmth and excitement that she had been no stranger to all of the loveliness of that in the past. She reached across the table just at that moment and touched my hand. I was instantly and totally overcome with a boiling and practically violent lust: I could during these very first moments have torn right into her with a breathless force – though yet with such ease and sweet-ness – and there, right there, on the chequered floor of the Bar Italia.

'So you're now at, um . . .'

'Pasadena, yeh. It's not too bad. Some good things we're doing. Left that other place, oh – seems like ages ago. Bit of a dead end, you know? Remember I said that? Going nowhere.'

'Uh-huh. Well obviously at this place, you're really quite . . .'

'Yeh. I get to do what I want, pretty much. You're looking good, you know. I really go for what you're wearing. Really works.'

'You're the only person on earth who would say so. You're the only one who'd even see it . . .'

'Well . . . we always had that. So is this a good time to ask you why you were molesting Portia in the foyer, Tom . . .?'

'Ah that, yes. The "unfortunate incident". Sorry for that. Something of a, uh . . . what shall we say . . .? Misunderstanding.'

'Misunderstanding . . .?'

'Mm. On my part. Doesn't matter. Too dull, too stupid to go into. Just good that you came when you did. Do you want another coffee . . .? I think I might have another coffee. So anyway, K.T . . . how have you, uh . . . well – what have you been , uh . . .?'

'If you mean did I ever get married, the answer is yes.'

'Ah.'

'But that turned out to be . . . well. Didn't work.'

'Ah. I see. Well . . . I'm sorry to hear that.'

'Really . . .?'

'Oh God no – Jesus! Not *really* . . .!'

And she laughed, the angel.

'You don't change, do you Tom?'

'I don't. I mature. The very last stage, the euphemism we cling to just prior to the onset of rot and decay. But listen – I'm just thinking: you maybe weren't actually all that surprised to see me, yes . . .? I mean – the *circumstance*, yes okay. I can see that you might not quite have been expecting that . . . but presumably you know all about Alexander and this bloody part that he has or he hasn't got in one of your films, and who actually gives a bugger either way . . .? Not that I want to talk about Alexander . . . it's you I want to talk about, K.T. I want to talk about you.'

'Us' is what I was really yearning to say, but I hadn't the nerve.

'I know about Alexander. Who doesn't? Didn't immediately make the connection, though. Lo and behold: can this be an example of what they call a . . .'

'. . . small world?'

'That's what I was going to say.'

'I know. Maybe it's just . . . meant. If you know what I mean.'

257

'I'm going out for a cigarette. I will have another coffee, actually.'

'Oh? This a new thing? You never used to . . .'

'Not that new. Everyone says I'm crazy. But I like it. What about you, Tom? You still . . .?'

'Oh yes. Odd cigar. When I get the chance.'

'Actually, Tom – what do you say we go round the corner and get a drink? Fancy that? You haven't got to run, have you?'

'Drink? Yeh – drink's fine. All the time in the, um . . . where were you thinking of?'

'Oh I don't know – French, maybe?'

'French, Christ. Haven't been there for . . .'

'Me neither. Let's go there then, yes? I can have a fag on the way.'

And during the very short amble along Old Compton Street and then into Dean, I really was feeling so terribly . . . alive. Oh – not just in the sense of being happy for once and feeling like a true human being, a man again . . . but actually being tinglingly aware, almost childishly thrilled by the fizzing and pop of a thousand so sudden and brightly coloured bubbles of thought – daring propositions . . . pleasing whims, antique desires, and wild ideas. K.T, she strode down the street beside me (beside me! Beside me! K.T – she was walking beside me . . .!) like the lithe and capable supermodel that really she always was – the lope of her long and perfectly dazzling legs, that poised and studied clip and then clop of her fuck-you shoes. Singlehandedly she was raising the smoking of a cigarette to the level of an art form – the style and elegance, they were things to behold . . . but it was the sheer bloody sex of it that was getting to me: stirring me up, and troubling me badly. I wished that the journey could have been longer, so that I might at least have decided by the time we got there quite what ripe and gorgeous avenue of possibility I was determined to launch into first . . . but all I found myself doing was hoping we might actually be able to bag one of the very few seats at the back – because the French House, it was busy at all times of the day, packed out with a jostling and mutating, disparate and gregarious mob of people, though seemingly very largely made up of those who didn't have to trouble with work, and others who never even got the chance: it's a good, good feeling in there, and Jesus I could barely remember it . . . was aching now to be there . . . oh yes but if we didn't, you see – if the tables at the back of the place were already taken and we were going to be standing, the two of us, at the horseshoe bar, well then in that case . . .well then she was going to be visibly taller, you see . . . and I never did care for that. For although it must be understood that always I have harboured an abiding and tremendous respect for K.T, and always looked up to her – that was a given, and maybe even mutual (I can but hope – but who ever can say?) . . . still though, it's looking up *at* her that I never could stand.

'Hello, Annabel. All right? Usual for me, my darling. What are you having, Tom?'

She'd got there first and done that. Hadn't been here for ages, she said . . .

'Oh. You know . . . I remember they used to have a really very good Alsace here, in the old days.'

'You want Alsace?'

'Yeh, why not? No – hell with it. Whisky. Malt, if they've got it. Course they've got it. Glenmorangie, maybe.'

Yes and there was no chance at all of a seat at the back – you just had to look: rammed, and I'm pretty sure with the same old battered and piratical faces who had more or less colonised the

259

place two or three years ago, which is the last time I can have been here. They maybe never left.

'Well . . . cheers, K.T. What's that you're drinking . . .?'

'Cheers, Tom. Vodka.'

'On its own?'

'Well . . . ice.'

'Ah. Because you always used to drink . . .'

'Yeh I know. But I don't now. I drink this. Usually, not always. God I wish I could have another cigarette. This bloody smoking thing . . . I know it's been around for years, but I never get used to it – having to go out in the bloody street all the time. And particularly in here. Do you remember, Tom? Blue with smoke. That's my phone. I'm going to turn it off.'

'I do. Stung your eyes. And I was adding to it with a Havana . . .'

'Always loved the smell of those. So I'm just nipping out, okay Tom? Can you get us in another?'

'I'll come with you. Same again then, yes?'

And I quickly knocked back in two the rest of my whisky, because her vodka, that was gone.

'Same, yeh. It's coke I could really do with . . .'

'What – vodka and Coke . . .? Oh right – I see. Another new thing, then . . .'

'I don't often. But it relaxes me, you know? That's the downer of the job. Can be pretty stressful.'

'I don't doubt it. Oh Christ I don't believe it . . .! Look, K.T – some people have just left a table at the back. Shall we take it? Yes? Got to be quick. Tell you what – you go and have your fag, yes, and I'll bag the table, okay? Okay. Here's your drink. See you in a bit. Just grab my change . . .'

More or less had to push out of the way this small old woman wearing a purple fedora, the lapels on her coat weighed down by maybe more than a hundred tin and enamel badges ... it had to be done, you see, in order to secure that table. She didn't seem to mind. I offered her a drink – always a sound policy in this place, I remembered. She didn't seem to hear. The bar girl had picked up on it, though, and put a large glass of red directly in front of her, which the old woman then drank very quickly. She didn't seem to notice. I gave the girl a fiver, thought that should cover it, and I was busy settling in – apologising to the people to either side of me (one of them was laughing, the other nearly snarled) because I'm telling you, it's a hell of a scrum back here, really tightly packed, last place on earth you want for any sort of a tête-à-tête with not just an ex-mistress, but truly the one and only love of your life ... yes but look, what are you going to do? This is where we find ourselves. Little in this life is perfect. You play the cards you are dealt. Oh dear ... all of that so very trite and jittery nonsense. Hear it? It would appear then that I am beginning to get just a little bit nervous, and honestly I can't imagine why. Why should I be nervous, with the only woman on earth who has ever made me easy ...? Oh and look – here she comes now ... I'm waving to her, but I'm not sure if she's ... oh, she's stopped at the bar. Laughing about something with the girl there, who she seems to know quite well ... just got herself in another vodka, looks like ... yeh ... yeh. She's drunk that now. Seen me, yes ... and here she is. Clearly she knows the man who had been laughing – was laughing still – and the other one too, who nearly snarled.

'Get us one more, shall I K.T ...? The girl at the bar – I think she can see us from here. I can just signal to her, maybe ...'

'Be great, Tom. Thanks. Now listen: you've got to tell me just all about yourself, okay? Are you still doing the ...?'

261

'Oh yes. Still doing all of that. Christ knows for how long. To be honest with you, I've let it all go to hell, just lately. And it's stupid of me, I do know that – and dangerous too, because I just can't afford to lose any of those pitifully few contracts I'm still just about clinging on to. Still – there it is. But you don't want to hear about any of that. Too boring. Oh – there she is . . . has she seen us . . .? Yes – she's very good, isn't she? Same again, please . . .! Can she hear . . .? Yes: same again. Thanks so much.'

'She's great, Annabel. We're quite good mates, actually. And still got the, uh . . .?'

'House? Oh yes. Nothing's changed at all, really. Well – Alexander, of course . . .'

'I know. Quite the star. How do you feel about that, Tom?'

'Hm . . .? Oh . . . I don't feel anything about it at all, really. All that, anything about Alexander, that's all to do with . . .'

'You can say her name, Tom. I shan't have the vapours. But only once . . .'

'Yes. Right. Well it's all her thing, really. Always was. Mission. Life's work. And since this bloody film business has come up, well . . . I mean to say, up until a while ago it was all on a fairly even keel, in a nuts sort of a way . . . but since, oh God – "Hollywood" has come calling, well . . . I think she might actually have gone a bit mad, quite frankly.'

'You know she was at the office earlier today?'

'Well – Portia said that, I think. Didn't know what she was talking about.'

'Willy Ouch: he was not pleased.'

'Oh Willy, yes. He's like apeshit, apparently.'

'Oh really?'

'According to Portia. Difficult to know what she's ever actually talking about . . .'

'And talking of Portia . . .'

'Ah – drinks! Very good. Thanks, Annabel. It is Annabel . . .? Right – thanks. Here – take this. And do have one for yourself, won't you?'

'That was nice of you, Tom.'

'Well – Christmas Day, isn't it? Presents all round.'

'And . . . Portia . . .?'

'Yes well . . . clearly not about to let it go, are you? And no – why should you, actually? You hear this godawful commotion, you're the boss, you come to see what in Christ's name is going on . . . um – are you, actually? K.T? The boss? Is that what you are?'

'Well – not exactly. Sort of. I'm about on a par with Willy. We work on different projects – so I've got nothing to do with Alexander, you may or may not be pleased to hear.'

'Am pleased. Well – don't care, actually. I honestly, really and truly just so don't *care* about a single part of it . . . and I can't even see quite why I'm meant to . . .'

'You're a funny bloke, Tom. Anyway. You were saying . . .?'

'Yes – what was I saying . . .? Oh yes: you arrive in the foyer of Pasadena Pictures – terrible name, by the way, not your fault, I suppose – and what should you see but your ex-lover . . . is it all right for me to say that, K.T? I can say that, can I . . .?'

'Why not? True, isn't it?'

'It is. It is true, yes. It's just that I didn't know if . . . well anyway. So: you see me there, and seemingly intent upon the defilement of Portia, a lady in your employ who so very evidently hails, as I am sure you will have observed, from the United States of America . . . while at the same time attempting his small and puny best to fend off the plump-fingered and actually pretty hopeless attack from the thing they call Harry . . .

well yes I can see that you might well be requiring some little stab in the direction of an explanation . . . out of curiosity's sake, if nothing else . . .'

'Annabel, my darling . . . could you just . . .?'

'Oh no, K.T – not for me. Honestly, I'm really okay . . .'

'Sure?'

'Oh yeah.'

'Okay, Annabel – just vodka, then. Thanks. So what is this explanation, then, Tom? Can't wait. All ears. But don't be ages because I've got to nip outside for a ciggie in a minute.'

'K.T . . .'

'Explanation, Tom. Waiting.'

'Yes I know, K.T, but . . . can we not maybe just talk about . . . us . . .? Maybe . . .?'

'Thanks, Annabel. Sure you don't want one, Tom?'

'No. Fine. I'm fine. But look . . . what I mean to say is, well . . . who would ever have imagined it? This – all this. Us. Us – just sitting here together in the French, and having a drink . . .! Just like we . . . I mean – when I woke up this morning, I suppose I had a sort of idea of what I intended to do, hadn't worked out any of the details . . . and yes okay – you want your explanation of what in Christ's name I was up to with Portia, well okay, then, here it is, then: I imagined I was . . . no, I didn't imagine that . . . I *wanted* – dreamt that there was an unspoken mutuality. Between us, yes. That I was in love. With Portia. You see? I wasn't – well of course I wasn't, nowhere close. Good-looking woman, of course, oh yes, easy on the eye all right, but that was more or less it. I know it now, but I didn't then. It was all a ridiculous fantasy – can hardly believe I . . . But I mean . . . let's just take one little instance: every single time she opened her mouth, it drove me absolutely barmy. Noise she made. I

264

pretended to myself . . . I really did make a pretty good job of convincing myself that I actually found it quite . . . charming, or something. But it wasn't. Isn't. Isn't, is it, K.T? Noise she makes. Disgusting. Sounds like one of her nostrils is permanently bunged up – as if she's constantly pressing a finger to the side of it – well like all these bloody Americans, I suppose, but it's worse with the women, of course. Makes them sound like a cartoon. Anyway . . . that's the bones of it. Doesn't make sense, I know. You're the only one I could even begin to tell it to. And yes I know it makes me sound completely crazy – and that's what she called me, Portia. She called me a crazy person, and she could well have been right. But clearly . . . well, it's suddenly become rather horribly clear to me that I'm in a bit of a state. I maybe didn't know how bad I was . . . but now . . . now . . . it's as if, I don't know – a light has gone on, or something. Cliché I know – but it really is like that. I could put it better if I . . . but a light, yes – and that light . . . well it's you. Christ knows, K.T – it always was. It always will be. I know that. At least I can say that I do know that. Known it for ever. And I hope . . . well I hope . . . that you do too. And that's . . . all I can say. Really. Except that I haven't ever stopped thinking about you – not for a single day, I don't think. Since you went . . . since you left me . . . well – life without you, it's been . . . it's been . . . well it just hasn't been *anything*, you want the God's honest truth. And just being here, like this . . . just this . . . just being here now, and with you . . . it's the best thing that's happened to me since . . . since . . . well since the last time we did something like this. Sorry. Very lame ending . . .'

And the man who had been laughing said, 'Bloody hell, K.T – you got to marry him after that little lot,' while the man who nearly snarled was muttering darkly, 'Fuckin' tosser.' And

K.T . . .? She smiled. She smiled her beautiful smile, and in the wave of a wand my heart was lifted.

'Let's go, shall we, Tom?'

'You want to go? Okay, if you like. Where?'

'Don't know. Nightcap somewhere?'

'It's early afternoon, K.T – it's barely . . .'

'Okay – early nightcap, then.'

'Fine. So you don't have to . . .?'

'No. PA can deal. And anyway – it's Christmas Day, isn't it?'

'It is. It surely is. So where, then? Oh K.T – meaning to ask: where, actually, do you, um . . .?'

'Notting Hill now. Portobello really. But we're not going there.'

'We're not?'

'Uh-uh.'

So we went somewhere else. Some bar in Frith, can never remember the name. My stomach now, it was filled with the dark unease that whisky may always be depended upon to bring along to the so-called party, after all the fire has gently subsided – so now I was watering it to so ridiculous an extent that it was looking like, I don't know . . . an albino's urine, or something (not that I've ever seen any). But honestly – it wasn't that much less clear than K.T's vodka . . . which she still seemed to be able to sink at will, and quite utterly endlessly. Wondrous, really. And there was no real sign of inebriation – well, fairly giggly, of course, but she was always that: one of the very many things that I absolutely loved about her – she was never a downer. K.T, she would never bring you down. So now then I am aware that this lady certainly has the ability to hold her drink . . . a thing about her I didn't really know before, because I never have witnessed her drinking anything approaching this.

Normally with us it had been most of a bottle of champagne, and then sex. And after, wandering off to the bathroom or the kitchen, one or other of us would be sure to kick over whatever was left in the bottle and that would go flying just everywhere, but we never did mind too much about that because the dark blue-and-red Persian rug she had there (eighteenth century, silk, and a rather good one, so presumably she has it still) – that effortlessly absorbed a multitude, and the champagne, it was anyway sticky and flat by then, so we'd just open another bottle.

Okay, then . . . so . . . all this is fine . . . all of this . . . it's perfectly fine, so far as it goes – more than fine, it's largely terrific, of course . . . but still . . . but still – I couldn't really pretend any longer. That it had been just another little element, inconsequential and fleeting, one of so many others, dropped into a fitful and episodic conversation. No – I really did have to know more now, you see. I really did have to know the lot.

'K.T . . .?'

'I've got to go out for a ciggie.'

'Jesus . . .'

'Oh God's sake, Tom – I won't be long! I'm never long, am I?'

'No. Okay, then.'

'Won't take a minute, will it?'

'No. Fine. It's just that I want to . . . ask you something, K.T.'

'I know. Well of course you do. Well I'll have my fag, and then I'll tell you all about it, if you really want to know. Okay?'

'Tell me all about what . . .?'

'My marriage. That is what you want to ask me, isn't it?'

'It is, yes. Yes it is.'

'Right, then. Back in two seconds.'

So that's what she did: had her fag . . . leaving me to attempt to very deliberately quell any dark design in what I would eventually be saying to her. It must emerge as mere conversation, with no hint whatever of an inquisition. Because, yes, K.T had just promised that she would tell me all about it . . . but she wouldn't really, of course. Not her way. She says, of course she *says* she is going to tell you all about it – maybe even means it at the time – but she never ever will. She just will construct a reasonably plausible narrative around a careful selection of sanitised facts and laundered opinions – lazy chronology, and trivialisation – while the omissions will be monstrous. Sometimes, to her credit, this is simply to spare my feelings. More often, here is merely a gauzy disguise for shame, the cloak thrown obliteratingly over all wrongdoing. Jesus: I do already sound very judgemental, though – and I mustn't, just mustn't: fatal at this stage, that would be. What I'll do is . . . all I have to do is just listen to whatever she decides to say to me, and then I'll just . . . probe a little bit. Not invasively, I hope. I must not cause irritation, not at this point. I must on no account remind her even in passing of just what a self-righteous, nit-picking and unjustifiably jealous fucking nuisance I can so very easily turn into. So casual, that's the key. And encouraging. Wholly understanding. Any dark design must be deliberately quelled.

'Okay . . .? How many of those things do you actually go through in a day . . .?'

'Oh – not many. I don't really smoke at all, not like some people do. But today, well – today's different. And these – they're not meant to be so bad for you as the ones I used to smoke. That's what they say, anyway . . . probably balls.'

'Okay. So, K.T . . . after we . . .'

'After I said I just couldn't stand it any more – yes, Tom. After you simply refused to commit yourself to me, when I had practically begged you to . . . Have you ordered any drinks?'

'Hm? No. But I can – I will do. Yeh well that's not quite how I remember it, K.T . . .'

'No well of course it isn't. Wouldn't be, would it? You were the married man. You still are, aren't you . . .? Amazing. I didn't honestly think that you would be, you know Tom. Not by this time. I sometimes thought that you just used being married, you know – having children. Just used it as a shield to keep me away from you. Oh Christ – if you're not going to get the drinks in, then I will. Back in a mo.'

And she was gone again: my fault, I suppose. I should have provided a whole fucking vat of vodka for her, should I, and rigged up some sort of a mask for her face and a funnel going out of the window so that she could drink and smoke quite eternally and seamlessly, and then maybe she'd bloody stay put for more than two minutes. But Jesus: how could she ever think that I was trying to keep her away from me . . .? How could she think that . . .?

'They didn't have Glenmorangie, so I got something else. I think he said it was an Islay – very beautiful bottle, squat and round, bit like Laurent Perrier rosé – remember that? We had that a lot. *Whoops-ie . . .!'*

'You okay, K.T . . .?!'

'Yeh yeh – I'm fine. Just didn't see that stool there, that's all. So anyway, Tom – you know how I wanted you. I mean permanently. I told you, didn't I? How many times did I tell you that, Tom? But you said – you remember what you said? You said it was "difficult". Men always say that – as if for the woman it's a stroll in the bloody park, I don't know . . . I needed commitment, Tom. I needed to *belong.* So . . . I changed things. That's all.'

'I thought it was commitment from *me* that you wanted . . .'

'It was! It was! But you weren't about to give it, were you? So . . .'

'So you went with someone else . . .'

'Don't you dare go saying it like that! I'm not a *hooker*, Tom . . .! I met someone, I liked him, we were together – and then we got *married* . . .!'

'Christ's sake, K.T – keep your *voice* down . . .'

'Jesus . . . same old Tom . . .!'

'Look. Look. I understand wholly. Honestly. Of course I do. I mean . . . not *pleased* about it, obviously. Can't actually bear the bloody *thought* of it, you want the God's honest truth . . . but yes . . . I knew . . . of course I knew . . . woman like you . . . you were hardly going to be *alone*. One of my greatest agonies, actually. If you want to know. Not just the sheer bloody awfulness of being without you . . . but knowing, always knowing, that you were with somebody else . . .! Even now – kills me. Just kills me . . .'

'Yes well. You were with somebody else, weren't you? All the time we were together. But that was supposed to be perfectly okay – oh yes: that was completely fine. And you're still married to her . . .!'

'Yes well, I . . .'

'Yes well you what, Tom? I mean . . . do you – *love* her? You can't, can you?'

'Well I . . . I can't really see that . . . look – I don't want to *argue*, K.T . . .'

'No, Tom. I know. You never did. How's the whisky?'

'Hm? Oh . . . I haven't, er . . .'

'Well taste it, then. Go on – taste it. Okay . . .? Yes . . .? Good, is it?'

270

'It's . . . yes. It's fine. So anyway, K.T . . .'

'Is it one of the smoky ones? Must be very different from a Highland, I should have said, but I've never been really into whisky, even the malts. What was that one you always used to drink after dinner, Tom? I can't believe I've forgotten the name. God, I bought it often enough . . .'

'I don't, um . . . look, K.T . . .'

'Was it Laphroaig? It wasn't, was it? It was that other one – oh God it's driving me crazy: what was it *called*, Tom . . .?'

'Talisker. It was Talisker. But listen K.T . . .'

'Talisker! That's it! Oh of course – Talisker, oh yeh . . .'

'K.T . . .! For Christ's *sake* . . .!'

'Okay, Tom – okay. I'll spare you the trouble: I'll give you the lot, okay? I'll tell you all of it once, and then we bury it. Deal?'

'The lot? You'll tell me the lot?'

'If you want it. Do you want it, Tom?'

'I . . . I'm not sure . . .'

'No well. I'll just start talking. And you say "when". Okay . . .? Okay. First I'm just quickly going out for a fag . . .'

'Oh for the love of Jesus Christ in heaven, K.T . . .!'

'Okay – okay, Tom. I'll tell you really quickly, then, because I really do feel like a fag, okay? So . . . where shall I start . . .? I was . . . and you can believe this or not, but I hope you do – I really hope you do, Tom . . . I was very low, okay? Really not in a good place, you know . . .? After we . . . when we weren't seeing one another any more. And it didn't help when you kept on calling. I couldn't see you – you have to understand that I couldn't see you, Tom. You maybe do now. Because we just would have drifted back together, I know we would – and then it would all have been exactly the same as it had been and I would have had to do it all again, break us up all over again, and that was going to mean more pain, wasn't it? Would have been even more painful than the first time. Because I had to . . . I thought I had to . . . well what . . .? Re-establish myself. Be me again, yeah . . . instead of, well – just half of *us*, if you know what I mean. Decided to grow out my hair . . .! That was the first thing. Big step. Leon – remember I've spoken about Leon? He's my hairdresser, had him for years – he just went absolutely crazy when I told him. And yeh, I have to admit it did look pretty scuzzy for just ages afterwards. All layered, you see – well: you remember. So it didn't grow in properly – all uneven, bits sticking out and the back still really short. I looked like a scarecrow! Even took the scissors to it myself sometimes, when it was looking particularly shitty. Pretty good now, though – don't you think? Yes? Really . . .? Good. I'm glad you like it like this. I did wonder, you know. I actually did say to myself: "Tom – I wonder if he'd like it . . .?" And I decided you would. I like it too. Lot less bother, I can tell you. Before, I had to get it trimmed and shaped about every two bloody weeks . . .! So that was that, anyway. That was the hair. And then . . . what happened next . . .? Well I got a new place – studio flat, I've got now. Not very big, but it is quite stylish: I liked the shape, and the light. Window's huge, and there's a decent Victorian mantelpiece and a bit of original panelling – and you know how well all that goes with the modern stuff, and when you bring a bit of red into it. I think I've done it quite nicely – not finished yet, of course. Rooms – they never are, are they? Top floor, but there's not really much of a view. Just patched-up roofs and chimneys. I *love* it, actually. Oh and *Tom* . . .! I finally got that Aalto chaise . . .! Yes! You know I've always wanted that. Yeh and I know you've got the stool, haven't you . . .? Yeh – thought so. And the trolley . . .? You got the trolley as well . . .? Yes. It's gorgeous, that trolley. So expensive, though. Anyway – so I got the chaise. I knew you'd be pleased. And then oh my God . . .! You just won't believe . . .! I found some original Lucienne Day fabric . . .! I know! On a stall in the market – just literally around the corner from me. 1957 – never been used, nearly a whole bale of it. Had to pay quite a lot – they knew what they were selling – but oh, it was *so* worth it. I felt quite bad about having it cut, actually – but I did, I had it made up into curtains. There's this woman, quite local, and she does all that. She's really good and actually very cheap. They look fantastic – and there was just enough left over to cover that ottoman of mine – do you remember it, Tom? That square sort of footstool thing, yes? All good. And so then . . . what happened then . . .? Well – got this job, one I've got now. That was lucky – somebody told me about it. Money's nearly double. And that's been definitely a step in the right direction, because I was really in a rut in that other place. Only got my promotion a couple of months ago. It's exciting. I can commission now, which I've never done before. Only one movie at the moment – it's just gone into pre-produc- tion – but lots more ideas in the pipeline. So all that – that's pretty good. And . . . it was at Cannes, actually – film festival – that I met him. Guy, his name is. Don't wince, Tom – it's only a name. Not French, or anything – he's from Newcastle, actually. He's with Working Title. Anyway . . . blah blah blah . . . and after about five months, bit more, we decided to get married. He'd been married before, actually – got a little boy. Had this really big house in Earl's Court – his uncle left it to him, which I always thought was a bit odd actually because his whole family, all of his relations – and there's loads of them – they're all still living in Newcastle, so God knows why his uncle had a house in Earl's Court, but there you are. So that's where we were

273

– but I kept my studio going though, and thank God I did, way things turned out. Maybe I knew. Maybe that's why I kept it. Don't know. Guy, he was always saying that it was a waste, paying the rent on it and everything . . . and okay, I could have done with the money, but still I thought no, I'll keep it. Also . . . I didn't want all my . . . stuff . . . to be . . . well, you're about the only person on earth who'll understand this, Tom – but I didn't want all of my things muddled up with his, you know? Yeh – I knew you'd get that. And the décor, the furnishings in that house – oh God, Tom, you would have died . . .! Really pretty bad – all the things you hate. We never did get round to changing it. Doing it up. Because I wasn't really there that long. It all became . . . I don't know . . . it wasn't what I meant . . . it wasn't what I hoped it would be. Because it was stability I was after . . . I needed to feel settled – you remember that's what I always was going on about . . .? Yeh well – I didn't feel it. Settled. And I don't think I was being unrealistic, or anything – I don't think I was after the moon. But it was just . . . it was all just so . . . I mean – he isn't a bad person, Guy, it was nothing like that. I didn't suddenly uncover this, I don't know – darker side, or something. There was no great sudden war, or anything. I just thought . . . I'd be better off on my own. You know . . .? Selfish, maybe. Probably was, actually. Anyway. So that's it, Tom – that's the rather sad story of my marriage. Short . . . and not really very sweet. Shall we have just the one more . . .? Yes, Tom? Did you like that whisky, or do you want something different . . .? I'm just going out now quickly, okay? Bloody gasping. So you can decide. You get in whatever you want, yes? And I'll have the same.'

And so once again, yet once more, and due to her seemingly insatiable craving for nicotine, I was left on my own. In order to do what . . .? Well – buy yet another round of bloody drinks, for a start: it's amazing she can even stand up and get herself outside the door with all the booze she's put inside of her. And during the course of her narrative, she didn't actually come to mention that, did she? How she came to take up smoking along with this very evident new reliance upon alcohol. . . not to say her 'occasional' use of Class-A drugs, by way of a top-up. All maybe part of . . . what did she say? What did she call it? 'Re-establishing herself', I think is what she said – some such female mumbo-jumbo. Bloody hell. But it wasn't that, was it? Course it bloody wasn't. Guy – it's all down to Guy: obviously a chain-smoking drunk who likes to get high. Not that that was the only omission, of course: that little story, well – it was simply riddled with omission: more holes than substance. Just as I knew it would be, of course. She didn't lie to me, K.T, and nor did I expect her to – because that, all of that, it all rang true. It's just the stuff she didn't say. Although that aside, one thing that I am thinking now, can't help myself, is that I would just love to go to this studio flat she's got – it really does sound absolutely terrific. What with the Aalto chaise, and everything – really so pleased she's got that now. Like she said, she always did want it – way ahead of all the other designer furniture on her very long list, that was always at number one. And I wonder if I will . . .? Ever see it. This studio of hers. Is that the way it's going to go . . .? Difficult to say. She's been frank, but only in a woman's way. Throwing out no hints at all concerning the future.

So . . . what do I think? About all that. Yes and about Guy, in particular. Apart from it's a fucking stupid name, in my opinion. I mean to say – what sort of parents can cradle and nuzzle and gaze down lovingly at their new-born, pink and cherubic baby boy and think, oh yes I know: out of all the names in the whole bloody world, I think we shall christen him 'Guy'. Just stupid, isn't it? Might as well call him 'Bloke', and be done with it. Anyway. And this Guy person – did she say how old he is? She did not. Not a kid, presumably, if already he's been in and out of a couple of marriages. What sort of a marriage was it . . .? This – Christ – *marriage* between K.T and Guy? Well – who's to say? What are marriages ever like? Jesus: what's mine like, for Christ's sake . . .? Yeh well: you see what I mean. And many times I have heard it said that there can only ever be two people who know what is going on within a marriage, and that is the couple whose marriage it is. To which I say: *two* people? Really? Are you quite sure about that? You mean to say – *both* of them know what's going on . . .? Mm . . . well I've always considered that to be a considerable exaggeration. And here's something else: are they actually divorced? K.T and this fucking Guy person. Or just separated? Or merely 'taking a break from one another'? Finding their own fucking *space* . . .? Well she didn't say that either, did she? Nor did she tell me how gorgeous-looking or hideous he is, this Guy. Going to be gorgeous-looking, isn't he though? Tall and dark and muscle-bound and bloody out-and-out gorgeous-looking, that's what Guy's going to be, God damn him to hell. From Newcastle though, on the plus side: that bloody ridiculous accent – how on earth did K.T stand it? I couldn't – I know that. And then there's all the ins and outs – including, but of course, the big one: how was the sex? Better than with me . . .? Because there will have been sex, won't there? Bloody loads of it. She likes sex, K.T – she likes it, yes, and she's good at it too. The way she told the tale, it was just a couple of people with the film industry as their common denominator who went to live in a house and held hands happily ever after. No . . . there will have been sex. Bloody loads of it. In Cannes, for starters. What's the point of meeting someone in Cannes if you don't have sex? So yes – sex in Cannes, then, and every bloody day after I should think, knowing K.T as I do. Which kills me. It's stupid, I know – but still it does: it just kills me, it bloody kills me. I knew . . . well I told her that, didn't I? I said to her that I knew that she was never going to be *alone* . . . and so if you're with someone, okay . . .? Well then there's going to be sex. Because otherwise, why bother?

And here's another thing: what memories, I wonder, has she taken away with her? What shared emotions and experiences between her and the blighted Guy will always be a part of her fabric? Well Cannes, for one. But what other places, songs, moments, tastes and atmospheres will always and for ever remind her of Guy? Like Aalto and Talisker and that ottoman have made her remember me. Well I shall never know. Which is maybe just as well. And if she's with Pasadena Pictures and he's with Working Title . . . is it not likely in the extreme that they will again coincide? Even if – and here's a thought – even if she has stopped actually seeing him in the first place. Maybe they text and tweet. Maybe they meet up once a week in that sweet little bistro that they made their very own, and where they always order exactly the same thing for the both of them. Maybe they are 'bestest friends', Christ help me. Maybe . . . maybe, because everything between them had been a total and utter washout barring the bloody sex, they have decided to remain on fuck-buddy terms. Jesus. And what about before this guy called Guy? Will there have been someone else, if only briefly? And what was his name, then? And how gorgeous-looking or hideous was he? And what was the sex like? Hey? Better than with me . . .? And how long has she been out of this marriage, and the big house in Earl's Court? A long time?

And if a long time, with whom did she strike up a relationship next? Or maybe there's been more than one. And what are all their names? And how gorgeous-looking or hideous is this newest mob of bastards then, hey? And what's the bloody sex like? Better than with me . . .? Not going to ask her. Can't. Obviously. And she's not going to tell me. Won't. Obviously. Yes . . . and so in light of all of this . . . how am I actually feeling? Do I want her? Still? Do I want to know her again? Be a part of her life, just like it used to be? Have sex with her again? Do I . . .? Well do I, *punk* . . .? Joking. Course I bloody do. Well look at her, can't you? Just look at her. *Inhale* her, Christ's sake . . .! Jesus – for K.T, just to be with her again, I'd give up willingly my soul and lungs, and within a single beat of my bursting heart.

'Oh bloody hell, Tom . . .! You really are useless, you know. What's wrong with you? You haven't even *budged* . . .'

'Oh God sorry. Thinking. I was thinking. About all that you've been saying. Right then – um . . . you really do want another one then, do you?'

'Well *yeah* . . .! We haven't finished talking yet, have we? Or have we? You want to go, Tom? Say goodbye? Part as friends . . .?'

I looked at her. Just looked at her. Wished I could *inhale* her, Christ's sake . . .!

'I'll get us another drink.'

So I did that. And then we talked some more. Didn't really get anything said, it ought to be understood – all we did is . . . we just talked some more. You see, the nitty-gritty here was that she wasn't giving, and I wasn't asking. I do remember that at some point she said to me that I – *you*, Tom, she said – quite accusatory, and yet with roguish cheek and a twinkle, neither of which I altogether cared for – that I, I couldn't possibly have been an angel, not me, not for all the time we had been apart.

278

And I imagine I must have looked really quite affronted, because I very much was. *What . . .?* I said: you mean another woman . . .? Which of course is exactly what she meant, well of course it was – what else could she be meaning? Oh *no*, I assured her – I haven't, I couldn't. All true. Until even less than just twenty-four hours ago, when I came to crave, be mesmerised, utterly smitten, by that idiotic Portia, the chewing-gum Yank. Who the hell, actually, is *Portia*, I suddenly was asking myself. From where did all that befuddled and perfectly asinine nonsense so suddenly spring? From the pit of desperation, is all I could imagine. And then I looked at K.T directly as I asked her if she was sure, if she was absolutely sure that we weren't, in fact, going back to her no doubt quite delightful little studio flat in Notting Hill, Portobello really, and she said yeh I'm sure Tom: we aren't. And so . . . what else . . .? What else did I say . . .? Oh yes: I said that it was a pity, really a very great pity, on balance, that she didn't actually have a say in whether Alexander did get the part in this bloody film, whatever the bloody film was destined to be (because no one has actually said). And K.T, she said, oh *Jesus*, Tom – you're not now doing what your preposterous wife (is what she said: preposterous wife) was trying on with Willy, are you . . .? And I allowed myself just the faintest of smiles: no no, I said – not at all: by no means. I was merely thinking that if you did actually hold any sway at all in that direction, I would now beseech you, as a friend, to kill it. Stone dead. Give the part to the other bloody boy. Why, she said: are you *jealous*, Tom . . .? And I said, oh Christ, K.T: don't you start . . .! *No . . .!* It's just that then we could all stop talking and thinking about it (not that I'm thinking about it). I told her that I didn't suppose that Alexander would really mind very much – although possibly he would, possibly he would mind very much indeed: I don't really know him, so it's difficult to say. Ah no maybe not, said K.T – but your wife would (never calls her Amy, never does) . . . *she* would, *she* would – *she* would mind, that's for sure. Yes, I said: she would. She'd mind, all right.

And . . . we drank, oh God – even more, even more, and then I asked her if she was sure, if she was absolutely sure that we weren't, in fact, going back to her no doubt quite delightful little studio flat in Notting Hill, Portobello really, and she said, yeh I'm sure Tom: we aren't. So then she went out for yet another bloody cigarette, and I tried hard to think – because by this time I was completely plastered, please let's face it – to find some subtle way, some gently nuanced and delicate manner by which I might have some way of divining just exactly what, if anything, she might have in mind for the future . . .? For us . . .? And fairly naturally I came up with absolutely nothing at all and so when she came back in and berated me for not having got another drink in, I said to her, look listen, K.T: what, if anything, might you have in mind for the future . . .? For us . . .? And she said, oh Christ's *sake*, Tom. So I nodded to that, and then I asked her if she was sure, absolutely sure that we wouldn't, in fact, be going back to her no doubt quite delightful little studio flat in Notting Hill, Portobello really, and she said, yeh okay, then: why not? Which serves to demonstrate either that dogged if not addled and bone-headed persistence can be a thoroughly fine and positive thing – or else, rather more likely, that she too now was just as legless as I was. And about time too, don't you think?

And so how did all that go . . .? Was it heaven . . .? Or that other thing . . .? Oh God oh God oh God . . . I'm so not going to think about it yet, not yet – no no no, not quite yet. I'm going to wait – I decided even on my way back that I wasn't going to think about it until I was all tucked up nicely in my own bed at home. In my study. Been sleeping in there for just ages, as a matter of fact – a rather too narrow sort of a pull-down affair, it is: looks like a wardrobe in the daytime, really rather neat, and I suppose that, yes . . . it's comfortable enough. Can actually barely remember what the bedroom – what used to be our bedroom, that barren battleground, the place where Amy and I used to put ourselves at night . . . do you know, I can actually barely remember what it even looks like. Used once to be rather smart, that I do know – black and white, my scheme, my design, and all the better to show off my lovely and elegant Mackintosh Willow Tea Rooms side chair . . . yes but Amy – Amy, at some point when I was hardly looking, long beyond caring, had it completely redone, the room, in a shade that I can only describe as apricot, and I am very surprised that she actually likes it, Amy – she says she likes it, anyway – because it's exactly the sort of colour that I would have betted good money she would archly have pronounced to be plebeian. Which shows how much I know, I suppose. And the chair – my Mackintosh chair – that now looks perfectly ridiculous in there, of course it must do, as well you may imagine.

Anyway . . . wanted to go to sleep, talking of sleep – yearned to, actually – the moment I walked through the door (because, you see, apart from still pretty smashed, I was in turmoil – turmoil, I tell you) . . . yes but I couldn't do that, as things turned out, because Amy – Amy, she started up on one of her exceedingly tiresome little 'conversations', didn't she? During the course of which I learned, among quite a few other rather unsettling and highly surprising things, that the house, this house, is about to be sold from under me – and I severely doubt if there's anything I can do about that. Well what am I saying? There's nothing, is there? Not when Amy is utterly committed to a thing. Well yes but it's done now, all that – the little 'conversation', that's now all over and done with, thank Christ . . . so at last and finally, I'm climbing into my bed. I quite some time ago, you know – don't know why I'm thinking of this now, quite why it's occurred to me – bought one of these memory-foam mattress toppers, have you come across any mention of these . . .? See them advertised just every-where now. Rather good it was too, actually – well at first it was, anyway . . . but now all its comfort, its moulding and cosseting – all of that has departed: the sunken troughs from the slump of my body . . . they stubbornly remain: this thing now, it seems quite wilfully no longer to recall me. I feel that it is true to say that as far as my memory-foam mattress topper is concerned, I have transcended into becoming a quite wholly forgotten person.

But now . . . I am in my bed, finally, such as it is. All is quiet . . . an enveloping peace that hugs me . . . and now . . . the light is off . . . and now . . . I can wholly give myself over to thinking . . . thinking, yes, all about it. About when K.T and I, just a few hours ago – can that really be . . .? When we did, very drunkenly, and after, Jesus, just how many more 'ones for the road' fall into the back of a cold and welcome taxi, she somehow almost man-aging to articulate a fair deal of the address of this little studio flat of hers – and it is, you know: quite delightful – in Notting Hill . . . and of course I can see now exactly what she means when she says it's Portobello, really. But . . . oh dear God . . . I can't. Actually. Give myself over to thinking about it at all . . . no, it would appear not . . . cannot, in fact, even think of giving myself over to thinking about that or, indeed, anything else, oh no . . . because Amy . . . Amy, she's somewhere down the corridor, it would surely seem – could be she's on the staircase, maybe. And Amy . . . she is shrieking quite wildly.

'Jesus Jesus *Jesus* . . .! I do not . . . I cannot . . . *believe* this . . .! Terence . . .! *Terence* . . .! Are you awake? *Get* here, can't you . . .! Where are you?! Oh God come *here*, for Christ's sake . . .! You simply will not *believe* this . . .! Are you *awake* . . .? Oh here you are. Look at this . . .! Just look at this . . .! I just simply cannot *believe* this . . .!

'What in God's name is it, Amy . . .? I was asleep . . . What are you . . .?'

'What in God's name is it . . .?! What in God's name *is* it . . .? I'll tell what in God's name it bloody fucking is . . .! A courier's just been, all right . . .?'

'Oh really? Didn't hear the bell. This late? I was asleep . . .'

'Yes, so you keep on saying – and how very terribly pleasant for you, Terence. Lucky, lucky you, to have been asleep. I wasn't. Don't remember the last time I was. And the courier . . . this bloody courier, he has just given me, oh God . . . *this* . . .!'

'What is it . . .?'

'It's a letter, Terence, you absolute moron. It's a letter, yes, couriered over in the middle of the bloody night from Pasadena fucking Pictures . . .'

'Oh. Really?'

'Yes, Terence: *really*. And do you know what it says? I just can't—! Have you any idea what it—?!'

'I don't, Amy. I don't.'

'It says . . . it *says* that they've given the part . . . the part in this fucking film of theirs . . . to the other bloody *boy* . . .! I just can't—! And after all I've—! That Ouch, that fucking bastard Ouch, I am telling you . . . that bloody Willy Ouch . . . I'll *kill* him . . .! I'll absolutely just *kill* him! Do you hear me, Terence?

283

I'll *kill* him! *Kill* him, *kill* him, *kill* him . . .! Do you hear? The next time I set eyes on that bloody man again, I am just going to *kill* him . . .!'

She stared at me, totally aghast. She was scandalised, and shivering with a fury that I had seldom beheld. Her face – shock white, and spattered with blotches of scarlet. Her rigid fingers were holding out to me the crumpled letter – she had been mashing it repeatedly against her thigh – holding it out to me, yes, and almost in supplication. There was hurt – amazement too, but hurt, mainly hurt – and also pleading, deep within the lit-up caverns of her two blazing eyes.

'Ah . . .' I said.

CHAPTER SEVEN

IT'S NOT AS IF THERE IS CHAOS

Maria, she were saying to me other day that she reckon in this chambermaiding game, you walking hundred mile a day. I tries to get out of her if she were just like saying hundred mile a day because it like a really long way and she making a point sort of thing, you know what I saying – or else she like been into it and work it out and we really does walk hundred mile a day. I thought about it, and I thought nah – can't be. Because hundred mile, right, that like from here to . . . I don't know – Brighton or Glasgow or some place like that. You know what I mean? So it can't be, can it? Still got to be a pretty fair whack, though – because we on the move all the bleeding time. Yeh well – on my break at the minute. Cup of tea. Some of the girls, they kicks their shoes off, but I never: don't reckon I could get the bleeders back on me, if I'm honest: don't know if it just me, but my feet, they swells up something chronic. First thing I does when I gets back home, yeh, and even before I gets Kenny his tea, is I sits on the side of the bath there and give them a right good soaking, and I got a bit of Radox in.

I don't mind the job, though. I'm all right. I don't like hate it like I thought I were going to. After the second day of it, I were that knackered I were like going to just jack it in, whole bleeding thing, and it were Maria what say to me to like give it another go. She been right nice to me, Maria – and I pleased I listen to her, because I sort of got into it now – so yeh: I'm all right. It bloody hard – hard graft, I'm meaning. All of the humping and the bending and them bleeding mattresses. But what I likes about it is I on my own, see, and I gets a lot of time to think – and I been doing a fair little bit of that lately, I have. I been thinking this, for starters: okay yeh, I earning a bit, a little bit of money for myself – not much, but a bit . . . yeh but still, it just ain't never going to do it. Ain't going to come close. Because style, yeh – all what I after – it take a lot more . . . because I sees it all around me, don't I? Looking at the women here and everything, lucky mares – yeh and what I sees is that it take a lot more than just having a Louis Vuitton handbag hanging off of your arm, you know what I saying? But just take that as a for instance, now we on to all of the money thing. I work it out: not like Maria with her hundred mile – I really work it out. Pen and paper. Yeh so listen: money what I gets after stoppages, if I was to put aside the lot of it, right? Not ever spend a bleeding penny of it – you know how long I got to work so's I can go into Vuitton's down Bond Street there and say, yeh well right okay – that the bag I wanting, thanks for asking, wrap it up for us, will you? Know how long? Tell you, will I? More than two and a half month. Two whole bleeding month, near on three . . .! And that all on account of I ain't on full time. Reckon I could be, if I was going to go and ask, like, because I think they took to me, Mumtaz and the rest of them – yeh but with Damien and Kenny, it just ain't never going to happen. Couple kids I got to look after – ain't hardly nothing between them: Damien, he bigger, that's all. Christ, don't get me started – telling you. And

I ain't going to get it in two month and a half, am I, this bloody Vuitton bag. Course not – because I got to spend. Got to. Keep it all going. And not just on make-up and my magazines and that – because other night when I couldn't no matter what I try get to thing – sleep, couldn't get off to sleep – I gets this really good idea of what I thought it might be worth blowing couple bob on. Because all of them American actresses, yeh? They can all of them do it – real good, they do it: amazing, really. Angelina and Renée and Gwyneth and Scarlett and just like piles of them, really. They does it more proper than what the English ones does it. So if they can pull it off, I don't see why I can't and all. Be good, that would. It'd be like a investment, is what I says to Damien. And he go:

'*Elocution* . . .? What's that then when it's at home?'

'What – you saying to me you really don't know? You got to know the *word*, Damien . . .! Bloody hell – you stupid, or what? You really don't ever know nothing about nothing at all, does you? Hey? It's about *talking*, ain't it? Talking not like we bleeding talk, but like real sort of nice. Like Amy, and that. And Terry, yeh?'

'Sound like couple ponces . . .'

'Yeh but listen, Damien – it all right speaking like what we do if you's *famous* . . . if you's like a reality star or a presenter or a model or a movie actor or a footballer or on the BBC or something. Then you just like does what you want – be as common as muck, you want to be – because you God, basically. And you, you see – you all right, Damien, working in the garage because you don't even got to talk much, does you? Just fix up the motors. But for me . . . for me, it different.'

'What – on account of you being a bleeding chamber-maid . . .?'

287

'Won't always be a chambermaid, will I? Wouldn't have to in the first place if you was any bleeding good at all . . .'

'Oh ta very much. Very nice, girl. Yeh but look so tell me why's it different then, Dolly. Ay? Why's it different for you? Why you always going on about all of this sort of total crap? Why you always got to be different? Why you think you so bleeding special, Dolly? Why you always like that? Ay? Why can't you never just shut your bleeding mouth and just fucking get on with it? Ay?'

I could of kicked him. I could of. I also could of cried.

'Oh just piss off Damien, can't you? Anyway. I going to do it. I decided. I going to learn. To talk nice. It's what I want.'

Yeh and I didn't say that I were going to be a lady, and all. A lady, yeh – a proper lady, and one what got real *style*. No – I never said that to him on account of he would of just laughed in my face. He can be a right bleeding pig sometimes, Damien. Yeh and often I looking at Kenny and all I can see is a right bleeding pig in the making. Is it just blokes? Is it? What they're like? That what it is? Can't be though, can it? Nah. Not all blokes is like that – you just got to look about you. Gentlemen – they isn't like that. Not people likes of Prince Charles and George Clooney – they ain't pigs, they does it proper, yeh . . . like gentlemen. And the geezer what I gone to, yeh? Because I meant it, I did mean it, I weren't just saying – yeh so the geezer what I gone to, I gets him off of the internet. Trouble with internet – you don't know what to do, do you really? You looks up something and they just like thousands of it all over and you just think oh blimey, I dunno – where do I go, then? Which of these is any good? Because all of them, they looking the bleeding same. So I just picks this bloke, basically. He live quite near is most of why I goes for him, I suppose, and I gone over there on an afternoon I ain't up the hotel. It's for a hour, this first like . . . what-do-they-call-it lesson. Introduction lesson, whatever – and it half of the usual price. Thirty quid. Thirty bleeding quid. Which mean normally I be looking at sixty, right? And me, I getting eight. Yeh well – that a pretty good lesson in itself, ain't it really? Yeh and before I even walks through the door. So first thing he say to me – and he ain't so old as I thought he be, because I maybe thought that anybody what going to be learning you something, they got to be old, you know? And wearing all beige and real cheap clothes he were, yeh? Like out of the Chums catalogue, or something: zip-up cardigan, you can believe it, with sort of dark beige kind of snowflakes on a light beige bleeding background, I don't know. Even his hair, what he got of it – that beige and all. Yeh and the first thing he go and say to me is, 'You're early.' And I says to him, 'Yeh I am – you want me to go back outside and sit in the street for ten minutes, or what . . .?' And blimey – it only look like he thinking it over . . .! Anyway – I goes in. Miserable little room he show me into. Ain't no woman living here, tell you that straight off – tell you that in a flash. It all just a table and a couple manky chairs and all sort of computer stuff. Mashed up Venetian blinds, and they beige too. George Handley, his name is. Not sure I taking to him, this Mister George Handley. Me he looking at as if I smelling.

'Right then, Dolly – let's get cracking, shall we? I can call you Dolly . . .?'

'It's my name . . .'

'Right. Okay. And I'm George. All right? Okay, then. Well to kick us off, as it were – would you like to tell me quite what you hope to achieve from a course of elocution . . .?'

'Ay . . .?'

'What you – you know – want to get out of it. What made you think of it in the first place? Why in fact have you come to me?'

'Why have I come to you . . .? Well why do you bleeding think I come to you? I want to talk good, don't I? I want you to teach me how to talk good. What you do, ain't it?'

'It's . . . yes. Yes it's, um – part of what I do. But just from this little conversation so far I can see rather clearly that there are, um – two problems facing us here.'

'Oh yeh? Here – this part of the hour, is it? Or do it start when we cut all of the chitchat and get down to doing it proper?'

'I assumed, yes, that the hour had begun, but . . .'

'All right, then. It's not that I minding. It's just so's I know, all right? So what are they then?'

'Sorry . . . what are . . . what . . .?'

'Problems.'

'Ah yes.'

'Two problems, you said.'

'Yes yes. Well you see – I can of course, over time, teach you proper enunciation. Phonetics. Euphony. This is – as you said, didn't you? – what I do. But . . .'

'Fonetics, yeh. What was the other thing what you said . . .? You . . . phoney . . .?'

'Exactly right: euphony, yes. But I wouldn't get too hung up on the words, you know, if I were you. Practice – that's all of it, really. And enunciation.'

'That's like all Mrs Pankhurst and that, isn't it . . .? I heard of that.'

'I don't think . . . Look: let me make plain what I mean about the problems facing us, yes? I can, as I say, very significantly improve your speaking voice – vowel sounds, the crisping up of consonants, pacing, general timbre . . . but still, Dolly, you will be left with the problem of grammar, you see.'

'Grammar. You don't do grammar?'

'Well no. That would be an English course, wouldn't it . . .?'

'I do speak *English* – what you on about?'

'Yes but you see what I am trying to explain to you Dolly is that it's not going to be terribly helpful to you if you learn to pronounce each word perfectly, if they are the, er . . . wrong words, if you see what I mean. And in the wrong order . . .'

'Right . . . so okay then, Mr Handley – if I got you right . . .'

'George . . .'

'Ay? Oh yeh – George, okay, got you. So what you saying is that I don't know, like – all of the words, and that. Yeh and I don't know how to put it good. Like I doing things all sort of wrong . . . yeh well I know I does that. Course I do. I knows it all the time because I listening to other people, aren't I? Like you, George – you speak lovely. Yeh but then you would, wouldn't you? So what I going to do about it all then, ay . . .?'

'Well . . . there are courses, as I said. English grammar. Syntax . . .'

'Sin tax . . .? That sound cheeky . . .'

'Um . . . yes. I don't think you'd actually have to study in a school, or anything. Correspondence course, you know? Very good indeed, some of them, these days. But as far as elocution is concerned, well that really has to be a one-to-one, of course. So that I can hear you, and you can hear me.'

'Right. Well . . . I got to think about it. All of that. What I going to do. Time, that's the trouble. Don't know how I going to . . . yeh but here, George: why don't you start me off on a lesson, yeh? I going to think about all of the other what you said, yeh?

But just for now, okay, I think it would be real nice if you could just, like . . . learn me to say something proper.'

He smile at me, George do then. He not a bad geezer, really. He not so beige as everything about him. I could see he were on my side, like – and I don't reckon it were just on account of my thirty quid. So he got me doing all of these like tongue twisters, I suppose is what they was. Won't never forget them neither, I says them to him so bleeding often. 'Tony tastes the tip of his tongue and teeth.' And he go to me – no Dolly, not 'Towny' – it's *'Tony'*, you see? Not 'teef', is it Dolly? Look at my tongue, he go: look at my tongue, you see? Pressing against the back of my . . . the back of my *what*, Dolly . . .? Yes! Yes! Well done! Except that it's 'teeth' not 'teef', all right . . .? He say I all at the front of my mouth, when I want to be at the back: I know – don't ask. Then he say to relax my muscles. Then we goes on to this one: 'Richard and Robert's revolting Rottweiler retched rancid rabbits.' Which kind of like really grossed me out, you know? Anyway, I says it for him: keep him happy. Then he say to relax my muscles. And I ask him: ain't we going to do 'how now brown cow', then . . .? What – no 'rain in Spain' . . .? And he say that he be very happy for me to say them, if I wants to, so I does. And I done it all wrong, of course. 'Hah nah brahn cah' is what I comes out with. 'Rine in Spine'. Yeh but by the end of the lesson, all right, I were doing it real proper, is what he say to me: 'how now brown cow' – yeh lovely. And them sounds in my mouth . . . I don't know . . . difficult to like sort of say . . . but it made me feel . . . different. Like when you put on heels, yeh? And you walks different, and you feel more good about yourself? It were like that. I were like all sort of lifted up, you know what I saying? I were real happy about it – proud of myself, you know? And then he say to relax my muscles and I go to him – here, listen up George – I relax my bleeding muscles any more and I going to fall off the bloody chair, aren't I? He laugh at that – he ain't too bad at all, old George. And then I go to him – here, you remember right at the beginning, does you? When you was asking me what I were hoping to achieve, yeh . . .? When you was needing to know what I want to get out of it, yeh . . .? Well what I want . . . what I really, really want is to be like a lady, you know . . .? A real proper lady – yeh and with *style* . . .! And he say to me – you know what he say to me? He say to me, well Dolly, I think that is a very wonderful ambition – wonderful ambition, what he said – and I feel quite sure that with persistence and application, is how he were putting it, with persistence and application, yeh . . . you will be sure to attain your goal. Yeh. That what he said. How about that, then?

I could of kissed him. I could of. I also could of cried.

Didn't last though, did it? Me feeling good about myself. Didn't last – never do. Because once I got myself back home to Damien and Kenny, yeh? Well it were all just the same old. Like what it always are, basically. Damien, he's fetched Kenny back from his school – least he never forgot – and then he gone and made tea, look. Bleeding wet teabags just dumped on the table there – yeh because it somebody else going to be clearing all of this lot up then, that right is it? Yeh, and that whoever, that wouldn't be me then by any bloody chance, would it Damien? I don't know: pig, he is. And they was doing one of them stupid games on the telly – each of them with the handsets there and pressing all of the buttons and making noises and that, all yelling and whooping like they was on one of them game shows like what you sees on cable. Never even notice I come in the door. So I just hangs about there for a bit, feeling like a bloody lemon, and then I thought oh sod this, and I starts up a sort of a dead slow hand-clap, like. And Damien then, he look round at me, okay (Kenny – he never) and he go, 'Oh it you, Dolly – never hear you come in. Oh fuck me – I gone and lost a life now . . .! Look what you made me do, Dolly! Nah – ain't fair, Kenny – can't count them, weren't looking, were talking to your mammy, weren't I? Here, Dolly – you getting our tea, or what?' Yeh. See? See what I got to put up with? 'How now brown cow,' I goes to him – all high falutin', like what I was just learned by Mr Handley. And he laugh, Damien. Damien, he just laughing at me, and then he get back to his moron gaming. Yeh well: how now brown *pig* . . .

Next morning I were back up the hotel and there were this like bunch of people hanging about in the lobby, there. They all got their cases and that about them – reckon they waiting for a coach, or something. They don't all know one another, nor nothing – they just all of them on the same bus to maybe the airport or somewhere. But they chatting away there, is what I getting at, and it just sort of occur to me, like: all of them people – they together, but they ain't really together at all. Know what I saying? By dinner time, they scattered about all over the world, shouldn't wonder. Just met by chance, like. Don't know really what to like make of what I thinking. Can't, like . . . sort of say what I feeling . . . just it funny, ain't it? How we all of us just go and bump into somebody, yeh . . .? Or else . . . well or else, we just don't. Like – if I never gone and met Damien that time . . . well, I be with someone else now, wouldn't I? It just that I did do. Meet him. Yeh and then one of them, woman in the group there, Jap she were, Chink, one of them – she go to me, oh hello, I recognise you, don't I? You do the fifth floor, don't you . . .? And I goes, yeh – who want to know? Turn out she gone and left a bag, yeh, carrier bag, up in her room, bag from Harrods she telling me, and she want to know if I can find a porter to go and fetch it down for her and there a bit of hurry up about it on account of she off in a minute. I says to her, I tell you what: I fetch it down for you, okay? Quicker than arsing about. Yeh – so I does that: straight up and down in the service lift, don't take two minutes. Were going to have a peek inside of the bag – see what she gone and bought, like – but whatever it were, it all done up in like tissue paper with like stickers on, so I never touch it. I gets back down and she ever so grateful because the bus, it come now, and the porters, yeh? They loading on the bags, and that – and she turn round to me, this Chink lady, Nip, whatever she were, and she go and give me a twenty note . . .! Couldn't hardly believe it: I says to her, oh no honestly (and I already thinking why I saying oh no honestly . . .? You needs it, don't you? She can afford it, can't she? So what you saying oh no honestly for then, you dozy bleeding mare?) – yeh and she say, no go on, take it: so I takes it. Very nice. Twenty quid? Near on three hours' work, that is. Blimey – I in the wrong game: I want to be a porter.

Yeh so then I gets myself back up the fifth floor and I got to get a right move on now on account of that gone and put me a bit behind – and so I dragging my trolley out the service room, checking on all of my supplies and that, all of the doings, and then I shoving it real fast down the corridor like I in some sort of a motor race or something . . . yeh and then, oh no . . . oh blimey . . . oh bloody hell . . .! I only gone and wheeled it right slap into him, didn't I? Never even see him come out the room! Yeh and just look at him: he standing there and rubbing at his arm where I gone and bang it. Got a smile on him, though. Still: I feeling just awful about all of this. In the normal way of it, I ever so careful.

'Oh my God I am so really really sorry, sir . . .! I never see you . . .! So sorry!'

'All right. Quite all right. Should have been looking where I was going.'

It could of been the voice what make me do it – lovely voice he got; he don't need no elocution lessons, that for bleeding sure – but it only when I hears it I takes a proper look at him: yeh and then I twigs what room it is what he just come out of. Who he is, right, is that really nice gentleman what I seen here on my very first day when Maria were telling me all about how everything work – and bloody hell: I gone and slammed right into him on that day, and all . . .!

'You must think I ever so clumsy . . .'

'Not a bit. Simply a very great pleasure to meet you again . . . Dolly. Remember you, of course, from . . . when was it? Couple of weeks ago? Something like that, I think. Dolly . . . charming name.'

He read it off of the badge what we all of us got to wear on our pinny, like.

'Thank you. That ever so nice of you. I remember you, of course. Surprised you remember me, though. So . . . you finished in your room now, has you sir? Do it, can I? Your wife, she not in there, is she?'

'Not my wife, as a matter of fact. Merely a lady friend. And no – not actually accompanying me on this particular trip, as it happens. Quite alone. Oh but look – thought's just occurred to me: now you're here, Dolly, it'll save me ringing down. There is actually something in the room that I've been meaning to mention. Would you mind stepping in for a moment, maybe, so I can . . .? Not too busy, are you . . .?'

'Nothing wrong, is there? What's wrong . . .?'

He hold open the door for me and I walks in and I having a good look about me: well . . . room wants making up, yeh well obviously – why I here, ain't it? But I don't know what else can be wrong with it. Can't see nothing – not at first sort of wossname, anyway. Yeh so then the bloke, right – he come in now and he shut the door after him, so I reckon he going to tell me. Yeh but he never. He don't say nothing: he just look at me. I were going to start thinking, oh blimey – this a bit creepy, ain't it? What he up to? Yeh but funny thing were, well . . . not creepy at all, you wanting the truth of it. Maybe because . . . I don't know . . . well he quite old, that maybe a part of what I were thinking – yeh and then there his face, right? It ever so soft and kind. Nothing weirdo about it – know what I saying? He weren't like no Jack Nicholson in one of them psycho parts what he always done, if you know what I meaning. I never thought he were going to like stick no knife in me, nor nothing. He ever so well dressed, just like he always are . . . beautiful suit he got on him, sort of grey with a bit of blue going on in the stripes of it . . . real nice shirt and tie and all, just sort of like that Cary Grant in all of them old movies when he looking real sort of smooth, you know? Yeh because I seen him about since the first time, this geezer, well course I have – he seem to stay here all of the time, far as I can make out. And I tell you something else and all: I were really liking the way what his hair – thick grey hair he got, I maybe said – yeh and, like I say, I were really liking the way it just covering the top of his ears, like, and you can just see it going over his collar round the back, look. He still weren't saying nothing though – which yeh, it do got to be a bit bleeding odd, no matter what way you want to be looking at it.

So I says to him: 'Yeh and . . .? What was it you were . . .? What wrong, then . . .?'

'Oh there's nothing wrong at all actually, Dolly. Merely a quite possibly wholly reprehensible little subterfuge on my part

I'm afraid – and I apologise for it. I just didn't really want to be out in the corridor when I put it to you, that's all.'

'Right. I get you. So there ain't nothing wrong in the room at all then – that right?'

'No there isn't. Nothing. Awfully sorry.'

'So what is it, then? What is it what you want to say to me? Only I really behind this morning and I still got the whole of this floor to do, see . . .'

'Oh please do forgive me – I really shouldn't be taking you from your duties. I am so very sorry. Quite unforgivable. Well look – I shall be brief then Dolly, shall I? And I shall quite understand if you . . . I mean, I don't wish you in any way to take this at all in the wrong way, as it were – and of course I shall perfectly understand, obviously, if you, er . . .'

'Yeh – excuse me . . . but what you on about . . .?'

'Well it's just this, Dolly. As I said, I'm here in London alone upon this particular occasion – doesn't happen that often – and I, er . . .well actually, I wondered whether . . . well look, you're probably most frightfully busy and all the rest of it . . . but I was wondering, in fact, whether you might consider having, well – dinner with me, maybe . . .? This evening, possibly . . .? But as I say, I shall of course quite understand if you, um . . .'

And I looks at him. Stares at him, really speaking. I just goggling up at him, you want me to be honest. Can't hardly believe what I hearing. I don't know what I thinking, what I feeling . . . no and I don't know what to say to him, neither.

'You what . . .? You – *serious* . . .?'

'Oh. Well yes of course – but . . .'

'You want *me* . . . to have, like – dinner. That what you saying? With *you*. This *evening* . . .?'

'Ah. Right. Yes. Well – bad idea, obviously. Very sorry. I do hope you don't think I'm, um . . . anyway. Very very sorry to have put you in this position, Dolly. To have embarrassed you in such a way. Don't know the first thing about you, after all. Your, er . . . position, and so forth. I can quite see that it was . . . anyway. Let's just forget it, shall we? Can we do that? I'll just get out of your way now, yes? Leave you to your, er . . . let you get on with the room, and so on. And, um . . . once more, Dolly – please let me say that I really am most terribly, um . . . All I can do is . . . well, I just very much hope that you can accept my apology, that's all . . .'

'You ever going to stop talking, or what . . .?'

'Oh. Sorry. Sorry. I was just . . .'

'What your name, anyway . . .?'

'Oh yes. Bad manners. Sorry. Should have said. Richard. Richard Cleveden. Sorry. Should have said.'

'Richard, ay . . .? Wish you'd stop saying sorry.'

'Sorry. Oh God . . .'

'Yeh well I likes it, Richard. Nice name.'

'Oh really? Well – so very pleased that you, um . . .'

'Yeh. Likes it a lot. So okay listen to me Richard, yeh? This dinner, all right? Where we going, then . . .?'

Livid. Is what I am. That will do – that will certainly do, yes, for the way I am feeling. Livid, mm – and with just about everyone, actually: every single person whom I have encountered, spoken to, during the last . . . well I don't know . . . God, it's only a day or two, can't be longer, since everything suddenly has started to . . . oh Jesus, Jesus: what in Christ's name now is actually happening to my life? All my plans. Why me? And why now?

299

Oh yes well . . . but look . . . I am rather exaggerating here, overstating the reach, I do see that: it's not as if there is chaos. It's
not as if Alexander . . . well it's not as if he is in decline, or
anything unspeakable of that sort: that will never happen – well
obviously: you just have to look at him, alongside all that I have
already achieved. But setbacks. There have been setbacks.
Severe. One in particular, perfectly clearly. And obstructions.
Interference of various kinds, and from various sources. And I
don't want it – any of that. And nor do I want what is boiling
within me – sometimes subsiding into merely acid, at other
times flaring strenuously into a hot white sheet of anger . . .
anger, yes, and considerable pain. Inner fury – don't want it,
you see? Vast resentment, and a need for vengeance . . .? No no
no – all that, it's not what I want to be filled with. Clutter too
– don't need any of that: stuff that muddies the clarity of my
one true single purpose. And I look at myself in the mirror.
Literally. Gaze at myself, I have no idea for how long. I know
that face, it's a good face, even beautiful (it certainly pleases) . . .
but still it seems so thoroughly strange to me. As if someone,
someone I used to know so well (we might have been sisters)
is staring blankly back at me: and who is she, I wonder? What
can she have become? My intimate insight into her character
and core, how certain are they now . . .? 'Hello, Amy,' I say: yes
– I actually do say it, right out loud . . . and the voice, even my
speaking voice, that too . . . it sounds to me quite perfectly alien.
And yet that is how I look, for God's sake – that is how I know
I look – and this is the voice I have always had, that cadence,
the inflexion . . . so why, then? Why do I feel . . . apart from me?
So very distanced. Divorced from all that I clung to: quite cut
off. No longer at one with all I am. I hate the complication –
because really, you know . . . all I want . . . all I've ever really

300

wanted for myself . . . well the truth of it is, I only ever wanted to be nice. Yes. That simple thing. Is all. Forever I've wanted to be that. The sort of person who, when my name might arise in the course of an idle conversation, some or other inconsequential chitchat, people would smile with fondness at a pleasant and abiding memory – a kindness I had bestowed upon them, a jokey aside that had made them just bubble up with spontaneous laughter: my cheery and generous disposition. They would say, 'Ah yes – *Amy*: she's nice, isn't she? So nice. Really lovely, Amy – always is.' And everyone around would nod then with enthusiasm – maybe even rush to contribute a sheaf of colourful examples that would gloriously illustrate, underline, my inalienable niceness.

So. What I am going to do . . . what I think I really have to do now is try to, um . . . I don't know . . . sort out each of the factors, all the things that are disturbing me, and then attempt to – individually – make some kind of sense of them, I suppose is the way. Yes: and then find solutions, quickly. But *individually* – that is the key to it. Because in the past – and certainly before I came to manage Alexander – a stingingly sharp and sudden awakening that was, when I had very rapidly to force myself to be ruthlessly efficient – yes but before that, I had been very prone to bludgeon all of my woes or anxieties into a shapeless and unmanageable lump, and then I would simply gaze up in awe and terror at its sheer and totally daunting face . . . or else just disconsolately gouge and chip at it with a lowering sense of inevitable hopelessness. It's just not the way, and I've learned that. Right: so let us please begin then, Amy, shall we, with . . . well I rather think the lesser things, yes. See if they can't be tidied up and resolved, in order to leave your mind . . . well – freer, yes? More receptive, so as to be capable of handling . . .

301

grappling with, more probably . . . oh – all of the rest of it: the serious and primary items on the agenda. So to begin with . . . Lizzie, then. Now this morning, when I was awoken – awoken, mark you – I was immediately aware that something was unusual. In the house, didn't know what. There thrummed around me a sort of tremor, a hum, hard to describe – something anyway unfamiliar. I was rather sure that I had heard Lizzie cry out – one single discordant note of . . . I don't know . . . anguish, was it? Not pain, not fear – that much I did divine. Not the start to the day that you wish for though, is it really? First thing in the morning: so bloody early. So I thought well I'd better go and see to it, I suppose – find out what silly crisis the girl is now convinced has befallen her – and so I dragged on a gown and went down the stairs to the hall . . . that's where I thought she must have been calling from, the hall. And yes indeed, there she was, just slumped into the chair there: head bowed, and her hair hanging forward to form that permanent – and, lately, really rather greasy – shield and blind, this ritual disguise of hers. And so I asked her, perfectly straightforwardly, what was wrong, what was troubling her – and Lizzie, oh so quite predictably, said to me nothing at all. But naturally. Didn't even look up – no well of course she didn't look up: might have given me an actual glimpse of her face then, mightn't she? No: just shook her head slowly from side to side, this intended to convey to me . . . well what, actually? What was I supposed to read into this exceedingly annoying and robotic gesture? Despair . . .? Disbelief . . .? Dread . . .? Depression . . .? Desperation . . .? Or is she just a self-absorbed teenager and downright *dumb* . . .? Oh Christ – how am I supposed to know? Not a mind reader, am I? All these *games* . . .! Why doesn't she simply *talk* to me, bloody girl . . .? And it was just at that moment, actually, that it

302

crossed my mind that it was I in fact who was supposed to be talking to her, wasn't it? Had said I would. So all right, then – might as well get all of that over and done with, is what I was thinking, while trying at the same time to prise out of her whatever it was this time that seemed to be driving her into a decline: kill two birds, as it were.

'Lizzie, my darling . . . please do try to tell me just what is wrong with you, yes? Because Mummy, she can't help you, can she? Not if you refuse to tell her exactly what's wrong . . .?'

Perfectly reasonable, I should have said: direct, though not without tenderness and concern. Yes well: no words. Not a syllable from Lizzie. All she did was flutter her hand towards the window.

'And just what are you attempting to signify, Lizzie? That you like the curtains? That you don't like the curtains? Could you not, please, just simply *speak* to me Lizzie – yes? Make it so much easier, wouldn't it? Because I want to talk to you in a minute, you see – various things. All right? And I really would appreciate it, my darling, if you could bring yourself to actually say something to me in return. All right . . .?'

And all I receive in return for that is a considerable increase in tempo with all of this perfectly infuriating head-shaking business, and again her arm is thrown out in the direction of the window. So all right then: humour the child. I walk across to the window. And look out of it. And now I think there must be escaping from me the same sort of noise as that broken exclamation that Lizzie had come out with just earlier, when she had woken me up. For here before me is a sight that I quite literally can hardly believe: girls. The girls. And oh yes I know I had been predicting just this exact same scenario to the obdurate Terence – but with Terence you have to overstate just simply

303

everything you say or else no portion of it at all has the slightest hope of even penetrating his consciousness. But this . . . this is . . . this is worse, oh God . . . this is *so* much worse than anything I had seriously imagined . . .! The garden . . . the garden . . . well it is full – just literally crammed full of them. So close together – they're jostling for their precious piece of ground. And there are more, even more of them beyond the gate and all over the pavement, look – in straggled little knots, way up the street and as far as the corner. All of them seem to be so very innocently happy . . . prattling excitedly and very visibly so utterly thrilled simply to be here – repeatedly putting their heads together for selfies, with twisted noses and stuck-out tongues, and then immediately reverting to photographing the house . . . and now as they catch the twitch of the curtains that my panicked fingers must just have caused, there rises high upon the air an eerie and collective scream, this subsiding only with reluctance into croaks of disappointment – practically sobs – and then just the contagion of a wistful murmur. Some of them, though – they seem to be far less girlish: quite short skirts, and so much make-up I'm amazed. I glance quite aimlessly about me, truly not knowing just what I should do. Uncertain and alarmed I most certainly am . . . though still I would be lying were I to deny that within me, and immediately, there now is welling the most tremendous pride and adoration for dear sweet Alexander – my son, the star – and all that I have achieved for him. I am actually feeling the girls' excitement . . . I am myself excited by all that must be surging through their glittering imaginations and pretty little bodies . . .!

Yes . . . but still . . . something must be done. I am quite surprised that there are no police . . . very surprised indeed that the meddling old bat Sylvia next door had not immediately seen

304

to all that side of things: God, that woman . . . she so must be stewing in envy. And here's another thought: what about this? Why aren't they all on their way to school, these girls . . .? That, clearly, had been Lizzie's intention . . . until she, what . . .? Swung open the door and was greeted by a shrill and terrifying shriek, this straight away arrested and supplanted by the lowing of let-down, a yelp of jealousy, and maybe then even the hiss and seething of severe resentment . . .? All these girls . . . neglecting school, hoodwinking their parents, ganging up with glee and following helplessly the pull of their hearts . . . and all of this simply because Alexander's home address had clearly and recently gone viral – very probably as a result of some sort of cyber-storming following his quite brief appearance on the BBC breakfast programme: we went to film it days ago, nearly a week, but it only went out this morning, I've just remembered. Well goodness: what a long way we have come. Yes . . . but in terms of the absolutely here and now . . . what exactly shall I do, I wonder . . .? Lizzie over there is simply moaning – no good to me at all – while Terence, no doubt, is still locked into that blissful oblivion that has come now to mark his entire existence upon this earth . . . yes but oh heavens . . .! What am I *thinking* . . .? Never mind all that . . .! What about *Alexander* . . .? He's the one I should be . . .! What is the time anyway . . .? Lord – it's actually quite late . . . how can I have overslept? Did I oversleep? I never oversleep. No well – after all the upset of last evening, I barely slept at all: must just have drifted off finally some time towards dawn. Oh dear – it's just . . . all this – it's just . . . well the trouble is, it's just *everything*, isn't it? Everything's . . . not quite right any more. And yes, I suppose I must admit to being just the slightest little bit, well . . . overwhelmed. By it all. Yes. Well . . . as I've already said to myself, and really quite sternly . . . never mind all that: just think of Alexander – he is obviously the most important factor here. And he'll be down soon, of course, so I just have to think quickly. Should I go up to him? Phone the school? Phone the police? Should he actually be seeing this, Alexander . . .? Do I want him to . . .? Always I have shielded him from the worst of what some of these girls will write in their letters (so very shocking – still it shocks me, and I'm reading it every day, all of their extraordinary excesses) . . . but if he actually comes to meet them en masse, and in person – goes out there, greeting the hordes – well what then might they actually *say* . . .? What then might they actually *do* . . .? Oh . . . so many questions! Let us just thank the Lord that his mother is here to protect him.

And then rather suddenly I was aware of . . . I don't know . . . there seemed to be some sort of a flurry of action just outside the house – voices were raised . . . yes, there was a shifting of volume, and then an erratic splicing of high-pitched and piteous squeals of not quite protest, but certainly discontent: whining against a perceived injustice – part of a young person's daily rediscovery, I suppose, that life indeed is so not fair. Because there were now police – word, clearly, had finally reached them, so at least I no longer had to worry about all of that side of things. Three of them, so far as I could make out, one a woman – well girl, seemingly hardly older than this mass of largely prepubescent children she was attempting to chivvy away and out through the gate, her arms stretched wide to either side of her, as if to gather geese, or corner a startled calf. I was squinting through the window in such a way that I might not be seen, so although I was hardly getting the whole, um – what do they say? Big picture, whatever, I still could see that the sight of police had clearly rather rattled many of the more tender of

306

them (thoughts of consequences at home and school suddenly looming large, conceivably) – but still there seemed to be dozens loose and milling on the pavement: I suppose it's perfectly legal to stand on the pavement, but not on private property, is that it . . .? If such a thing is what you are inclined to do with your time.

Then there was the doorbell – the policewoman and one of the others. Both were trussed up in those very ghastly stiff and bright yellow, what are they . . .? High-viz, is it, or something, jackets, jerkins . . . and that poor young woman was positively waddling, though she wasn't really *that* much overweight, under the burden of all the rather menacing-looking equipment that was loaded about her waist and hips, even more of it bulging from pockets and pouches. Some sort of radio type thing quite close to her chin was crackling and spitting incomprehensibly, rather in a manner reminiscent, it occurred to me, of those perfectly ludicrous staff announcements they pointlessly and constantly put out over a supermarket tannoy. But before I had opened the door, I quickly ran up the stairs in order to head off Alexander: didn't somehow really want him to be a party to this. As ever, he didn't ask questions, didn't demur – just smiled at me happily, and quietly returned to his room. Would that Lizzie could bring herself to be anything approaching so pleasant and amenable: wouldn't that alone make my life a very great deal easier?

'I expect you get a lot of this sort of thing, do you, madam? Quite used to it, I expect.'

I am looking at the policewoman as she is saying it – really quite a dumpy little thing she is, but clearly appreciating the situation, then: quite obviously she knows all about Alexander. A cheeky young grin on her face, though, and not good skin.

Rather as if this, all this, is really something of a . . . I don't know: lark, maybe – as if she were really quite joyously enthused by putting her whole heart and soul into thoroughly enjoying a good day out.

'Actually, officer, this has never happened before. Oh – one or two, you know, just lately, but nothing at all like this. I'm really quite shocked by it. I have always taken very great care to keep this address a secret. But somehow, obviously . . .'

'Oh really? I'm surprised it didn't get out before. Kids now, they can get anything. Find out anything.'

'Net,' said the policeman now, who was fingering a silver-framed and actually perfectly stunning black-and-white photograph of Alexander – Rankin, I think that one was: for *Vogue*, as I recall – and I told him to stop doing that.

'Well thank you both for clearing them all away. Most of them, anyway. How come you . . .? Were you, what – just passing . . .?'

'Had a call. Neighbour, I think – wasn't it the neighbour, Bob?'

'Neighbour,' said the policeman. You know . . . I don't think he had been fully wound up by whatever patient toymaker had in some or other factory created him.

'So what happens next?' I said – not really understanding my own question.

'Nothing more we can do. Of course, if there's any trouble – if one of them tries to break in . . .'

'Break in . . .! Lord – I hadn't even thought of that . . .'

'Oh you'd be surprised. Fans, they can be very determined. You remember, Bob, when Justin Bieber was at that hotel in Kensington . . .?'

'Bieber,' said the policeman, nodding solemnly.

'They were up the drainpipes, down the garage, in through the kitchen . . .'

'Yes well,' I said quite shortly, 'let us just hope that . . . anyway. Well look, officers – thank you very much indeed for your time. For all you've done, and everything. And now if you'll excuse me . . .'

And they went, eventually. I don't know if I imagined that the policewoman – not, obviously, her moronic colleague – seemed extremely inclined to linger. She maybe was hoping that Alexander suddenly would be walking down the stairs. Who's to say? Maybe why she took the call in the first place. She could quite easily be an ardent fan – though if she had wanted to meet him, surely she was to be disappointed: Alexander would stay in his room, of course he would, just as I had asked him to. And by the time I shut the door behind these police people – the remaining girls on the pavement, the older-looking ones, they regarded them sullenly: the thick wet blanket summarily thrown upon their party – Lizzie had vanished from sight to God knows where. Not sure if she still had been there while I had been talking to them, the police, didn't notice. I telephoned the school then and explained to the headmaster – quite a nice man, I suppose he is, though hardly, I've always thought, with the sort of accent that you might have imagined a headmaster ought to have – and of course he quite fully understood. But it can't – simply can't go on like this for a moment longer. I am today going to engage that tutor I spoke to – should really have done it immediately – and then see how soon I can get Alexander into Highgate: they did seem quite amenable, when I talked to them, as to dates, and so on. And then a further priority: estate agent. Put this place on the market straight away, and then start hunting. For something new, and maybe rather out of the way.

309

Hotel in the meantime, I suppose: nothing too grand, but certainly somewhere that befits Alexander's position, and affords us both a degree of comfort. Oh Lord . . . so very much to attend to . . . and all on my shoulders. Yes well: I expected that. And I can do it. Because look: it must be done – so who else? But first – before all that – I'll quickly pop upstairs and talk to Alexander, explain, without going into too much detail, the current situation . . . and after that, yes . . . I think I'm just going to pay a little visit to my dear next-door neighbour, Sylvia: get to the bottom of all of this Lizzie nonsense – see what in effect is going on, and what business she actually imagines it can be of hers.

So I did that, saw to my sweet Alexander, and yes of course he was quite perfectly happy to hear that he wasn't going to school today – oh my goodness, he can be such a little imp! – and I was just about to step out of the back door (didn't at all want to confront all those beastly little girls on the pavement – I actually was finding their continued presence really quite menacing, by now) – when I had a sudden brainwave: before I speak to Sylvia, before I speak – if ever that day would come – to Lizzie, why don't I try to get something out of Sophie . . .? About whatever it is that might in fact be troubling the girl. Sophie being the nearest that Lizzie would appear to have to an actual friend, though I don't think for a moment that the two of them are particularly close, or anything: Sophie, she's really quite a dynamic sort of a girl, bit of a beauty, very outgoing – Sophie, you see, she has a life to lead, so I can't quite imagine why she has any time at all for Lizzie, really. Anyway. Now what is the time . . .? Yes, not quite school time yet, so I might just have a chance of catching her . . . let's try, anyway . . . okay, then . . . well it's ringing . . . it's ringing, anyway . . . and yes! Amazing! She has actually answered: not for once tweeting,

310

then, or whatever it is they do. She didn't want to talk, of course
– these young people, they never ever do. Said she was in a rush
for school, said I was 'breaking up' (such an old and very silly
lie, that one) . . . but I was extremely persistent, as she must
know I can be, and eventually managed to stop her hanging up
immediately by promising her that if she did, I would continue
to phone her every single minute of the day and night . . . and
then I did prise out of her one or two grudging and fairly inar-
ticulate and stilted sentences, along with a great deal more that
I could make no sense of whatever because it . . . all of it . . .
seemed to be centred around, well – technology, if you can actually believe that for a single moment.

It turns out that Lizzie . . . oh look, I'm actually fairly hopeless, really quite bad with all of this. I'm only versed in, well
– all I have to use a computer, phone, whatever . . . for. So I was
scribbling down words as the girl continued rather vacuously
to prattle to me . . . but it seems, if I got all of this right, that
Lizzie, well, she does not Skype – well yes all right, I do know
what Skype is . . . and she doesn't do Twitter and I think 'Tinder'
is what Sophie said then (she wouldn't mention 'sexting', of
course, and nor should I have expected her to) and Instant-
something, pretty sure, and Snapshot, Mylol – had to get her to
spell that one, no idea what it means or might stand for . . . yes
and so basically, because all the other girls and, maybe more
tellingly, boys . . . because they do all of these things, it shows
to them – is what she said, is what Sophie said to me – that Lizzie
has no FOMO, is what she was saying to me, this girl. I see, I
said: and tell me, Sophie: this FOMO – and already she had
delighted in telling the old crone to whom she was speaking
that that is how you spell it – it's not a *detergent*, I am assuming . . .?
Acronym, it transpires: fear of missing out – being omitted, and

missing everything . . . and as a consequence of this, well . . . she is omitted, you see, and misses everything. Ignored. The modern equivalent, I can only think, of being a social outcast. Sent to Coventry. Pariah, sort of thing. Apparently the only time that communication is made with Lizzie – and I was very angry indeed when I heard this – is by way of cyberbullying, because we all well know how very sickeningly cruel that is: how young people can be to one another. And then Sophie said that she really had to go . . . but not before she told me that there was this one time recently when she had been trying to get Lizzie to lighten up, okay, and so she had said to her YOLO. And I said to Sophie, YOLO . . .? What in God's name is YOLO . . .? And again she spelled it out for me, or I wouldn't have had a clue. Stands, apparently, for You Only Live Once. Which is a truism, yes – but so what, exactly? I said to Sophie, I hardly think that Lizzie imagines she is going to live *twice* – what, like in that silly James Bond film? Don't quite think so. But Sophie told me I didn't understand – which must by then, I suppose, have been rather startlingly obvious: YOLO, she explained – and not that patiently – is what you say when you're about to do something new, something daring, something fun, okay? Okay, I said to her – okay yes: and . . .? Well apparently, when Sophie said it to Lizzie . . . Lizzie said . . . well Lizzie, if Sophie is to be believed . . . Lizzie said that she didn't care if she lived at all. That she actually . . . didn't want to. And as I simply stared at my phone, Sophie, she was telling me very hurriedly that she really really really had to go now – and so I quickly rushed in with, Yes but listen to me, Sophie: why? Why? Why would Lizzie say that . . .? Feel that . . .? Why would she . . .? And Sophie, she laughed. Don't *laugh*, I snapped at her, very strictly: why in God's name are you *laughing*, Sophie . . .? It's obvious, she said: it's so like *obvious* – just everyone knows *why*. Oh is that so, I said to her – and really very sternly, insufferable little girl: well I am her *mother*, all right? Understand me, Sophie? And I do *not* know – so tell me, please: immediately. And again she said that she just *so* had to go – but before she did, before she just hung up then, and cut me dead – she said to me one word. Just one word. And that word . . . was *Alexander*.

Which . . . well . . . well that just has to be nonsense. Doesn't it? Of course it does. Makes no sense whatever. Well just look at it: she is his *sister* – Lizzie is his elder *sister*, for God's sake: how on earth could she, of all people, be feeling . . . I don't know – resentment. Is that what is being inferred here? At his success? No. Oh no. I simply refuse to believe it. Not a word of it. My God – you would have to be a very small and deeply mean person indeed even to think of behaving in such a way . . . yes and whatever else she may be, Lizzie, with all of her very evident faults, still I simply could never even begin to credit my daughter with that. Oh well there you are: my fault for asking that idiot child Sophie in the first place. Because these teenagers, honestly – they just get worse and worse, and I'm not the only one who says it. I can't imagine really what can have got into them all, because we were never like that. Were we ever like that? No – I can't believe we were, not for a moment. Because these kids now, they either say nothing, or else they will come out with the most unutterable rubbish. Yes and all the while imagining that they are oh so *mature*, oh so very *wise* – implying with that awful rolling of the eyes, the sniggers, those maddening and elaborate demonstrations of such absolute *boredom*: simply this sheer and bloody wall-to-wall *rudeness* – that older people, proper people, people like me . . . that we know nothing, are incapable of the slightest understanding. Yes well – just let

313

them grow up a little bit, that's all – then they'll see it for themselves. Then they will come to experience just what it's truly like, what it's actually about, being a responsible adult in this, oh . . . in this awful bloody world. Yes. So anyway . . . I think I will, now . . . go to see Sylvia. She, at least – if she is actually and genuinely aware of anything relevant at all, which is something I severely doubt (Sylvia not being someone, I shouldn't have said, who is possessed of any insight at all) – yes but at least she will not babble at me inanities on the level of that perfectly ridiculous Sophie girl. So I will, then – I'll see her, Sylvia. Can't harm: just hear what she has to say.

'Amy . . .' said Sylvia at the door. '*Quelle surprise* . . .'

'Hello, Sylvia. Is this a terribly bad moment . . .? I just . . .'

'Come in. Come in. *Entrez*. You'll have to excuse everything . . .'

'Oh don't be so silly, Sylvia. Your house is always perfect.'

'If in only a very unstylish way, I suppose. I haven't yet got to the hoovering . . .'

'Oh well I'm sure I shall be able to cope with that . . .'

'Will you be staying? Do you want tea?'

'No, I . . . in here, should I go? This room, yes? I don't want to take up too much of your time, or anything. So no tea, Sylvia I think – no, thank you.'

'I see that most of them have gone, then. Stupid girls . . .'

'Yes. It was you, presumably? Phoned the police . . .?'

'Are you quite sure you won't take tea? It was, yes. Stupid girls.'

'I don't think they mean any harm, or anything . . . They just love him, that's all.'

'Stupid girls. Do sit, won't you Amy . . .? So, then – *une tasse de thé*. Yes? No?'

'Well . . . some tea would be quite nice actually, Sylvia. Thank

314

you. I haven't even had any breakfast, now I come to think of it. It's been a bit of a morning . . .'

'I could do you an egg . . .'

'Oh good heavens no, Sylvia . . .! I didn't mean . . . no no. Let's just talk, shall we? It's just what you, er . . . well, it's actually about what you said to Terence, you know . . .?'

'Ah, Terence. How is he? Poor man.'

'Poor man . . .? Why on earth did you say that? What a perfectly extraordinary thing to say! Why should you imagine that Terence is a "poor man", Sylvia . . .?'

'I'll make the tea. Are you happy sitting there? Or would you prefer the sofa?'

'Answer me, Sylvia. What is "poor" about Terence?'

'Well . . . just all he has to cope with, I suppose . . .'

'Oh *really* . . .? All he has to *cope* with . . .?'

'Mm. Can't be easy. I have Earl Grey. Would you like Earl Grey . . .?'

'Sylvia . . .'

'Or just the ordinary? I have both, so it doesn't matter to me remotely.'

'Look – let's just forget about the tea, shall we? Come here, Sylvia. Sit down. Let's just have a little talk, all right?'

'Very well. We're to talk about Terence, are we . . .?'

'No, Sylvia – no. I'm here to ask you what Lizzie has been saying to you.'

'Lizzie, ah yes. Not a happy girl. Not happy at all.'

'Why do you say that?'

'Well because it's true. Why, Amy – do *you* think that Lizzie is happy . . .?'

'I – I don't know *what* she is. Young girl, isn't she? They all behave so . . .'

315

'Well she hasn't spoken to me. Not really. Not as such. It is simply the impression I receive. The way she walks. The way she . . .'

'What? The way she what . . .?'

'The way she never smiles. It's sad. Don't you think it sad, Amy?'

'I don't know why she's like that. Alexander – he's never like that.'

'Mm. Well it's Alexander, of course, who in all probability is at the root of the problem. Though of course he'll be having problems of his own . . .'

'What on earth are you *saying*, Sylvia . . .? What absolute and total *nonsense* . . .! What problems could *Alexander* possibly have? He's sailing on top of the world . . .!'

'At the moment, that would appear to be true. What with this film role and everything, on top of all the rest of it, yes of course. But what then? You must have considered it, Amy. What when some other pretty little boy comes along to take his place? Because it's the way of it, isn't it? Fashion. It inevitably is what will happen, because it just *has* to. Always something new – that's what fashion is, as I well remember from the sixties. Whole point of it. And what is this film, by the way, Amy? That we've all been hearing so very much about . . .?'

'We, um – there aren't any details. Not yet.'

'Really? How odd. I mean – I know absolutely nothing, obviously, about the film industry, but I would have thought that by now you would be talking about, ooh – all sorts of interesting things. What part is he playing?'

'Look – could we please get back to the . . . oh . . . oh . . . it's no use. Is it? No use talking. Pointless. You know as much as Sophie, and that is precisely nothing. I'm sorry I came, Sylvia.

Wasted both our time. Foolish of me. Don't know what I was thinking. I'll go now.'

'Well – if you like. Who is Sophie? Not sure I know a Sophie. . . Anyway, Amy – I'm sure you have a great deal to be getting on with . . .'

'Well I do, actually. You wouldn't believe . . .'

'Mm. What with tending to three broken people. Three ruined lives. Four, if you count yourself, of course . . .'

'Broken . . . *people* . . .?! Sylvia – can you truly be quite as mad as you so very frequently appear? Oh – I understand you, Sylvia: I understand you only too well. What you can't stand . . . what you simply cannot bear . . . oh . . .! You, you're just so completely consumed with jealousy – you're so very bitter that your time, your "moment", if ever you had one, is now just so completely *over*, and you cannot bear the success of others. Warped. You are warped, Sylvia. Do you know that? You talk about broken people – Christ, Sylvia . . . just take a look at yourself, some time, why don't you? You want broken? Jesus – you, you're in *pieces*. . .! And Alexander, my Alexander . . . is a *star* . . .!'

'For now. And my, don't we seem to be getting a lot off our chest this morning . . .? But listen to me: what about the other two members of your family, Amy? Do you remember them? Do you ever look at them, at all? Think of how they might be feeling? Are you really as selfish as that? I mean I knew you were selfish – I have always known how very terribly selfish you are, Amy . . . but can you *really* be so selfish as that? Not to say blind . . .'

'Sylvia. I am leaving now. You have been extremely insulting, and . . .'

'*I* have been insulting . . .?! You think it is *I* who has been insulting?! Oh my dear Amy . . .!'

317

'Yes I do – and I do not wish to speak to you for a moment longer. All right? Because basically, Sylvia, all you are is a complete and utter *idiot* . . .!'

'I see. Well there we have it. *C'est ça*. But before you go: who is this Sophie? And what about tea . . .?'

'Mad. I actually do think you are *mad*, you know that? Christ – I hope you choke to death on your fucking *tea*, Sylvia – you crazy old bat . . .!'

'Well: that's very nice. Very nice, I must say. To hear that in my own house. But then this is the *real* Amy, isn't it? Oh yes – it's the *real* Amy that we're seeing now . . . and it really is, isn't it? Absolutely *horrible*. Oh yes – none of us likes it, no one can frankly abide it . . . and least of all *you*, Amy . . .!'

She was speaking perfectly implacably. A steady, and very smug tone, as if to . . . I don't know, I don't know – tease me, maybe? Test me, is probably rather more what I am meaning – and do you know . . . she was even faintly smiling, a twinkle of quite open contempt very evident in her eyes. And . . . looking back on it all later, rather later, when finally I was back in the sanctity of home, and had sort of pulled myself together with the help of quite a large slug of Terence's Scotch, something I practically never will think of drinking . . . I hardly could believe what had happened. What next I had done. Because . . . oh my God: did I *really* . . .? Can it truly be *possible* . . .? Oh yes indeed: I had simply hurled myself at her, I'm afraid. I remember the terror first of hearing this stark and jagged shriek, ugly in the air – realising then that it had just and hoarsely been torn out of me. I was aware of Sylvia's wide and startled eyes – all of that smugness and contempt now quite shattered into bits – while she was panicked and flinching as I just launched myself at her with my two hands hovering up high, and forming so very dangerous claws . . . and my teeth, my teeth – they must have been quite horribly bared, because I could feel the hardness of my lips dragged so far back from them in an aching contortion of sheer and utter fury: all of me was molten, quite ecstatically elastic, with the release of this avalanche of pent-up suffocation, this glorious and spectacularly uncontrolled eruption of all that had been filling me right up to the edge . . . oh yes, but now it had burst so very cataclysmically, I was actually – from somewhere black and deep, swimming behind the crimson mist – seriously fearing for Sylvia's life. She cried out once, stepping backwards just a moment too late to have any hope at all of deflecting the full and furious force of me, and we both of us careered back and over, just as if we had impacted into a weighty collision of sandbags – then were sprawling askew and all across the length of that quite perfectly dreadful sofa: even at that very appalling moment, still I was wholly aware of the absurdity of it, in all its sheeny, damask, Dralon and ecru horror, these tiny tapestry cushions once just so, and now with the fringes of them maddeningly caught up in my face and eyes. And then as I scrambled to get a good and tight hold of this very beastly woman's throat, I was aware with a jolt of something cracking: not her neck, but some little fiddly side table, can it have been – and that sent a clustered collection of all her silly little figurines and knick-knacks flying about briefly before coming down hard, and many of them in splintered pieces – which, even in the state I was in, I cannot pretend didn't utterly delight me. It was then that nothing short of what I really am forced to describe as a bellow of rage – surprisingly dark and genuinely menacing – rose up from very deep within her, and she began quite suddenly to fight me back with frank and terrifying ferocity. The side of her hand had caught me once

319

and then again right across my cheekbone, and I felt its burn as I was tugging hard on her vile and tightly set hair – sticky and stiff in between my fingers, with the actual coarseness of a scourer. I somehow then was face down on the floor, my twisted nose and flattened cheek quite cold, and now sopping – I could see the flowers, disgusting dahlias, scattered out and away from the broken vase – and now the woman's very considerable weight was pressing down hard upon my spine as she grappled for my flailing hands, in a strong and shockingly determined effort to first subdue, and then utterly conquer me. And very immediately, it was absolutely no longer the life of Sylvia that was of the primary concern, here: if I could not somehow throw her off – yes, and very bloody soon – if I could not in some way manage to revolve my pinioned body so that at least one of my legs might just possibly be gaining even a modicum of leverage, then I really did think that here and now could very easily be the end of me. I bucked myself upwards, clawing at the sodden and garish Axminster with all of my strength, kept on bucking, up and up, as hard as I could possibly manage – I heaved against all of her seemingly unshiftable bulk … and only then did I hear from her a grunt, and was suddenly and blissfully aware of a shifting of this most terrible pressure that truly painfully was so very badly crushing my back. By now I was feeling I could just about crawl – and then I crouched, and was panting desperately – all the time kicking out quite wildly and blindly to the rear of me, sometimes connecting with a muffled and gratifying thud … and then, and then … and then I could wriggle, squirm myself free – and I staggered up and just dashed headlong for the hall without even thinking of glancing back – flung wide open the front door then, and left it clangingly ajar. And those bloody little girls who still very gormlessly were hanging about on the fucking pavement – Christ alone knows what they can have thought, or to what degree they were startled and hopefully scarred and traumatised for the rest of their futile little lives by my wild-eyed and tattered appearance – and even then I just knew that this very beautiful Gucci silk shirt was destined for the dustbin – as briefly I was wheeling about in aimless circles before I lurched back into my own front garden – and yes, at last and finally, to the sanctity of home. The sheer and near demented slam of me into the porch sent fluttering into the wind an immediate cascade of, oh . . . all these multi-coloured Post-its, with scrawled-on messages and hearts – and as if I wasn't in quite a bad enough state as it was, I nearly broke my bloody neck in the hall skidding quite giddily on one of quite a few of the furry teddies and so on that had been rammed through the letter box. One of my knuckles was bleeding with reluctance, and all of my head felt as if it were just one looming protuberant bulge, and somehow the colour of indigo. I sat down, panting – hot, and amazed.

In my office, now. Lizzie is gone – school, presumably. Terence, he isn't here – Christ knows where, and who can actually care? I really can't mind about that. Alexander, the love – he is perfectly fine, of course: perfectly happy. Opened his door just a smidgen, called out hello – solely to reassure him of my presence, really: make him feel safe, and at peace. Didn't actually show my face, because one of my cheeks is still rather flushed as a result of my recent and impossible encounter, and just a little swollen: I didn't wish that to in any way upset him. Some ice in muslin is helping it along, but all my bones are aching badly. So . . . I am in my office, yes . . . trying to think, and also . . . trying very hard not to. I have emailed the tutor, the new school, the estate agent. Each of the messages read quite

321

well, I considered – all quite perfectly calm, the writer clearly wholly in control . . . so very much more so than I had been feeling while composing them. And in my inbox . . . oh, so much nonsense, all of the usual . . . though I see that here is a message from an indie record label . . . and yes, I think I have heard of them, asking me if there is a reason why I have not responded to their previous email, and strongly urging a meeting 'to our mutual advantage', as they not just crudely but hideously phrase it. Well I am totally unaware of any previous email. Though I shall respond. Could be exactly the diversion we are seeking, now. Maybe here, then, is the future direction – a single . . . do they still make them, single records? Or maybe no . . . not a single . . . straight into a debut album for Alexander . . . called, quite simply, *Alexander* . . . a perfect black-and-white close-up of his beautiful face . . . we could maybe get Bailey to do it: Bailey, I think I'm right in saying, being one of the very few photographers who so far hasn't . . . and then, I suppose quite inevitably, utter stardom, and all of the attendant mania. Which I am sure we both can cope with, once we have all of the new and essential structure firmly in place. I wouldn't obviously actually ever say this to anyone, but I do have to confess that he isn't really that much of a singer – just a little reedy . . . but whenever did that matter? So yes, we can consider that, I suppose . . . I suppose we can . . . now that it has been made quite absolutely clear to me that he is not now, Alexander, in fact about to appear in a – *film* . . .!

And there: I am red with anger, I just can feel it. Livid: I am livid again. Because all of that bottled-up *hate* . . . oh God – all of that *violence* that I had so completely unthinkingly unleashed, inflicted upon the simpering idiot Sylvia, well . . . I was aware, of course I was, that it was not she, not she at all – but Ouch who should be hurting. It is he who deserves just all of the pain. And I do hope that he does not for even an instant imagine that he has the remotest chance of escaping it, either. Oh no: that man . . . and yes, here comes all that I have been avoiding, shying away from, so terribly fearful of actually dealing with . . . that man . . . he crossed me, he deceived me, he utterly duped me – he . . . *used* me, yes, and perfectly repellantly. Oh God . . . when I think, when I remember just what I *did* for the odious little creep . . .! Well maybe he still fails to realise quite the calibre of the woman he is dealing with here: for I shall never forget – and as to forgiveness, oh well: you can just fuck all hope of that for simply ever. Vengeance will be mine, oh yes: because if that was good enough for the Lord, well then you can be perfectly sure that it's quite bloody fine by me, thank you very much.

Livid: I am livid again. And, I realise now, angry too with Terence, of course. No, that hasn't passed from me either. Because just sitting here as I am in my office, and idly glancing about me, soothing a rib where I feel sure there is going be bruising, if already I am not quite horribly black and blue . . . well it offends me, that's all – it deeply offends me, to know that he has been in here. Looking. Touching. Breathing in this air. My very most private place. A trespasser. And why was he . . .? How did he get in? Well – key, obviously: he must somehow have got hold of a key. All right, then: this is very easily remedied, anyway – I'll get the lock changed: simple. But still, though – the invasion, it has happened. Hasn't it? And why? Why was he in here . . .? He isn't interested in me, in what I do – he isn't remotely troubled by any of the intricacies of Alexander's career . . . so why was he? Well . . . I don't know . . . I simply don't know, and I suppose I never shall . . . but at least I can repay the intrusion: I shall go into his room. Why not? Not to seek out or steal something – it's Terence we're talking about here, and let us please not forget it: what of interest could there possibly be? No – and nor even to defile his space, for what would be the point of that? But just by the subtle shifting of, oh . . . I don't know . . . something or other. Looking. Touching. Breathing in his air. To make it quite clear to him simply that I have been there. A trespasser. Yes. And do you know . . .? I am going to do that now, yes I am. I am going to do that, right this very minute.

The room . . . his room . . . it does sort of smell of him – although I don't really know, couldn't quite define exactly what I can actually mean by that, because Terence, well . . . I should not really have said that he ever was in possession of any very significant . . . odour. Aroma. Aura, charisma, call it what you will . . . or even base essence. Though of course I am now just so far distanced from anything of this sort that I couldn't even tell you what aftershave or cologne he might be using, these days. He has his own cabinet in the bathroom, and it has not once occurred to me to open the door. That Givenchy . . . I think it was Givenchy, thing – what was it called . . .? Oh yes – Pour Homme, that's it, that's what it used to be . . . yes, he used repeatedly to make that very feeble joke about its translation being Poor Bloke: jolly good, well done Terence, ho ho ho, a veritable laugh a minute. Yes but of course that was a very long time ago indeed. In the days when I actually used to buy it for him myself. And wrap it up nicely – a little surprise gift: pre-history, then. And Terence, he is the sort of man who . . . well how can I put this . . .? All right: if I actually minded, or any-thing, and were to ask him outright whether or not it is still Givenchy Pour Homme that he uses, he would either look

324

slapped and frankly amazed and say to me well of *course* I do
– what: you haven't *noticed*? Aways have, always will – it's my
brand, don't you see . . .? Or else he is equally perfectly capable
of affecting quite the same expression of frank amazement and
then laugh at me with considerable indulgence: Givenchy Pour
Homme . . .? Oh my God, you just have to be *joking* . . .! Haven't
used that in simply *years*: not awfully observant, are we Amy?
So you see . . . well what I am probably meaning to say is that
Terence, he's utterly predictable, yes he is, but only up to a point
– because generally there will always be a stark alternative to
what you imagine his reaction so very easily could be. There
are no shades in between, however: with Terence, it is much like
flipping a coin – it is never going to land upon its rim.

So I sit in his Eames Lobby Chair in a rather pleasing shade
of burgundy leather in front of his immaculate desk – knowing
that this is an Eames Lobby Chair because when he really quite
recently acquired it, he told and told and told me that it was. It
isn't uncomfortable, I have to say – I never before have sat in it,
obviously. But . . . I am wondering now . . . what actually do I
imagine I am doing in here . . .? I lack all curiosity – and this is
really the point, I think: I just simply so don't *care* what is in this
room, nor what the man gets up to in here. Well – his work, very
largely, I suppose . . . if he still does that, work: he certainly
hasn't mentioned it lately: maybe he foresees a lifetime of lei-
sure, relaxing into Alexander's income . . .? Yes well – he can
rather think again about that. Oh Jesus, you know . . . it is still
quite early in the morning, and already this has developed into
such a very strange day . . . yes, and I am doing such wholly
uncharacteristic things: look at me earlier – look at me now. I
feel . . . thrown. Thrown, yes – that merely I am reacting to circumstance. Outside influences. And in a way, of course, I hope

it is just that – that that's all it is, you know? And that I am not going . . .well, just a little bit crazy. There can't be any of that . . . I just must keep a very firm check on myself – I must be in control, I must be – well I have to be: for Alexander's sake. Oh . . . I don't know . . . I'm anyway going to go now: this is stupid. Can't go on staring at Terence's colour-coordinated files, his state-of-the-art speakers, this Campbell's soup tin jammed full of red sharpened pencils – and when in Christ's name does he ever use a pencil? Well he doesn't, of course – why they are all of uniform length and so perfectly bloody sharpened. What, however . . . is this . . .? A couple of pieces of paper, conspicuous only for not being part of a perfectly ordered stack – because really, you know, this entire quite ludicrous desktop has the air of having been very painstakingly arranged in advance of a photoshoot, assembled with care for a catalogue or feature extolling some sort of slickly aspirational, though actually utterly vacuous lifestyle.

Oh . . . it's not a piece of paper . . . it's a photo, in fact. The other one is – the other, that seems to be a letter. You don't much see them any more, handwritten letters . . . well *I* do, of course – oh God *I* do. They come in absolute droves for Alexander – I used to think it was just because I have been very careful with all our email addresses, and so on, but I do believe now that the actual creation of a letter is important to these girls: it maybe forms a sort of connection . . .? And although people tweet about Alexander just constantly, from the beginning I decided that we ourselves would maintain no direct input: remain aloof from it all, as it were. This was no shrewd strategy – I just didn't have the time or the know-how even to think about it, because I knew it would have to be done properly and regularly or not at all – but it had all worked out really rather well: a sort of glittering

326

and tantalising unattainability had come to surround him, which I think has worked to our considerable benefit. But now . . . now, everyone knows where we actually *live*, so the sooner we can get out of here the better: can't go on living through scenes like this morning. And these letters that all the girls send to this sort of *poste restante* I had the wit to set up in the very early days – well God, the time they must spend on them is extraordinary. All very touching, really. Like those Post-its in the porch, I suppose, and all the soft toys piled high in the hall . . . well, that is how I think I would look upon them, anyway, were I in a rather better mood, and if one of them, bloody teddies, hadn't nearly bloody killed me. And little drawings, they will often so lovingly include – gifts such as a keyring or a badge or something. Some of the things they write, though . . . well they really are quite shocking: I was astonished by the very first I read. Where do they even learn of such things . . .? Oh well: internet, of course. And parents – they just have no idea, do they? They just have no idea – what their little girls are up to, what they can be thinking. But I suppose it's natural . . . is it natural . . .? I don't know – but obviously I never let him see them, not any of those. Pictures too, of course – lots of photographs, have to be selfies, some of them semi-naked, oh dear dear, usually a name or some little message written on them, or a kiss, often the impression of a mouth, in lipstick.

And this . . . and this . . . this picture on Terence's desk . . . is, I can barely believe . . . Jesus Christ Almighty . . .! This is *one* of them . . .! I am . . . speechless. I simply just cannot . . .! So *that's* what he was up to in my office . . .! That's what he was after! Oh my God . . . that is just . . . that is just . . . that is just so perfectly . . . *disgusting* . . .! I never would have dreamt that Terence . . . that he would be . . . that he could even . . . well.

Well. That shows me, doesn't it? That just shows me how little I understand of him. Yes and the more I learn . . . the less I wish to. Never mind not knowing about his fucking aftershave – look at this, now . . .! This letter . . . what is it . . .? It is from someone called Scarlet . . . *Scarlet* . . .! And oh yes, I do actually remember this one, quite incredibly: this is one of the very worst. My inclination was to destroy it, along with many others . . . and then I thought, well – do I have the right, actually? Because it's a sort of archive really, isn't it? History in the making, maybe. And the picture . . . this picture is of a child . . . a very provocative and bare-breasted child, whose name is Linda. Yes. And, very clearly, this has appealed to Terence. Well . . . I don't know . . . I just don't know . . . what to think about this. I am stunned. I truly am: quite stunned. I never would have said that Terence possessed the power to stun me – but there: I am completely and utterly floored by this. So: another thing . . . yet another bloody filthy mess for Amy to knuckle down and deal with. Yes, but the thing I have to ask myself, though, is . . . do I mind . . .? Well do I? How much do I honestly actually care about this . . .? Before I think further, before I actually *do* anything, that, I think, is what I just must decide. And how much more of this stuff has he taken? Stolen from me? These drawers, the cabinets – they could be stuffed to bursting with titillating semi-pornography written by pubescent girls. And pictures. Which he will pore over. And then what? What then? And so this is what Terence has come to. Well . . . we had better find out then – just how far it has gone.

In this drawer . . . is nothing. Yellow legal pads, which I'm sure he never uses – simply heard from somewhere that creative people do. Old copies of *Architectural Digest* and *Wallpaper** in this one: don't know why he keeps them – they're all the same.

Every issue, from one year's end to the next – because I used once to flick quickly through them, can't for a moment imagine why – is largely identical and completely interchangeable. And . . . what's this . . .? A box, black box. And what might he keep secreted within a black wooden box, do we think? More photographs? Actual correspondence between himself and an infant inamorata? *Worse* . . .? Well let us see – let's just find out then, shall we? It's actually quite heavy – can't just be pictures, I don't think. And no it isn't . . . there's a sort of a velvet bag with a drawstring . . . and inside that is . . . feels like a . . . oh fucking Jesus . . . I do not believe it . . . I do not . . . I do not . . . I just do not believe this . . .! This must be the day when finally I shall lose my mind . . .! Because . . . it is . . . a gun. Black . . . pistol, it looks like . . . and it has that thing on it, on the handle part – that Nazi thing, what is it called . . .? I can't remember what it's called. Oh my God in heaven . . .! And suddenly, as I weigh the gun within both of my hands . . . all of it is back with me again: I am hot from the crimson mist: livid, I am livid – at just every single one of these horrible and destructive people who are ganging together to drive me mental . . .! Sylvia . . . Terence, of whom I now and so very brutally suddenly learn that he nurtures twin, dark and secret passions for both Lolita and illicit firearms . . . yes . . . yes, but most of all, the worst by far – the damager, the ultimate bad man: Willy Ouch. The man whom I hate, and shall never ever forgive: the man whom I absolutely know must be damaged in return. Well. So I'm going to take this. I'm going to take this away with me. Replace everything else, and quite precisely – the position of the Eames Lobby Chair, Scarlet's letter, Linda's photograph: all of these actions being the reverse of my original intention. He must not know, Terence, that I have ever been near: we cannot have so

329

much as a trace of suspicion of my presence in this room. The black wooden box is back in the drawer, in exactly its original position: everything looks the same. So I leave now. I leave. I am calm, and I am leaving. Taking with me the gun, the gun with the gold insignia on the handle, though I still can't remember what it's called . . . along with, oh – such thoughts, and surprising ideas. Somewhere else, though – in another, rather darker and inexpressibly disturbing chamber of my mind . . . I am faintly aware that I ought not really to be behaving like this: that this, all this . . . it isn't really me. And no, it shouldn't at all be to my liking, this: I should be struggling to deflect it . . . and yet apparently I am taken. Yes and even as I close the door behind me, I am saddened – because this is not something, you see, that I ever wanted for myself: the weight of having to be like this: to be filled right up to the very verge with just . . . everything. Because all I ever wanted to be . . . was nice. You see? Swastika . . . that's what it's called.

CHAPTER EIGHT

WAITING FOR
THE MAGICAL HOUR

Still dark. The very next morning, when I practically ran away from home (that's how it felt – and what a true and head-spinningly magnificent feeling that was, I can tell you – felt so young, felt just dangerous enough, and I was charged to the verge of explosion with an uncut and beautifully boyish lust, thrilling in itself, as I was hugging to my heart this one big secret venture) . . . yes and I only realised as I closed the front door as softly as I had the patience to be bothered with, that still the sun had yet to rise. When was the last time that had happened, I'd like to know. Christ – can't even remember the last time I was *returning* at so unthinkable an hour, reeling and gaga, following a roaring and gaudy night on what I so very much adored to call the toot. And even that early in the morning – can't have been six yet – there were hanging around on the pavement a few young girls in the cold and yellow light of a street lamp, shivering in inadequate clothing, their faces quite gorgeously tarted up: obviously young and generally tiny, but no less exciting for that. In the old days, I would have been on to them, it just has to be faced. But today, today . . . ooh, sod all of that, sod just anything – because I just had to get back to K.T: my K.T, and her studio flat . . . can't imagine how last evening I ever dragged myself out of the door . . . and already the essence of her was flowing so hotly, bubbling up in my veins. Oh Christ . . . finally – a life force: that necessary, thudding and so frighteningly pervasive a thing. Nothing like it for letting you know – telling you straight to your face with quite shocking energy and the wagging of a cautionary finger, just how very worryingly close to dying you had come. Within, I mean: all hope, closed down. And before I had left her, K.T, after that actually miraculous, thoroughly alcoholic, and practically delirious afternoon – and then after, when at last she had taken me home . . . before I finally left her, peeled myself away from her with pain, she had whispered almost as if the thought had just come into her head that the following day she did not have to work. I nodded, and didn't believe her. Because what she meant was . . . well this is what I am absolutely sure she was meaning: that she wanted more, more of this, a great deal more of all that we had, all that we were sharing, and so therefore tomorrow . . . well tomorrow – work could just go and fuck itself. Because . . . unless I truly know nothing any more, and there is no way at all that that can be true . . . we had become ignited. Lit, yes – a thing I had hardly hoped for. Hadn't dared even to think about. And life now, you know . . . it has suddenly spun me. Twenty-four hours ago, I was a desperate and laughable idiot (I cringe away from the thought, the memory of all my contortions) who was besotted with some or other thing called Portia – so therefore deranged – and coming so very dangerously close to being arrested and charged with her physical assault.

Now . . . well now, I am back in love with my very rescuer, the woman who has taken me away from all of that, the woman

whom I never even for a moment have ceased to adore . . . and yet the daily, hourly memories of her, over how many years, only served to leave me burnt. Well of course they say it, don't they? There's a saying: 'What a difference a day makes.' Is that a song, or something? Bit of a lyric? Or just a trite old adage? Sort of thing anyway I've never really had the time for – yes because look at it: in life, one bloody day is pretty much like any other, isn't it? Same old thing. Whole point: why we're all just sick to death. But just as tragedy can strike in an instant (no one leaves his home in the morning expecting to be hit by a bus) so then, very mercifully, can something else entirely. Winning the lottery – that, I suppose, would be the undreamt-of instant that most people will crave. But it's nothing, that. Not really. All that can mean is that you're the same old bugger, with added cash: all ready and primed to make a world-class fool of yourself. Love . . . real love . . . there is the true transformation. And I hadn't actually fallen into it, of course, because already I was right up to my neck in it – yes and have been for just about ever . . . since first I had met K.T. Simply now it is gloriously undammed, the river of love, and no longer do I feel mauled, and bit by vicious teeth. Love laps up and into me now, and so richly, with such lavish indulgence: I am warm, and kissed all over. Being with her . . . just to be with my own K.T . . . oh – it's wonderful, so wonderful: simply no other word for it. And yes, people say that – I know, I know . . . people in love, they say and say it, don't they? Their eyes all a-dazzle, as they constantly and genuinely irrepressibly will continue to tell you, oh . . . all of this sort of nonsense, seemingly pap, until frankly you need to just slap them, and beg for the bliss of silence. Yes and the reason for that is because you are an outsider, you see: it's the way of it. You cannot know, you cannot even hope to

333

understand remotely any of what a lover is meaning, feeling, nor all that he is relentlessly, compulsively trying to convey to you from within the shudder of a rapturous cocoon. No . . . you simply cannot know what it's like, nor how it is. Well then let me spell it out . . . it's like this, you see: this is how it is:

'Christ . . . oh my Christ . . . oh *Jesus*, K.T . . . that was just . . .!'

'I know.'

She leant across the bed then, her lips lightly brushing my forehead, just that little touch of warmth setting me ablaze. I heard my gasp as her breasts were tumbling into me. The sweat that glistened just stickily within the hollow of her collar bone, it smelt so sweet. The whole of her body was utterly hairless, a thing I love, and so much more than smooth – sheeny, and even polished, its softness beneath the hover of my tentative fingers so utterly yielding, and at once alarming. Then I could study that perfectly wondrous sweep, the length of her spine, the notching of each of her vertebrae, as she turned aside and was scrabbling about among all of her bedside clutter, I just knew for a cigarette: scraped alive this turquoise plastic lighter – sucked in smoke, so greedily.

'I'm surprised that you have a . . .'

'I know. I terribly want this quite amazing Dupont. Gunmetal. Until then, anything'll do, really.'

'Yes, but of you I would have thought . . .'

'Yeh – well I did go through a Swan Vestas phase. For the box, obviously. But they rattle. In your bag. They rattle. Annoying. Tom, shall I make us some . . .?'

'Not really hungry. Are you? I wouldn't mind a, um . . .'

'Is it too early for a . . .?'

'Christ, K.T – I would have said so, but . . .'

'Well champagne, then – that doesn't really count, does it?'

The fridge – Westinghouse, stainless steel, tall and double-doored, with a water dispenser and some sort of a green electronic screen. And I somehow had registered even last evening, from amidst the shadowy, then quite hurtfully jagged perspectives that cast such strange and menacing shapes, and then were invasively piercing my quite staggering drunkenness . . . that this fridge, it was pretty much jammed with it, champagne. Clicquot, the whole lot: a drink for lovers – I see it like that, because here is a drink that we used to drink. So . . . a gift? Left over from one hell of a party? Does she drink it on her own? With someone else? And who would that be? And how is the sex between them? Better than with me? Yes because even from within the tremor of those bending and alcoholic distortions, the blur of fragmented imaginings, these are the tainted questions that had immediately assailed me. And now . . .? Doesn't matter. Now . . .? Couldn't care. She's with me, you see. I just know that she is. It all starts here. Again. The past . . . is over. It's the way of the past: it's absolutely how it goes. All I have to do . . . I've just got to get her to . . . well: she just has to say so. That's all.

'I'm so-o-o lazy . . . too lazy to move . . .'

'I'll get it if you like, K.T. And shall I do us a bit of . . .?'

'Gets in the bed. All the crumbs. I'll fix us some eggs, or something. Later on.'

'K.T . . .'

'I know.'

'I haven't said anything . . .'

'I know.'

'But you . . .? What I was going to . . .?'

'I do.'

'And so you . . . what do you think? Will you . . .?'

335

'Get the champagne, darling . . .'

'I will, K.T. I will. But do you . . .? Are you . . .?'

'Champagne first.'

'Okay. Okay, fine. But *do* you, K.T . . .? Think we could . . .?'

'I think I could . . . drink a whole bottle of champagne. Oh *go*, Tom . . .!'

So I did. I did that. There's food too, in the fridge. Good stuff, naturally. Some proper foie gras – not goose, but still. Cheeses, a few, in greaseproof paper. What looks like a decent cut of breadcrumbed ham. Yogurt. Eggs. In the freezer, just a sack of peas, and vodka. Two martini glasses and a couple of Baccarat flutes. She is . . . an independent woman. She always was, of course . . . but here, clearly, is someone who lives her life the way she likes to. So how open would she be, I wonder . . . to a shift in that? Maybe, after some, or quite possibly a very great deal of champagne, she will tell me. But even as I was dealing with the cork, though – all I was thinking was that I had to, just had to get back to her: if soon I could not touch her, feel her – fill up both my hands with just all she has to offer . . . then I think I might just wither, diminish; either that, or simply disintegrate: here, and right now, all over the chequerboard floor . . . shattered splinters and hard particles, scattered in a glossily crimson pool of all my yielding parts.

I gathered all I could carry, and more or less cantered back to the bed – immediately struck and startled, then . . . simply gloating upon the form, the swell and curve of her, beneath a tangled sheet – that fabulous tousle of all her hair betraying only the peeking rudeness of her glinting, warm and gloriously rounded shoulder . . .! I nearly dropped the bottle: I nearly yelped out loud. I hurtled the Clicquot into an icy flute as she knelt up to take it: the sight of her body as the sheet just was clinging to those, oh – quite mind-numbingly arrogant breasts of hers, before it fell away . . . it brought me close to tears, and then a boiling desire. We drank and spilt the wine – set aside the glasses, and just anywhere, certainly to topple over and hiss out their resentment as the champagne set to seeping in, or ran away . . . and then we were rolling and clutching and so quite breathlessly consumed, truly an act of feasting as we hungrily devoured just everything we needed – and those great and wide black eyes in her reddened face were excitingly shocked as I rammed back with joy into the heaven and heat of the only place on earth where now I can truly any longer belong. It all was so . . . *so* just like the old days – and yet, very invigoratingly *new* . . .! That alone would make me dizzy.

And after . . . K.T, she said something quite wholly surprising:

'I'm sorry . . . he didn't get the . . .'

'What? Who? What are you . . .?'

'Alexander.'

'Oh. Him. Forgotten all about that. Doesn't matter. Probably good. Doesn't matter.'

'I just want you to know that it wasn't . . .'

'I know. Of course I know: nothing to do with you – I know that, K.T. Doesn't matter anyway. As I say. Look – never mind all that. Listen, K.T . . .'

'Let's just enjoy it. Can't we . . .? Don't have to speak . . .'

'I am. Enjoying it? Christ I am. I'm in heaven. I'm at *home* . . .'

'Not, though – are you?'

'Well . . .'

'You see, my darling Tom? It's the same old thing, isn't it? Here we are again, the two of us – doing what we always used to. And loving it, oh yes sure. But you, Tom – you're going to

337

go. Aren't you? Like you did last night. Like you always did. When you've had enough, when you've had everything you want, you're just going to get up and leave. It's that that broke me: it's that that I simply couldn't bear any more . . . not again. This, maybe . . . all this that we're doing, now . . . it's maybe, I don't know . . . maybe all a mistake . . .'

I turned to look at her. I well remembered that expression, how it used to flicker with hurt and uncertainty, fusing with all of the tenderness in the light of her beautiful face: the look, it is one of gentle resignation – indulgence, against a backdrop and the familiarity of despair. Her eyelids were half closed and heavy, simply with the weight of knowing who I am. And I said to her:

'No.'

She held my gaze for a good long time. And then she blinked.

'No . . .? What do you mean "no", Tom . . .?'

'I mean no, K.T – no I'm not going to leave. Unless you want me to. And actually – maybe not even then, if you're really asking me. Because I want to stay. I do. I need to. I mean it. Really mean it. This time. I do. It's us, K.T – it's us, just look at us, can't you? We were always, well – we were always just *meant*. Weren't we? Weren't we? You know we were – you know it's true, you've got to. Who else . . . what other two people have you ever met in the whole of your life, K.T, who just have so much . . . *style* . . .?'

My eyes, I think they must have been wide in my eagerness to impress her with all that had suddenly rushed up and into me, all that I was striving so desperately to even half adequately express. And those eyes of mine, maybe blazing . . . she held them, K.T, in the steadiness of her gaze.

'You do . . .? You really do . . .?'

338

I nodded at her then – yes, and with what felt like an unnerv-ingly ferocious vigour.

'For ever.'

She laughed, and kissed my cheek. She reached across me for her glass of champagne. Mine was rolling around the floor. She fumbled then in the packet for a cigarette.

'It is pretty ghastly, this thing . . .'

'Turquoise plastic: of course it is. Your only slip-up, K.T. The one disappointment.'

'I'm ashamed . . .'

'No you're not. It's not within you – and nor should it ever be. You know . . . I . . . love you, K.T. I really, really do. Always have. Always will. Simple as that, really . . .'

'Will you buy me a gunmetal Dupont lighter . . .? Love me enough for that . . .?'

'I will, K.T. I will. I do – of course I do. And you . . . will you stay with me now, and for the rest of my life?'

Her eyes were gleaming as very deliberately she exhaled a column of thin blue smoke.

'Will you . . .? Answer me, K.T, for the love of God. I mean it, K.T. Will you . . .?'

She eyed me sidelong, a finger flicking at the cigarette's tip.

'You mean it . . .? You really do mean it . . .?'

'K.T – just *look* at me, for Christ's sake . . .!'

'Well then I . . . will. Yes, Tom. I will . . .'

'You . . . will? You will? You really will, K.T . . .?'

'Oh *Christ* yes, Tom – I will I will I *will* . . .!'

And then she hugged me tight. We were laughing so appal-lingly uproariously, the two of us bonded into a mass, and rocking in each other's arms. As she kissed me repeatedly, I licked with hunger at the tears that were jolted out of her.

And so for all who simply cannot know what it's like, nor how it is . . . well then: it's like this, you see: this is how it is.

'Where you off to, then?'

'Told you Damien, didn't I? Why don't you never listen? Late shift, yeh? Remember I said?'

'Yeh but why you all got up like that, then?'

'Bloody hell. Maria – gel there, yeh? Birthday, ain't it? *Told* you, Damien . . .! She having a little bit of a drink and that, after we come off. Be nice.'

'Yeh? So, what – you going to be like late then, or what?'

'Don't know, do I? See how it go. Just make sure Kenny in bed by nine, all right? Don't go playing all of them stupid games with him into the bleeding night.'

'What about my tea?'

'There's a ready meal for the two of you. Pasta bake. Freezer. Got sausage in. Got to go – all right?'

'Yeh. Suppose so. All right.'

'Yeh and have a lovely *time*, Dolly, won't you? You going to say that to me, are you Damien? And don't go *working* too hard, will you Dolly, hey? You going to say any of that to me, are you? Nah – because you never.'

'I work and all you know, Dolly. Sometimes I reckon you forgetting that.'

'No, Damien – I not ever forgetting that, am I? On account of you never stops telling me it. Why don't you remind me we got a mortgage, while you about it. Might of slipped my mind, yeh? Anyway – I'm out of here.'

What I were wanting to say to him, bleeding pig, is that I

340

never had no shift at all in the hotel tonight – tonight, it one of my nights off. Not Maria's birthday neither – crap, all of that. I going up West, you want to know – up West, yeh . . . and with a older gentleman, all well dressed and with proper grown-up style what is going to take me out to dinner – real like dinner of an evening time – and only in one of them restaurants what's coming up all of the time in blogs and the magazines what I get, I just so can't believe. What I got on is a Jasper Conran at Debenhams black sort of maybe what they's calling a cocktail dress because it ain't no tea dress which has got flowers on and it not tea I going to, it dinner. It got sequin sleeves, and I never thought when I got it that I'd get to wear it ever on account of it ever so glitzy, but not too showy, I reckon – I not looking like some slag on the pull. It were on the very last day of the sale and there were only the one of them hanging on the rail there, and then I seen it were my size (10 now – I starved and puked myself back down to a 10) and it were ever so cheap, like less than a third of the original price, and so I just thought oh fuck it – I get it, yeh? And now I ever so glad I did because look at me, okay? I only going up West – I only going to Scott's for my dinner, which is where outside of it on them smoking tables what they got there that bleeding creepy Saatchi bloke gone and strangled lovely Nigella couple year back, and then he pick her nose, or something – how creepy can you get? But you sees all sorts coming and going in and out of it in the magazines, and all of the Hollywood set when they in London, they going there all of the time on account of it ever so expensive and if you want to smoke a fag or a posh cigar or something they got these tables outside of it where you can go and choke your wife, you want to – no, just kidding. George Clooney and Sandra Bullock and Scarlett Johansson and even Brad and Angelina . . .! Oh my God

341

– what if I goes and walks right bang into Brad and Angelina . . .?! Reckon I like die on the spot, you know? And I got black tights, they called midnight mink but they black tights basically, and a little red handbag what is Asos and I telling you it is so like Céline, and dead high heels which I not too used to so I got to go easy. And it only now in the taxi I putting on all of the slap – blusher, eye shadow, mascara and real red and shiny lippy, yeh? I looking pretty good, I says it myself. Haven't had no time to get nervous about it, nor nothing: I not crapping myself. Don't know what I going to do though, don't know how I going to handle it if the, I don't know – doorman or waiter or whoever go and get all right sort of sniffy with me, don't know what I going to do. Just got to see what'll happen. I wish I got in couple elocution lessons: only bleeding thing I can say good is How Now Brown Cow, and that not about to come up, is it?

So I paying the taxi – can't hardly believe what it costing me, ain't been in a taxi since I can't remember, can't hardly believe what he charging me, this bloke: maybe a cabby I want to be, then – they all of them pulling down film star money . . . yeh and so anyway I pays off the taxi and it were twenty-one quid something, you want me to tell you, and I only got two tenners and some bits on account of I never thought, did I? And I gives him the tenners and I says hang about, I only got bits, have to find them, and he say that okay, twenty's good, which nice of him, I suppose. It look ever so classy, Scott's do – and when I come up to all of the doings, there this geezer in all like a top hat and a coat with brass wossnames all down the front of it and he open the door and he kind of like salute me and I only just stop myself saluting him back – and I sure I seen him, this very bloke, in the pictures in my magazines when all of the stars is leaving. 'Good evening, madam,' is what he say to me:

'Welcome to Scott's.' Well blimey. I give my coat to the gel there – even the hall, whatever they calls it, it ever so lovely, and all sort of with what look like crystal twinkly lights and that. I pleased to be shot of that coat, you want to know, because it were spoiling the whole of my outfit, but I don't got a good coat, not nothing I really want – it only a mac what I got in Primark what look like a Burberry if you practically blind, but it ever so thin . . . yeh and the gel there what I give it to, she got beautiful hands and long sort of real dark red nails and I don't know if it just in my head but she sort of go all funny when she take it: don't reckon she ever touch a cheap coat before. Then there this bloke, ever so tall and with a suit and tie and everything and he say to me, 'A very good evening, madam. Mr Cleveden is at his table, and looking forward to the pleasure of your company: may I escort you?' And I go yeh go on then – but I thinking, how the bleeding hell he know that who I meeting? It like he got radar.

So I follows behind him, yeh – and I trying to do like a thousand things at once: I trying to do that walk like what the models on the catwalk do, yeh? Sort of with the top of me – it kind of like hard to describe it, but sort of with the top of me further back than what my hips and legs is, you get what I meaning, and then this long sort of loping, really – like a animal, and my face, it got to look real pissed off with just about everything – yeh but them heels, they well high you know? And if I goes and falls over with all these like people watching, then I decided I got to crawl off to the Ladies' and just top myself: end of. And also I wanting to have a good look about me – if Brad and Angelina's around here somewhere, I don't want to be missing them, do I? Yeh well I nearly done the journey, and I got to stop looking like an angry mare now because I got to the table and I want to be smiling all nice for my new gentleman friend, don't I? Only polite. And here he is now, look – he stood up for me, and he looking ever so hand-some for an old person. Lovely clothes he got on him, as like he always does. Cartier watch, he got – bit like Terry's. Last time, it were a Jaeger-LeWossname: blimey. The table – oh, it just lovely: sort of a snug little corner it is, and you can see the whole of the restaurant and this amazing sort of bar thing they got right bang in the middle of it – but it ain't a bar, not really, it really beautiful, and all of the people up on them stools all around, they not just knocking back beer like in a boozer or something – they eating: all of these silver like plates and towers of big pink seafood with bottles of bubbly in all of these shiny buckets. It only then I remember it famous for fish, this place – and that okay: I don't mind a nice bit of fish of an evening time. It then I get a fit of the shivers: I just can't *believe* I here . . .! I just can't *believe* I doing this . . .!

'Dolly, my dear. How very good it is of you to have come. You look quite perfectly delightful, if I may say so. Extremely beautiful. If it isn't actually illegal to compliment a lady, these days. Please do sit, won't you? There: all right . . .? Now – what, I wonder, can I get for you? Champagne, possibly? Glass of champagne? Something else?'

'Oh yeh, Richard – that'd be lovely. Yeh lovely – thanks ever so much.'

You hear what he said? He said I were beautiful: extremely beautiful. That what he said. And that he were complimenting a *lady* . . .

'So, Robert – a couple of glasses of the Laurent-Perrier, I think. Rosé, yes?'

'At once, Mr Cleveden. And I shall leave you with the menus.

344

Although for you, sir, I expect it will be your customary order . . .? We already have a particularly fine one waiting . . .'

'Ah, Robert – you know me too well. But you never can be sure though, can you? This might well be the evening when I surprise you! And so Dolly, my dear – I hope you are comfortable? Table to your liking? Have you been here before, I wonder?'

'No. No I never. I heard of it. But no. No I never. It ever so nice. Really really nice. And, like – from what that waiter were saying, you coming here a lot then, yeh?'

'A fair deal, I suppose. If I'm in town. When you get older, you know – you'll have to take my word for this, Dolly, young little thing such as yourself – but when you get older, your parameters, they tend to shrink rather, you know? There are three, maybe four – yes: four, I'd say, four restaurants that I seem to return to regularly. And why not, actually? That's what I say. I have my usual table, the welcome is warm . . . good grief, they even know what I'm going to order . . .! So why risk somewhere new? Very dull of me, I daresay, but there it is. Now then – have you an appetite, my dear? That's the question. I do so very much hope so, because the food here, I have to say, is really quite wonderful . . . but it's actually rather funny: although the fish and so on is clearly the thing . . . ah, Robert . . .! Wonderful, wonderful. There we are. Splendid, splendid. A toast then, Dolly . . .!'

'Lovely colour. Isn't it a lovely colour?'

'Very pretty indeed – though not nearly so pretty as you, if you'll permit me. May I propose a toast, then . . . to you. To Dolly. Welcome – and may you have everything in life that your heart desires.'

'Ha! Bit of a tall order that would be, Richard. Ooh – it's lovely. Ain't never had fizz like this before. Tickle your nose, don't it? The bubbles, like.'

You hear what he said? He said the champagne, yeh? It pretty, but it not nearly so pretty as what I am. That what he said. And he want me to have everything what my heart desire.

'So you harbour ambitions, do you Dolly? Things in life you aspire to?'

'Yeh. Yeh, you could say that. I want stuff, yeh. All the bleeding time, you want the truth of it. Sorry if I'm, like . . . oh my God . . .! Oh look, Richard – look at that! Blimey – look at that! That's that woman, ain't it? What's her name? It's that woman, sure it is . . .'

'Long sight isn't too great, I'm afraid. I'm anyway not really too up in all of this celebrity business. Is that what you mean? Somebody famous, is it? I'm told they do come here – I really wouldn't know. Doubt if I'd recognise the name even if you said it to me.'

'Oh yeh I know! I got it! It's that Carol Vorderman. Off of that programme she ain't on no more. Bloody hell . . . that Carol Vorderman sitting over there, having her dinner . . .! Bloody hell. She look lovely, don't she? Ever so glamorous. Beautiful eyes. Sorry, Richard – what was you saying? Was you saying something? Oh look . . . only I got to be honest with you, okay? You know I just ordinary. Yeh well, course you do – stick out a mile. You know what job I got. So being here, right . . .? It a thrill for me, you know? Can't describe. A right thrill – can't hardly get over it. I ain't never been nowhere like this in all of my life, you want to know – and I ever so grateful to you, Richard. Because this . . . all of this . . . well it part of what you was saying to me earlier, yeh? All of what I want. Yeh well – all this. What I want. Style. Real style, yeh? Well that's it. That's it, basically. What I want. What I always did. Oh look, Richard . . . you must think I'm so . . . I'm really sorry if I'm, like . . .'

346

'No apologies required, I do assure you. We can maybe have a bit of a chat about it all – a little later on, shall we? You never know – I might even be in a position to help, in some way. But why don't you glance at the menu in the meantime? Can't have you going hungry, can we? Oh yes – that's what I was saying, I remember now: mind like a sieve. Yes – you see, although Scott's is probably one of the two most famous fish restaurants in London, whenever I am here – and you will think this most frightfully absurd – but whenever I am here, I tend to order a steak. Well: I say *tend* to – I always do, actually. Is not that quite thoroughly perverse of me? I don't really know quite why I do it, but I do. Oh I'll happily enjoy a seafood starter, lobster generally – but when it comes to the main, well then invariably I plump for the fillet steak. That's what Robert meant – that's what he was alluding to, you see. Silly, really . . . but there you have it.'

'I reckon you should go for what you wanting. Reckon everyone should. Blimey . . . it do go on, don't it? Menu. All sorts here . . .'

'Anything I might help you with, Dolly? Suggestions, maybe?'

'Think I might have a bit of smoked salmon . . .'

'Sure? It's very good here, of course . . .'

'About the only thing I know what it is, you want the truth. Oysters I heard about, but they disgusting. What is a . . . don't know how to pronounce it . . . what is a . . . langoustine?'

'Rather large prawn. Taste is kind of prawn, slightly lobster. Talking of which – why not have a lobster cocktail? Sublime. That's what I'm having. That's what I always have, actually.'

'What – that a drink, is it?'

'No no. It's a whole small lobster, that has been grilled and diced. Bit of salad. Sauce. Really good.'

'Never had it, lobster. Do like prawns, though . . .'

'Well why not try something new, yes? I know I'm a fine one to talk – but after all: this evening, well – different, isn't it?'

'I should bloody say so. Ooh sorry – I keep on swearing like that, don't I? Never mean to – don't know why I does it. Habit. Got to stop it. Yeh okay, then – let's have a lobster cocktail. Why not?'

'Good girl – that's the spirit. And to follow . . .? Don't go by me, I implore you – I'm an absolute idiot to be having the steak, I know I am. But I am told that the Dover sole here is quite the best to be had. Plain grilled is probably the thing to go for . . . pan fried, if you prefer . . .'

'Never had. Is it . . . what is it?'

'Flatfish. Very delicate. Succulent.'

'Like plaice, is it?'

'Similar shape. Very much superior.'

'Yeh? Well I'll have a go at that then, if you says so.'

'Excellent. Now wine. We can happily stay with the pink bubbles, if you'd care to. Or maybe something white . . .?'

'Yeh. White. Or pink bubbles. Whatever. Oh look – I don't know, do I? Leave it to you Richard, yeh? Thank God you here, that's all. You wasn't here, I would of . . . I don't know . . . I would of run off by now, I reckon. Stupid thing to say, of course – on account of if you wasn't here, well then me – I wouldn't be nowhere near, would I?'

'Well I'm very pleased indeed that you haven't run off, Dolly. I honestly cannot recall a time when I have been privileged to dine with so very lovely and charming a person as yourself. Ah Robert – perfect timing! Two lobster cocktails, if you please. A grilled Dover sole for the lady – think you'll enjoy that more than meunière, Dolly – and possibly a few beans with that, do

348

we think? Spinach, conceivably? Bring both, Robert. Think that's best. And yes . . . for me, I am afraid, the usual. I know, I know – I am wholly incorrigible. The Meursault, of course . . . with the, um. Still got the . . .? Yes? Oh good. And then I'll have my Lynch-Bages, if it's still the 2000 . . .? It is? Perfect. Thank you, Robert. Excellent. Well that's that out of the way, then. So, Dolly – happy?'

'Yeh. Yeh I am. Very, as it happens. Thank you, Richard, yeh? Thank you.'

You hear what he said? He said I a very lovely and charming person. That what he said. And being with me, yeh? It a privilege.

'Ah good – so pleased the food has arrived promptly. Rather peckish, you know. Well then – here it is before you, Dolly: your lobster cocktail. Attractively done, isn't it? Wouldn't you say? They do that here – make everything look rather lovely. So let's just tuck in then, shall we? And do tell me what you think of the wine. To your liking?'

Well blimey: it all a bit much to take in, you want the honest truth. I don't mean take in like sort of through my mouth, you get what I saying: just looking at it all. Just, like – *being* here, yeh? Because when I got up this morning, yeh – when I fall out of bed and were moaning to myself oh Christ here it come, then: another bleeding day . . . well did I ever reckon I later on be in Scott's, with a like gentleman? And Carol Vorderman over there, look, having her dinner? It just go to show, don't it? You don't never know nothing about nothing what going to happen – not really speaking.

'Oh it lovely, Richard. Lobster, I meaning. It more like meaty than sort of fish, isn't it really? I like it ever so much. Wine and all. Don't never drink much wine, you want me to be honest. Not

349

much of a drinker all round, not me, not really. But this lovely. It don't cut you in half, like some what I had. So yeh I'm . . . Oh . . . my . . . *God* . . .! Oh . . . oh . . . Richard – look! I so like do not *believe* . . .! You see who just gone over to that table there . . .? Who she with . . .? You clock it, did you? Oh . . . my . . . *God* . . .!'

'Someone else, is it? Someone else famous, that it . . .?'

'Well it only Paris *Hilton*, that's all . . .! Can't get much more famous than that! And I just can't . . . I just can't *believe* I in the same room what Paris, oh my God – *Hilton* just walk into . . .! Who that she with . . .? And oh she got such fantastic *style*, that one, I always thought it. On the red carpet and at openings and the Oscars and all of that – always just this real and ladylike *style*, you know? Look at that dress – you see it Richard, does you? Could be Armani, what I reckon – dead simple, yeh? I pretty sure she not wearing nothing underneath of it. You can't get it all sort of smooth like that, not if you wearing anything underneath of it. Who that she with . . .? I never seen him in the magazines, nor nothing. Unknown admirer. New squeeze. I pleased. I pleased for her. Because them last two what she had, they was never right for her: could of told her that. Expect it'll be all over the papers and that in the morning – then we'll get to know who he is. And I were, like – *here* when it happen . . .! Oh my *God* . . .! Oh look, Richard – I so sorry if I being . . . it just that I'm so . . .! Can't hardly *talk* . . .!'

'Not a bit of it. I'm simply so very glad indeed that you are enjoying yourself, Dolly. Now then – drop more Meursault, possibly . . .? Do eat up though, won't you? Not lost your appetite in all the excitement, I hope . . .'

'You not . . . you not . . . *laughing* at me . . .?'

'Oh my good Lord *no*, Dolly . . .! How could you ever even think such a thing . . .?'

'Yeh well it just because I never knows, not really – not with people, like. And yeh – I can see how all this, all of this . . . all of what I just come out with, it must seem just so like . . . *stupid*, to someone such as yourself. But me, you see . . . well with me, Richard – I don't know why I saying it to you, because I ain't never told it to no one before – but in my life, see . . . it all I got. Them . . . celebrities, yeh? They, like – take me right out of it, you know? The chambermaiding, all what I got at home . . . when I reads and sees pictures of what they all of them up to, it make me feel like somebody else. Outside of it all. I not putting it right, I know I not putting it right . . . but just knowing about all of their doings, seeing them in all their lovely clothes, and that . . . it take me beyond. It like, just for a minute . . . I up in the stars. No . . . I not putting it right. It real difficult to explain . . .'

'Well now I find all of that extremely interesting, Dolly. I surmised as much in you – and I might just possibly be in a position to help. Do you remember I said so? A little earlier on? Well look, tell you what: you finish up your lobster – don't have to, of course – and then over the mains, we'll have a little chat, yes? During the course of which I shall not remotely object if you feel unable to drag away your attention from this young lady over there, whom you evidently hold in such high regard.'

'Paris *Hilton*. What – you never, like – *heard* of her . . .? Don't believe you. You must of. You kidding me . . .'

'Well I may have done: who's to say? I think you are immensely more attractive than Miss Hilton, and it is you in whom I am interested, Dolly. And I really do believe that you in turn might well be interested in what I have to say to you.'

You hear what he said? He said I immensely more attractive than what Paris Hilton are. That what he said. And it me what he interested in.

'Here we are, Dolly – that's a rather fine-looking sole, I'd say. Thank you so much, Robert. Off the bone we think, do we . . .? I think so, yes – would you, Robert? So much. And for me . . . well there, you see Dolly? My habitual fillet steak. Frites. Béarnaise. Ideal. And with typically perfect timing . . . the sommelier: splendid. And I shan't have to taste it, shall I? The claret. No I thought not – because you already will have done so, yes? Capital.'

While I were waiting for my fish to be, don't know – gutted, or whatever they does with it, I looks at his steak, and I goes, 'How Now Brown Cow', I don't know why I done it. And he laugh, Richard, and his eyes, they goes all crinkly. He says I said it beautiful. And yeh – I did say it good, I knowed I did. And that, it make me even more determined: I going to learn to talk proper, even if it bleeding kill me. Oh yeh and that fish, I got to say – it were just wonderful, you know? Never had nothing like it. Beautiful, it were, I really just got to say. And then he gets to talking, Richard . . . and I can't hardly believe what it is he got to say to me. I thinking back on all of it now, and still I can't hardly believe it. Because when we leaves the restaurant, right . . . we come here. This flat what he got, couple streets away. First thing I says to him: listen, if you got this here flat, Richard – and it ever so posh a place, all like full of antiques they got to be, and these dark brown pictures all in like big gold frames? – if you like got this lovely flat, okay, well why you go staying up the Marriott? He say: this place, it not exactly mine, but I gets the use of it. So how this all come up, right, is that after our dinner were done – and I had this amazing like jelly which were all looking like it were made of glass and had these different colour berries floating in it? – he say to me listen, Dolly: I got something to show you

– something what I like you to see. And it just around the corner, all right?

Carol Vorderman and Paris, they both gone by this time – I really were looking at Paris when she walk past me, really quite near, but she never look at me back. In and out so quick because she don't never eat nothing, Paris, that a known fact – also she be going on now to Boujis or Mahiki or Whisky Mist or whatever, should reckon, with her mystery lover, oh wow. Carol Vorderman, she eat, you only got to look at her, yeh but then she were there before us, weren't she? Anyway, they was ever so nice to us in the restaurant when we was going – and when we come out in the street – there's like all of these paparazzi . . .? And like, they all taking a million pictures? So I looks behind me and there this actor, ever so gorgeous, but I can't remember his bleeding name and it really annoying me, you know? He American, that I do know, with these like bad-boy eyebrows like what Colin Farrell got, but it ain't Colin Farrell who are Irish anyway, but he do a lot of American parts with a pretty crappy accent. And the doorman, yeh? Bloke in the top hat? Richard, he bung him a twenty, can't hardly believe it: blimey, it a doorman I want to be – they hauling down film star money.

Yeh . . . but what were I thinking, then? Ay? What were, like . . . going through my head? When Richard, he go to me he got this thing, yeh, what he want to show me, something he wanting me to see. Yeh and just around the corner. Well . . . you want the truth, I were right excited. Not ashamed to say it. I weren't thinking oh *yeah* . . . here it come, here it bloody come! Men, they all the same – and old men, they the worst, shouldn't wonder: what – I got to pay for my dinner now, that it? What he think I am? Slag, or something? Nah . . . nah . . . never was thinking none of any of that. I were thinking I were right pleased

353

he said it. I were grateful, I were that relieved – on account of the thought of just leaving here, all of it, this world what I been dreaming of and I never even seen, the thought of just leaving him, Richard, and going down the Tube what are all I got the money for and then getting back to bleeding Damien and all of the mess what he left for me to deal with because I the bloody muggins and he a bleeding pig . . . well I just about were crying with the thought of it. And Richard, well . . . he old, yeh he is – but he ever so attractive. And so I thought . . . I not going to mind this. No I not – I going to like it, actually. I want it, is the truth. I want it, yeh.

He weren't joking when he say it just around the corner, this gaff he got. Ever so nice round here – all of the buildings, yeh, they looks like they kind of made out of sort of flowerpots, but all real tall and with like a lot of decorations and twiddly bits on. Bloke in the hallway behind a little desk there – nod to Richard, smile, almost like he bowing at him: me, it like he don't even see. We goes up in a lift – ever so small, bit of a squeeze, and when we sort of pressed together like we was, I looks up at him, Richard, but he never look down at me, nor nothing. Don't know what floor it is we get out at – weren't looking at the wossname. Then we got a little corridor with real thick carpet, and it all kind of bouncy when you walks on it, just like up the Marriott – but this a lot classier. Then we in a box of a hall, and he take my coat. I hate that coat, hate the bleeding sight of it: sorry he had to see it on me, sorry he had to put his hands on it. Then we in the lounge, but he call it something else, can't remember. It beautiful. All old-fashioned, and really beautiful. Then he go: you want something do you, Dolly? Digestive, maybe? And I'm like nah ta, Richard – I eat any more and I going to like burst: ain't used to it. And he say to me no, Dolly – I

354

meaning a drink, like a liqueur, and I going oh blimey no: I has any more booze, I be falling over. And then he come out with this lot – straight out, like: come in here then, come into the bedroom: something I really do want you to see – think you'll like it.

Bedroom, it ain't big – whole of the flat, it ever so posh, but it ain't all big and grand like what Scott's was. Bed there, it nearly filling the whole of the doings. And there this wall of cupboards with mirrors on, and it over there he taking me, look like. Yeh and then he open all of the doors . . . and I just . . . gaping, really . . . and yeh I were – I catch a sight of me in one of them mirrors there, and I look like I been hit in the face.

'You like what you see, Dolly? You'll remember some of it, I expect . . .'

'Yeh . . . yeh I do. Recognise that suit, for starters. Chanel, right? Yeh thought so. It lovely. Oh yeh and that dress – that Miu Miu. Took it off and got it pressed one time for your lady friend up the Marriott. Here – this where she live, or what? What we doing here? Why you show me all of this? What going on, Richard?'

'Well yes, Dolly – I do feel I rather owe you some sort of an explanation. This whole evening – while I very much hope you are enjoying it . . . it must of course appear to you to be some-what, um . . .'

'Weird? Yeh, it do, you want the truth.'

'Well, Dolly – permit me to explain. Now you're absolutely sure I can't get you anything at all, no . . .? Champagne, maybe? More pink bubbles? No? Very well, then. Well you see, Dolly, my "lady friend", as I took to calling her . . . well she wasn't really that at all.'

'Right. So wife, then.'

'No no – I have no wife. Used to, of course – used to, oh yes. But that was a very long time ago indeed. No – that lady, she was an employee of mine. On the staff, you see? And now, well . . . she is no longer. So this has presented me with something of a problem, you see – well two problems really, I suppose. Firstly – how to replace her. How to find a fine-looking and extremely able young woman who is up to the demands of the job. And secondly, well . . . what on earth to do with all of these beautiful clothes. For she left in something of a hurry. Size 10, you know. Oh yes and the handbags and shoes – they're in those other wardrobes over there. Size 5, the shoes . . .'

'I'm a 10. I'm a 5. I'm them.'

'Yes . . . I rather surmised it. So pleased to discover I was correct.'

I looks at the clothes, and I looks at Richard. And then I says to him: 'So this job – and let's be straight, yeh? Because I don't know now what you taking me for, Richard, but I ain't a bloody fool.'

'Oh my dear Dolly . . .! But of *course* you aren't a . . .'

'Yeh well just listen, all right? This here job – you meaning what I think you meaning, or what?'

'I, um – doubt it. What is it that you imagine I, um . . .?'

'This woman of yours. This "employee". She on the game, right? Upper-class Mayfair hooker.'

'Dolly . . .!'

'I right disappointed in you, Richard. I thought you like me . . .'

'Dolly, please – you must let me explain—!'

'I really did think you like me. Feel stupid, now. Insulted. Best go, I reckon.'

'Dolly. I implore you. Listen to me. Please. No no – I insist:

you mustn't leave, you mustn't. I refuse to let you leave this flat until you've heard me out. Please, Dolly: please.'

'Yeh? Well make it bloody quick, that's all.'

'Thank you, Dolly. Shall we sit . . .? Let's sit down Dolly, yes? Little sofa, here. Right, then. Comfortable? Right, then. Good. Well let me say immediately – because it worries me to see that you are so very evidently upset – that you are wrong, utterly wrong, in all of your surmise. You rather unforgivably diminish the two of us, Dolly, if I may say so, by imputing any such thing. I *respect* you. Do you see? And of *course* I like you, Dolly – I like you very much indeed. I have done so since that very first time we collided with one another in the hotel corridor, whenever that was. There was always something special about you. I saw it immediately. You have life – you have intelligence. And you also have beauty. The job I am offering you – for yes, you have certainly divined that much, anyway: I am, of course, offering you a position: the ulterior motive for my having invited you to dine. And that position I am offering . . .well, it involves travel. Which I think you might rather enjoy. No? Short-haul, generally. Sometimes rather further afield. And because during these journeys you would in effect become my, well – ambassador, if you like . . . well then it would please me very much were you to feel free to indulge yourself to the utmost in all these beautiful clothes and accessories – accept them, as a gift, from me to you – so that finally you may be able to fulfil your absolute potential. In your own eyes, yes? And before we discuss such vital matters as reimbursement – salary, and so on – may I just say in passing that in addition to this, every one of your incidentals is allowable: they will form a part of your rather generous expenses package. You see? Oh – you know, all those little extras such as hairdressing, beauty treatments, taxis, entertaining – all that sort of thing. Yes? You see? No – please do wait a moment, Dolly. I can see that you have plenty of questions, I'm sure you have – but all I am attempting here is merely to fill you in on the general picture, the broad brush-strokes, as it were: so please just do me the goodness of hearing me out to the finish, would you? Not much more of it, I do assure you. So as to the actual remuneration, should you choose to accept the post – which I very earnestly hope you will, it goes without saying – well that tends to be pro rata, you know. Which is to say, you are paid immediately following each individual trip, depending upon its duration. For something fleeting – up to twenty-four hours, say – you might just receive as little as a thousand pounds, but that, of course, you have to see as being simply the beginning of rather more serious earnings. Over the years, we have found cash to be generally the most mutually convenient method of payment. Well now, there are details to be gone into, quite naturally – on both sides, I daresay – but still I think I have told you sufficient for you to at least be able to consider the matter, anyway. No great tearing hurry for a deci-sion – though the sooner the better all round, I should have said. Of course, should you choose to take up the position, that would entail your leaving your current employment. Would that be a great hardship, Dolly . . .? Inconvenience you at all . . .?'

You hear what he said? He said there always were something special about me. That what he said. I got life and intelligence. That what he said. And also I got beauty.

'I hope, Dolly – I do so very sincerely hope that the expression upon your face, the light within those startlingly delightful eyes of yours . . . that they betoken a "yes" . . .? Yes? You do say yes . . .? Oh how perfectly *splendid*, Dolly. Well there, you see: I told you I might be in a position to help you . . .'

358

'Think I'll maybe have a digestive, now. And can I . . . can I . . . look at the clothes, and everything . . .? Like, maybe – try something on, yeh . . .?'

'Dolly: the clothes, and everything – they are yours. Remember? And now . . . you must please excuse me for what I am about to do, for I simply can resist no longer . . .'

I were fingering this real nice MaxMara two-piece in king-fisher crêpe when he come up to me. I held on to his shoulders while he done it.

'That . . . that . . . were the most tenderest kiss what I ever had . . .'

'And you . . . the most wondrous of women. Now I perceive, Dolly – from your lips, and the way you are holding me now, that you might well be desirous of . . . more. Well . . . I *can* do this, if you'd really like me to. I am far from absolutely ruling it out. I have pills, you know – little blue pills – that will assist me very greatly in the accomplishment of all your wishes. I leave it to you. Might take half an hour, or so – to get weaving, as it were. Bit longer, conceivably . . .'

'Not very . . . romantic, Richard . . .'

'No well – old man, you see. What are you going to do about it, really? Pain, but there it is. I could take two, if you're in an absolutely fearful hurry. Not too sure if they work like that, but still. Otherwise . . . our friendship – and I do hope I may safely assume that we two now are nothing but the very best and closest of friends, Dolly – well then our friendship, our relation-ship, if you will, could of course remain as merely . . . what shall I say? An affectionate connection. Perfectly happy to leave it to you. Oh but I can tell you, Dolly, who will very much please you in other departments, however, and that is James, of course . . .'

359

'James . . .? Who James? This coat . . . oh my God: this *coat* . . .!'

'James? Well he's my sort of right-hand man, I suppose he is. He sees to everything on the business side – travel arrangements, and so on. Nitty gritty, as it were. Everyone on the staff appears to utterly adore him. They call him Jimmy Blue Eyes, I'm afraid . . .'

'Joking. Jimmy . . .?'

'Blue Eyes, mm.'

'So what – he got . . .?'

'Yes. Very blue, his eyes. Can't miss them. Quite intense. You'll like him, I'm sure. In fact, if you are agreeable, you would be able to meet him very soon indeed. Just say the word. Possibly you might even be game for an inaugural little trip – within, what shall we say . . .? Next couple of days? What do you say? Something brief: Amsterdam, maybe? James – he could fix that up in no time. How do you feel about that, Dolly?'

How I feel about that? Good, that how I feel about that, you want to know. Amsterdam? Jimmy Blue Eyes? Yeh great, mate – bring it on, baby! Feeling a bit ashamed, of course – little bit embarrassed, yeh sure – about me telling him I thought he were wanting me to go out, like – whoring for him, picking up tricks: can you bleeding imagine? All of them fat Arabs and Chinks and loaded Russians – and like Richard, he some kind of a pimp, or something. Well he ain't never that, is he? You only got to just look at him. He a gentleman, Richard is – I knowed it, just knowed it, very first time I clap eyes on him up the Marriott: he a right and proper English gentleman, that what Richard are. Ever so glad I never just gone and walked out like I said I were going to: ever so glad he stopped me. Else I would never of knowed, would I? Yeh and just look at what I would have been walking away from . . .! Yeh . . . and so how I feel about . . . oh Jesus, all of them *clothes* . . .? Oh God oh God oh God . . . I just can't keep my hands off of them – and they all fitting me just perfect, them what I gone and try on, and I ain't even bleeding started on the most of it. Ain't even close to getting to the shoes – and I remembering them shoes, course I do: Manolos, Louboutins, Jimmy Choos, all of them. Aren't even daring to look at all of the bags, on account of I just going to be fainting on the bleeding floor. And what he don't even mention, yeh – what he never think were even like worth sort of telling me about, okay, is all of them big red leather boxes we got here with all, like . . . *watches* in them? Like Le Must de Cartier, and Tag Heuer and Dior and Hermès and oh bloody hell I can't hardly *stand* it . . .! Think I joking . . .? Well I bloody ain't. And not just watches neither but all of these like necklaces and bangles and a whole bleeding spadeload of kind of these dangly-type earrings, and that . . . Can't hardly believe it. Can't hardly believe it . . . everything, just everything what I ever wanted in the whole of my life – it all right here, and in this flat . . .! What yesterday I never even knowed it exist – and neither did I got a clue that today, right, I be actually *dining* with Carol Vorderman, never mind Paris, oh my God, *Hilton* . . .! And listen to this: I don't got to go humping no mattresses no more – no and I don't got to wear no nylon pinny with my bleeding name on, neither. And remember what he go and ask me? Jacking in my job – would it be a *inconvenience*, is what he go and ask me: well now let's have a little bit of a think about it, will we . . .? Well no, I don't hardly think it going to be too much of a bleeding inconvenience, do you? And now – I going to travel. Hear that, did you . . .? Bloody *hell* . . .! I going to *travel*, me . . .! Short-haul, generally. Sometimes further afield. And what more, I going to get paid for it – yeh and proper money, and all. Only a grand, for twenty-four hours. Only a bleeding grand . . .! Yeh and best of

361

all . . . it *style*, yeh . . .? All I ever want. And now I going to get it: it going to be mine.

Later, I drags myself away from all of the wardrobes – there just the lot in there, I telling you: Céline, Chloé, McCartney, McQueen, Gucci, Prada, whole bleeding lot – and Richard, he back in the lounge there with a drink in a glass what looking like a bleeding goldfish bowl. We has a bit of a cuddle on the settee, like – but it don't go no further on account of he ain't gone and had his pill what he were on about. I don't mind too much. But I would of, he wanted. And my mind – my, like, brain, yeh? It all buzzy, you know? And over the fireplace there – and I just seed it, I just looking up at it – there this picture in one of them big fat gold frames like is all over the shop, and it of all of these dozy-looking cattle sitting down in a field, and the whole of the picture, yeh, like all of the others what he got here, it the colour of Bisto Granules. And I laughs. I laughs, and I shouts out: *How Now Brown Cow* . . .! Richard, he nodded off, look, so he never hear me. Then I sees the time: can't hardly believe what the time is – so I got to get back to the other world then, yeh? Got to be getting Kenny up in couple hours for his school. Yeh well. I don't care. Do I? Nah – couldn't give a shit about none of any of all of that – why would I? Ay? It only for temporary. Because my life . . . the whole of my life: it different, now. Like that what he said to me at dinnertime, Richard: all what my heart desire. Yeh and best of all . . . it *style*, yeh . . .? All I ever want. And now I going to get it: it going to be mine.

The question is, the key question here is . . . and I have thought about this, well of course I have, of course I have thought about

362

it, yes, and in considerable depth, I might say . . . and so the question is, the key question here is . . . well, perfectly simple, really: entirely obvious. Who first am I to kill . . .? The order, you know. Ah but do you, I wonder, assume me to be speaking merely figuratively? Well if you do, you are wrong. Do you imagine that here cannot possibly be a true and pure determination, but is merely masquerade, a weary expression, the semantics of pique . . .? Well if you do, you are wrong. Because although I quite freely admit that it would be something of an exaggeration . . . well, in truth, it would be rather more akin to nothing less than total fabrication to suggest that thus far into my thinking, I have formulated anything that might even in a very dim light indeed be passed off sensibly as an actual plan of action . . . nonetheless I am clear, reasonably clear, upon the . . . well, what shall I say . . .? Direction, at least – the direction, yes – of each of the very most pressing problems which now, like it or not, I clearly have to deal with.

I am in a café, actually. Yes – at the moment, that is where I am, in a café, yes I am, coffee shop sort of affair it is, not unpleasant, and all I am so far guilty of having killed is a reasonable proportion of the morning: time, then – only the passing hours have so far been my victim. As I wait. For I am waiting, yes. Waiting for the magical hour, and how I do yearn for it, when finally I can get to him: have him alone. As alone, anyway, as ever one can be in a restaurant at lunchtime. And then kill him. For there, directly across the road, is the once very fashionable brasserie in which, when he is not himself entertaining or has not been invited elsewhere by a client, my quarry will habitually dine on his own. How do I know this . . .? I made it my business to know this. If your calls are purposefully blanked, if entry to a building is barred . . . well then from within such deliberately unhelpful and wilfully obstructive circumstances you are forced to, aren't you? Simply forced to . . . fall back on information previously garnered as a matter of course, and conjure for your own convenience alternative and workable arrangements. Yes but meanwhile, you see, I am finding it impossible, quite impossible to decide – it really is so awfully difficult – quite which of all the so many other tasks starkly now confronting me is actually the most important. Is it to kill the next person down on the list . . .? Is it that? Can that be the numero uno? Or duo, technically, I suppose – once I have already killed the first. Well it surely would appear to be. Wouldn't you say so? Go through the lot of them, like a scythe in a cornfield, while still it is at the forefront of my mind . . .? Or is it to follow up upon the particulars of what looks to be a very charming four-bedroom house in the nicer and quieter part of Highgate Village with a walled and enchanting garden which could, on the face of it, prove to be quite perfectly ideal for Alexander and myself . . .? Dilemma, you see. And then, of course, there is the business of the tutor . . . the school . . . the appointment, finally, of a professional managing agent . . . and then – and maybe it is this, actually, maybe it is this that truly is the most important of all: the acquisition of a bodyguard. I stared into my cappuccino, until it went cold. I ordered another: same thing would appear to have happened. The waitress, she is regarding me oddly. I cannot imagine why.

Talked to someone already – potential bodyguard. Got in touch with a detective agency. Do they call them that? Investigators. Pages and pages of them on the internet. I selected a website at random, as ever one must, where it was made plain that in addition to the general run of down-at-heel gumshoes who will shiftily shadow an errant husband, act as an industrial

364

spy or whatever, they also could supply you with 'doormen and personal protection', which I interpreted to mean (correctly, as it turned out) bouncers and bodyguards. Following on from my initial enquiries, a further gentleman fairly promptly telephoned me. Wasn't a gentleman, though – you could tell, and not solely by the voice alone, though that, clearly, was forming a major part of it. We were chatting fairly airily – I did not name Alexander, but was deliberately talking more generally, and tentatively sounding him out – and then, from out of a clear blue sky, it quite suddenly struck me: something of a brainwave, I considered it. Why don't I ask this man – Frank, he was called, or so he told me – why don't I ask him to do all of the killing for me? Because that then would leave me quite blissfully free to follow up on the school, the tutor and this lovely little house in Highgate Village. You see? And in his line of work, I reasoned, he could hardly be shocked at the suggestion. If it doesn't shock me, then why on earth should he be fazed? So I put it to him:

'I'll be frank, shall I Frank? How would it be if I wanted someone . . . erased, as it were? Just the one initially, you know, and then quite possibly more, should your work maybe prove to be satisfactory.'

'Erased . . .? What you mean . . .?'

'Well – you know what "erased" means. It means rubbed out. Doesn't it?'

'What – *whacked*, you talking about? What's this? You a reporter?'

'No of course not.'

'Wind-up this, is it?'

'I'm perfectly serious.'

'Lady . . . I'm going to hang up now, all right? I ain't no hitman . . .!'

'I see. And why are you laughing now . . .?'

'Well I were just thinking. I say I ain't a hitman – and it's true, course it is. But nor am I a strokeman or a, well . . . caressman, you take my meaning. I could, on occasion . . . be a smackman, if you see what I'm saying. We talking serious money, though . . .'

'Serious money?'

'Yeh.'

'As opposed to what? Silly money?'

'Nah! *Silly* money – that's even more serious than serious money. Know what I mean?'

'Not really, no. You seem to be talking complete and utter nonsense. And anyway, Frank, for whatever sort of money, this is no good at all to me, I'm afraid. Goodbye.'

I didn't even for as much as a moment consider pursuing the possibility of his guarding Alexander, this man Frank, because he sounded far too common and I shouldn't wish for my son to be consorting with such a person, and nor did I at all care for the flippancy of his general attitude. And for some time following this rather ridiculous conversation, you know . . . I stared at the phone in the palm of my hand. I suddenly was aware of myself quivering – quivering, yes, and with doubt, of all things. Can you believe it? Wholly unlike me, of course, but do you know . . . well it is barely credible, but I had actually come to question . . . my reason . . .! To wonder whether this, all of this – the way I was thinking, the deeds I was planning . . . whether all of it could actually be seen to be altogether, well . . . quite sane. But I was very relieved when it proved to be fleeting – this hesitance, such needless uncertainty. Oh good heavens: of course it is *sane* – well of course it is. Because look: it's making perfect sense to *me* . . .

The waitress, she has just come over to me. 'All right?' That is what she said. I did not think that she required an answer: was unsure quite how I could anyway frame one. I ordered a further cappuccino – for still there is time that just has to be frittered – and silently, she removed the abandoned cold one. She was looking at me oddly, I can't imagine why. My body is hurting – in some places, just dully aching . . . and in others, an area of stiffness. The cheek – that still throbs. Big-boned, you might say of Sylvia. That, anyway, is how they used to describe some misshapen and broadly rather mannish woman: big-boned. When all they meant was lumpish – possessing the lithe and antelope grace of a grand piano: a buffalo, wearing a frock – and brutal, when roused. It must, it occurs to me now, be simply quite utterly dreadful, mustn't it? Being Sylvia. I mean to say – just imagine it: every day and every single night, each and every moment of your entire life on earth from the very moment you were born . . . to be *Sylvia*. Oh well – the poor old dear, she will have to suffer it for not much longer. Because she, I have decided – she is to be numero duo: I shall release her from the considerable burden of her simple existence. I shall deliver her, yes. From evil. Which is good of me, I'd say.

My phone . . . my phone, now, is ringing. I wonder, though quite without interest, who it can be. I let it ring. My answer-phone, that cuts in. Silence. Then a bleep. Someone would appear then to have left me a message. The waitress, she places a cappuccino before me. I glance at the screen. It is school, Lizzie's school. Well what on earth are they bothering me for . . .? Don't they know I'm *busy* . . .? There is no spoon in the saucer: just so slack. I listen anyway to the message – for still there is time that just has to be frittered. The headmistress, she says she is – we have spoken rarely: I simply remember her as imperious, yes, and aquiline in profile. She says it is a matter of

367

urgency . . . well yes and what isn't, these days? You answer me that. She says she would like me to come to the school immediately. Come to the school *immediately* . . .? Extraordinary behaviour: doesn't she know I'm *busy* . . .? She says there is evidence of Lizzie self-harming. Well. Self-harming. Harm, yes. Well. I, of course – I have people to do that for me. To me. No shortage: queuing round the block. Oh . . .! Look at the time! Oh good, it is finally time . . .! I can leave here now. So I shall do that, yes. Cross the road, and enter the restaurant – that is where currently I just have to be, you see, in order to execute the initial stage of my grand operation. Execute, yes. I place a ten-pound note adjacent to my cooling cappuccino, though as I stand and pick up my bag, the waitress is telling me that this is insufficient. So I place a further ten-pound note upon the table, while eyeing her enquiringly. It would appear that this now, as I wave away change, is quite amply sufficient. The waitress smiles, though still she is looking at me oddly, I can't imagine why.

The road is rather busy. Cars, I mean – a virtually constant stream. I hadn't noticed it, hadn't been aware of all these cars, while I had been sitting in the café. Everything had seemed to be perfectly serene. They must have installed this . . . what is it? Glazing, special sort of glazing, whatever it is they must have installed, these places. Otherwise it would be perfectly deafening, wouldn't it? Last thing you need, when you are looking into a cappuccino, and thinking your thoughts. There is a traffic light a little way up. Should I walk to the traffic light, I wonder . . .? It's a bit of a trek. Or just wait here where I am, and hope for a break in the flow . . .? No . . . no . . . I think I will – I'll walk up to the traffic light. Yes because I know me, you see. Eager – I'm now very eager indeed to confront the man and have done with him, and in such a frame of mind I am

368

thoroughly capable therefore of darting quite recklessly into the thick of the traffic – yes and what will that get me? Then where will I be? Hospital, I should think. Or a mortuary. And that's no good to me at all. I cannot, obviously, risk injury or death – because who then would there be left to take care of Alexander? I am pleased to notice that I am thinking sensibly. That I remain aware of my responsibilities. And so I do that, I do that – I walk up to the traffic light, and it's not really that far at all, when it comes to it. Cross the road when the little green figure appears, turn abruptly right, walk a little further . . . and here I am, at the door of the restaurant. Right, then: the rest of it, the essential business, that shouldn't take me too long. And I know that I have what I need, nestling snugly in the internal side pocket of my Prada bag. I know it's there because I placed it carefully – but still I feel for the comfort of its bulk through the delicious folds of soft chocolate leather.

'Good afternoon, madam.'

'Oh. Hello. I'll just go on in . . .'

'Do you have a reservation . . .?'

'Meeting someone. Meeting someone, yes.'

'Oh I see. And the name . . .?'

'Name doesn't matter. I'll find him. It's quite all right.'

He isn't really pleased about it, this front-of-house person – and how much do I care about that? I'm not here for *lunch*, am I? You stupid man. I'm here on a *mission*.

It's larger . . . it's larger than it appears from the frontage, this place. I suppose, to have earned its fashionable and buzzy repu- tation – not now remotely as vibrant as it was – it would have to be, would it, a considerable size . . .? Well who cares? Not the point, is it? So . . . I am looking. Scanning the tables. A party of four women, each of them quite laughably badly dressed, and

369

clearly almost hysterically pleased with all that they have done to themselves. This is the sort of thing, I suppose, that must eventually have made the real people, the proper people, all the fashionable and regular lunchers and diners, rather begin to wonder. That, and the increasing availability of tables: something they never like – for what is the point of having the secret telephone number and your regular table if just anyone can walk in off the street? One or two quite discreet and respectable couples, though, of the sort that in the old days you would fully have expected to see here, so clearly the place is still just about hanging on, in the face of all the hot new and must-go-to restaurants one is constantly hearing about. And now . . . I see the table. The table I am looking for. Yes, there it is . . . way over there in the corner. He would appear to be taking soup. And he dabs his lips with a napkin: quaint in itself, these days. I am not going to speak: I shall not stand just a little to his side, maybe looming over him, until he is bound, feels constrained, to glance up enquiringly to see who this can be. My intention is to sit quite boldly in the chair immediately opposite him: I need to savour the instant of his absolute amazement when he is stunned that I am here. He might even let his soup spoon clatter back down into the bowl: this would be an unimaginable bonus. And as I slip into that seat and now am concentrating the whole of my blazing gaze upon the whites of his eyes . . . I am feeling, oh – let-down . . . quite severe disappointment. He clearly is surprised – this is not what he had been expecting – but his entire demeanour. . . I am desperate to see that it is so far short of candid astonishment.

'May I . . . help you . . .?'

'Evidently not. I thought you were going to help me, Mr Ouch. I will not call you Willy. But apparently not. I, however, helped you. Wouldn't you say? Why are you looking around you, Ouch? There is no one here to help you now. You are no longer protected by your minions. Oh yes – I helped you, all right. For when in your life could you ever have hoped to be . . . approached by a woman such as I? In my sort of league. Looking the way you do. Well never. Don't talk – I'm talking. Never, Ouch. Not ever – that's the truth, as we both well know. But worse than that – so very much worse than that: you foolishly and unforgivably passed over an extraordinary talent in Alexander.'

And now, the odious little man, he is staring about him almost frantically, seemingly waving at waiters. Is he intending to order me a *drink* . . .? He does not look at me, but he is about to speak:

'Look . . . I am terribly sorry, er . . . but I think . . .'

'You have forgotten my name . . .! You have actually forgotten my *name* . . .?'

'Look . . . would you just leave, please? I am expecting someone. I do not think you are actually quite well . . .'

'You aren't! You aren't expecting anyone. You're in the middle of soup! And anyway, you only ever come here when you are lunching alone. You think I don't know this? You think I haven't been *in*to it all? Then you do not know me, Mr Ouch.'

'No – I do not. And I am not . . . what did you call me? *Ouch* . . .?'

And now I simply stare at him. I had not expected an arrant denial of his actual existence. A denial of our carnal involvement, if vile and mercifully brief . . . a dismissal of blame and all wrongdoing – oh yes, of course he was going to do that. But this . . .! This goes beyond anything I had anticipated. And now I am conscious of someone who is standing quite close to me.

'May I be of assistance . . .?'

371

'Yes, Marco – you bloody well may. And what took you so long? Been waving like an idiot, here. Would you please ask this woman to leave? I cannot imagine what she is doing here. I think she might actually be a bit . . .'

'Oh I'm not standing for *this* . . .! You can't seriously imagine you can wriggle out of all the trouble you're in simply by denying who you *are* . . .! Do you think I'm *mad* . . .? I know exactly who you are, Ouch – and I am here to *kill* you . . .!'

'Madam. You will please leave immediately, or I must call the police. I cannot apologise enough, Mr Stanley. She said she was here to meet someone . . .'

'Mr . . . *What* . . .? What did you just call him? What sort of a conspiracy is this? What did you just say? He has *aliases* . . .? This is Ouch! Ouch! Are you *blind* . . .?!'

Now, though – before the waiter lays a hand on me, before he fulfils his threat to summon the police – I simply rise, and in silence I am looking down at the man . . . his eyes quite hard with something approaching true fury. And now I turn to leave, and am blanking the stares from adjacent tables. And I have walked the length of the restaurant and am soon back outside, the traffic's roar assailing me as I am standing in sunlight. Though in defiance of all this brightness, there is the faintest gauze of a shower. Well . . . I shall go now. Back home. Deal with the next thing on the list, I suppose is what I ought to do: must keep busy. Because that man . . . that man . . . well he wasn't, was he? Willy Ouch. It seems quite plain to me now. He was someone else entirely: Mr Stanley, it would seem. No resemblance whatsoever. Well now. I don't really understand quite what can have come over me.

CHAPTER NINE

A LACQUER OF UNDERSTANDING

Lizzie is with Sylvia. I couldn't think what else to do with her, quite frankly – I really am just so totally hopeless at this, anything at all to do with the children. And when the phone rang, my mind, as ever . . . well naturally it had been thoroughly absorbed by completely different things: my things, selfish things, exclusive things – things that are wholly to do with me. I was still in bed. With K.T. Well of course with K.T. Don't answer it, is what she said: I thought you told me you'd turned it off? Had I told her that? Can't remember. Probably – if she asked me to, well yes I would have said that. But I hadn't, quite obviously: turned it off. And I nearly did, I nearly did ignore the call: because face it, in my life as it has become, what could be more urgent or desirable than the here and now? So I nearly left it – because I knew it wouldn't be work: that I knew for sure. It never is. I can't even begin to think about my work, these days – and largely because there is none, and therefore nothing whatever to think about. Neglected it utterly. Shameful, really – no excuse for it, none at all. And when you're a freelance struggling hard within a very crowded field . . . well: just you ask any one of them. And there are

373

millions of us, you know: quite literally millions: terrifying to think of. Because it's the definition of a freelance whatever it is you might be up to, these days: very crowded field. We will think nothing of standing with heavy boots upon a rival's face, badly mangling his features, simply in order to be up there, and able to breathe. So if you stop – if you even pause – well then you are soon on the way to being finished. You have to keep calling. Posting. Reminding, underlining the truth to this blank, remote and anonymous world outside that still you are standing, if only just about. You have to keep on coming up with fresh and bright ideas, together with a rush of reasons why a client simply cannot live without them.

Yes but you see . . . my expertise, what there was of it . . . it's all quite common currency, now. It happened quickly, as I had known that one day it simply just had to. It's not really seen to be clever any more, all that I used to be able to provide. All that I've done, anything I've ever achieved, well . . . some savvy kid with maybe five grand's worth of equipment could effortlessly manage the same: surpass it, probably, maybe as a result of a young and fertile mind – God curse the savvy kid, and all the others like him. And because this cocky arriviste is unaware of any rules, he can therefore quite uproariously break them – he will glory in shattering them into ancient smithereens, the crumbled and powdery splinters of something quite obsolete, and with thrilling and glittering results. And God knows he'll be faster – because look at me: I sit in front of my computer now and it can take me a morning to remember what I'm actually supposed to be doing. So add all of that to my recent, um – preoccupations, will we say, and what you are left with is . . . well what, now? A duck . . . a duck who really would be very well advised indeed to continue paddling extremely hard within the

374

diminishing and increasingly scummy circumference of his already quite diminutive pond . . . but simply he continues to bob about, soon to be dead in the water.

Anyway . . . Lizzie is with Sylvia: I couldn't think what else to do with her, frankly – because when I got the call, well obviously I had to *go* to her, didn't I? My little girl – my innocent angel, Lizzie. I was wounded when the headmistress, I'm pretty sure she said she was the headmistress, told me so baldly that Lizzie was hurt. Harmed. Harmed, yes, and by her own hand. Can it be true? Can it really? How awful. How very terrible for a child – well anyone, I suppose, but particularly a child – to be . . . moved to do that. So I had to go. I had to go immediately. Still, though . . . having expressed my concern to the woman over the phone, I of course had gone on to mutter to her something about Amy. I didn't actually want to say the name too loudly because K.T she still was languorous beside me, and she's always been a little bit funny about it, you see, my saying Amy's name . . . but still I felt compelled – through indolence, cowardice and just sheer habit – to suggest that maybe Amy, you know, would probably be the best person to approach here, the best equipped to be dealing with this, yes? Being the mother, and all. Supposedly. But Amy was unreachable, apparently: a message had been left for her, swiftly followed by another, though no response had resulted. And hence, concluded the headmistress tartly, I now am attempting the father. So you see why I had to go. I had to go immediately.

'So that's it then, is it?'

'Christ, K.T – I've explained the *position* . . .!'

I was tugging on my trousers, and in something of a hell of a rush, as one might imagine: got my foot caught up in the twist of one of the legs – and whatever the circumstance, I find it impossible not to feel utterly absurd, when I do that.

'Yes but the point is, Tom – you're *leaving*. Aren't you? Just like you always used to. Because of your other life. Because of your family. It's always your *family*. Why must I always come second? Why is that, Tom?'

Buckling up the buggers now: and where the hell did I kick my shoes . . .?

'Mind that cigarette, K.T – it's going to fall on to the duvet. And what the hell are you *talking* about . . .? You're *never* second, K.T. You're not just the first – you're the *only* . . .! You know I want to stay with you – you must know that, you've just go to. Look at the way we've *been*. But this . . . this is my . . . this is just a little girl, K.T . . .'

'Not that little . . .'

'She needs help. Her mother isn't there. Her mother never is. And she is little – she's only thirteen. Do you know where my jacket is . . .?'

'Yes but what about the *next* time, Tom? When there's something else wrong with Lizzie. And she's fourteen – fourteen, she is: not little at all. Or someone has locked themselves out. Or there's a . . . I don't know . . . break-in, or something. Something. Anything. You'll drop the lot, Tom – and then you'll just *go*. And that's exactly what you used to do. Isn't it? And I can't . . . I told you I can't . . . I just can't stand it. Not again. I won't. I won't.'

'The other sock has to be somewhere . . . doesn't matter. If you find it, well . . . look, K.T: it's different now. I love you. Don't I? I've told you I love you, and I've told you I want to be with you. What more can I do? You just have to believe me. My daughter . . . my daughter is in trouble, and I've just got to *go*. Okay . . .?'

'It can't be that bad. Can it?'

'What are you saying . . .?'

'Well can it? She's not in *hospital*, is she? It's probably just a – what do they say?'

'I don't know what they say, K.T. I've just got to *go* . . .'

'Cry for help. That it? She just wants attention.'

'Yes well maybe. Christ knows she never *gets* any . . .'

'No well nor do I. So what are you going to do about that, Tom?'

'Jesus, K.T . . . I don't believe this. This is just how you *used* to be . . .'

'Yeh well whoopy-doo! Big surprise . . .! Here we are: same two people, doing the same old thing . . .! No *good*, is it Tom? It's just no *good* . . .!'

'K.T. Please . . .'

'I don't want you to go out of that door, Tom. Do you hear me? I do not want you to leave. If you go now, you needn't ever bother coming back. I mean it, Tom. I'm not prepared . . . I'm just not *capable* of going through all this again . . .'

'K.T . . . what can I say? You might understand a bit better if you were a *parent* . . .'

And maybe, just maybe, there might be something I could have said that would have been worse, more barbed, even more injurious to the two of us than that . . . but even now, as I am bounced about in the back of a taxi, and still I am wracking my brain . . . I have utterly failed to come up with whatever more than quite shockingly terrible thing it could possibly have been.

'Oh . . . *well* . . .!'

'K.T – oh God . . .!'

'Oh . . . well . . . that's . . . just . . . *perfect* . . .! Now you're throwing in my face the fact that I'm not a *parent* . . .?!'

'Jesus. Oh Jesus Jesus. *Please*, K.T – I wasn't thinking. I . . .!'

'And why, Tom? Do you remember? Why I'm not a parent? You don't? You do? Because I could have been, couldn't I? But you – you didn't at all *care* for the idea, did you?'

'K.T . . . how many times have I apologised for this . . .?'

'She was a little girl too. Would've been. Remember? So tell me why, Tom, you have to rush off to attend to *one* of your "little girls", but the other "little girl" you ordered me to have *murdered* . . .?'

'*Order* you . . .?! I didn't *order* . . .! Oh bloody hell, K.T – you know it wouldn't have been right for you. For us. Not at that time. We talked about it. It wasn't just me. We talked about it, just . . . *endlessly* . . .'

'Oh . . . get out, Tom. Just go. I'm sick . . . I'm just *sick* of it . . .'

'K.T – *please* try to understand. I want to stay, I want to hold you, I want to hold you for ever. This is the only thing on *earth* that could take me from you now . . .'

She just looked at me, K.T. Her eyes grown dull, and filled with tears that soon would roll. And I wanted to fuck her. When she raved that she hated me, and her eyes were fierce and suddenly blazing . . . I so did want to just fuck her. And how many night-times can I tenderly remember, when her eyes were closed, and flickering in sleep . . . and I still just wanted it: to fuck her hard. She could be making an omelette, pouring a drink, flicking through a magazine . . . there was no time ever when I was around K.T and couldn't want to, oh – just fuck and fuck and fuck her. And now she was telling me to go. Though before that, she was telling me that if I did go, then I could never come back. Christ. But I didn't dare speak. Not now. So . . . I went.

And then when still bounced about in the back of a taxi on my way to Lizzie's school, I tried to settle down, and I tried to somehow reflect upon it all. Yes but you see . . . when I said to her, K.T, that this, that Lizzie who is hurt, that this is the only thing on *earth* that could take me from her now . . . well it was utterly true, of course: here was the absolute truth of the matter. So I just am forced to ask myself: why did it have to happen? Why has this arisen, how could this occur, and just at this particular moment? Why am I dragged from K.T by the only thing that could? And then I think this: there was something worse, you know: something worse, more barbed, even more injurious to the two of us that I could have said to her. I could breezily have assured her that once we were truly together again, living as one and in peace as always we should have been, that then, dear K.T, we can have babies galore . . .! Yes because she can't, you see. This is what they told her. Following the procedure. Jesus.

She seemed the same, Lizzie, when eventually I got to the school. To my eye, anyway – admittedly inexpert, quite woefully so. The headmistress – it was the headmistress – after her curt and rather formal greeting, she had requested, if I wouldn't mind, a 'quiet word'. I smiled, with a bit of luck reassuringly – maybe quite manically – at little Lizzie, as I followed the woman into an adjoining room. She didn't meet it, the smile, my little girl – there was to be no spark of contact. It occurred to me that she hadn't actually looked at me at all, not once. As if she was unaware that I even was present in the room. I yearn, at moments such as that, to scoop her up and whisper into her ear all that I would do for her – to feel her grip, to see her eyes ablaze with love for me. Jut as, long ago, they always used to be.

'As Lizzie's father, you will well be aware that she is going through a difficult time. That is evident. It is not an easy age for

379

a girl – I'm sure you are aware of that also. But in her particular circumstance . . . her brother, you know . . . the attitude of her contemporaries . . . well: not easy, as I say. You might wish to consider seeking professional assistance . . .? Guidance? Please do be assured, however, that I do not ever suggest such things lightly. I am not one for *enhancement* . . .'

'Enhancement, really. *Enhancement* . . .?'

'I never wish to be seen to . . . indulge a child's concerns. Which is not to doubt or disregard them. In my profession, one is constantly walking something of a tightrope. One must never neglect a very apparent need, though nor must one ever be perceived to be investing the problem with a unique significance. Do you see what I mean?'

'Yes of course. No – not really. That's a contradiction, isn't it . . .? Anyway – doesn't matter. I'll take her home now. Talk to my, um . . . And then we'll decide quite what we're going to, er . . .'

She nodded at me, the headmistress. Quite dismissively, I thought. There might even have been contempt in it, that briefest inclination of her head. Don't know. Can't really juggle with it. Don't care. She then went on a bit more about the delicacy of handling an adolescent's mental fixations, 'his or her unspoken concerns'. She said that the most important thing of all was *focus*. Direction too. According to this woman, as she became more animated and increasingly caught up in the welter of her own oratory, all manner of vague abstractions appeared to be the most important thing of all – easy and nebulous conveniences which, while making no concrete sense whatever, were deliberately difficult to disagree with. She concluded with considerable vigour by way of a final trumpet blast that the absolutely key element with all of her charges was that they should at all times behave as responsible young adults who appreciate and take full advantage of the level of education that is being offered to them, and must, as a consequence, be turning in work that is proof of their very best ability. Then she wished to make it perfectly clear that in no circumstances whatever – when all was said and done – could she have them turning in *tomatoes*. I know. I would have queried it, but look – I was tired, so tired . . . I was so very tired and jangled, and I just had to be out of there, then. That school . . . it was reminding me of my own, and as a result, all of my confidence – that small, and yet somehow still constantly shrinking reserve – was draining out of me and into a thick and oily puddle on the floor. They're all like that then, are they? Schools? I rather think they must be: simply crushing. And also – Lizzie, she still was just sitting next door, all on her own, with heaven knows what going on in her mind. So I didn't react in any way at all to the tomatoes thing. I just thought: maybe she's raving. I don't know. Maybe I am. I don't know. Can't juggle with it. Don't care.

And in the taxi home, I did try my damnedest to coax a little out of Lizzie: oozing, though diminutive, queries in my very gentlest voice – tender, never prying, and coated in a lacquer of *understanding*. Didn't work, predictably. She just hung her head low – shook it from side to side. She said 'I'm fine'. She said that quite a lot. And I said but you're *not* fine, are you Lizzie? Lizzie . . .? You're not, are you Lizzie? *Are* you, Lizzie . . .? And she said I'm fine Dad, honestly: I'm fine. I'm fine. I'm fine. I'm fine. So I nodded to that (well look – there's a limit, isn't there?) and then I as subtly as I could be expected to manage squinted down at my phone to see if K.T had called me. She hadn't. Didn't expect it. Just hoped. Maybe she's texted . . . maybe she's emailed . . .? She hadn't. Didn't expect it. Just hoped. That's all.

Yes and then when we got back here, the taxi driver said blimey – because there rose up upon the air this little birdlike flurry of discordant trilling from the few young girls who had been sitting cross-legged on the pavement and now were darting towards the cab, fluttering their hands and all caught up within a collective tingle of excitement. They looked so very crestfallen, those big sad eyes pressed up close to the window, their noses distorted and misting the glass – close to quite poignantly heartbroken, actually, when they absorbed the awful truth that it was only us.

And then I thought well look, okay – we're home now, right? But what in Christ's name am I supposed to do next? Even when we're inside, Lizzie . . . well she isn't going to speak to me, is she? Plain as day. All she'll do is fly upstairs and into her room. Maybe she might be prepared to speak to her mother, but from what Amy's been saying about her lately, I severely doubt it. And anyway – Amy isn't here, is she? No. Amy – she would appear to have dropped off the edge of the earth. So I took her round to Sylvia's, Lizzie – couldn't think what else to do. And Sylvia, she welcomed Lizzie in, she did that, yes – but she was looking at me terribly strangely, I thought: can't get any further with it than that. I attempted to fill her in just a little – *sotto voce*, I hoped – about all that had just been going on, or as far as I understood it, anyway. All the self-harming, and so on – which, I had been considerably relieved to discover, was not what you'd call severe: a couple of plasters, is all, one applied to each of her inner arms, though nothing approaching the swaddling of fully fledged bandages. She said she had to speak to me, Sylvia, and urgently, sometime very soon. *Mais pas devant l'enfant*, she was whispering. Didn't actually go so far as to request a 'quiet word', but from the narrowness and intensity of the set of her eyes, that is more or less exactly what she was after, you could tell.

And as I was turning the key in the front door, one of the girls – such a sweet little face she had – she was forming her two hands into a megaphone and her message was apparently directed at me: 'How's Susie getting on . . .?' is what it actually sounded like, from where I was standing. And I found myself waving like a bloody fool and airily calling back to her 'Oh yes she's fine, thank you. Lizzie's fine. She's fine, she's fine, she's fine . . .!' Jesus . . . it was a relief to get that door shut behind me, I can tell you that. This day – Christ Almighty. I'm in turmoil: turmoil, I tell you. Phoned K.T, then: *'leave a message'*. Didn't. Phoned Amy – thought I ought to: *'leave a message'*.

'Amy – it's me. Where are you, actually? Did you get those calls from the school? About Lizzie? Well I've gone to get her, so you needn't worry. If you were worried, don't suppose you were. So anyway – she's back at home now, okay? Seems all right. Not too bad, anyway. Difficult to say. Headmistress thinks we ought to . . . well: talk about it later. Okay. Anyway, she's . . . well she's actually next door with Sylvia, at the moment. Yup. I've got . . . well: one or two things to catch up with, so . . . if you get this . . . you might give me a ring. Tell me what's going on. Right, then. See you when I see you, I suppose. Well okay . . . that's it, really.'

And I'm just wondering, now . . . and I called K.T again, of course: no answer, *'leave a message'*, didn't want to text, because it's just not like that, all that I have to say . . . yes . . . and so I'm sitting at my desk here in my office and just wondering, now . . . if Alexander – well, whether he's with Amy, wherever that might be. I don't know – maybe they have eloped: they might as well. Gretna Green. Do people still do that . . .? I can't really think that they do. Oh God . . . I don't know what I'm thinking about, quite frankly: all becoming rather silly. And now . . . I'm hearing something – something across the landing: bathroom, I think it must be. So he is here then, Alexander. Well . . . maybe have a word. Shall I? About what, exactly? Don't know – but maybe I ought to anyway, just have a quick word with the boy. Can't remember when last I did. He'll be about as unresponsive as Lizzie, of course: far more polite, oh Jesus yes – immensely more forthcoming on the surface of it . . . but at base, oh yes – equally unresponsive. So I wander down the corridor with no intention whatever in my mind, and simply incline my head to the panels of the bathroom door: yes . . . soft and muffled plashy noises. So I knock. Nothing. So I go in. And the girl in the bath, she looks up brightly and says hi to me. And I realise that still I am staring right down at her, the whole of my face just electric with all that is jumping up and down and simply all over it. She makes no attempt to cover any part of her . . . that slim and taut, quite breathtakingly beautiful youthful form, the budding and curve of her so just subtle, and perfect . . . it does, it takes my breath – it takes my breath and it makes me remember . . . just how young girls are.

'Can I help you . . .?' she asks, quite helpfully. 'I'm Susie.'

'Ah yes. Sorry, um . . . Susie. I'll just go. I had no idea. I was just . . . well anyway. Sorry to, um . . . I'll just go. Lizzie – she's back now, if you want to, um . . .'

'Who's Lizzie . . .?'

'Ah. I thought you must be a friend of, erm . . . but evidently not. Ah . . .'

'Are you looking for Alexander? You're his dad, aren't you?'

'Well . . . vaguely. I mean – vaguely looking, is what I mean. For him. Not, you know . . . vaguely his dad . . .'

'He's in his room. He asked me into the house. I hope you

384

don't mind. He's just . . . wonderful. Isn't he? Don't you think? And then I thought I'd quite like to take a bath.'

I am staring hard at the door. My back is turned away from her, and I am staring hard at the door. Don't want to be, no – but there is such a thing as decorum. I suppose.

'Right. Oh well no of course. But I really do think, however, um . . . Susie . . . that you ought to maybe get going now, yes? Alexander's mother, she'll probably be back quite soon, and, er . . .'

'Yeh. Got to go anyway. I was just about to get out.'

And now there are noises of splashed and displaced water, as if she surely now is doing that very little thing. Want to turn round so that I can see it. Yearn to. Am longing to envelop her in the biggest and fluffiest bath sheet – peel away the heavy wetness of her hair where it will be slung across the sparkle of those two great blue and glittering eyes. But I keep on staring hard at the bloody fucking door.

'Right. Well I'll leave you to it, then . . .'

And I did that, yes. She said it had been a pleasure to meet me. She did. And now I'm back at the desk in my office again . . . and more astounded than ever. I mean to say: what is going on . . .? Hey? What is going on? I do wish someone would tell me. I mean . . . I mean . . . well look: let's just review the position here, shall we? K.T . . .well K.T, she won't talk to me. Last time I rang, it said that I ought to hang up because the messages thing was full. Yes well it would be: full of messages from me. She doesn't want to talk to me. We never before have been so very close – never so absolutely together as we were this morning . . . when I told her that I loved her, when I told her that I was finally prepared to commit, and spend the rest of my life with the woman. Well of course I do, of course I am – what sort of an idiot would I be otherwise? I mean, Jesus – miracle that we met again at all. Isn't it? And it's beyond all hope and reason that after all this time still we would be, oh . . . just so wonderful together. Well there you are: second chances – all too rare. And what you do is, you grab them. K.T and I . . . a true pair, an utter match, just as we always have been. And so you don't mess about – not again, not any more you don't. What you do is, well . . . you just reach out for it, hold it tight – hug it close to you, yes oh yes, and this time for ever.

All very well . . . but now . . . now . . . now, she won't talk to me. Simply refuses. And the reason she won't talk to me, so far as I can make any sense of it, is that I just had to rush off to collect my daughter from school because Amy has vanished from the face of the planet and won't talk to anyone at all, seemingly. And Lizzie, she is in the grip of anxieties so very severe – and it's only now just slowly dawning upon me – that she has had recourse to . . . self-harming (can hardly bear to think of this . . . or even *pronounce* it). And according to her headmistress – who is never given to enhancement – she might easily require psychiatric treatment. And Lizzie, she won't talk to me. And one of the causes of all this is apparently Alexander – which of course I can very easily understand: saw it looming, warned Amy of the consequences of all she was undertaking, oh – how many times? How many? And over how long a period? Not Alexander's fault, of course it isn't: he goes where he's put – Amy's plasticine, between her fingers. And Alexander too – he won't talk to me. Admittedly I haven't yet even attempted to talk to him, but even if I did, he wouldn't, I just know it, talk to me back. Sylvia – she wants to talk to me, but I can very much do without talking to her, quite frankly: there was something about her this time that was positively unnerving, can't put a

386

name to it. The only person who has, then, talked to me is Susie, a naked teenager who may or may not still be in the bathroom down the corridor. Or possibly now back in Alexander's room, who can say? Doing what, exactly? Hey? I mean . . . what was in the boy's head when he invited this pretty young girl into the house? And how, incidentally, did he avoid being savaged by the others whom he didn't? Because Susie . . . from what I saw of her (which was all of it, Christ . . .) has got to be, what . . .? Fifteen? Younger? Bit older, maybe? Lizzie's age? Hard to say. No body hair, you know: none at all. Does this denote merely prepubescence, or else what is these days perceived to be no more than essential grooming? But anyway clearly at the very least four years older than Alexander, is the point. So what was he thinking, the boy . . .? What was in his head? And what, actually, can have been in hers? Is this . . . sexual in a way I am yet to understand? Don't know. Can't juggle with it. And here's another thing: why did she suddenly, Susie, decide upon having a *bath* . . .? Don't know. Can't juggle with it. But I do rather care.

Yes but now I've got to abandon all this – not that it's getting me anywhere at all – because that was the front door, no mistaking it at all. It has been slammed with an appalling force – so much so that the building juddered and that framed reproduction above my desk of one of Mondrian's very earliest colour block compositions has jiggled on its hook in the wall . . . though it's settled back down now. Right, then: Amy is back. This must now be faced.

'What in Christ's name do you *mean* by this . . .?!'

'Amy – you're back . . .'

'How *dare* you . . .?! How *dare* you, Terence . . .?!'

'Dare what, actually? Where have you been? Why are you so bloody angry? It is I who should be angry. It's Lizzie who should

387

be angry . . .'

'It's Lizzie I'm talking about! Why in Christ's name have you given her to *Sylvia* . . .?! Is she still there? Is she?'

'Well yes . . . far as I know. Haven't collected her, anyway . . .'

'No well collect her. Collect her now, Terence. Because if you don't, how can I do it? How can I do it, you absolute *fool*? How can I be expected to do it if *Lizzie* is there . . .?'

'Do it? Do what? What on earth are you—?'

'And who in fuck's name is *this* . . .?!'

'Hm . . .? Ah – this. Hello again, Susie. You arrive at an awkward moment, I'm afraid. This is, um – Susie. Susie, yes. She's just leaving. Aren't you, Susie?'

Susie is beside me, smelling quite deliciously of pine and childishness. And cool though she is, looking understandably uneasy. Any other young girl, I imagine, would already have bolted, screaming wildly – because Jesus, the way Amy is staring right at her, I'm telling you – it's enough to unsettle Alexander the Great. Bad example.

'*So . . .! So*, Terence – I come home unexpectedly and catch you in the act! You *dirty* and despicable man! I never truly believed that you would actually go through with it! I gave you the benefit, Terence! I thought that here was no more than the murky fantasy of a *dirty* and despicable man! But no – be quiet, Terence! I am speaking! But no – you actually did go through with this . . . *crime*. And in this *house* . . .! And after I had given you the *benefit* . . .! Scarlet – leave immediately, before I do damage to you.'

'I'm Susie . . .'

'She's Susie. Listen, Amy – she's Susie. She . . .'

'She's *Scarlet*! Do you think I am mad? Do you think I have no eyes? I know her from the letter you stole from me and have

388

been pawing and lusting over and God alone knows what else that I can't even begin to *think* of . . .! She is the scarlet *woman* . . .!'

And Christ, never mind Susie's safety: it's me who's worried now. Jesus – just look at her, will you? Her face, Amy's face, it's practically . . . *purple* . . . and her eyes, her very pupils, they're actually *contorted*. She's breathing hard, and her hands, oh Christ – they're forming into claws. Never seen her like this: I've seen her get bad before . . . when her temper takes a hold, I've seen her go practically crazy – yes but not like this, never like this. Both Susie and I – I can smell it – we both of us now are in considerable danger. So I turn to her, while affecting my shabby approximation of a reassuring smile.

'Susie: go now. All right? Go straight out of the door, yes? Sorry about, uh – all this. Off you go. It'll be fine. Really. Off you go. Go: go now.'

And she does, thank Christ: doesn't say anything, doesn't look at me, just goes. What she'll be madly gabbling once she's back outside with all of the other girls, well . . . anyone's guess, isn't it? And Amy, now . . . hasn't budged: she's still just seemingly rooted in the same position in the middle of the hall. I'm wary. She did not blink as Susie passed her: her eyes now look to be struck for ever into permanent and uncomprehending surprise, her face shock-white, each cheek smarmed with a livid flare. And even as I ready myself, as well as I am able, either to withstand or flinch away from whatever more than awful thing might next be coming my way . . . her eyes are suddenly softer . . . she visibly relaxes the bunch of her shoulders: her fingers, not now rigid . . . they are slowly uncoiling. She looks directly at me . . . and holding my gaze, she slyly smiles.

'I think I'm going to make tea. Do you want some, Terence?

389

Tea?'

And now I'm more wary than ever: because this . . . this is
something new.

'I really have had the most beastly day. What about you,
Terence? What sort of a day have you been having? I'm actually
going to sit down. Are you coming into the room? Suddenly
quite exhausted. Did you answer me, Terence? About the tea?
Oh my goodness, you know – oh how awful: I'm sounding
exactly like Sylvia! That's what she kept on saying to me when
I was round there: *tea*, Amy? *Tea*? Do you want *tea*? As if it can
ever matter: tea. Oh yes and talking of Sylvia – do you think
you could now please, Terence? Go and fetch Lizzie? I can't
really imagine why you thought to take her there in the first
place, but what's done is done, I suppose. So would you mind?
Awfully? Just slipping round to collect her? And then when I
know she's safely back at home, I can go and do it. Get it out of
the way. And that's *all* I'm going to do today, I can tell you that.
Suddenly quite exhausted . . .'

I'm looking at her. Don't know what else to do. My brain is
working, though not at all productively. And then I hear me
speaking:

'Don't you want to know how she is? Lizzie?'

'Yes of course. How is she? Lizzie?'

'Not too good, I think. I mean – the cuts, they're superficial.
But mentally . . . emotionally . . . I'm not too sure.'

'Cuts . . .?'

'Yes. You know: you were told. She . . . cut herself.'

'Really? I was told? Well how terribly clumsy of her: she really
must learn to take more care. So will you then, Terence? Go and
get her, yes? Oh Lord, you know – I will not be at all displeased
when this day is over. I must go and see Alexander. He will be

missing me so much, the poor sweet lamb. I went to see him, you know. Not Alexander, I don't mean. Ouch. Willy Ouch. Remember? Had to, after what he did. Raped me, I mean. And of course after all that he did to Alexander. His career. He has to suffer for that. Well obviously. The ultimate price. Why not?'

Still I continue to look at her. And my brain . . . I'm not sure it's working at all, now.

'Oh yes . . .? And how . . . was he . . .?'

'Well I haven't the faintest idea. Because when it actually came to it, I didn't at all. See him. Saw someone else. In a restaurant. The restaurant he goes to. I wasn't there to eat, or anything – not hungry: I'd been looking at cappuccinos. It was meant to be Ouch. Or cappuccini, I suppose it is, strictly. Meant to be Ouch, yes, but it turned out not to be. Can't imagine how *that* happened . . .'

'I'll . . . go and fetch Lizzie. You're . . . all right here, are you Amy . . .?'

'Oh God yes. Completely fine. Who was that who was here just now? Person who left. Was that a friend of Lizzie's?'

'Um – yes. Yes it was. Friend of Lizzie's.'

'Oh good – I was beginning to think she didn't have any! Well go on then, Terence. You keep on saying you're going, but you're still here and just hanging about, aren't you? Such a dawdler. You get Lizzie, and then I can go round to Sylvia's myself and do it. Get it done. I do hope Mike isn't there though, because he's really been quite perfectly blameless in all of this. If he does happen to be there, though . . . well then I'm afraid that's just his bad luck then, isn't it? Can't have loose ends, can we . . .?'

'You keep on saying "do it", Amy. Do what? What are you actually talking about?'

'Oh really, Terence – you haven't at all been *attending*, have

391

you? Do *what* . . .? Can you truly be serious? Do *what* . . .? Well *kill* her, of course . . .! What else? Honestly, Terence – sometimes, I just can't understand what it is that's actually *wrong* with you . . .'

And it is only now I am seeing, I think, just about all that I find myself up against. Trying not to: doing all sorts of things with my face, some of them involuntary, all of them hinting at the desperate: acrobatic eyebrows, a wry and lopsided grin or so – willing her to crack, willing her to concede that this, all this, is no more than simply just the hugest joke . . . but no, her face is remaining absolute, and rather eerily incurious: didn't really expect anything else – just hoped. So it is only now I am seeing, I think, just about all that I find myself up against. Have to get round to Sylvia's, then. Christ knows what I am to say to the woman, but certainly I have to get round there, no option. I ask Amy tentatively to once more assure me that while I am away . . . she will be . . . all right . . .? To which she is predictably dismissive and snappy. Says she will be with Alexander. Says that Alexander, he will be needing her now: says he will be pining. Well that should be safe enough, then: because Alexander, he is the Messiah, after all. Amy, she can honour him – go over once more, and in glorious detail, just how it is to be for the two of them when finally the keys to the kingdom of heaven are bestowed upon him. While he, in turn, can wallow neck-high in the warm and heady swamp of her ridiculous and quite merciless indulgence. So I more or less hared around to Sylvia's. No girls outside the house: maybe they all are attending Susie's hastily convened and packed-out press conference at the bloody Marriott Hotel. Sylvia, she opened the door more or less immediately, and I was grateful for that: didn't want to be hanging around.

'Terence. Glad you're here. Relieved. Come in. Come into the room. Lizzie is upstairs. She seems . . . not too bad. For now, anyway. She's watching television in my bedroom. We only have the four channels, but she seemed to find something to interest her. She's a thoughtful girl, Lizzie. Always was quiet. But . . . how is Amy? That is the question. Can I get you anything, Terence? Tea, maybe?'

'So she's . . . okay then, Lizzie, is she . . .?'

'Well . . . I wouldn't say okay, no Terence. Are you coming in or not?'

'Yes. Sorry.'

'She's . . . well – what I said: all right for the moment. But there are problems there, Terence. To be dealt with. I do hope you realise that.'

'Well I do. I do now, Sylvia – yes. But it's Amy I have to . . .'

'So do you . . .?'

'Huh? Sorry? Do I what?'

'Want tea.'

'Tea? No – no tea. In here, do I go? Listen, Sylvia – I've just got to talk to you about Amy . . .'

'No, Terence: it is I who must talk to you. About Amy. You know she was over here earlier, do you? Mention that, did she?'

'She . . . no. No she didn't. Said she went to see Ouch.'

'Ouch . . .?'

'Doesn't matter. Well what did she want?'

'I couldn't tell you what she wanted. I know that she attacked me. That I do know. Are there still marks around my throat? Do you see? Where it's red? Tried to throttle me.'

'She . . .?'

'Completely out of the blue. I was telling her what I've told you – that I have concerns over Lizzie. And she just flew at me. Madly. I thought I was going to die. Saw her off, of course – she's

393

really quite flimsy, when it comes down to it. But she managed to break my favourite vase. The dahlias were ruined. I've only just cleared up all the mess. In one way, I was very pleased that Mike wasn't here to witness it all. It would have upset him greatly. On the other hand, had he been here . . . well he might have been able to prevent it, who knows?'

'Oh my God . . .! I can't . . . I just can't . . .!'

'I know. Well there it is. Things aren't really going terribly well for you, are they Terence? At the moment. What with Lizzie. And now Amy. I suppose . . . Alexander – he is a consolation, is he?'

'Alexander? No. Not really. But listen to me, Sylvia: I don't . . . know quite what to do. Listen . . . I have to . . . *confide* in you, all right? In the light of what you've just . . . because now, just now when I left her . . . what she said, what Amy said to me was that I should go and collect Lizzie, yes . . .? Because then she was going to come round here . . . and . . .'

'And what?'

'And . . . *kill* you . . .'

'I see.'

'Why would she want to do that, Sylvia? Why does she want to? Kill you.'

'Well you see, Terence – this is a classic error. You are attempting to invest reason into the ravings of one who now is clearly, I'm afraid to say . . .'

'Yes? Yes . . .?'

'Well . . . deranged, actually. Not to put too fine a point on it. And make no mistake – she means it, you know. When she says she wants to kill me, she is not merely venting her anger. This is no overwrought *expression*. She means it. Literally. I have read about this sort of thing. *Reader's Digest*. Everyone pooh-poohs it, but they really shouldn't. It's very good. A great deal of sense in the *Reader's Digest*. You see – people in the grip of whatever psychosis it may be – I don't know all the technical terms, obviously . . . well, they seem to imagine that once so-and-so is safely out of the way, then everything will be all right again. But soon – and this is the real danger, this is when it starts to take a hold – soon, some other little thing in their lives upsets them, you see, and so they decide that someone else, some other perfectly blameless bystander is wholly responsible for this new discomfort, this new inconvenience, and so therefore they too – they too must now be despatched, so that peace may be restored. It is never-ending, of course. Eternally propelled. Because the guilty party is invariably the self, you see. The cancer lies within. Are you really absolutely sure you won't, Terence? Take tea? I don't at all mind making it. I see from your expression that you know I am right. Does she . . . see someone, Amy? Psychiatrist, sort of thing? I'm told it's quite normal, among the stylish set. I wouldn't know, of course – being defiantly unstylish in all my words and actions. As I am sure you are aware, Terence. Doubtless you and Amy will have talked about it. Laughed about it.'

'We don't, we haven't – laughed about anything. And no, she doesn't see anyone. Therapist, or something. Not so far as I know. Which doesn't mean very much . . . But listen, Sylvia – tell me: tell me what I'm supposed to do. I mean . . . well the awful thing is that by the time I get back home, she might have forgotten all about it.'

'I doubt that.'

'No well but she seems to . . . swing, you see. Hot and cold, if you see what I mean. All very new, this: never seen it before. But listen, Sylvia – here's another thing: what will *you* do . . .?

You know – if she, if Amy comes round here and . . .'

'Tries to kill me . . .? Oh, I don't think that will present too much of a problem. I dug out Mike's old bat.'

'Mike's old . . .?'

'Mm. Cricket bat. He hasn't played for decades, but he insisted on clinging on to it. Silly – but sweet, in a way. Still keeps it oiled. Anyway – it's in the hall now. If she threatens or attacks me again, I shall hit her with it.'

'You'll . . .! But Sylvia . . .! You can't . . .! You can't just . . .!'

'Well why not? Very good of me not to have called the police, I think. I only didn't for your and Lizzie's sake. But you simply have to face it, Terence: she's not well. Not at all well. And forgive me for saying so, but I do think that this, all of this, it's a great deal to do with, well . . . the way you live. The way you . . . go about things. I mean – Alexander, obviously: his situation. But everything else too . . . it just doesn't seem to be *genuine*, somehow. And now . . . well now, Amy would truly appear to have departed from reality altogether. So I'm afraid it is your job, really – to restrain her. In the short term, I mean – have to seek treatment for her, obviously. Sooner the better, I'd say. Because otherwise . . . well if you don't, and she does come round here again and threatens me with violence, well then I'll do as I say. Hit her for six. The bat might relish a bit of action. Last chance to change your mind about tea, Terence.'

Don't know what to think. Don't want to think at all. Can't speak. Just content to sit here, in Mike and Sylvia's famously dreadful front room . . . and I am finding it really such a comfort. I don't actually want to leave it. How can that be? I mean to say – just look at it: glance around you, drink it in. Dralon and damask sofa. Tapestry cushions – 'scatter' cushions, probably. Upright piano – with sconces. And propped upon its little fretwork easel, the sheet music for *Some Enchanted Evening*. Half-moon rug on top of the wall-to-wall carpeting, the pattern of which is green, and queasily energetic – and this in front of the fireplace. There is a fireplace. Electric heater with fibreglass and flickering coals. Standard lamp – chintzy shade. And fringe. Two reproduction Constables, amid an abundance of gilt rococo. Knick-knacks, in clusters: porcelain figurines – one of a Regency beauty in a full-length crimson coat and an ermine muff, the other of a crone, selling balloons. A Limoges cigarette box. An elaborate candelabrum. The thud of a clock that periodically chimes. Pelmet: there's a pelmet – yes and tie-backs too. Silver-framed photographs of Mike. Silver-framed photographs of Sylvia. Silver-framed photographs of Mike, with Sylvia. Roberts radio. A magazine rack: *Radio Times, Daily Telegraph* . . . and a brick of *Reader's Digest*s. Cornice. Picture rail. Cactus. A panelled mahogany cupboard with brass drop handles which I feel sure will be concealing an analogue television. A large tin of Quality Street. Cut-glass chandelier. An onyx table lighter, with matching ashtray. Apricot emulsion, and a wallpaper dado. And – had it not been for the tumult of Amy – Sylvia's favourite vase, amassed with dahlias. Ghastly. Famously dreadful . . . and yet I am so much loving it. Sitting here. I feel embraced. Safe. And I don't want to go. But I do – go, I mean. Got to. Got to get back home: see what Amy's up to. Sylvia – she calls upstairs for Lizzie. Who comes down. And looks at the floor. We leave. I say to Lizzie: say goodbye to Sylvia, but she doesn't. And Sylvia, she says it doesn't matter. And then I hear myself offering to reimburse her for her favourite vase – maybe buy her dahlias – and she is telling me not to be so silly. As the door is closing behind us, I look at my phone: no messages.

I enter the house very stealthily – wary, though feeling like the clumsiest burglar – not quite knowing what exactly I am dreading. Lizzie does the usual – she's up those stairs in seconds flat, and I hear the slamming of the door to her room. Can't locate her, at first – Amy, I mean – and then I track her down to the dining room. She is sitting at the mighty Saarinen table, and angrily flicking through a magazine – *Harper's*, I think. Is it anger? That staccato drumming and thump of her fingers? Just impatience? Don't know. Soon find out, I expect. I don't actually much care for it, however – her sitting there. And the magazine on the white marble surface. It is so much better, the table, when left quite alone: pure – you know? K.T, she would understand this.

'So she's back now, is she? Lizzie? Honestly, the trouble that girl causes . . .'

'Yes, she's – yes. I wouldn't bother going out, if I were you. Cold. Quite cold, now.'

'I haven't the slightest intention of going anywhere. Really quite exhausted. I thought we could have a nice family evening at home. The four of us – like we used to. Doesn't that sound nice? Plenty in the freezer. I've checked. Boeuf stroganoff, we could have. Does that appeal? Or there's lasagne. Do you think a bodyguard should charge more than a tutor? Per hour, I mean. That seems to me . . . somewhat skewed. And the only one I've so far spoken to, well – no use at all to me. Didn't even want to consider killing Ouch. Didn't even let me raise the possibility. So there was no point at all in discussing Sylvia. Was there? I think I'll phone some others.'

'It's quite late, Amy. It's really quite late, now . . .'

'It is, yes. I think I'll phone some others. Terence – could you be a dear and fetch my phone? I've got all the numbers on it. I thought I'd brought it in with me, but I seem not to have it.

Could've sworn. Anyway – could you? Be an angel? And maybe we ought to open some wine. Yes? What goes with Boeuf strog-anoff? Claret, I suppose. Possibly a Rhône . . .? Or there's lasagne, of course. If you prefer. I think it must be in my bag . . .'

'Well . . . either thing. Don't mind, really. They both sound, um . . . so you are definitely staying in, then? Not going anywhere.'

'I told you, didn't I? So are you going to get my phone for me or not, Terence? In my bag – I think that's where it has to be.'

So, I am thinking, as I wander back out to the hall – because I saw it, Amy's bag, I saw it on the chair there – and I am thinking, wondering, quite what to make of all this: I mean – she's rational, after a fashion . . . but at the same time, nuts. Nothing is quite . . . cohering. Is it? It's all . . . not right. I am relieved, however, that she no longer seems determined to go and kill Sylvia . . . which in turn relieves her of the serious pos-sibility of being brained by a cricket bat. On the other hand, if she is quite decided upon staying in . . . then that completely scotches the nearest I have come to developing a plan. With regard to K.T, I mean. Because it is utterly clear now that she is quite wholly set upon cruelly and, I think, very stupidly ignoring all of my attempts to make contact . . . and so the only thing for it, I thought, was to go round there. Demand entry, if need be. And then comfort her. Do whatever it takes to make her see reason, forgive me for whatever heinous sin she imagines I have committed . . . abase myself, if necessary, so that she remembers who I am, and takes me in. Lets me be close to her again. Because I need it. I do so need it. And I am dying from the fear of just losing it for ever. Yes but . . . I just can't risk it, can I? Leaving Lizzie here with Amy. How very awful, even to think it . . . that you cannot trust a mother with her child. But I simply don't know, do I? Quite what she might be capable of. And also, of course – once this fresh and reasonably breezy mood of hers erodes, as surely it must – then she might remember her impassioned vow to assassinate the next-door neighbour. So . . . I've just got to be here, really. To prevent any . . . unpleasantness. Or bloodshed. Yes but that means, then, that I can't go to see K.T. I look at my phone: no messages. And now I am looking for Amy's phone, amid the depths of this absurd great handbag. And what I find is . . . a gun. My beautiful Luger . . .! Oh good Christ. But where on earth did . . .?! How has she . . .?! Oh good Christ. So when she was talking, raving about killing people, she actually did . . . possess the means . . .! A Luger. My beautiful Luger. And as I continue to hold and look down upon it, knowing once again – rushed by the warmth of familiarity – just how appallingly fittingly it is cradled there within the cushion of my hand, and how very charged I am by not just the feel, but the heft of it . . . quite bizarrely the only thing to enter my mind is that headmistress's perfectly ludicrous comment about her never being one for *enhancement*. And then, although my head is fretful – thick and clouded – I suddenly get it. A brilliant flash. That tomatoes thing. Her pupils – that she couldn't have them turning in tomatoes. It isn't what she said at all. What she said was . . . she couldn't have them turning into *martyrs* . . .

What I were expecting . . . well I don't rightly know, really – what I were expecting. But, like . . . going by his nickname – Jimmy Blue Eyes, yeh? Well I suppose I sort of reckoned he were going to be a bit of a Jack the Lad, know what I saying? Like sort of the cheeky, bit iffy one in a movie – real like kind of

400

good-looking and he know it, sort of style: yeh, and probably pretty shady with it, and all – up to no good. Sort of geezer your mum, she don't want you to got nothing to do with. Well nah – ain't like that at all. Gentleman, is Jimmy – just like what Richard are and all. Right pair of gentlemen, and me – I ever so lucky. Except for he really are bloody good-looking, though – yeh, and he do know it, course he do. And the eyes what he got – oh blimey. Blue – they ain't just blue: blue, that just don't come nowhere close. It like they lit up, or something – like real electric, yeh? And they goes right through you. Can't see them now, them eyes. On account of they closed. He still asleep. Just lying there under the sheet, and all kind of warm and beautiful, and them long eyelashes what he got and all – I wouldn't of half mind them, telling you that. I had to bung on these fake ones, old days, I want to be looking like that – yeh and then a whole bleeding load of mascara on the top of it and all. But one of them, left one, always the left one, it keep on peeling apart, nearly falling off of me, don't know why it were: right one were always okay – it were just the other of them bleeders what wouldn't never stay on.

Maria, she were that sad, when I gone and jack in my job up the Marriott. Brung her pinny up right to her face, she did, and she dabbing at her eyes with it, all weepy. I were right touched by that – and I tells her I were. I bung her a bottle champagne – Bollinger: Jimmy, he say it a good one, I dunno do I? She say – what's this? What you going spending your money on me for? And I never tell her it didn't cost me no money at all. Round at Jimmy's, it all over the place: champagne, vodka, you name it – it just all over. He got a fridge, it the size of my bleeding kitchen, I ain't being funny. Mr Mumtaz, he weren't pleased. He say I a real good worker, and he don't want to lose me: yeh

401

well – he never say nothing like that when I were working so bleeding good for him, did he? And then he say I got to see out my notice and I goes to him I can't, on account of this new job I got, right? It start today. And he say then I won't get no money, and I goes and tells him to go and stuff his bleeding money, basically. Jimmy – he give me five hundred quid, yeh? And I never even done nothing yet. Maria, she say to me – so what this new job then Dolly? You in another hotel? And I goes nah – I travelling now, that what I'll be doing. And her eyes, yeh? They goes all big like I joking or something, but I weren't. And then she go to me I really do like your coat – lovely colour, and it ever so soft. I chuffed about that, of course – pick it out myself. Only Yves St Laurent, that's all. Bright yellow, like in a boiled egg. And I got Ferragamo shoes, you can believe it, and that lovely little navy blue Chanel handbag with the chains all wove into the leather wossname over your shoulder, and yeh – I looking bloody good, I says it myself. And Mumtaz, he get all sort of nasty then, he do, little fucker. He go to me: so what truth then, Dolly? You on game, is it? And his head all go wagging about side to side, and his eyes dead dirty. He still howling at me when I walks down the corridor and out of that bloody hotel for ever – because I only gone and clock him one, didn't I? Right round his bloody chops. Yeh and if he come after me, I would of killed him, filthy bleeder.

It didn't take him long, Jimmy, to get me to do whatever he like. Reckon I want it even before he do: ain't felt nothing like it, not in bleeding ages. Damien . . . I don't never even think of him like that no more, not in that sort of a way, you know? Can't hardly remember when I did. Must of once, I suppose – on account of Kenny, if nothing else. Sometimes, he get too much beer inside of him, and he start all sort of pawing me and I goes

to him bleeding get off of me Damien, can't you? What you
think you doing? And he stinking of the beer and he go oh come
on Dolly, come on – what wrong with you? Ay? Never used to
be like this, Dolly. Did you? Ay? Yeh well, I says to him – I like
it now, aren't I? Give over slobbering on me, will you? Just go
to bleeding bed, can't you? And he say well you come with me
then . . . on and on, he go. Yeh and sometimes I done it: just to
shut him up, basically: get it done with. I know what do it for
him, so it never take too long. Minute, tops – and then he snoring
and gurgling and belching out all of his horrible beery stink.
Yeh but with Jimmy . . . oh blimey. Oh bloody hell. I ain't never
felt nothing like this. I mean – I would of done it with Richard,
yeh I would of. Because I had a bit to drink and he were ever
so nice to me, and he were ever so clean . . . but Jimmy, oh
blimey. Oh bloody hell. He touch me . . . when he first go and
touch me, I just go to bleeding bits. And then he go and look at
me with them amazing, just amazing blue eyes what he got . . .!
Yeh well . . . and that just done it, really.

You want to see his flat. Apartment, he call it – duplex, what
I thought were a rubber johnny, and he laugh at that, but not
unkind nor nothing. He got white settees, size of a bleeding
boat. It right high up in a modern building with all big like
windows what slides open and he got a sort of a little garden
going on out there on the wossname and you can see Big Ben
and the Shard. Telly on the wall like in the bleeding Odeon and
all big sort of like paintings what look like someone gone doo-
lally with the Dulux, you asking me – yeh but what do I know
about art? I don't know nothing about nothing – and now I
meeting the like of Richard and Jimmy, I sees that I knows even
less than what I thought I knowed. I tell him, Jimmy, about how
I going to get elocution classes, and he say I like how you

talking, Dolly – I like it. And I go why you like it, Jimmy? Is it because you think it sound funny? You laughing at me, or what? No, he says – course I ain't laughing: yeh, but he laughing when he say it. And then I'm like – here listen, Jimmy: got an idea. Hard to keep my mind on what I saying, you want the truth, because we was in bed at the time – when I not on a trip or clothes shopping and seeing to Kenny, time to time, that where I seem to be, most the day – and he got this bleeding feather, I ain't joking. Bloody great thing, it is, sort of reddy mauvey colour, ostrich he says – and he just sort of stroking my tit with it, what make me go ever so funny. But no listen, Jimmy, okay? When I talking – when I talking, right? When I saying whatever, okay? If I goes and says it wrong, I wants you to tell me. Tell me how to say it proper. All right? Not just wrong words and that, but the way I says it – because I want to be all sort of 'How Now Brown Cow', all right? And then you can learn me. All right? You don't have to stop with the feather. Yeh but he do – he packs it in with the feather, and he looking at me dead straight and he go to me: are you serious? And I'm like, *course* I'm serious – what you think I say it for? And he says: what – every *time* . . .? And I goes bloody hell, Jimmy! What you mean every *time* . . .? I can't be that bad! I ain't that bad, am I . . .? And he go . . . well yeh, Dolly. Actually. So okay: I takes it on board: got a lot of work to do, then.

Won't never forget that very first trip what I done for him. Didn't hardly get no sleep the night before, I were that nervous – and even before I get myself to bed, Damien, even Damien, he notice I all like sort of keyed up. He look at me odd. Never says nothing, though. He were playing one of them stupid bloody games with Kenny: all kind of cars crashing and blowing up and they laughing their bleeding heads off. It were that sort of thing

404

what make me always think that men, boys . . . I don't know . . . like they was all defective, some way – not sort of exactly mental nor nothing, but just bleeding pathetic, basically. But I knows now: they not all like that. And the next morning, I does all of my make-up real careful, and I puts on all of my get-up – all ready for my trip. I decided it be best for me to go up the Marriott for the look of it, and then they got me a taxi booked and I going to Heathrow, all right? And then I flying in a plane to Amsterdam in Holland. Can't hardly believe it. Last time I were out of England it were on honeymoon in Magaluf and Damien were off his face every night on the lager and my nose got all burnt and then it go and peel and rest of the holiday I were looking like Coco the bleeding Clown and getting sick on the sangria: were pleased it were only the five-night package. Yeh and the day before this trip to Amsterdam I got my hair done. Jimmy, he send me up Nicky Clarke and it shorter now, and with a fringe? Ever so smart and classy, but sexy with it, you know? And that a bit why I never sleep all night: didn't want to mess it up. So I put on the dark pink bouclé Chanel suit, patent courts with a kitten heel, same bag what I were wearing with the yellow St Laurent coat . . . and I set. You know what Damien say when he see me . . .? He say: you look nice. And I go: ta. And then he say: you on all day up the Marriott, or what? And I go: yeh. And he say: so I picking up Kenny again, that it? And I go: yeh, Damien – that's it. And he nod. I don't know . . . what sort of a man is he, ay? I ask you. And yeh I were thinking of Jimmy – course I were. Wanted him again real bad – and it only the afternoon before we been going at it like we was in a marathon, or something. He wear me out. He near kill me, Jimmy . . . yeh and then I want it all over again. Jimmy: that what he do to me.

Yeh but if people knowed about all of this, I can see what they be thinking. They be thinking: what she think she up to? Ay? This Dolly person: she stupid, or what? Why they sending her to Amsterdam? She asked them, or what? Why they give her all of them luxury doings? And the money. She asked them, or what? Well no – I never, as it happens. Because I thought, well . . . their business, ain't it? Really. Not bleeding idiots, are they? Richard and Jimmy – bleeding idiots? Don't hardly think so. So no: I didn't ask no questions. Not my place to, I reckon. So anyways – I gets to Heathrow, yeh, and I been told to go to the what is it . . .? Business Class lounge of British Airways, yeh, and I done that. And then these ever so nice people, they takes care of everything for me. All the men in there, they was mostly men, was dressed ever so nice in suits, and that – not like all of them losers queuing up for EasyJet on the concourse in all like bleeding nylon football strips and real naff bumbags, and their great big podgy wives is in like onesies and sweats and stupid T-shirts with stupid words on, just like their great big podgy kids – they just don't care: got no style at all.

I don't got no luggage nor nothing, obviously – just a Vuitton holdall in dark red epi leather, real class, with magazines and make-up in, basically. And ooh . . .! I were ever so pleased when Jimmy come in then . . .! I having a glass of champagne what they was doling out for nothing because I got to quite like it, and I goes and all splutter it out when I sees him walking through the door, like – because he say to me, Jimmy, that some-one'll be meeting me there just before the flight, yeh? But he never say it were going to be him! And he give me a kiss and that, and then he give me a packet. It sort of the size of them Ferrero Rocher boxes what I always get of a Christmas time, and it all wrapped up ever so nice and with a ribbon and a bow and all like it a birthday present or something. And I says: that nice, Jimmy – it for me? And he go: no, Dolly – not for you. What I wants you to do, okay, is bung it in your bag, all right? And take it to Amsterdam. Have lunch in that restaurant what I told you. You got the map? Yeh? Sure you got it? And then you has yourself a bit of a walk about – it a lovely little city, think you'll like it – and then you takes the 4.50 flight back home again. All right? Then you come round the apartment and give it me. The packet. All right? And . . . well . . . I just sort of looks at him. I a bit worried, to be honest: thought I missed something. Thought there must be something important what he just gone and said to me, and I never picks it up. So I asks him to say all of it again, and he do. And it just like what I thought. And no – I never asks him why he want me take a gift-wrapped packet to Amsterdam, and then bring it all the way back with me and give it back to him. No I never. Because Jimmy – not a bloody idiot, is he? Don't hardly think so. Know what he doing, don't he? So I just nods. Bung the packet in my Vuitton and I goes to him All right then Jimmy, I sees you when I sees you. And he go to me: no, Dolly – I'll see you when I see you. And I says . . . what . . .? And he go: it wrong what you said. It should be 'I'll see you when I see you'. And I say . . . that what I said, ain't it? And he go no. So I thinks it over – and yeh: he right. He keep doing all of this like what I ask him to and all sort of learning me, like – I be speaking proper in no time.

It all gone so perfect. The flight were ever so smooth, and we got there ever so quick. I had steak and chips for my dinner – lunch, pardon – and it right what Jimmy say: it really pretty, Amsterdam. Lovely sunny day it were, and all of the canals, and that. I were sorry I never had no time to go on one of them boats. Course, I been back a few times now, and I done that pleasure cruise . . . and I done the Rembrandt Museum and all

(I know people say he great, Rembrandt, but I can't see it, if I'm honest: his pictures, they ever so gloomy, and the most of them, they just got his ugly mug in – and you got to face it, he ain't no oil painting, is he?). And I done the Heineken factory – Damien, he be in his wossname, element: he'd want to move in, silly sod – be bladdered on the lager for the rest of his bleeding life, love that he would. Another thing what weren't up to much were the Anne Frank house, what was this girl what wrote a diary like what I done when I were at school, but hers, it just got to be famous and were in Dutch, of course. And when I come back from that very first trip, oh – I were right full of it all. Loved every minute. And when I give Jimmy back his packet, he were ever so pleased with me. And I says to him: but I done nothing, Jimmy – I just like been on a little holiday! And then I says to him – here, what's in the packet then? I really been wanting to know. And he go: open it. And I'm, like – really? You sure? And he go: yeh, Dolly – open it, go on. So I does that – tears off all of the paper and the bow and that . . . and it a plain white cardboard box. And inside of it . . . there nothing. Nothing at all – not a bleeding dicky bird: it completely bloody empty. So I says to Jimmy: what's the game? What's going on? And he say to me that this, this here were a trial run, is what he say. This were to see if I look the part, whatever that mean. And I come through . . .! So next time, he say – next time, you be taking a packet like this, yeh? Could be smaller, won't never be a lot bigger, is what he say to me – and sometimes, yeh, could only be a envelope. And then you leaves it somewhere. Else, you goes out with nothing at all, not even a envelope . . . and you brings something back what someone'll give you. Sometimes it both. Won't always be Amsterdam, course: could be anywhere – all right? And I go yeh – yeh, Jimmy: all right. And then, he

408

only go and bung me another five hundred: can't hardly believe it . . .! He give me some champagne, and I says to him: Jimmy . . . I want sex now. I want it bad. And you know what he come back to me with? He say – no, Dolly: you want sex badly. No, I goes – I want it good, like what you always does. And he go: that not what I mean. And I says well you want to say what you mean then, don't you? Anyways – we in bed in no time after that. Blowed my head off. Yeh. And after, he give me a snort of charley – ain't never done it before, only ever seed it in movies, and he show me how to stuff the rolled-up fifty in my nose: would be a fifty – he got a lot of style, Jimmy. Two white lines, all chopped out, and on a mirror. I were blowing it all over, at first I were, and then I kind of got the hang of it. It were amazing. Like everything, with Jimmy. Yeh. I getting ever so fond of him.

CHAPTER TEN

A REALM OF SOPHISTICATION

'Alexander who . . .?'

Look: I can barely bring myself to recall it, but this is what she said to me, you know. Amy, she actually did say this to me, her eyes struck open with wonder. And yes, okay, she rallied round almost immediately, yes she did: '*Oh!*' she said. '*Alexander* – oh of course, Alexander. Well why didn't you say so, Terence?' Yes but nevertheless, it was then, it was at that moment that I just had to face up to what I'd been ducking for just ages – despite all the lunacy that had been forced right into my face, and several times daily. But when she said that, when she came out with 'Alexander who . . .?' . . . well . . . I couldn't really hide any more – and that's quite something, coming from me, because I'm really very good at it: hiding. Amy, then . . . she has a rather serious problem. That the very existence of the sun and moon, the centre of her being and universe, could actually have slipped her mind, if only for the briefest of moments . . . well that was a worry, a very great worry. Wouldn't you say?

Because up till now, I had been trying my damnedest to become accustomed to the nearly constant . . . oscillation, I have come to call it. One moment she's the old acerbic Amy, sharp as a knife – glinting with menace, and a capacity to wound – and then she would be elsewhere: staring at her phone which she cradled in her hand, when she hadn't even turned it on. Plucking at the shoulder of her angora sweater, fastidiously picking away at a series of wholly imaginary bobbles. Which is another thing: her appearance. Sometimes immaculately dressed and made-up, her hair just so, quite like the Amy we know, and occasionally have loved. Other times, well . . . in a state I can barely describe, actually – a state which I never could have dreamt that Amy could get herself into: bare and shiny face – hair scraped back into a rubber band, nothing on her feet, tracksuits . . . didn't even know that she owned a tracksuit. Well there. And then suddenly she could be highly energetic and determined, though with no discernible direction or intent. The old obsessions would recur: Ouch, Sylvia. Sometimes she still wanted them dead, while at other times she was completely convinced that they had already been despatched. She told me that she had shot them. They both had been cowering on their knees before her, babbling for mercy. And she had shot them. First Ouch, through the head – and Sylvia, when she bolted, in the back: it took, said Amy solemnly, several shots to bring her down. On another occasion, Ouch had been strangled with a silk Hermès scarf – a limited edition. While Sylvia had merely passed away peacefully in her sleep – from old age, Amy said – thereby cruelly depriving her of the much anticipated pleasure of beating her to death with a carpenter's mallet. And subsequent to that, Sylvia had apparently plummeted to a thundering demise following a footling miscalculation during an elaborate stunt on a rope at Niagara Falls. I also seem to recall a reference to Ouch having been drowned in his lavatory.

Is that enough . . . ? It is, isn't it? It's more than enough – and

I'm bloody worried, I can tell you that. And throughout, I have been attempting to behave ... well, drinking hard, as you might expect, barely sleeping ... but still I have been attempting to behave quite normally – though I am fast forgetting how even the conception of normal actually *goes*. And in terms of the basic everyday running of the household (is that what we have here? A household?) I am being very much tested. Well: let us put that another way, shall we? I am making a complete and utter dog's fucking breakfast of the whole bloody business, is the truth of the matter. Sometimes I am assuming that Lizzie is at school, and then I discover that she isn't. Haven't actually done anything about Lizzie yet, of course: she's so silent, she's so absent, she's so very wilfully invisible, that it is rather easier for now to go along with the illusion that she doesn't actually exist. Shameful, I know: but Amy, well ... in the loony stakes, she's completely taken over. You see? I mean, Lizzie – she's disturbed, quite clearly – we can all agree on that. But Amy, Jesus – she's making the Mad Hatter seem an exemplar for sagacity and quiet good sense. I've suggested – well of course I have, and more than once, loads of bloody times actually – that she see someone, and she says that she doesn't want to see anybody. And I say yes but if you see a, you know – *professional*, Amy, he really might be able to help you, you see. She says she doesn't need any help, and then she's suddenly staring at me and looking quite alarmed as if I am the crazy one here: she just shakes her head in ... I don't know – possibly pity. Well I don't know. What's going on? I'd dearly love to know. And what in God's name am I expected to do about it? I wish there was someone to tell me. Because I've got my own things, you know – other things that I really ought to be thinking about, and putting some effort and time into. Yeh well – can't at the

412

moment. Want to – want to more than anything, but can't: not at the moment, the way things are. Christ: you know it ain't easy.

And then there's . . . Alexander. He's very rapidly gone from being thoroughly contented, as well as frankly nothing to do with me, to very much less so on the contentment front, and something of an increasingly tiresome burden. Positively surly, last time I encountered him. Said he felt sure that he was due at a shoot that morning for he thought it could be *Style* magazine, and hadn't the booker called about collection and where is Mummy? I said no, no shoot – not this morning: no booker called. Hadn't a bloody clue, as should be quite perfectly obvious – and it was no good at all consulting Amy on the matter because that morning, she had decided, was to be devoted to putting all of her books in alphabetical order, commencing with M. So yes – positively surly, he was: no other word for it. And yes I do know why, and it's all my fault. Well it's Amy's fault, actually, for going so bloody nuts in the first place . . . but my fault too for being so very demonstrably unable to pick up the slack and just get on with taking care of business. Literally business in the case of Alexander, as already we have seen: and it's all a bit dire. It's sort of in danger of . . . unravelling. If I'm not very careful (and the trouble is, I'm not) everything just might . . . come apart. And while I know this . . . what I do not know is even remotely how I can go about keeping it together. Case in point: just yesterday, I picked up the phone. It had been ringing for a while. Can't think what came over me though, because it's something I'd been actively avoiding, picking up the phone. Some American person. The last time I heard that accent, it had emanated from the ludicrous Portia, and that was a thousand years ago.

413

'Hi. Bob Horwitz. Amy there . . .?'

'Amy – no. No I'm sorry. She can't speak at the moment. Would you like to leave a message?'

'She can't . . . speak? It's Bob Horwitz.'

'Yes, you said. So – any message?'

'And you are . . .?'

'I am Terence. Amy's husband. Yes.'

'Oh right – so you know all about Alexander then, yeah?'

'Oh yes. Course. Well . . .'

'So I'm kinda . . . surprised, I guess. Which is why I'm like – calling? That she hasn't gotten back to me?'

'Oh yes?'

'Yeah. Time sensitive, you know? Like I explained. Tick tock. If we gonna do this album, it gotta be out in a month, buddy. We need to ride the wave. Tick tock, yeah?'

'Uh-huh. Album . . .?'

'Look . . . lemme speak to Amy, yeah? Put her on, Terry.'

'Well as I say, she can't speak. And it's Terence, actually.'

Yes and when I said she can't speak, it happened at that moment to be quite literally true: she was in bed, alternately strumming her lips and forcing between them a succession of chocolate-coated marshmallows while watching an endless stream of vintage *Kojak*s. I suggested that five straight episodes on the trot might just be going it a bit, no . . .? But she just shook her head angrily and went back to a fairly heavy and energetic bout of really quite serious lip-strumming. Well, I thought: at least she's out of my way . . . although she's managed to get chocolate all over the duvet. I'm not cleaning it: you know – washing it, or anything. I shall throw it away, and buy a new one. Or, more likely, just leave it.

'Look, buddy . . . I sent her over everything. I talked with her

414

about the situation. Money is top dollar. If this is about the money, buddy, you can just forget it. Money is top dollar.'

'Right. Well look Mr, um – Halfwits, is it?'

'Horwitz.'

'Fine. Well I'll be sure to tell her you called.'

'That don't cut it, buddy. I'm now rethinking this whole goddamn deal, you know? I'm thinking it ain't about to come off . . .?'

'Well you never know, do you? I'll get her to call you, Amy – all right? She's, erm – got your number and everything, has she?'

'She's . . . she's got the whole enchilada. What's going on here, buddy . . .?'

'Well she'll ring you, then. I promise.'

Mm, I thought, as I put down the phone (yes and I shan't be picking it up again in a hurry, I can tell you that): no good asking me, Halfwits, what's going on here, because I'm bloody sure I haven't the least idea: *buddy* . . .

Alexander is now a pupil at Highgate School, it would appear. I had no idea he had actually been enrolled (that Amy, she does work quickly, she surely does get things done – used to, anyway). First I knew of it was this morning when an official letter of welcome arrived in the post. I only opened it because it was addressed to Mr and Mrs, and this did strike me as something of a quaint and really rather charming novelty: simply can't remember when anything arrived that was addressed to Mr and Mrs. Also enclosed 'for your consideration' was a comically staggering invoice, this to cover the entire current term, and also the successive term in advance. Not much short of what I used to earn in a year, when I was just starting out: well – not quite. More though than it had cost me to have installed a loft

415

conversion at my lovely old flat in Belsize Park – also to have had the entire place redecorated, and all the busy fireplaces and cornices removed. So tomorrow – too late today – I'll have to try to remember to order a taxi or something to get Alexander up to Highgate. Has he got the uniform . . .? No idea. Has he actually met anyone there? Will he know where to go and who to speak to . . .? No idea. Oh Christ – I don't have to go *with* him, do I . . .? Well I can't. Can't actually go anywhere. I'm jailed. That's the absolute pain of it. It's Amy – well of course it's Amy: don't dare leave her. Can't imagine what she might *do*: well I can, actually – that's the trouble. And this is why . . . yes, and this is the part of this completely ridiculous nightmare that is so terribly getting to me, of course – this, this is why I still haven't yet managed to be with K.T. And I need to, I need to – oh God I do so need to. And it's all a bit dire. It's sort of in danger of . . . unravelling. If I'm not very careful (and the trouble is, I'm not) everything just might . . . come apart.

Did eventually get to speak to her on the phone, though. The messages box had been cleared, and so I left a dozen more. And then . . . and then . . . she actually called me back . . .! I was amazed – thrilled, of course, utterly thrilled, oh God yes – but amazed, quite astonished, that she had actually called me back . . .!

'K.T . . .! K.T . . .! Oh *God*, K.T . . .!'

'Yes. It's me. What do you want, Tom?'

'What . . . do I *want* . . .? What do I . . . *want* . . .?'

'Yes, Tom: what do you want?'

'Well I want . . . are you *serious*, K.T? What do I *want* . . .? Well – you. I want you, K.T. I said. I told you. You know that's what I want. It's you – it always was. It always will be. Just you. The way we were.'

'Well . . . we ought to talk.'

'Yes! We ought. We must. Been trying to. For days . . .'

'Okay . . . well I suppose you'd better come over, then.'

'Ah . . .'

'Ah? What's "ah", Tom . . .?'

'Well at the moment, you see – I can't. Not just – at the moment.'

'Right. Terrific.'

'No no – it's just that . . . well I'm sick. As a dog, actually. Don't know what it is – just suddenly I was . . . and then I was . . . it might have been something I . . . don't know. But I'm flat on my back. Feel terrible. Yes.'

'Oh. Poor you. Okay, well . . . call me when you're better, yeh?'

'Absolutely. Of course. Will do. Can't wait.'

'You don't . . . *sound* sick . . .'

'No well I'm pleased. Sparing you, you see. Because I *have* sounded sick. Christ yes. As a dog. Not good. Not nice. But tomorrow – I'm sure I'll be fine tomorrow: I'll come and see you tomorrow, okay? Or maybe even later today – I might be feeling absolutely fine, later on. Never know.'

'Well . . . whatever, then. Look after yourself, okay?'

'I love you, K.T . . .'

'Just take care. Bye then, Tom.'

And why did I say that? Why did I go and say to her that tomorrow I'd be fine – that I'd be coming round to K.T's tomorrow? Or even later today . . .! Why in the name of Jesus did I ever say I might be round there later today when I know, I just know, that the bloody situation here with Amy, it isn't going to *change*, is it? Not going to alter in any way – not by tomorrow, anyway. And certainly not by bloody later on today.

417

So why did I have to go and *say* that . . .? Well . . . because . . . because I wanted it to be so. I want to see her. It seems as if we have been apart for simply *years* . . . and I want to see her. I've got to see her. If I don't very soon see and touch her, I'll completely lose my mind. And this house, it's already pretty well stocked with fucking lunatics, wouldn't you say? Without my adding to their number. Oh Jesus . . . oh Jesus . . . what shall I *do* . . .? And then it came to me: a delirious and blinding eureka moment: *Sylvia* . . .! Yes! She can *babysit* . . .! Look, look, listen to me – just hear me out: I know it seems mad, at first sight. But if you just stop and think about it for a moment, and soon I will do that . . . well then it all makes perfect sense. Because look: okay, Amy, she wants to kill Sylvia, yes I do know that. Or else she imagines that Sylvia is already dead. And if she comes round here, Sylvia, then she'll know that she isn't dead, and so therefore will want to kill her. But in a way, you see – and this is why I really do think she might go for it – in a way, this *rescues* Sylvia from all danger, because then she'll be in the prime position to keep a very close eye on the only person on earth who wants to kill her, you see. She's a big person, Sylvia – what used to be called a handsome woman: she can easily take care of herself. And if it comes to it, there's always Mike's old cricket bat, isn't there? And then if Sylvia is here . . . and Lizzie is here (she likes Sylvia, Lizzie) and Alexander is here . . . well then there is nothing to stop me effecting an instant and miracle recovery from whatever it is that ails me, and shooting round to K.T, the love of my life – finally, yes, and for ever . . .!

And now . . . some minutes have passed: twenty . . . twenty minutes, could be . . . half an hour . . . and still I'm just sitting in the hall . . . pondering, thinking over all of that. Nonsense, isn't it? Did I truly imagine that Sylvia would ever agree to it? That she would clap her hands in glee and congratulate me warmly for having come up with so terribly neat and logical a solution? Whatever Sylvia is, she is neither insane nor suicidal. She will never again be agreeable to setting foot in this house, and rightly. So . . . am I raving . . .? Am I also in danger of losing my grip? No . . . I don't think so. It's desperation, is all it is. I am desperate to bend the actuality, to twist up a wild and flailing possibility into any distortion at all that might, if not dovetail, then somehow be manhandled and battered into forming some sort of a grotesque misshapen effigy of the true conclusion I had been aiming for. Which is K.T. To see her. Got to – got to get to her. And so . . . that's just what I'm going to do. Leave. Got to. Take a chance on it. Hope that Amy will be fine until I get back. Hope that she won't feel the need to kill someone. Hope that she won't take it into her head that the thing to do now is just, I don't know . . . set fire to herself, or something. So I'll take a chance on it. Got to. And I won't actually say it to Amy, that I'm going – because however she reacts, whatever mood grabs an instant hold of her, it means there will be talk, and I'm done with it, talk. The only person I want to talk to is K.T. This is quite literally essential to me. And no point at all in knocking gently on Lizzie's door and whispering lullingly through the panels that Daddy is just quickly slipping out for a moment . . . because Lizzie neither knows nor gives a single damn wherever I might be at any hour of the night or day, so why would she now? And Alexander . . .? Joking. So . . . I am putting on my coat, now . . . and I am leaving. Taking a chance on it. Because if K.T isn't worth a chance, well what is? And yes she'll say Christ, Tom – what are you doing here? I thought you were supposed to be sick. Yes, she'll say that, bound to, something like it, anyway. But so what? I am resilient, I shall say to her – look at me! I have bounced back.

419

There is a person, man, in the hallway as I walk into the building. K.T, she has just buzzed me in – after one hell of a while, frankly. Sounded quite as amazed to hear my voice as it was echoing over the intercom as I sort of supposed she would be. Had collared a cab reasonably quickly, so I got there in no time, really. Well – other side of London, obviously, but still the journey seemed surprisingly fast: maybe because I was willing it to be. And my heart was stopped as we swung into the road: soon now, and I would be with her – we would be together again, K.T and I, snuggling within her actually quite delightful little studio flat in Notting Hill, Portobello really. He seems to be waiting for me to pass him, the man, and he does loom rather large. 'Awreet . . .?' That's what he is saying to me, just as I am reaching the first-floor landing: 'Awreet . . .?' He is nodding his head, and quite curtly. Really is quite massive, this man – big black beard: looks like the villain – what's his name – in *Popeye*. 'I'm fine, thank you,' I answer automatically, and quite like the perfect moron – and then I continue plodding on up to the top. K.T is standing at the open door, when I reach it – her eyes struck open, I'm noticing – ablaze with something, hard to tell. I'm just so totally caught up within the welter of simply *being* here again . . . oh, I just can't tell you.

'. . . K.T . . .!'

'Hello, Tom. I didn't . . . expect you. Not so soon. I thought you were supposed to be sick.'

'Was. As a dog. All right now. Tip-top. As you can see. I should have . . . yes, I should really have brought champagne. I didn't. Should have, though. But you've got some, haven't you? You seem to have piles of it.'

'Come in, Tom.'

'Thank God you rang. I was nearly going out of my mind . . .!

420

Why did you wait so long? Why didn't you take my calls? Jesus – all those bloody messages I left . . .'

'I was thinking. I've been thinking.'

'Uh-huh. Where shall I put my coat? Just stick it here, will I . . .?'

'About us. About the two of us.'

'Well . . . that's good. That's a good thing. Me – I think about . . .'

'Yes I know: nothing else.'

'Yes – that's what I was . . .'

'Going to say. Yes. I know.'

I drape my coat over the back of a bright red lacquer Magistretti chair – wonderful thing, about 1960 I think, with a rough rush seat. Pluto – that's the name, isn't it? Villain in *Popeye*? Or no – that's the dog, that's the Mickey Mouse dog, pretty sure: not Goofy, the other one, the orange one. Bluto, it might just conceivably be . . . though I can't bring myself to address exactly why I am seemingly so very deliberately exploring all of this – can't imagine why I am padding out the moment with rubbish about where I'm to put my coat, the name of the stupid fucker in *Popeye* . . . but still I continue to sod around with the thing – and it's a nice coat, good coat, Crombie, midnight blue, velvet collar – forever elongating the instant, as if to defer for ever the next one, though already I can sense its coming: its silent introduction is enormous, and so very throbbingly loud as to jangle me utterly. And while I continue to fool with this bloody coat, something heavy is tumbling from the pocket – it clonks quite decisively upon the floor.

'Jesus, Tom . . .! What in Christ's name . . .?!'

'Oh that – oh God yes. I know. Gorgeous, isn't it? Do you want to . . . feel . . .?'

421

And I had been quite as amazed as K.T, when first I saw it just lying there. Remembered, of course – how I had quickly stuffed it into my coat, just slung there in the hall, after I had been so completely astonished to have come across the thing during a cursory rummage of crazy Amy's handbag. I stooped to pick it up, knowing once again – rushed by the warmth of familiarity – just how appallingly fittingly it is cradled there within the cushion of my hand, how very charged I am by not just the feel, but the heft of it. My finger is folding so blissfully naturally around the welcoming curve of the trigger, and as I look across to K.T, I imagine my face really just has to be so ridiculously wide-eyed with wonder, and smarmed all over with a childlike delight. Her smile is sly, as I move to pass over to her this perfectly glorious thing – and her hand is out, and eager . . . but then we both are instantly stunned, and suddenly spiked by fright – I feel it instantly in all of my heightened and electric senses, and see so plainly the vivid alarm alive on K.T's face – as the door to the flat is immediately crashed and burst open, and before I can even scream or run, a giant of a black-bearded man is on and then all over me, bellowing as if enraged beyond endurance by an absolute agony, and grappling at once for my throat and wrists, while winding me severely, forcing me to retch. K.T screeches and is attempting her pitiable best to wrench him away from me – but this man, Jesus, he is twenty solid tons of bulk, with ten outrageous sets of big and bony hands . . . and I am sinking to my knees, now, invaded by decline and weakness, I am feeling gradually so very sweetly exhausted and utterly bruised – but as he wrangles for the gun in my hand ... well then immediately I become so completely angered . . .! I sense the smoulder of true indignation, and I am fighting back now with all that is in me – and K.T too, she's trying, she's trying to tug and claw at the beast, but she's no match at all for this perfectly wild and fearsome thing – and nor am I, and nor am I . . .! She is mewling, he is roaring . . . and he has it now – he has it in his enormous mitt, and I know with dreadful certainty that it would be nothing short of madness for me to lunge towards him with all the strength I have now still within me, my fists upraised – and I lunge towards him with all the strength I have now still within me, my fists upraised in fury, and then this extraordinary *booming* . . .! There is . . . a resounding plangency, and it is stinging in my ears, and I clutch at this rush of hot then scalding pain so close to the very heart of me and try to shriek, though knowing I'll never be able to rise to anything close to shrieking . . . and I'm falling now, I can feel myself going . . . I'm falling, keeling over, yes . . . and I want to, I need to, I am needing to fall, to fold, to crumple and collapse, to lie down quietly, and to close my eyes: I think, now, I might just have to die . . .

'Oh Jesus Christ in heaven, Guy . . .! What have you done? What have you *done* . . .?! What did you think you were *doing* . . .?! Why are you here? Why are you even *here* . . .?! I thought you'd gone. You went – you left! Tom! Tom! Are you all right . . .? Oh my God. Phone an ambulance! Don't just stand there, you—! Phone a bloody *ambulance* . . .!'

'He was coming for you . . .! He had a gun, Christ's sake . . .! You're my *wife* . . .!'

'Oh you don't *understand*, Guy . . .! It wasn't . . .! Oh – you just don't *understand* . . .! Wait a minute – he's speaking . . . get a cushion, Guy. He's trying to speak. Oh my God . . . there's blood all over the . . .'

'No . . .'

'What? What did you say, Tom? Well at least he's *talking* . . .'

423

'No . . . ambulance. Be fine. Have you got an Elastoplast . . .?'

'Oh bloody hell, Tom – I don't even know if you're trying to be funny . . .! Where's that cushion, Guy? Get a towel. Oh Christ *do* something, can't you . . .?'

'Warn't my fault, K.T. He had a gun. He had a *gun*, man . . .!'

'Yes and you've gone and bloody well *shot* him with it, you absolute moron . . .!'

'Oh Jesus . . .'

'*Towel!* How many times? *Towel* . . .! And get a fucking cushion. Tom . . .? Tom . . .? I'm just going to try to take your jacket off, all right . . .? Tell me if I'm hurting you . . . is that all right? Yes? I'm not hurting you, am I Tom? Oh look . . . I think it's just . . . it looks like it just grazed you, Tom. Well – more than *grazed*, obviously – but I don't think you . . . it doesn't actually look like there's a bullet in you, or anything. Jesus. Can't believe I'm saying all this . . . All right, Tom? Just try to rest. Christ – you could have been killed . . .! What did you have a . . .? Why have you got a . . .? No – don't answer – just lie still. Guy . . .! *Guy* . . .! Where the fuck *are* you with the towel . . .? Oh – forget it: I'll just use kitchen roll.'

I may or may not have slept a bit, after that. Passed out, maybe. Yes – I must have, because that's surely the last I remember of that little scene. And now . . . I seem to be sitting, half lying, in the very comfortable Aalto chaise. My shirt is off – nice shirt, good shirt that was, Hilditch & Key, bloodied rag now, I suppose – and there's some sort of a bandage around my shoulder and under my arm. Frayed edges – probably a torn-up sheet, or something. Hurts like bloody hell: raw, it feels, and as if it's on fire. K.T's here . . . and there is love in her eyes, I'm certain of that. K.T's here . . . oh thank Christ: it will all be all right now: K.T's here . . .

424

'Feeling a little bit better, are you Tom . . .? You've been asleep.'

'How long . . .?'

'Not long. Hour or two. Can I get you anything? Drink? Good idea? Is the smoke bothering you . . .?'

'Has he . . .?'

'Yes – yes of course. Gone. I'm really so . . . sorry, Tom . . .'

'But why was . . .?'

'He was here because . . . well because I'd asked him to be, if you want the actual truth. You said you were sick. I didn't think you'd come. I'm . . . confused. I needed to talk to someone.'

'Why him?'

'I don't know why him. Why not him? Do you want a malt?'

'He said you were . . .'

'Yes well – I'm sorry you had to hear it like that. I'm amazed you heard anything at all, actually – you seemed so woozy, so totally out of it.'

'But is it true . . .?'

'Well – I told you I got married, Tom. Didn't I? I told you that.'

'Yes but he didn't say ex-wife . . . he said *wife* . . .'

'Yes well.'

'Yes well what?'

'Do you want that whisky?'

'Of course I do. Answer me, K.T. Is he still . . .? Are you both still . . .?'

'Technically, I suppose . . .'

'So you haven't . . .?'

'No. Not actually. Separated, obviously. That green Conran vase got broken. Someone knocked it over, during all the . . .'

'And are you . . .?'

'Going to? Well – that was always the intention.'

425

'And it still is, is it? The intention? Get me that drink, could you K.T?'

'Course. Well that depends, doesn't it?'

'Does it?'

'Yes it does. On you. As always.'

'But I've *told* you, K.T . . .! I've *told* you . . .!'

'Okay – here's your drink, Tom. Can I help you to sit up . . .? No? Sure you're okay? Well – let's get all of this quite straight then, shall we? You're finally going to tell . . . that woman that you're leaving her. Yes? For good. And then you're going to leave her. For good. And also for me. Right? And all that's going to happen right now. Is that it?'

'Well . . .'

'Ah. And here we go again . . .'

'No – *no*, K.T: it's not like that. It's just that, well . . . a hell of a lot has happened since I last – well, since we spoke. If you'd taken my calls, I could have told you . . .'

'Told me what?'

'Well it's not just Lizzie, you see – I mean, she does have problems, no doubt at all about that. Oh Christ . . . Lizzie . . .! I do hope she's all right. I hope *everyone's* all right, actually – because I'm just remembering: I left. Didn't I? I just left. It's Amy, you see . . .'

'Who . . .?'

'Don't, K.T. Please. Just let me tell you: Amy – I can't keep avoiding her name, so just listen. Amy – she's gone a bit . . . well – crazy, really. Really very odd. You know? Worrying. Very. And everything's a bit going to pieces . . . and Alexander, well – she takes care of all of that, usually, but . . . she isn't. And I can't. Obviously. So Christ knows what will . . . and then there's our neighbour. She wants to kill her.'

426

'Why does your neighbour want to kill her?'

'No – other way round. Amy wants to. Kill the neighbour. Among others . . .'

'So what are you actually saying, Tom . . .?'

'Well . . . what I'm actually *saying* is that . . . it can't happen immediately. You do see that. It will happen – I want it to happen, I need it, need it to . . . but, well . . . it just can't happen immediately. You have to see why . . .? And now – well look at me: I've been shot. So I'll be even more useless than usual . . .'

'Uh-huh. So . . . when your wife is fine, and your daughter is fine – no listen to me, Tom, don't interrupt, because this is how it is – and when your son is fine and then when *you* are fine . . . then you'll get around to me. That it? It is, isn't it? That's exactly how it is . . .'

'Oh come on, K.T . . .'

'No *you* come on, Tom . . .! This is just like it *was* . . .!'

'No! No! Ow! Ow . . .! Christ this *hurts* . . .'

'Well don't move about, then.'

'Can you not keep blowing that smoke in my face, K.T . . .?'

'You never used to be so sensitive.'

'No well – you never used to smoke.'

'Why did you bring a gun, Tom . . .?'

'I didn't *bring* it . . . I just happened to . . . have it on me . . .'

'It's beautiful . . .'

'It is. Very. Dangerous, though . . .'

'As we've seen.'

'Where is it? Have you got it safe? Haven't got a licence for it or anything – Christ alone knows how many laws I'm breaking. But I only wanted it as a – well you know me, K.T: it was only ever an *object*. Of desire. Wasn't meant to be . . . fired. Particularly not at me. Because at first, well – I just had the Luger itself . . . found it in a sideboard, if you can believe it. Scandinavian. Doesn't matter. But then . . . well it's just that I thought I had to have the bullets, you know? Which cost an absolute fortune, I just can't tell you. Completely under the counter, of course. Dark side of the internet. Hell of a rigmarole. Took for ever. Completely terrifying, actually – but I had to do it, had to . . . because otherwise . . . well if I didn't have the proper ammunition for the thing, you see . . . well then it just wouldn't be . . .'

'Complete. Yes. I understand. I know you, remember? So. Back to the other thing, Tom: are you leaving your . . . oh God: *spouse* . . .? Yes or no?'

'You leaving yours . . .?'

'Christ, Tom . . .'

'I'm sorry about that vase. Sylvia's vase got broken too . . .'

'Who the fuck is Sylvia?'

'Neighbour Amy wants to kill. Doesn't matter. But listen, K.T – when he was here. When Bluto was here . . .'

'*What* . . .?'

'No. Not that. Bloke . . .'

'Guy . . .'

'Whatever. The man – your . . . the giant who shot me. When he was here before I arrived, you didn't let him . . .? I mean – you didn't, the two of you . . .?

'You men. Always the same . . .'

'You haven't answered me.'

'I'm going to make coffee. There's chicken in the fridge. Hungry?'

'I'd . . . I'd really better go . . .'

'Uh-huh. Tom is leaving. Well there's a shock. Tom is leaving.'

'I don't *want* to . . . and you still haven't answered me.'

'No. You never want to, do you, Tom? Or so you say. But still you just keep on leaving . . .'

I shook my head. K.T, she flounced into the kitchen, and I closed my eyes. She hasn't answered me. Has she? I gave her the opportunity, but still she hasn't answered me. And so therefore she has, of course. Yes. Of course she has.

Damien, he moaning like anything, bleeding pig: all he ever do. I tells him he don't want to be moaning – don't he see the money what I putting on the table? Ay? Not peanuts, is it Damien? More than paying my whack, wouldn't you reckon? Ay? Well wouldn't you?

'Yeh . . . yeh, course. It ain't that, Dolly. But still I don't get it – all of the money. Why they paying you so bleeding much?'

'I told you. What's wrong with you? I told you before. It a responsible job I got now. Them Marriott people, they reckons me, don't they? Seen my talents. Why I got to go all over. See what the other hotels is up to. What they does different. Why I goes on all them planes. News to you, all of this, is it? Told you it all, haven't I Damien? How many times? You got cloth ears, or what? You ain't really very concomitant.'

'I ain't very bleeding *what* . . .?'

'Ignorant, that's you. You know that do you, Damien? That you just plain ignorant? Don't know no words. Me, I trying to improve myself. Better myself. You won't of noticed it, on account of you don't never notice nothing – but these days, yeh? I well on the way to being a lady. And concomitant, you want to know, it mean . . . well it don't matter what it mean: you wouldn't understand it anyway.'

'Right. Well ta very much. But listen, Dolly . . . it Kenny, really. I mean – I can see to him, all of that. I ain't saying I can't see to him – and I don't mind it, nor nothing. It just that he say to me: where's Mum, Dad? Why she never about? You know what I saying? Break my bleeding heart. What I supposed to keep on saying to him?'

'I *explained* it all to him. Didn't I? When I gets him them Nike trainers what he were on about – and that were just after he gets his own bleeding flatscreen. Like – not enough, or what? What's wrong with the both of yous, ay? I talks – I hear the words what's coming out my mouth, and somewhere along the way, it what . . .? All get scrambled, do it? Float away, do it – before Damien and Kenny gets to hearing it . . .?'

'It just that . . . it such a lot, that's all. You away a lot, these days. More than what you used to. And another thing is . . . you sometimes seeming, I don't know . . . a bit like . . .'

'Bit like what . . .?'

'Well . . .'

'What? Bit like what? Come on, Damien – bit like what?'

'Well, like . . . sort of, a bit like sort of out of it . . . Not really here, you know? Like you don't know what going on, or something . . .'

'Yeh well: these is the trials of a executive lifestyle. Jet lag. Never heard of it? Time zones. You too bleeding stupid to see it, but these days, I . . . what was it . . .? Oh yeh: I inhabit a realm of sophistication.'

I sometimes gets to thinking with Damien that it ain't just ignorant what he are, but a bit bleeding simple into the bargain. Been thinking back on it all – all the dumb things what he say to me, over all these years we been together. Like here's one: the very day Kenny were born, right? We never knowed if it were going to be a boy or a girl, like, because we never ask, and so we never done all of the names thing: you know – what about this one? What about that one? Me, I thought of a couple possibles, but we never like sits down and talks about it. So he come up the hospital and there's me with our new little baby in a cot there, and Damien, he got a bunch of half-dead carnations and this little furry turquoise duck in his hand. So, I says to Damien: what we going to call him, then? And he look at me and he say well it don't hardly matter, do it? And I goes to him what you mean it don't hardly *matter* . . .? And he say to me well . . . it only a turquoise duck, ain't it? You believe it . . .? Yeh but still and all, it dead true what he saying now about all of my going away all of the time. Were thinking the same thing myself. Says it to Jimmy, my lovely Jimmy. I just been licking and sucking on him, which I never knowed about before except from in that Sharon Stone movie, what were it, with Michael Douglas – and I just loves it. Everything what he showed or give me, I loves it all. We just done couple lines, and we swigging the Bollinger out the bottle. That why I can get so completely out of it – trashed ain't in it. Damien, he weren't wrong about that. But I'm amazed he notice it, because I ever so careful: never thought it showed. But I really likes it, I got to say. If I don't get my charley and champagne, I can be ever so grumpy: always has a line in the airport bog. It were Jimmy what tell me I inhabit a realm of sophistication. Only Jimmy I ever sees, now. Clock Richard just the once since I were over the flat that time, with all of them clothes – which was moved over to Jimmy's place soon after, whole room of sliding mirror wardrobes he got, so they all fits ample, and that make it ever so handy. It Jimmy now I deals with. Richard, I don't know . . . he maybe just the booker. Looking for girls. Because they always is: looking.

431

'Here, Jimmy . . . no look listen – get off of me for a minute, can't you? Listen to me you silly sod, because I being serious. You got to learn me a bit more about how all of this is working.'

'I have to *teach* you . . .'

'Yeh. What I said. Because listen: I go to Paris in the morning like what you telling me . . . well that four trips in couple weeks. Not going it a bit, is it . . .?'

'Not really. You're a natural, Dolly. The confidence you've gained . . . it's simply amazing. You're a complete and utter natural. And you don't mind it, do you? Last time we spoke about this you told me how much you were enjoying yourself.'

'Yeh. I do. I am. Just want to be . . . safe. That's all.'

'Well you will be. Of course you will be. Always look after you, don't we? We trust you, Dolly. Respect you, Richard and I. With you, we won't ever have to, well . . . do what we did with the last girl. That's a given.'

'Ay . . .? What you mean? What you bleeding do with the last girl . . .? And what – she don't got a name?'

'Her name . . . hardly matters. Oh forgive me, Dolly – I put it badly. No no: all we did was issue her with a very gentle warning.'

'A warning . . .'

'Well not even that, really, More of a reminder. Which we would never dream of doing with you, because we both know full well that we will never have to. It was simply that Richard felt compelled to, well . . . as I say, *remind* her that she is paid a great deal of money, and in return for that money, we do expect an absolute . . . fidelity. Loyalty – that goes without saying. Silence, naturally – subterfuge, if necessary: as it has proved to be, in the case of your husband. Immediate availability, at

432

whatever time of the day or night. And the carrying out of instructions to the letter. All the things that were clearly explained in the very first instance. No more than normal business practice.'

'Right. So you sort of saying, what . . .? That you owns her. And me: you reckon you owns me and all then, does you?'

'Well – a little dramatic. But yes, in a way. So long as we're paying you . . .'

He smiling his ever-so-lovely smile when he saying it, and his eyes – oh my God: them amazing blue electric eyes, they just makes me go to bleeding bits. Still, though – all what he said, it did make me feel a bit, I don't know . . . funny. Inside, like. Then we has another line, and he start up with all of what he do to me with his tongue, so that was that, really. But then just after, I walking over to the bathroom, like – and wham . . .! I just blanks right out. One minute I going across there quite the thing, next minute . . . I don't know: it like I suddenly can't see nothing, it all gone black, and my legs, they just folds up under me and I goes over. Next thing what I know, I lying on the bed there, and Jimmy, he looking down at me. He seem worried.

'Dolly . . . are you . . . quite all right . . .? I was worried.'

Yeh see: I said he seem worried.

'I'm fine . . . I think. Don't know what happen. I just gone all . . .'

'Yes. I saw. But you feel . . .?'

'Yeh. Fine. I'm fine, now. Maybe have a glass champagne. Buck me up.'

'I'm . . . concerned. Maybe we ought to have someone take a look at you.'

'No honestly, Damien – I completely fine now. Don't need no doctor, that what you meaning.'

'What did you just call me . . .?'

'Ay? Well what you think I call you? I call you Jimmy. My beautiful Jimmy Blue Eyes . . .'

'All right, Dolly. But . . . I'm concerned.'

Yeh well: me too, you want the truth. But I never said.

Anyway – stayed over at Jimmy's, that night. Ever such an early flight in the morning. Told Damien it were the evening before. He just nod. Whatever, yeh? I don't sleep good, though. Jimmy, he well out. One point, I goes to shake him, you know? Felt scared. Felt a bit lonely. Can't explain. Yeh but he never move, nor nothing. Took a big hit of shit before he turn in. Never seed him snort so much as that. So dead to the world, basically. Had a wander about the apartment. Drank a whole load of water: right parched. Looked at a movie, some movie, never took in nothing – not a bleeding word of it. Planned what I going to wear in the morning. Were already the morning: off in couple hours, not much more. I were doing Armani. Paris, they likes it if you going all Chanel and that, but it more normal there, that sort of look: chick, is what they calls it. But something else, they going to look at. What I like. Silly, I suppose, but that just me. And the Rolex – that the one I wearing more than anything, now. Ain't got no diamonds round the edge of it, but other than that it just like the one what Porsche had on that time, round at Terry and Amy's – yeh, and I remember how it were driving me bleeding mental. Yeh well: now I got my own. My make-up, I got that all ready. Bobbi Brown Creamy Concealer: go through a bloody ton of that – always looking so bleeding tired, these days . . . can't understand it. Benefit Benetint Rose-Tinted Lip & Cheek Stain: I so washed out, half the time – give me a bit of colour, bit of a glow. Hotter places I'll go a Clarins bronzer. YSL lippy I reckon still the best – but if I ain't going full-on, I don't mind a bit of Soap &

Glory Sexy Mother Pucker Lip Plumping Gloss: it only cheap, but it do the job – it do what it say on the wossname, you know what I meaning? I ain't saying my mouth, it end up like Angelina Jolie's nor Scarlett Johansson's, I ain't saying that – but at least it don't look like a tired little slit no more.

And then I just sitting there, and I thinking – well sod this for a lark: reckon I'll just get myself early to the airport. Have a neck massage and a nice glass of bubbles in the lounge: reckon that sort me out. So I gets togged up, check I got my passport, money, all of that . . . and I just walking out the door (ain't even light yet) and it only then I hears his voice. Jimmy, he call out to me: you got the package . . .? And I says, yeh I got the package – what you think I am? Stupid, or something? And then he just grunt. Like Damien would of. He never say: well have a good trip, Dolly. I'll miss you, Dolly. Come over here and give us a kiss then, Dolly. Nah. He never.

I must of been zonked in the motor, because I never even notice we was going the wrong way until we was in my street – we was nearly outside my bleeding front door . . .! Jimmy, he got this Mercedes E-Class, big black bugger, for getting me about – him and all, when he ain't driving that Maserati what he got – and it just seem to be waiting outside the apartment, day and night far as I can tell, and the driver, it usually Jason who also a big black bugger, but today it were Wayne what is pretty pathetic and dumb, you ask me, and I only had him the once or twice and he ain't nearly so good as Jason.

'What the fuck you playing at, Wayne? Where the fuck you think we going . . .?'

'Isn't this right? I thought you were going back to your . . .'

'Yeh well I ain't. Heathrow we meant to be going. Just as well I early. What you think you doing, Wayne?'

'Sorry, Dolly. Jimmy, he never said.'

'Yeh well he should of.'

Yeh and it were then I just looks out of the window, and I nearly has a wossname . . .! She just wandering about in the street – can't hardly believe it! Heart attack – nearly has a heart attack, because it's only Amy, I sure it's Amy . . . and she just walking about like she on a beach on her holidays or something but it only gone half five in the bleeding morning and her hair, blimey – it all over the place, what I never seed on her before, and God alone know what it is she think she wearing. That why at first I weren't too sure it were really her, but yeh – that Amy all right. So I says to Wayne to pull over, and he go: what – you want me to pull over? And I goes to him *yeh* I wants you to pull over, I just bleeding said so, didn't I? What's *wrong* with you, Wayne?

'Amy – hallo. Not seen you in ages. You all right then, are you . . .? Not too cold in just that little dress you got on? Where you off to, then? Ever so early . . .'

'Dolly.'

Are all she say. We stood on the pavement there, and all I knowed were it were bleeding freezing, real brass monkeys, ain't joking. Her hair, I telling you – it wild. Bleeding bird's nest. No make-up on. Look quite old, she do. Dress, it torn. And she just staring at me, real close. It like she trying to work out a sum in her head, or something. Look like she got blood on her arm. Paint, could be.

'You okay, yeh . . .? Can I drop you off somewheres? That paint you got on your arm, is it Amy?'

'Blood.'

'Oh blimey. You hurt? You cut yourself?'

'Dolly.'

And all this time, her face, it ain't moved. Like it a mask. No

436

smile, nor nothing. And I were just thinking what it is I ought to be doing, maybe go and knock up Terry, should I? Because something ain't right here, plain as bleeding day. And then suddenly she talking to me: 'Dolly. You are extremely beautifully dressed. And coiffed. And made-up, if I may say so. Never before have I seen you like this.'

And I were thinking yeh well same here with bleeding bells on, matey – but I never say nothing.

'And your dress, your coat . . . Armani, if I am not mistaken. And a Fendi bag, how lovely. The shoes . . . not Ferragamo, by any chance . . .?'

'Is, yeh. But listen, Amy . . .'

'Well I mustn't keep you.'

'Amy – look . . .'

'Well I mustn't keep you. I too – thousand things to see to.'

And before I can get out another word, she turn about and she off round the corner. And I just left standing there thinking well blimey: how bloody weird were that? She off her face, or what? Hitting the Pinot Grigio of a morning time, that it? Anyway – got a plane to catch, yeh? So I gets back in the limo and I says to Wayne right then, let's for Gawd's sake get going yeh? And he say to me where to. No, straight up: he do. And I goes to him Heathrow bleeding *airport*, you dumb bugger: I just *said* it to you, didn't I . . .? What's *wrong* with you, Wayne? Yeh: because you got to ask yourself, really speaking: can't think why Jimmy want to give him the time of day, to be honest with you.

Yeh and never mind we gone the wrong way and I done all of that with Amy – we gets to the airport and I still got ages to be hanging about. Ain't no hardship – not in the Business Class lounge, nah never. Has a glass of Veuve Wossname, then I has me another. What I usually does is I snorts a line in the bog

437

before I goes through security (yeh well obviously before – ain't a mug) but this time I never brung none . . .! Gutted, when I finds that out: gone all through my bag, and nah – nothing, not a bleeding dicky bird. Kill me when I thinks of it: in that shiny big black box in Jimmy's bedroom, there so much snow you could go bleeding skiing on it: and I never brung none . . .! So I has another glass of fizz: ain't the same, but it sort me out good enough for now.

Paris . . . well – what can I tell you? It were just Paris, you know? Never thought I like be saying that. Was a time not too long ago when I would of been excited if Damien and me, we was off to Bognor or Southend or somewhere. Even Hampstead bleeding Heath. Never went nowhere, never done nothing. Not with Damien. He always in the garage, or else he say he knackered. Yeh – never too knackered to play all of them stupid bloody games though, is he? So I been through all of the boarding, no trouble – never is no trouble on account of I never pays it no mind, to be honest with you. And I always ever so peaceful, what yeh is down to the drugs and booze, of course – but it were just the same this time really, charley or not. Flight, that take no time, course. Taxi to the Meurice in Rue de Wossname. Weren't staying over nor nothing – but Jimmy, he always make sure I got a nice big room to chill in, yeh? Put my feet up. Get a lobster omelette off of the room service, what I really like. Rue de Riverly, I think it called, what the Meurice are in. Drop off the package – it were ever so small. They not ever big, I ain't saying – but this one: real tiny. Wander down the Crillon, what is another great big posh hotel there – telling you, make the Marriott look like some sort of a fleabag doss-house. Used to think it were called the Crayon before I seed it wrote down: that what everyone call it, the Frogs and that – the Crayon. I don't know. I likes the bar there on account of they always got a piano player what tinkle away. Make me feel nice. Glass of champagne. About thirty quid. Don't even think of it no more. Got to thinking about Amy. What going on there, then? All-night party? Bust-up with Terry? Can't think. Got in another glass – coop, they calls it, couldn't tell you why: foreigners, they got stupid names for everything. And then before you knows it, I back at Orly. Yeh. And that when it all go wrong.

'Good afternoon, madam. Or evening, should I say . . .? Sort of in-between, isn't it really? I hope you enjoyed your time in Paris?'

'What? Oh – yeh. Yeh.'

Good-looking girl at the check-in, there – could be French, none of that stupid accent though. Ringer for the Duchess of bleeding Cambridge. Hell of a lot of make-up – skin, it look all clogged up. I been told they does it to cover how tired they always is on account of the shifts. I been told they does it because it in the rules. I been told they does it to catch the eye of all of them rich blokes what travel First and Business. I don't bleeding care why they does it.

'No luggage for check-in? Beautiful bag, may I say . . .'

'Ay? Oh yeh. Ta. Thank you, I mean.'

'Are you, um . . . are you quite all right . . .?'

'Ay? Oh yeh. Ta. Thank you I mean . . .'

And then I sees her face, it turn all sort of odd like, just before it all go and happen to me again. I just goes all blank and then I sees white and dancey colours and the last I remembers is all my bones just going like jelly. Next thing I knows, I in a room somewheres, all pale green and lit up, and there a bloke there hanging over me.

'Ah. Welcome back. You appear to have fainted, Dorothy. I am a doctor.'

439

'Yeh . . .? Oh bloody hell – I miss my flight? It Dolly, me . . .'

'I'm afraid so. Dolly, is it? That's nice. I was going by your passport. With your ticket, though, I am assured that there will be no problem at all in your catching the next – or any other you might prefer – so that's good, isn't it? So . . . how do you feel? Sit up, can you? Yes? Manage it? Well I've given you the once-over, MOT you know, and there doesn't appear to be any immediate problem. Had a little to drink with our lunch, did we possibly?'

'Ay? Nah. Lunch? Nah. Well – couple glasses.'

'Yes. Well no harm done. Now if you feel up to it, there's a gentleman outside who would quite like a word, I gather. Customs and Excise, you know.'

'What he want?'

'I haven't the slightest idea. Send him in, shall I?'

'You want . . .'

And he come in, this bloke, and he never smile – not like the doctor: he were smiling fit to bust a gut. Customs geezer, he say to me all real serious like that it his intention to examine my holdall, my handbag and my clothes. He were waiting for me to come round, he says, so's he could tell me and I can be present. Don't leave no leeway, do it? I says yeh go on then, son – I off to the bog, you don't mind. Yeh so I got to get him to go through my make-up bag the first, because I bloody well going to need that because I just got to be looking a right bleeding sight after all of that falling over, and all. Dead embarrassing, apart from anything else: ain't laddered my tights, though – so that some-thing, because I don't got no more on me. And I in there, I in the Ladies, and I trying to make myself look a little bit decent, and all the time I going over it: there ain't no traces of charley . . . and there ain't no return package, neither. There could of been. There

440

could easily of been. Usually there are – not always, but usually. But this time – nah. Nothing. Just the one on the way out. But I still all shivery. I looking at my moony eyes in the mirror, and I gone all cold and like shivery. Just thinking about it.

Feeling a bit more together, time I come out. Smiles all round, time I come out. Customs bloke, he even sort of half go and give me a kind of salute, you believe it. Sorry for the inconvenience, he go – hope you feeling better, and all is well. Girl there, she want to know if she can do anything for me . . .? Get something for me . . .? No, I says: I be fine. So I picks up my bag and I goes in the lounge and I has a quick couple glasses of I think it could of been Bollinger, weren't looking, that calm me down a bit. Be a bit of a rush for the next flight, I's thinking, so I thought well fuck it: comfy here, have a bit of smoked salmon, few of them langoustines, another couple glasses, and I be fine for the one after – because this time of day, they's ever so regular. London in no time flat, and then I gets a taxi, don't I? Queue, weren't too long, weren't too bad. Got back to Jimmy's, because that what I always does: he like it, when I been on a trip. What we generally does is, we has a drink, we scores a couple lines, and then we go like totally bleeding nuts in the sack: can't tell you. Rang up Damien on the way – tell him there's sausages, he want them, few peas and potato wedges, on account of I running a little bit late.

Were pressing on the buzzer for ever so long – which were funny, actually. Yeh – I remember thinking: that a bit funny, what's wrong with him? Because sometimes, Jimmy, he come down to get me. One time, he only got a big red rose stuck between his teeth, silly sod. Ever so romantic. Anyway, after one hell of a while, the door go click and I gets the lift up to the apartment and the door of it still closed so I got to ring on another bleeding buzzer. I done all of my make-up in the taxi, because I always likes for him to see me, Jimmy, when I's at my really best. I only been away, what – ten, twelve hours? Could of been more, what with all of the mess-up, and that – yeh but still, I already missing him. So the door swing open and I all smiles and waving about this great big gift box of Eau Sauvage, what is Dior and I got it at Orly at the very last minute: spur of the wossname sort of thing – because he like it, Jimmy, he like it, yeh . . . and I likes it and all: make him smell ever so manly. So I never expect it, do I? Ay? For the door to be opened by some woman. Some woman, yeh – some woman what I never clap eyes on before.

'May I take your coat . . .?'

I'm stood there, just looking at her. You know? She my size – long and thick black hair, like in a retro page-boy? Young, she look – younger than me. Lovely pointy red fingernails like what I never been able to get on account of I always gnawing on them like a animal. I got false ones, yeh, which is pretty good – but these is real, you can tell. She talk ever so posh. Like a lady.

'Who the fuck are you?'

'That's not very polite. Jimmy is in the drawing room. With Richard. They're waiting for you. May I take your coat?'

'I'll take my own bleeding coat, thanks very much. Off. Take my own bleeding coat off. Richard here too, is he? Blimey.'

So I barges in the room, feeling . . . well, I don't know what I were feeling, tell you the honest truth. But not that good. And I were tired. Yeh – I were tired now . . . all of a sudden, after all of that argy-bargy back at the airport, I were real tired now: all sort of weary. They both of them stand up as I walks through the door, which I always think is really nice. Gentlemen, they does it automatic.

'Dolly, my dear – it has been far too long.'

442

'Hallo, Richard. Yeh – ain't seen you for ages. Jimmy. All right . . .?'

'Do take a seat, won't you?'

'Let me get a drink. All right are you, Jimmy? Why ain't you talking?'

'Yes, Dolly – I'm fine. Champagne . . .?'

'Yeh. Lovely.'

'Samantha – would you mind? Clicquot in the . . . well, you know where it is.'

'So, Dolly . . . Jimmy and I, we'd just like a little chat, yes? If that's quite all right with you.'

'Who the fuck's this "Samantha", then? Ay? Something new what you just bought, is it Richard?'

'Just sit down and let's all of us have a little friendly chat, yes? Oh . . .! What's that . . .? What on earth did you do that for, Dolly . . .?'

'It a bleeding big box of Eau fucking Sauvage, you want to know. And I just throwed it against the wall because I bleeding well wanted to, okay?'

'Right. I see. Fine. Jolly good. Well now . . . just try to . . . calm down a little, yes? Ah – here's Samantha with your champagne.'

'Don't want no champagne. You drink it, "Samantha". Choke on it, all I care. Here, Jimmy – why ain't you drinking nothing? Usually by this time, we be into the second bottle. We be into a lot of things, by this time . . .'

'Dolly . . .'

'Yeh, Richard? What? And why ain't Jimmy bleeding *talking* to me . . .?'

'Well we rather agreed that I would, erm – talk to you, Dolly. Instead. Do please sit down, won't you? Oh thank you, Samantha

– just leave it there, will you? Yes, there – just set it down there. Perfect. Thank you. And now, if you wouldn't mind terribly . . .? Thank you so very much. Yes – off you go, Samantha, and we'll be seeing you later on, yes? Splendid. Now, Dolly . . .'

'Why you doing this? Why you . . . talking to me like this? Like you don't know me, or something. And Jimmy – he ain't talking to me at all . . .! I upset. I really am. I really am upset . . .'

'I am so very sorry that you are, Dolly. Have some champagne, yes? Little sip? You know it always makes you feel so very much better. My intention, you will be pleased to hear . . . is to be brief.'

'Yeh . . .? Yeh . . .? Brief about what?'

'Just this: you have served us very well and loyally, Dolly. Excellent work. Truly excellent. And as I am sure you will agree, your recompense has been wholly commensurate, if not even over-remunerative.'

'Ay . . .?'

'You have been very well paid for all you have done. Yes . . .? Yes. We agree, then. But, as they say, all good things must come to an end, and . . .'

'Don't! Don't talk like that. I had a hell of a day, and you being mean to me . . .!'

'Well yes – and here is the very point, actually. It is in fact the day you have just endured that has rather served to bring things to a head, as it were. You see, Dolly . . . scenes such as that at Orly, well . . . we simply can't have it. You see? Just simply can't have that at all.'

'At Orly . . .? How you know what happen at Orly . . .?'

'Oh really, Dolly – how can you ask such a thing? It is our *business* to know. You must understand that? We know . . . *everything*. In this business, it is how one survives. It is how one

444

prospers. We hardly got where we are by remaining in *ignorance*. You must surely see that . . .?'

'Yeh but . . . yeh but . . . nothing *happened*. Did it? Ay? They never find nothing. Never had nothing for them to find . . .'

'Indeed. But . . . and this will have occurred to you Dolly, of course it will, for you are very far from obtuse, as I divined immediately upon meeting you, or else we should never have, well . . . known one another. But, you see . . . what if there had been? Something to find. What if there had been a return package? As so often there is. And they had . . . questioned you. Traced it back to source . . .? You see? Everything we have for so long safeguarded against – blown asunder in an instant. And so in the light of all this . . . I am afraid that it is of course quite impossible for you to remain in our employ any longer. Highly regrettable, but there it is.'

'No . . .! *No* . . .! That not . . . *fair* . . .! I never got caught! I never! I would never of said nothing! Why you doing this to me? I good – I real good. You says it yourself. Why can't I go on? I *got* to go on. I don't know nothing else, now! This . . . this is . . . this is all I *does*, God's sake . . .!'

'But my dear Dolly . . . you got yourself *noticed*, you see. In quite the wrong way. And as a result of that, details of the incident will have been recorded. Next time, in whichever country you may find yourself, you will be extremely closely observed, I can assure you of that. Believe me – I know how these agencies operate. Suspicions were undoubtedly raised, otherwise you would not have been searched, and these things are never forgotten. In addition to this, I am informed that it is not the first occasion upon which you have quite suddenly blacked out, like that. Well you see, this sort of . . . frailty . . . this sort of susceptibility, well . . . we simply cannot tolerate it. Not at all. Far, far too dangerous.'

445

'So . . . no listen to me, Richard – just listen, okay? This . . . this . . . is like a warning then, yeh? Richard? Like what you give the last girl. Warning, yeh? Not the end. Can't be the end. Just a warning, yeh? Yeh? That it . . .?'

'The last girl . . . I regret to say that the last girl, Dolly, was an extremely different situation. She . . . transgressed. Betrayed our trust. And so what she received . . . well, let us say that it was rather more than a "warning". Yes – let's just say that, and leave it there. Now, Dolly – we must address ourselves to the question of termination. Yes? In the envelope on the table there you will find two thousand pounds. Not ungenerous, I think. This represents full and final payment. Our business arrangement concluded. And while I am sure I do not have to say this to you, Dolly . . . still there can be no harm, I'm sure, in this very gentlest of reminders: you will, of course, speak to absolutely no one about any of this. Addresses. Activities. Our very existence. Should you ever fall foul of this direction . . . well, I don't really feel that I have to go on. As you have seen, we *know* things, you see. We will find out, please make no mistake. And the consequences . . . well, we shan't go into it. Just always remember that we are absolute professionals: there can be no loose ends. Oh please, dear Dolly . . . do not upset yourself in this way . . .'

'Well how you expect me to feel . . .? Ay? I can't hardly remember last time what I go blubbing like this – blubbing like a bleeding baby . . .! Look what you made me do . . .! And I scared – I scared, now. Jimmy . . .! *Jimmy* . . .! *Say* something, Christ sake . . .! I *loves* you . . .! Don't just . . . turn away. What's *wrong* with you? What's *wrong* with you . . .? I *loves* you . . .!'

'I *love* you.'

'Yeh . . .? You does? You really does . . .?'

'No of *course* I don't, you utterly vulgar and stupid woman!

446

I am merely correcting for the umpteenth time your perfectly laughably appalling grammar, as you have repeatedly insisted that I do. It is "I love you", not "I loves you". You see? *Christ* . . .!'

'Steady, Jimmy old chap . . .'

'Oh well *honestly*, Richard . . .! She's been driving me completely insane for just how bloody long now? Just listening to her *voice* . . .! Jesus – quite apart from the ghastly accent, if I'd corrected her every time she made a grammatical error, she never would have reached the end of a *sentence* . . .! Pretty glad all this has happened, actually. She's a bloody good fuck, I'm not denying – but oh *Christ* what an absolute pain in the arse . . .! At least I won't have that trouble with Samantha . . .'

And that were it, basically: that just about done it for me. I gets a hold of the bottle of champagne what next to me and I up and I waving it like a club around my head as I just goes flying right at him and I want to beat his fucking brains out all over the floor is all I wanting to do, the bastard, the bastard, the fucking bloody bastard, and the champagne, it splattered on my face and down my arm and all over my beautiful Armani clothes and Jimmy he up and he hit me with something before I even get close to him, the bastard, the bastard, the fucking bloody bastard, and Richard, he got me by the arms now and he holding me back down on the settee and I just let him get on with it, yeh I just let him get on with it – because I had it now, I knows I just had it, I so tired, I so tired, and I so bleeding sad, and my chin, that hurt real bad where I just got hit and I can feel my mascara running down and over my cheeks with the mess of the sticky champagne . . . yeh, and all the bloody tears.

After, Richard . . . he say, do you want to use the bathroom? Clean yourself up a bit? I says to him to just fuck off. Jimmy, he gone by now. Don't know where. Getting hisself sucked off by

447

"Samantha", I suppose. Don't yet even know if I cares. He order me a taxi, Richard – no ride home in the big black bugger car drove by the big black bugger bloke, then. Not even stupid Wayne. I says I don't want to go, and he say to me don't be so silly and I tells him to just fuck off. He more or less put me in the corridor outside and he shut the door on me. I bangs on the panels and I shouting for him to just fuck *off*, yeh . . .?! I goes down in the lift but I ain't looking at me in the mirror like what I usually does because I just don't want to see it. And I don't want to go home neither. Well of course I don't want to go home. But where else I going to go? Where else?

Late, when I gets in. Were trying not to think about nothing all the way there. It quiet. They in bed then, Damien and Kenny. Well blimey – look at the bleeding time: course they in bed. Lights still on in the room though, bleeding pig he is. It the smell of the place . . . it's that what I just can't take. It smell old. It stink of stale. It the smell of all what I left behind me, when I finally gone out there and got for myself . . . oh, I don't know –just a little bit of style, maybe. And in the kitchen . . . there more lights on and half-eaten sausages and hell of a pile of dishes over in the sink there, look. Frozen peas is rolling on the floor. I'm stood there just looking at it all for I don't know how long. Don't know what to do. In the fridge . . . there ain't no champagne. There's two tins of Carling, a yogurt and a bag of Babybels. Which kind of like done it for me. Because this, this . . . this ain't no more in the realm of sophistication. I not so much crying . . . it just kind of seeping out of me, you know . . .? Like I bleeding, or some-thing. And I don't know what to do. I just don't know what to do about nothing. There ain't no one no more what'll feel my pain. Except for me, of course. So yeh: how now, brown cow . . .?

448

CHAPTER ELEVEN

THE IMPENDING SUFFOCATION OF THE NEXT

Ran into a fellow in the street the other day – face was maybe just about vaguely familiar, could never have put a name to it. 'Hullo, Terence!' he goes – seeming actually rather pleased to have encountered me. 'Ah,' I said. 'Well well.' He told me he hadn't seen me for ages, and I believed him. He chuntered on for a little while, wasn't remotely listening – for as usual, when-ever I am waylaid by just about anyone these days, my solitary yearning is to get away quickly, retire to the shadows so that then I might slink back with a black and guilty stealth into the simmering stew of all my contemplation. And then he said to me – this man in the street, whoever he might be: 'So anyway: how are you, Terence . . .? What's been going on with you . . .?' Yes, that's what he asked me . . . and do you know, I stood there in silence, probably gaping, and just for the flash of a moment felt myself to be lithely flexed and utterly ready, poised upon the very heady brink of just, oh Christ . . . *plummeting*. Flooding him with the answers he politely was pretending to be after. Slamming him square between the eyes with the whole unholy lot. Unburdening myself of the sheer and crushing bloody weight of it, and swooping maybe upwards then, to the clean and rarefied air. Could have taken days. Because, look . . . how *am* I . . .? What's been going *on* with me . . .? Jesus: where even to begin with it . . .

I had thought things bad when I was shot by Bluto, K.T's . . . husband. And it was bad, that was – but only the start of worse, oh Christ yes: so much worse than that. I had eventually left her in the wee small hours of the morning, K.T, soon after I told her that I had to: her legs were crossed and so were her arms, as she watched me go, the stillness of her face so very dull and heavy with a look that I knew – half the expression of sour satisfaction in the knowledge that she had been right about me all along . . . a hearty dash of uncut anger, the balance rounded out with that just about sneer of open disgust. I knew by now that there certainly wasn't a bullet in me – the pain still was searing, but I was breathing normally and could walk with comparative ease – and so in my typically trivial and frankly idiotic manner, I set to wondering where on earth it might have got to, this single discharged bullet. Probably lodged in one of K.T's walls – or could it have done for her green and handsome Conran vase? It could well have been the culprit. And talking of all that, I made sure I got the gun back, Christ yes. I cradled that Luger in the taxi home, while sensing amid the enveloping murk the warmth of seepage from my scalding wound. Only in the dazzle of the hall did I see the great red stain spread across this tattered and makeshift bandage. I stood for a moment: the house was quite utterly silent, and I was startled to be finding that circumstance absolutely terrifying. I thought that even before attempting to attend to my injury, I just had to find Amy – see what she was doing, where she was doing it, and how she was . . . behaving. But it was she who found me. She wandered

450

across the rug, looking like a battered and not altogether convincing waxwork of someone Amy once used to resemble. She was smiling so very expansively.

'You're back early . . . would you like a drink of some sort?'

'What do you mean . . . back early? How . . . *are* you, Amy . . .?'

'From the office. I'm fine, thank you. And yourself?'

'From the office . . .? I don't . . . I don't *go* to an office. Do I?'

'Of course you don't.'

'I work here, don't I? At home.'

'Of course you do.'

'And it's late, isn't it? It's very late indeed. What is that . . . in your hand . . .?'

'There is nothing in my hand. Look!'

'Not that hand. The other hand.'

'Oh the *other* hand. Well why didn't you say? In this hand, I have a hammer.'

'Yes – I can see it's a hammer, Amy . . .'

'Well why did you ask me, then? Rather foolish, if you knew all along . . .'

'Why are you . . . holding a hammer, Amy? What have you done . . .?'

'I have hammered. What else? Were it a screwdriver, then I should have screwed.'

'Amy . . . let's sit down. Let's go and sit down, yes? And you can . . . tell me, Jesus, just what it is that you've . . . *done* . . .'

'I can tell you that now: don't have to sit down. Murder.'

I looked at her. My chest, it felt upon the point of bursting – a jagged catalogue of faces was flickering over and under my eyes as I endeavoured to search in hers for anything, anything at all that she might want to give me. Tears now were pricking me.

451

'Murder . . .? Oh *no,* Amy . . .!'

'Oh *yes,* Terence! I have murdered that which you love. Would you like to see . . .?'

'Christ. *Jesus,* Amy . . .!'

'Come on. It's only next door. Won't take a moment. It'll be fun. Come and *see . . .'*

She was grinning, full of guile and girlish secrets – and then she actually took me by the hand. I waded on in boots of iron, my eyes so wide, yet needing to shield themselves from just *everything* that now very surely just had to be coming. I faltered – tugged her back, unable to face this . . . but her grip was amazing, so dauntingly strong, and she urged me on remorselessly. And in the room, I gasped – cried out. My knees, they simply were caving in beneath me as I was confronted by the utter devastation. Splintered shards of pure white marble, the liquid beauty of the table's base horribly chipped and dented from a ceaseless and demented battering. My eyes were stung, and I was bleeding from the shoulder.

'I knew that you loved Eero Saarinen more than you ever loved me . . .'

I continued to kneel, loose-mouthed and helpless. Never before had she said his name.

'Well? Well, Terence? Have you nothing to say? Not even a *prayer . . .?'*

I stood now, and confronted her.

'I do, yes Amy. Have something to say. It is this. Always I have known that you were small-minded, petty, vindictive, envious . . . and cruel, oh yes, very cruel. Now though, it is simpler. No, Amy – don't walk away. Not now. No good just walking away from it – you really have to hear this. You see, Amy . . . the fact of the matter is that you are mad. Quite

452

literally . . . insane. You may not even know it – in which case you are a great deal luckier than everyone who suffers the misfortune to be around you. But now there can be absolutely no doubt about it: you are seriously deranged. You have become . . . a dangerous lunatic.'

'I see. So what you are saying then, Terence, is that in your considered opinion, the balance of my mind is disturbed . . .?'

'No, I am not saying that, Amy. I am saying that you are a complete and utter raving fucking *fruitcake*, and the sooner you are put away for good, the better for all concerned. I am now going to phone the police.'

'Oh really? What – to report the murder of a *table* . . .?'

Was she mad . . .? Was she . . .? Or was she simply just goading me mercilessly? Well if goading were her game, well then it was bloody well working – because I saw with bitter pleasure that fat expression of hers very rapidly sag and deflate, the second she had registered the gun within my hand. She rushed at me immediately – I cannot ever know whether my finger did or didn't tighten around that trigger, but although I was keenly shying away from it, there came no gaudy explosion – because the gun had been abruptly knocked away from me, and Amy now was frantically wrestling with my upraised arms and grappling with her claws for the white of my throat. I was trying with desperation to prise her strength away from me – I didn't wish to actually strike her, though nor did I wish to die. Her dress was ripped, and there was blood – my blood – streaked all over her arms. It was then that I became engulfed by a sickening bewilderment as I still disbelievingly just had to come to realise that what she was attempting to do here was . . . *embrace* me: she struggled to hold my head – she was seeking to kiss my lips. With any power I had, I hurled her away from me, feeling

453

nothing but a profound revulsion. She was glaring up at me as she sprawled across the floor.

'I don't care . . .! I don't care if you don't *want* me . . .! Plenty do, I can tell you that. Willy Ouch – he wants to marry me. He told me so himself. Sylvia, she yearns – just yearns to possess my body; it is written all over her. But I need none of you – none of you! You all mean nothing to me – because how could you? There is only one man whom I truly love . . . and that is why I have just left his bed. He *adores* me . . . and I love him back. With tenderness, yes . . . and sometimes vigour . . .'

Again, once more, I was simply stunned. Again, once more, I just was standing there, as I gaped at her.

'You don't . . . you can't mean . . .'

'Well of *course* I do, you stupid man! And why do you look so shocked? It is not unusual, you know, to sleep with the man you love. You maybe do not know this – but I do assure you, Terence, that it is very far indeed from being in any way *unusual* . . .'

'But . . . but *Jesus*, Amy – he's your—!'

'I know. I *know* – you don't have to tell me! Of course I know that. And this is good. This is pure. Because you see, Terence – do you want to know the real beauty of it? Shall I tell you? It's this: you see, with him . . . I know where he's *been* . . .'

I gazed at the floor. I shook my head – in horrified wonder, yes, but maybe even to try to clear it. And within that flicker of an instant, she was gone. And back in the hall, she was holding wide the front door.

'What in Christ's name do you think you're doing *now* . . .?'

'Going for a walk. Want to come . . .?'

'A walk? A bloody *walk* . . .?! It's five o'clock in the fucking morning . . .!'

'You should never be bound by artificial concepts such as time, Terence. It will only make you dull.'

And then she was gone. Yes but it was only rather later that I knew that the gun, oh Christ . . . that the gun had gone with her. Because as soon as she had clanged shut the door behind her, I had dashed up the stairs, my heart still strumming like a motor, my mind a chaos of smithereens – ceaseless shattered fragments of sharp and stark possibilities, each of them even more terrible than the last. I do not remember the last time I had eased open gently the doors to each of my children's bedrooms, with all the love and stealth of a caring parent, this tinged by an unreasoning panic. They both had seemed quite perfectly at peace. Lizzie was wearing these tiny earpieces, that were faintly fizzing. I touched her cheek, and it was soft and warm. Poor Lizzie – my own little girl. Alexander, in sleep, appeared as no more than an infant, stirring slightly from within the flicker of an infant's dream. Now, though . . . I had to leave them once again – because my mind had flown irresistibly to Sylvia. So many minutes now had passed since Amy had wandered away from the house . . . and right next door, oh God, was Sylvia – Sylvia, yes, whom Amy repeatedly had vowed to kill, and now quite absolutely was in possession of the means to do so. It is true that I had heard no muffled explosion, but during that awful dawn, the whole of my head was booming, and only just about contained.

I suppose I was banging on her door really very loudly, and certainly with escalating desperation. I had rung the bell, but because there was no absolutely instantaneous response, I attacked the knocker like a wild thing. I was picturing Sylvia and Mike, dead in their beds, the sheets a sea of sappy crimson. Or Sylvia, shot through the heart in the hall, with Mike – awoken and startled – summarily dealt with on the first-floor landing . . . and from a striped pyjama sleeve, one arm protruding with awkwardness, stiff and still, askew through a splintered banister. So I only really could breathe again freely when finally Sylvia opened the door. She was not dead – she was not even apparently wounded, and nor was she tousled and trussed up hastily into a dressing gown, her hair either awry or pinned away neatly into a net: across her face, there was spattered no expression of enquiry that spoke at once of confusion, alarm and the lingering vestiges of interrupted sleep. No no – Sylvia, she looked the way she always did: neatly turned out, her face just so. The sight of her, oh I just can't tell you . . . it was simply quite devastatingly reassuring.

'Terence. Quite the early bird . . . *entrez, entrez s'il te plait.*'

'Sylvia . . .! Are you – all right . . .?'

'As you see me, Terence. Won't you come in? We're just having breakfast.'

'Breakfast? Really? Well I will just, maybe. For a moment. But oh . . . I've just got to *find* her . . .'

'This is Amy we are speaking about, I presume. Well do come in then Terence, won't you? There's a draught.'

Sylvia led me through to the kitchen, and I'm not actually sure that I've ever been in there before. So very different from ours, and in so many ways it would be ridiculous to count them. But they haven't broken through walls like we have – first thing we did – so this little kitchen of theirs, it's still quite intimate and kitchen-like: not just acres of gleaming units, appliances and islands like ours is, and Christ alone knows what it is she can be keeping in them, Amy, all those bloody units. Mike looks up in greeting from his cup of tea. Says to me hallo. Says to me I'm quite the stranger. Says to me I look like I've been in the wars. Gingham cloth on the table – yellow, and a green that's practically kingfisher. Small Welsh dresser with quite a lot of that blue-and-cream striped Devon ware and a small array of Oxo tins. Sylvia is pouring me tea from a big Brown Betty pot, and although there are triangles of toast in a chromium rack, she insists upon making me more. Mike is eating Bran Flakes now, and glancing from time to time at the folded *Daily Telegraph*, which he keeps to the side of his plate. I say to him something along the lines of him being up bright and early, and he laughs and says oh no, we always do, we always are – best part of the day, this: get a lot done, first thing in the morning. And he jerks his thumb in the direction of what look like the casing and internal pieces of a rather old mantel clock spread out over old newspapers on the draining board. Sylvia wags her head and rather theatrically chucks up her eyes towards heaven, before casting across to Mike the merest glance, the quickest gleaming of what could possibly be quite coy affection . . . but who knows? For apart from the anointed couple, who can ever know whatever is slipping between them, in silence? And . . . I . . . really am loving all this. The comfort. More than I can say, or even remotely comprehend. So it kills me, it absolutely kills me to have to spoil it all. To have to broach the dreadful subject.

'So then, Sylvia . . . you haven't . . . actually seen her? I can't tell you how relieved I am about that . . .'

'Oh – we've seen her, Terence. Haven't we, Mike? Oh yes – we've seen her all right. You haven't long missed her, actually. There's marmalade there, if you're partial – it's got bits in, I don't know if you like it with bits in . . .? Butter's in the dish. *Le beurre.*'

'What . . . you mean – she *came* . . .? She actually . . .?'

'Mm. Didn't stay long. Did she, Mike? Said she couldn't stop.'

457

Mike, he was now reading the *Daily Telegraph* with intense concentration.

'Well what did she . . .? You see – I'm really *worried* . . .'

'Yes well you should be. No doubt about it. She's mad, as I said.'

'I . . . know. Well what did she . . .?'

'Well she came in – looking most awfully dishevelled, I have to say: not like Amy at all. Blood all over her arms. Torn dress . . .'

'Mine. It was mine.'

'The dress . . .?'

'Blood. It was mine. See? Bleeding. Actually – it seems to have stopped . . .'

'Well of course I did notice the terrible state you're in, Terence, the moment I opened the door, but I didn't really like to say anything. I thought, poor man: he's got enough on his plate. Anyway . . . she said she had come to kill me. Didn't she, Mike? As promised. And then she showed us this . . . gun. To prove it, I suppose . . .'

'Oh God I'm so *sorry*, Sylvia . . .! So what did you . . .?'

'Well. Didn't know what to do. Did we, Mike? Not the sort of thing one has ever really prepared for. In the end . . . well in the end, we didn't actually have to do anything, because she then went on to say that she had decided that she wasn't, in fact, going to kill me. Didn't she, Mike? That's when Mike, he put down his cricket bat. Then she said something rather curious – said she had murdered a table. It was a table she said, wasn't it Mike . . .? Yes. Well I didn't enquire. Silly, isn't it? With mad people. No point going *into* it. Said she was going to give herself up. Whatever that means. *Je ne sais pas.*'

'Give herself up . . .?'

'Mm. That's what she said. Sounded very . . . she sounded

really very weary by this time. Didn't she, Mike? And even almost normal. And he said, Mike said to her then: do you mean the police, Amy? Or do you want the hospital? Because either way I can run you up. And I was thinking yes well: hospital, fair enough – but I have no idea where you'd go to even *find* a police station, these days . . .'

'I see. So . . . well . . . she's all right, then . . .?'

'Well – as all right as one could expect, I suppose. As all right as a madwoman can be. But listen – can we do anything, Terence? Can I do something about your injury? Really does look rather nasty. I could, I don't know . . . clean it up a bit, at least . . .? What on earth did she *do* to you . . .?'

'Not her, actually. Someone else. Doesn't matter.'

'I . . . see. Well if you say so. But how are the children bearing up in all of this? That's our worry – isn't it, Mike?'

'Well fine when I left them but . . . you know, I think I will have to call them, the police. I mean . . . she's just wandering about London with a *Luger*, for Christ's sake . . .'

'Oh is that what it is? But listen, Terence – where did it *come* from . . .?'

'Germany. Look: maybe I'll go and see them – talk to them properly. Wherever they are. The police. But yes, Sylvia – if you wouldn't mind popping round a bit later? Seeing they're okay? Lizzie and Alexander?'

'Of course. We had already decided we would – hadn't we, Mike? Anything particular they ought to be doing today . . .?'

'I . . . I simply haven't the faintest idea, Sylvia. If you want the truth. I've lost it, all of that. I just don't know . . .'

'Poor Terence. Oh dear. It's all gone a little bit wrong for you, hasn't it? All the beauty, all around you. It's all gone a little bit wrong for you . . .'

459

She was smiling weakly – fondly, I think.

'It has, Sylvia. Yes it has.'

I left that house – the comfort – with huge reluctance: more than I can say, or even remotely comprehend. And . . . even as I was walking out of Mike and Sylvia's front garden, I could see that there was a policeman in mine. Wasn't dressed as a policeman – no uniform, but I just knew that that's what he was. These plainclothes people, no one could ever argue that their horrible clothes are anything but plain, but still you always do know. It is a little to do with authority, the right to be there, but rather more down to the unveiled suspicion, if not outright accusation with which they confront quite brazenly and routinely simply everyone they encounter. And, almost unbelievably stupidly on my part – even in the midst of all of this – my first thought was that he might have been there in connection with the dispersal of all the little girls who are silly enough to congregate here . . . except that they don't, not any longer: haven't seen one for a long while, now – yes and naturally I know why: my fault. Well of course it's my fault – but I can't get into all of that, not yet I can't: another, yet another, just one more of my monumental failures, yet to be sifted, if not faced up to. But of course the policeman was there about Amy. It took just ages, all of this. Some of it in the house, more of it down at the station, the bulk of it in a psychiatric hospital; I nearly was fainting from lack of sleep, hunger, anxiety, bewilderment, you name it. And had I known about the weeks and months more of it to come, I might just simply have lain down upon the floor there, and willingly died.

The gist of the initial business however was that Amy, so early that morning, had told a taxi driver to get her immediately to the nearest police station, and the taxi driver – taking just the one look at her – did exactly that. There she presented to the detective on duty a Luger . . . and of course (and why hadn't I thought of this . . .? Why hadn't I been dreading the potential consequences . . .?) the first thing he asked her was where she had got it from. She told him, apparently, that she had found it. Come across it. In the street. The detective then informed her that this was a rare, highly collectible and expensive firearm in very fine condition (and it was, it was – it was all of that, and more: for he had failed to mention its stern and absolute beauty). So, he probed: was she quite *sure* that she had found it? Come across it? In the street? And Amy had said well of course I'm sure! Why do you doubt my word? Do you think that I don't even know my own *mind* . . .? And maybe – who can ever tell? – maybe, at the time, she even believed it. The blood on her arms was duly noted, and she was subjected to a medical examination, whereby it was established that she was quite uninjured, and that the blood – not her group – had emanated from another party. It was further established that a single bullet had been recently discharged from the gun . . . and that is the point when the whole of the inquiry was cranked up into a major investigation. And so when the plainclothes detective in my front garden saw me caked in blood, now gone hard and brown, his eyes . . . they looked as if they were having a party. But there was no bullet in me: I explained that I had foolishly hurt myself with a Black & Decker (which yes I do possess, actually – well a DeWalt, to be specific: very superior, it's a fine design) and that Amy had simply been attempting to help me stem the considerable flow. Not great, I'll allow – but still not too bad for the spur of the moment, no? He didn't actually ask to see the Black & Decker, the DeWalt, which was highly remiss of him, and of course an absolute godsend. Later in the day, I actually cut

461

myself afresh with a Sabatier vegetable knife and smeared some blood all over the jigsaw attachment, just in case a brighter detective happened to pick up on it later.

And no of *course*, Detective-Sergeant, I know nothing of any gun. A *gun* . . .? Amy had a *gun* . . .? I am amazed – where on earth did she get a gun from? Yes sir, he said (his voice as flat as flat): that is what we are attempting to establish. And here's something else: to my extreme relief, no one ever asked me to explain how then, in that case, the Luger came to have all over it several partial though clearly identifiable sets of my finger-prints . . .? No, because astonishingly, Amy – amid all of her distraction – still had had the wit (I learned all this much later) to wipe it down before she handed it over. What can she have been thinking . . .? What had been struggling for clarity amid the blackest tangles of her mind? Something else we'll never know. Among the many partial bits of information I have been able to piece together over the next oh Christ knows how long was that they had presumed the gun to have been stolen from a specialist dealer or collector, maybe here, maybe in Europe, maybe in the United States, but no such theft had been reported – and nor had any murder or gunshot wound where the bullet could be matched to that of the Luger. And as here was no street weapon, as commonly traded by hoods . . . well maybe, they had concluded with enormous reluctance . . . maybe this clearly very disturbed woman had simply found it. Come across it. In the street. They nonetheless continued to question her endlessly, of course, until the doctors had felt forced to intervene. They expressly forbade it, then: said that their patient could be expected to endure no more – but not before the detectives had independently decided to discontinue anyway the entire line of inquiry. A bit in the way that Sylvia had been meaning, I suppose: because it's silly, isn't it? With mad people. No point going *in*to it.

A more or less total mental breakdown: that had been the ultimate diagnosis. Almost certainly brought on by abnormal levels of stress, over an extremely protracted length of time. Well. And I had thought, if I thought of it at all, that all she had been doing was dickering about with getting Alexander's face all over the magazines, while obsessing with his eventually conquering the universe – as well as things even more stupid than that, such as handbags. And so do I feel . . . sorry for her? Well – it's rather hard to say. Knowing the broader truth, viewing the wider picture, as I am uniquely placed to do. I mean . . . one feels . . . one feels . . . well in the abstract, of course, one does feel compassion for any stricken creature, well of course one does. Particularly when once the creature in question was so very undeniably mentally agile and . . . close to me. But Amy . . . she has come so very near to having ruined lives. I suppose not intentionally . . . but still, though: so much damage has been caused. And Amy, she is not mad, I am given to understand, in the sense of being terminally insane. There has been no unearthing of a latent and encroaching illness such as, I don't know . . . schizophrenia, say. She is simply, I am told – this if I am correctly interpreting and paraphrasing the endless earnest jargon and smilingly cautious reassurance – taking a holiday, a long overdue holiday, from the world that has harmed her. And with proper care, soon she will return to us, refreshed and revivified. Uh-huh, I said: and how soon is soon? Ah, they replied: that is rather harder to predict – it varies from individual to individual. And from the insistence of my enquiries, the doctors may easily have construed an eagerness on the part of the husband to have back his wife. To the hearth and home. Yes well

463

– there is none. I cannot conceive of it, having her back. Because how will she . . . be . . .? How can we be expected to . . . live . . .? I simply cannot think of it . . . in any way at all.

And so . . . we wait. Although I don't at all think that's what I'm actually doing, not consciously anyway: I am not waiting. Waiting for what, actually? For everything to return to, oh God . . . 'normal' . . .? Hah – I hardly think so. I am not even dealing with things – not at all 'soldiering on', you know? The time when I could maybe have begun to deal with things, well . . . that is long gone. That was when, exactly . . .? Well maybe around the time when Amy was committed. They don't say that, of course – they don't call it that: committed. But for now, anyway – that's certainly what she is. Everything around that time, well . . . it more or less unravelled – and pretty much unstoppably, so far as I was concerned. Fell apart. Hadn't needed much: already it was well on the way. On the rare occasions when I would open a few token letters . . . or glance at Amy's message box which was listing, I don't know – three hundred unopened emails . . .? I would pluck something out, utterly at random, and yet always it would be filled with outrage, disappointment, even menace. Welshed deals, broken appointments, cancelled photoshoots, interviews, auditions . . . botched and forgotten promises. Long overdue invoices. Lawyers' letters. The bank, they helped me out a bit – because despite Alexander's earnings to date, there was alarmingly little liquid capital, this due to Amy – surprisingly wisely, I suppose – having locked up the bulk of it into a trust fund. So . . . the more appalling and urgent debts were somehow gradually more or less settled, or else the creditors appeased, though only because of this mind-numbing bank loan which I have no idea when, how or if it will ever be repaid.

464

My own work now . . . is completely non-existent. Not only have I been comprehensively overtaken, just as I knew I would have to be . . . but at no point did I make the slightest effort to remain ahead or even abreast of the game, to court my contacts, to concoct and launch the new and big idea. I have no ideas: I barely can tell you the day of the week. And Alexander's career, well . . . that too is now very much in the past, I'm afraid. It is quite over. All due to my passionate and unswerving neglect, of course – though still I find it perfectly appalling and extraordinary the speed by which a boy may be taken up, disproportionately lionised . . . and then just completely abandoned. And he is . . . suffering. I have to acknowledge it. His happy nature, his utter equanimity . . . that quite blissful temperament must have been, I now see it, wholly dependent upon his . . . well: stardom, I suppose. It is gone now, all that. He is normal. Just another boy at school. And he hates it. Hates it. He has become so very sullen, so very silent. If ever he looks at me at all, that look is charged with loathing. He used to ask constantly after his mother. Scream because she was not there. Biting at his clothes and shrieking out his need for her. He doesn't even do that any more.

He didn't at all like Highgate . . . but then he wouldn't have liked anywhere. The headmaster, he told me this. The boys, he explained – and gently, to give him his due – the boys were, um . . . aware of Alexander's alteration in status. And then I told him that it hardly mattered, because anyway the following term simply could not be afforded. He accepted the news with sympathy and a palpable relief: I know that already he saw Alexander's presence at the school to be an unwelcome disruption. God knows where I'll send him now. Back to the old place, I suppose – if they'll have him, no idea. Just nowhere that

465

charges fees, that's all. And the house, our house . . . that's got to go: it's on the market. Which, the estate agents tell me, is sluggish. When I bought the place for some quite stupidly astronomical sum, the market, perfectly naturally, was booming. We'll get something smaller, quite a good deal smaller, and somewhere I suppose quite nasty, with whatever is left, which of course won't be much. And a lot of the treatment that Amy apparently continues to require really very much ought to be dealt with in the private sector, it is repeatedly explained to me, otherwise the wait could in the long term be extremely detrimental. Alas, the BUPA cover that I discovered Amy had in place did not extend to the family in general: it was for Alexander, solely. Well fine, I said: we'll go private, then. I had no idea what these people charge. I have now.

And Sylvia . . . oh my God, without Mike and Sylvia, I honestly do believe that all of us – myself, Alexander and Lizzie – we'd all be just dead in a ditch. And particularly Lizzie – because, oh . . . throughout all this, she had been even more forgotten than ever. But my goodness . . .! How that girl has quite utterly transformed . . . Well I just never would have believed it! No hint at all any more, you know, of any sort of self-loathing – none of that expressionless silence and truly disturbing black introspection. It turned out, you know, that the bulk of the absolutely vile and corrosive messages which apparently she used to receive on her tablet virtually hourly . . . it turned out that the very worst of these . . . she had sent them herself. I . . . did weep, when I heard that. But now – oh heavens . . .! She smiles, she talks, she is beautiful again: she even calls me . . . Daddy. And all of it is down to Sylvia, you know. Amazing. I'm saying it to her, Sylvia, just all of the time – I suppose I'm clinging on to it, really: the only good and positive thing.

466

'Well I've honestly done nothing, Terence. All of it, it's coming from within her; you just can see it. It was always there. Well – you remember it, don't you? When she was very young.'

'I do. My little girl . . .'

'But I agree that it really is quite wonderful to see her blossoming – emerging, the way she is. Such a very pretty girl – I've always thought so. And now that her hair is so lovely and not all over her face, the way she used to have it . . .'

'I know! I know! You can actually see her eyes, her complexion. I know. Oh – I really am so terribly grateful to you, Sylvia.'

'Oh heaven's *sake*, Terence – I do wish you'd stop going on. Now listen to me: there are enough meals in the freezer – lower part, yes? Are you listening to me, Terence? They're in the lower part of the freezer, yes? Enough to see you all through, well – most of the week, anyway. You just have to heat them up – I've written it all down, as usual. And you're all of you coming over to me on Sunday, remember? So you don't have to worry about that. Your shirts are here. And I'll be bringing Lizzie and Alexander's things around this afternoon – all right?'

'Wonderful, Sylvia. I just don't know what I'd do if it weren't for—'

'Don't be silly. Gives me something to do. I like to be active. And I love it, actually, being involved with the children. I seem to be able to, I don't know . . . relate to them, children, in a way I never thought I would. Because . . . well . . . as you know, Terence . . . I never, we never actually had any of our own. Rather regret it. My decision, you know. Poor Mike – he wasn't even consulted on the matter. And then, of course . . . well, any sort of decision was removed from me. Anyway. I don't know if he minds. It could be that he minds most horribly – I've no

467

idea. We've never really spoken about it. Well as I say – too late now. Far too late for talk of that sort. We make our beds and we lie in them, yes? But this – all this, for me . . . well, it's really something of a rebirth, in a sort of a way. A second lease, you know? Which I never thought I'd have, quite frankly. Now – I'll make you some tea, shall I? While I'm here?'

'Oh God no, Sylvia – honestly, you've done quite enough. I know – let me make tea for *you* . . .'

'Mm. Remember what happened last time, Terence . . .?'

'Ah. Yes. I forgot to, um . . .'

'Put the tea in, yes. Look – I'll do it very quickly. But Alexander though, Terence. Still . . .?'

'Yes. Still, I'm afraid. No change there. Oh and it was so very kind of Mike to offer to take him out for the day – and I'm sorry if he was, you know – offended or anything.'

'Oh God no. Mike – skin like a rhinoceros. No, I just thought it sad from Alexander's point of view. He might have enjoyed it, steam engines.'

'Oh . . . it wouldn't have mattered where it was – that's the sadness, really. He just doesn't like to go anywhere.'

'I know. He told me. I said to him: why, Alexander? Why don't you like to go out? He said it was people.'

'People . . .?'

'Mm. The way they don't look at him any more. He just can't stand it, apparently.'

'Christ . . .'

'Well quite.'

'But . . . how can that happen so quickly? I mean . . . it's not as if he was a star of the silent films, or something . . . I mean . . . . it was only a few months ago he was just *everywhere*. How can people . . .?'

'Forget? Well they do. It's the nature of it. Particularly these days, I think. If something isn't constantly dangled in front of people's faces, well . . . in their minds, it just simply ceases to exist.'

'I suppose. Why things like Coca-Cola are advertising all the time, I expect.'

'Oh I really wouldn't know about any of that sort of thing. But Alexander, well . . . I don't know if this therapist I got for him is making any headway or not – I mean, I can't say I'm really aware of any sort of, I don't know – breakthrough, or anything. Are you . . .? No . . . nor I. But we really might have to think about calling in some other people, you know. If nothing . . . improves.'

'I know. Yes . . . I think I do know that. Oh dear . . .'

'Indeed. *Dommage*. But anyway: listen, Terence – I really have to be off. You'll be all right, will you? Got something to get on with, yes?'

'Hm? Oh God yes – fine. I'm fine, Sylvia. Got a call to make, actually. I'm sorry you were never a mother, Sylvia. You really do seem to be a natural, you know.'

'Yes well – there it is. But it's very sweet of you to say so. Right, then. Well I'll leave you to make your phone call. But do always remember that we're right next door, won't you, Terence? If ever you need anything.'

'I will, Sylvia. Bye. And thanks again for, you know – everything.'

Yes . . . got a call to make, actually. But it won't do a blind bit of good, because of course she's right back to not speaking to me. Her – yes of course. Whom I've been trying not to think about, and failing. It's amazing, actually: I can be talking to Sylvia, a barman, Lizzie, Alexander, a barman, a doctor, a barman . . . and still I just lust for K.T. Not even solely her body, but her actual presence, to make me feel whole. But . . . well, K.T, she doesn't understand all of what's been going on. Well how could she, to be fair? I barely can understand, or even believe the half of it, myself. She thinks I'm merely prevaricating. She thinks I'm being what she calls 'the same old Tom'. She said to me that she didn't want to hear another single word about all of my petty domestic problems. My petty domestic problems.

'I'm not your . . . *confidante*, Tom. I was meant to be your *lover* – not your bloody, I don't know . . . *sister*, or something. I don't *want* to be confided in. I don't want to be *told*. A bloody priest in the confessional . . .? That *so* isn't me. I am not in the business, Tom, of trying to solve all of your petty domestic problems just so that you can, I don't know . . . *feel* better. What about . . . me? Hey, Tom? You talk about just everybody bloody else on the planet, but what in Christ's name about *me* . . .?!'

And while my yammering mouth, my useless lips, were scrabbling with the formulation of some or other vaguely ameliorating response to that, my mind and loins still were throbbing with the truth that she had just said the word *lover* . . . and I so simply wanted to fuck her, there and then, with all the great abandon and spilled champagne of the old days.

'Anyway, Tom . . . I've come to a decision. About us.'

'K.T, I really do think we . . .'

'Ought to talk it over before I say anything hasty I might regret, yes I know Tom. But it isn't hasty – of course it isn't. I've been thinking really hard about us and . . .'

'But K.T . . .! I think of . . .'

'Nothing else. Yes I know. You keep on *saying* that, but it's just not true! Is it? Is it, Tom? You're thinking about everyone *but*! And so round and round we go – and I'm just completely fed up with it. Oh Jesus . . . don't tell me I've run out of cigarettes, now . . .'

'I can get you some . . .'

'Don't be . . . *menial*, Tom. You were never *menial* . . .'

'Just . . . trying to help . . .'

'You want to help? Do you, Tom? Do you really want to help me . . .?'

'Well . . .'

'Yes exactly: well. You want to help me – you'd be very happy to help me so long as there's something in it for *you*, right? Yes well there isn't. Not any more. I'm going, Tom. Or at least – you are. And this time for good. I mean it. I just can't go on like this. Not again. And not any longer. That's it, Tom. Final.'

I glanced around her really quite delightful little studio flat in Notting Hill, Portobello really, with a lowering sense of doom. Because as ever, there was something she was not telling me. She meant what she said – you could see it in her eyes – but if all she meant was simply all she had said . . . well then I just know there would be some way or another of turning it around. Sex. Champagne. And not leaving directly afterwards. These would go a pretty fair distance. But . . . as I look with fondness upon the Aalto chaise, the red Magistretti chair and so many other quite beautiful things which would dovetail so very perfectly with mine (those, anyway, that are left to me, subsequent to the murder of my most pure and precious possession, the Saarinen table – and never would I have told K.T of this wanton and cruel destruction, because I really do think that she actually might have wept . . . and when ever would I want such a thing?) . . . but as I take it all in, and for the very last time . . . I feel nothing but the weight of the moment, and the impending suffocation of the next. Because there is something she has not told me. She will, though. And it will not have to be coaxed. She requires termination, and so it will be both absolute, and coming soon . . . and my heart is full of aching.

'Let's be plain. Can we be plain, Tom?'

She did not require an answer, and nor did she receive one.

'You seem . . . I don't know . . . you seem more up to your eyes in all your bloody family – no listen, Tom, for God's sake: just listen to me, because I've got to just *say* this, and then that's the end of it. Your . . . family . . . has taken you over lately like it never has before – and no I don't want to hear any reasons, I don't, I really really *don't*, Tom. Okay? You are not going to leave them. That's completely obvious. I don't suppose there ever was a time, Tom, when you truly were. But now . . . no. It just isn't going to happen. If you were a man, a proper man, you would honestly have told me this – but you just blabber on about your petty domestic problems and some golden distant, oh God – *future* for the two of us that is going to be, oh – just so fucking *glorious*, but Christ knows when or how or bloody *if*. Well it's just no good any more. And . . . I'm pregnant.'

I think, on reflection, that they really have to love it, women, ending a statement with this. In context, it is rarely quite wholly unexpected, and yet always it detonates like a bombshell anyway.

'Well . . .' I tried. 'That's a . . . *good* thing, surely . . .? That's . . . *amazing*, K.T . . .! Because the doctor, all those doctors, they were absolutely positive that . . .'

'Yes I know. Of course I know. It's . . . not bad. It's okay. It's good – it is good. And I think I'm ready for it. But listen, Tom . . .'

'Ah . . .'

'Yes. So you see . . .'

472

'Mm. I do. Well, well.'

'Look – I did *tell* you, Tom! I've always been *honest* about it. I *married* him, didn't I? I *married* him . . .'

'You did. You did indeed. During the time I was stupid enough to be without you. And so . . . well what, then . . .? He is to continue to have and to hold you – that right? Better or worse?'

'Better. It will be better. *Got* to be better . . .'

'Uh-huh. Right, then. Well. That's that. That is . . . the end of me.'

'Oh don't be so ridiculously melodramatic, Tom! Of course it's not the *end* of you. You've got . . . well – you've got what you always, no matter what you said . . . what you always seemed to need to cling on to. You've got your . . . family.'

'If you say so, K.T. But one thing you must see – you just must. This . . . Bloke . . .'

'Guy. His name is Guy. Jesus . . .'

'Whatever his name is, this man . . . he has absolutely no . . .'

'Style? That what you were going to say? Well maybe not – maybe not, in our sense. But there are other things, Tom. Maybe it's time for you to learn that. There are other things in life apart from *style* . . .'

There are . . .? Well yes I suppose there are. Can't actually think of any, not just at the moment I can't. Not in my bloody life, anyway. And *style* . . .? Christ: I don't even have that any more. Can't even remember how it *goes*. K.T . . .? Well despite all that – and she can hardly have been clearer, you'd think – still I continue to ring her. Leave messages – alternately craven, and demented. She never calls back. She never will. I do know that. Yet still, every time the phone rings, I rush towards it, my throat just choked with all that can be mustered of my sore and battered love, together with a hope beyond stupid. And one time quite

473

recently, having suffered the crush, as usual, of hearing a voice that wasn't hers . . . I registered only after a severely disjointed sentence or two that the woman on the line . . . well it was Dolly, of all people. Virtually forgotten her existence. Was enquiring after Amy – said that Amy had been on her mind since she had glimpsed her in the street really very recently (though it can't have been really very recently) and was concerned for her well-being (I am, naturally, paraphrasing here – could never seek to emulate Dolly's perfectly extraordinary vernacular, which I had been stoically attempting to decipher, doubtless with variable success). She couldn't, she said, seem to be able to get through to Amy on her mobile. Which was hardly a surprise: she had had three of them, Amy, I discovered – and eventually I just threw them all away: it seemed the simplest option, really – rather than even attempt to tolerate their incessant and discordant warbling. So I had muttered to Dolly some damn thing or other – brief, wholly non-committal – and just as I was assuming she would then just ring off, crawl away, die somewhere quietly . . . she said she would really appreciate a word, Terry, and could we maybe possibly meet? What . . . with *me*, Dolly . . .? Are you *sure* about that . . .? Apparently she was. Well – last person in the world I could be expected to cope with, I should have said . . . but she did go on and on in that awful voice she's got, and when people go on and on at me, I do tend to end up saying yes. She suggested some or other coffee place which I'd never heard of – but I can't anyway be bothered with it, going out, not really, so I said to her well look here, Dolly . . . if you really think you have to, why don't you come round to the house . . .? For . . . I don't know . . . tea, or something . . .? And, I had added – wholly automatically – it's Terence, actually. She said yeh cool Terry, *Terence* – that would be luvverly. Christ.

474

And so I continue to be . . . in mourning. I am in mourning for all that is lost to me. K.T . . . well of course, K.T: the love of my life, and now she is gone from me. Again. She is to mother a child with her husband, Bloke. A bloody *Geordie*, of all things – can barely believe it of K.T: how can she seriously even contemplate living with that *noise* for the rest of her life . . .? Though, I can only suppose, she will try to make a go of it with him again. Seeking that 'stability', as she called it, that had always eluded her. Maybe surrendering her really quite delightful little studio flat in Notting Hill, Portobello really, and returning to the house in Earl's Court: more suitable, she might be thinking, for the raising of a child. Something the two of us had been quite convinced for all those years could simply never happen. And what though, I wonder, if it had been mine . . .? Yeh well: isn't. But listen: how can you overcome all of that . . .? Well you can't. Just can't. And then there's the sex: not just me not having it – although Jesus, that's very much more than terrible enough – but the vivid and searing, and therefore unstoppable, imaginings of her, my K.T . . . cavorting with Bloke . . .! And . . . is it better with him? Well is it? Amazing she was never completely pulverised by the sheer and towering bulk and tonnage of the man: he's built like a bloody house extension. The other awful thing . . . knowing me as I do . . . is that before too long I shall encounter a woman. A random woman. Who will look good. But apart from that, it could be just anyone. And – just as I did with the laughable Portia – I shall convince myself that here is love: the big, true thing. And so . . . just what sort of a colossal fool shall I make of myself this time? And how many more such pitiable and shame-inducing occasions still will lurk in the offing? How much ballast does it take? To fill the chasm, left by K.T . . .?

475

Then there's my table. Oh yes – people can laugh, but it was more than that to me, so very much more than just a table. That's why Amy murdered it, you see: for remarkably, she did possess that insight. I have kept the pieces. Would never get another . . . and not only because I couldn't even begin to afford it. And my Luger. I could have been killed, because of that gun. And I could have killed with it, too. Not to say spent many years in prison simply for having owned the thing. And so I regret ever having acquired it then, do I? No. Oh no. I'd buy another right this minute. I loved it. I love all of my things. All right . . . but do I see myself to have been pretentious and shallow, for having invested such illusory power and spurious importance into a clutch of inanimate objects and a wardrobe full of clothes, to the detriment, if not annihilation, of just everything else that I had ever possessed . . .? No. I don't. And so if there is a moral to be learned here . . . well then it stubbornly eludes me. I still feel exactly the same about just all of it . . . and despite the resulting mess of quite literally every single thing I have ever touched, I still would do it again. All I want is . . . everything . . . restored to me. And now . . . I am suddenly reminded of what that fellow had said to me. The fellow I ran into in the street . . .? The one I didn't know? Who asked me how I *was* . . .? What had been going *on* with me . . .? Just as well, don't you think? That I didn't flood him with the answers he was pretending to be after. Slam him square between the eyes with the whole unholy lot. Because Jesus: where to even begin with it . . .

Bit funny, being sat here in Amy's house, and Amy ain't at home. Not never happened before. Terry, he off making me some tea. I say to him I don't really want it, like he don't have to go to no bother, but he gone and done it anyway. So I looking about me. Trying to, like – keep it together, you know? All I can do, these days – because I been ever so knocked, just can't tell you. Yeh – I'm like . . . not in a good place? It Zen, what I trying to do. Read it in a magazine. Were actually reading about boob jobs because I were thinking if I get one of them done on me it might help me get a job. Because I don't know what to do. Can't go back to the bleeding Marriott, can I? What – go crawling to that bastard Mumtaz fucker and ask him for my old job back? Don't hardly think so. And anyway – I couldn't do it. Just couldn't. Not after all what I see. Not after all what I done. I gone over the other side. I knows what it like to live within the realm of sophistication, and there ain't no way I can ever go back.

But I got to get money – money of my own. I used to it. I likes it. I needs it. And Damien, he the same tight-fisted bleeding pig what he always were. So I well and truly stuck, really. And a boob job, I don't know . . . I were thinking it might be helping me get a job in one of them swanky nightclubs or whatever up West. Least I gets to drink champagne again. Score a couple lines. Wasn't thinking no further than just a hostess, though . . . yeh but you never knows, does you really? I a living wossname to that. What can like turn up. Yeh and then I gone off of the new-boobs idea on account of I couldn't never of explained none of it to Damien. And also . . . I don't got the money no more. All that money what I were earning, well it's just sort of went, somehow. Ain't hard to do. Still and all, though – I can't sort of really work it out, because Jimmy . . . he give me everything really, never was wanting for nothing . . . but still all the cash I got, it just sort of disappeared. Can't hardly under-stand it. And that last two grand what Richard bung me, well . . .

few days after I were still in shock, so I were scoring off of Jimmy's dealer real heavy: caning it with the coke, I were – swigging champagne from Lidl out the neck, weren't even cold: just so bleeding out of it. And them blackouts, I were getting them more and more, and real bad: could be there something wrong with me. One time I gone over, bathroom it were, I give my head one hell of a crack on the bog brush, and that shake me up, I can tell you: well it ain't too good, no matter what way you looks at it. I says to Damien I got the flu. He just nod like what he always do and then he turn up after his work with a bunch of daffs and a packet of Lemsip, stupid sod. Yeh and then word must of got out because the dealer, he don't take my calls no more. Yeh and it were the same with Richard and Jimmy, what I were ringing all of the time: numbers changed, must of been. Dead noise on the phone. Gone.

And in this magazine, see, there were a piece about Zen. Some Chink or Nip bloke he is. What you does is, you takes it one day at a time. Concentrate real hard on what you doing and what going on right now, yeh? And you tries to focus and enjoy it, if you can. Don't go dreading tomorrow on account of tomorrow, it coming down anyway. So now I just sitting here in Amy's front room, and I trying my real hardest to do that. Not to think about nothing else. And it a nice room, ever so posh. I thought with Amy out the way, Terry might of let it go a bit – but nah: ever so clean and tidy. He maybe got a woman what does. Because Terry and Amy, they so loaded – they always was. And Alexander . . . I got to say I don't see him no more in all of the magazines what I'm back to buying religious, but ain't he meant to be being a movie star soon, or something? So they just got to be rolling in it, lucky sods. And he come in now, Terry – with all a tray, look, and a proper teapot on it: not just couple

478

teabags hanging out of West Ham mugs, like what Damien would of done it, if he done it at all. And as he set it down, he say to me, Terry: You looking very nice, Dolly. You looking well, Dolly. How nice to see you again, Dolly. Only being polite, yeh I know – gentlemen, they does it automatic: and anyway, Terry and me, we ain't hardly said two words to one another in the past, but still I loves to hear it. Because I don't never get none, compliments, not no more. And I made an effort today – first time in hell of a while. Got on that Armani and the Fendi bag and the Ferragamo shoes . . . because they all I got left of the decent stuff, the proper stuff – not all of the knock-offs and Primark tat what I used to wear before: can't even look at all of that now. Yeh because I were dumped, right, with just the clothes what I were stood up in. And even them, you can believe it – I got a call saying I got to give them back . . .! I says to who-ever it were what rung me to just go and fuck off, yeh? But all of them other clothes, and the bags and the scarves and the watches and bloody hell the shoes . . . oh God I missing them so bleeding much. I weeps over them, they was all so beautiful – and that how they made me feel, you know? Beautiful – just beautiful. And that bastard Richard – he said to me they was mine! That evening, that evening after all of that posh dinner what we had – he show me them, don't he? Yeh – and he say to me they was mine! A gift, is what he say . . .! From him to bleeding me! Lying bastard. And now 'Samantha', yeh . . . she be wearing them now. No accident, were it? Ay? That she were my size – perfect 10, and 5 for the shoes? Nah. Richard, he go shopping for good-looking girls what is all the same size and wants a bit of money, no questions asked. And . . . I never did, did I? Ask no questions. Like what it were that happen to the girl before. Like what were in them packages. Like where all of

479

the money come from. Nah. Never asked no questions. Because I never wanted no bloody answers. I got off lucky, one way. Could of end up in Holloway. Make me shiver, when I thinks of it. Yeh so anyway – she wants to enjoy it while she can, 'Samantha' . . . on account of any day now, she put a foot wrong, and she be on the slag heap, and all.

'So Amy all right then, is she? It ever so good of you to go to all of this bother, Terry. Ever so grateful, but you really shouldn't of, you know . . .'

'No trouble at all, Dolly. Pleasure. And it's Terence – remember?'

'Yeh – Terence. Sorry. Tea's lovely. You growing a beard, or something . . .?'

'Hm . . .? Oh . . . no. Just haven't . . . shaved for a bit, that's all.'

'Okay. Suits you. Well . . . I don't know, actually. And so Amy? All right?'

'Well – on the mend, you know. Just been overdoing it a bit, that's all. You know Amy . . .! Biscuit, would you like . . .?'

'Ooh – chocolate. What's inside of them?'

'I . . . I haven't the faintest idea. I didn't actually, um . . . Sylvia next door – you remember Sylvia? Met Mike and Sylvia, have you? Can't remember. You must have done. Anyway, Sylvia – she, um . . . she's been helping me out a little bit, you know. While Amy's away. Children, and so forth.'

'Yeh I knows Sylvia, course I does. Well that nice, ain't it? Neighbours helping out, like? Real nice.'

'Yes. So anyway, Dolly – what was it you, uh . . .?'

'Ay? What was what?'

'Well . . . you wanted to, um . . . didn't you? Want a word? Why you're here?'

480

'Oh yeh. Yeh. Yeh course. Well it were Amy, really. Worried for her, you know? From when I seed her, like. Just sort of wandering. And it were ever so early in the morning.'

'Yes. Well she likes to do that, time to time. Take an early walk.'

Yes. In the freezing dawn, carrying a Luger. Having attacked her husband, still fresh from having murdered his table. Saying to her next-door neighbour that she intends to kill her, then explaining that she doesn't in fact intend to kill her, and soon after that taking a taxi to the police station in order to surrender the gun, together with all that was remaining of her tattered sanity. Yes. She likes to do that, time to time.

'Yeh well so long as she okay.'

'Soon will be. Right as rain. I'll pass on your, um . . .'

'Oh yeh do. When you sees her, like. Yeh – tell I were, er – yeh. Here – reckon she like a visit?'

'No . . .! Um – that is to say . . . she won't really be there for very much longer, you know, so it would be rather silly, really. And I go to see her every day, so . . .'

'Yeh righto, then. You knows best.'

'So . . . another biscuit, possibly? And then if that's all, Dolly, I'm afraid I really do have to be . . .'

'Yeh well it not quite all actually, Terry. Terence, sorry – can't never get it, can I? It just that, well – I got this real good job at the moment, don't know if you heard, or anything . . .? It real good. Travel. Lots of money . . .'

'No, I . . . well that's very good news, Dolly. Congratulations.'

'Yeh. It just that this month, well – them bloody computers . . .! You know? Total screw-up, basically – you know what I meaning? So all what are owed to me ain't gone into my wossname, see . . . and well look, it ever so embarrassing and everything, Terry, but I were wondering if you might be able to

481

sort of sub me few quid, you know? In the meantime, like – just till I gets sort of together, yeh? Get it back to you ever so quick, of course – just as soon as they sorts out all of the wossnames. What . . .? What is it . . .? What I said . . .? Why you laughing, Terry . . .? What I said that so funny . . .?'

'Oh . . . forgive me Dolly, please. No no – I'm just laughing because as soon as you told me about this highly paid job of yours, it immediately crossed my mind that you might be in a position to sub *me* a few quid, that's all . . .! Silly . . .! No, you see Dolly – I tell you this in all confidence only because you are a friend of Amy's, as it were . . . but what with one thing and another, just lately . . . well, we're not quite as flush as we used to be, I'm afraid. Far from it, actually. School fees. Hospital bills. Shan't go into it all . . . but the truth of the matter is, I am completely unable to help you, you see. Terribly sorry, but there it is, I'm afraid . . .'

'Oh. Right. Yeh I get you. Oh well look – I sorry to hear of that. I mean – don't you worry about me, nor nothing: I be all right, yeh course. It only temporary. Well look, Terry – I ever so sorry to of bothered you. Shouldn't never have said nothing in the first place . . .'

'No no, Dolly. Not at all. Just so long as you understand . . . the position. I mean to say, in any other circumstance, I should of course have been delighted to, um . . .'

'Yeh. Course. Well thanks ever so much for that, Terry. Oh blimey – that the time . . .? I really got to, er . . .'

'Yes well me too, actually. So, Dolly – thank you so much for, um . . . dropping by.'

'Yeh. No. Thank *you*, Terry. And . . . sorry, yeh?'

'No need to be. I'll see you out. And it's *Terence*, actually . . .'

482

Yeh so he done that, seed me out, and I says to him well goodbye then, Terry. Yeh – because I'm fucked if I going to call him *Terence*, it such a poncey name anyway. I wouldn't mind if he never gone *on* about it all of the time, Jesus. And what about all of that crap about him and Amy? They's what? Hard up? Yeh right. Amy and Terry and that bloody Boy Wonder – hard up? Yeh right. I would of liked it better if he just gone and told me to piss off out of it. Bugger about the money, though. I were feeling pretty sure he bung me a ton, no trouble. If only to get shot of me. Because I bloody penniless, you want the truth. Can't hardly understand it. See, I so used to taxis, and decent nosh and buying all of the perfume and make-up . . . and I know I blowed a fucking fortune on the powder and the booze, and I had to pay for eight bleeding elocution classes what I never turn up to . . . and what a bloody stupid idea that were – because face it, yeh? I ain't never going to be talking like no lady, not in a million bleeding year – but apart from that I just got some La Perla underwear, shocking pink and ever so lovely, it make me feel good about myself inside, you know? And that pair of boots – I got a pair of boots yeh, real nice, but they only Russell & Bromley so I just don't get where the whole of the two grand gone, but it gone. And even my lovely Rolex, what I were ever so fond of . . . hocked it down the Kentish Town Cash Convertors. And what they give me, well . . . that gone and all. Can't hardly understand it.

And . . . I needs a fix, I needs it real bad – the only thing what banging in my head. It were ever such a effort just to stay sitting on Terry's settee and drinking his sodding tea which were some sort of Chinky muck instead of climbing up the fucking curtains. And then when he say no to me, I could of rip out his throat, if he only knowed it. So . . . it got to be down to Damien, then. Got to get some money out of Damien, yeh . . . and trouble is, I know I should be doing all of the sweet talk, yeh I do know that . . . but I don't reckon I going to, on account of I don't reckon I can. Should be laughing at his useless jokes, he ever leave off of the Xbox long enough to be making any useless jokes. Blow job, maybe, what I now know how to do – but he never seem bothered about none of that no more, which were a relief, if I'm honest. Because after all of what Jimmy and me was up to, I come home, I were right knackered, telling you. I thinks of it, all of that – my time with Jimmy Blue Eyes. Been trying to hate him, but it don't work. Richard and all, really. I knows they was just using me like a mule – I knows all of that: I ain't stupid. But I using them and all, weren't I? Ay? To get what I want, like. And then I goes and falls in love with Jimmy, like what I suppose all of the girls does – and I knows I were just a good lay to him. Well – he say it, didn't he? Right in front my face. Yeh but still . . . when I old and looking all back on it, like – them is going to be the best days of my life. Blowed everything before it right out the water . . . and there ain't nothing coming up what going to top it, nor even come close. So I don't regret none of it, not a bleeding minute – why would I? And if I ever gets an offer like it from some other beautiful boy, I just takes it, I knows I will. But funny thing is . . . I been feeling lately I just got to tell Damien I been fooling about. Not the whole of it, just like the Jimmy and me bit. Thought of it days back, and the feeling, it just growed and growed. Stupid, I knows it stupid. Won't do me no good. Sure ain't going to do him no good. I just feels I got to. Won't even make me feel no better, neither. Just think I got to. Yeh – and if it money I wanting off of him, it a bloody funny way of going about it, yeh I do know that. But still. It mad – but I just feels I got to. Can't explain.

So I just had couple shots of vodka stirred in with the last of the flat champagne what are all I got left. It don't do what a couple lines would of done, but it do quiet me down a bit. Kenny in bed. Oh Gawd – Kenny. Ain't give him no mind for how long? Still and all though, whenever I does see him – shoving couple fish fingers at him, wiping his snotty nose – he still seem just a bleeding idiot, really speaking. Just all moony-faced and thick, like his father. Telling you: them two – I don't know. Well anyway – I just give Damien a Carling, and I says to him don't go playing no stupid game now Damien, on account of I wants to talk to you, yeh? Something I needing to tell you, okay?

'It going to take long . . .?'

'It take as long as it take. Bleeding hell, Damien . . .!'

'Yeh well get on with it, then.'

'Well . . . it, like . . . sensitive. Yeh? I wants to talk to you about . . . something what didn't ought to of happened. Something . . . not right.'

'Yeh . . .?'

'Yeh. A, like . . . relationship, okay? Between two people what shouldn't of been having it. Because . . . it not right. Know what I saying . . .?'

'Oh God, Dolly . . .'

'Yeh well. It gone and happened. What's done is done. But it got to be said. We got to, like . . . talk it through. Confront our demons. Feel one another's pain.'

'Bloody hell, Dolly . . . what can I say to you . . .?'

'Yeh well . . .'

'I mean . . . I ever so sorry . . .!'

'Ay. . .?'

'About it all. I never thought you find out about it, nor

485

nothing . . .! How you find out about it? It ain't nothing serious, Dolly – you got to believe that . . .! She . . . she don't mean nothing to me . . . honest, Dolly – it were nothing. I never plan it. It just come up out the blue, like, when I service her Mazda. And, like – you, you was never here, was you? See? But you got to believe it when I says she just don't mean nothing to me . . .! It were just a . . .well, sort of a – thing, you know . . .?'

And I looks at him. I just bleeding looks at him. And I just thinking oh fucking hell: I just so do not *believe* this . . .! I sat here – trying to, like, just keep all of my shit together and thinking I doing the right thing by making a clean wossname of it, and it turn out all the time I were away, bleeding Damien here, he been banging some slag in the garage . . .! Yeh – and it weren't just her Mazda what he were servicing, neither. Well I just had it. That's all. I just had the bleeding lot of it, now. And Zen . . . I don't really reckon that Zen are going to cut it, somehow. What do Zen know, stupid bloody sod: can't think why he so bloody famous in the first place. And Christ . . . I just screaming for a fix, mad for it now. Same time . . . I going all dizzy. I knows this feeling: next come one of them bleeding blackouts . . .

It's not too bad here, actually . . . really rather pleasant, on the whole. The room is clean and airy, the nurses always smiling. I cannot imagine how much it can be costing, but . . . well, the money, the money side of things, that has gone all rather wrong, of course. The reverse of what I intended. Together with a great deal else. Terence visits me every morning, I cannot imagine why. We hardly speak, and he doesn't stay for long. I do not ask him how he is managing at home . . . and he doesn't seem inclined to tell me. I certainly do not enquire after . . . people. And he in turn is kind enough, at least, to volunteer nothing. It may be that he is revelling under the illusion that the rigours of my illness have robbed me of all memory. Though I amply recall having been so very starkly confronted by his criminal and highly probably long-held enthusiasm and longing for prepubescent girls: something that I will always have to know. It could be he comes merely to reassure himself that still I am elsewhere, and captive, I couldn't say.

Anyway, he has just this moment left, having arranged for me some white anemones, of course while tutting over the nastiness of the vase . . . and so now I can relax. For it really is a considerable strain, you know, having always to remember to appear to be constantly upon the brink of something black and wild and deeper. Because I am not mad, of course I'm not. There were a few occasions when I maybe might have been, or anyway thereabouts . . . but they are blurred within my memory, this very largely down to my thrice daily intake of pills, I expect . . . but certainly there have been both words and actions over which I could exercise little control. Never *no* control, however. I am fully aware that the, um . . . what is it that they say? Call it . . .? Oh yes, I know: that the balance of my mind, it has been disturbed. Disturbed, oh yes, no doubt at all about that – but never for a moment completely off kilter, which I do believe to be rather important.

I could have knowingly plummeted, wild-eyed and headlong into the pumping heart of the illness – abandoned myself utterly to being caressingly enveloped and then immediately swallowed whole by a clamouring insanity. But I held back. Otherwise I would have killed so very many people. Willy Ouch, most obviously . . . had I not that afternoon been talking to someone else entirely: there, I confess, was a worrying moment. Dolly . . . well I might very easily have shot her, Dolly, when I met her in the street, so early that morning – because her very existence, actually, had been rather annoying me for quite some time. It was her clothes that saved her. Cannot imagine how she came to have them, such fine and beautiful clothes . . . maybe she has turned to prostitution, who can say? But certainly it was the perfect Armani, the Fendi, the Ferragamo that rescued her: I couldn't bear to be responsible for having ruined such clothes. Finally, to see Dolly actually exercising just a modicum of style, well well. Or *stoyal*, as she would have it. Then there was Sylvia. Well I would have – her I would have killed . . . but when finally I had gone round there expressly to do so . . . well Mike, he was there as well, you see, and . . . I don't know: I not only no longer had the stomach for it, but suddenly I did feel so very terribly tired. Wanted to finish it. Wanted rest. Wanted to leave and be left alone. So I did hold back, you see – I did possess that capacity. Just as I am holding back now from a complete and rapid recovery. I could do this: I could be quite well within the twinkling of a moment. But I am not ready for all that then I would be forced to confront. My marriage, of course, which is no longer. Terence and Lizzie – his 'little girl', as he always called her – I am sure that now, together, they can find true happiness. And then there is . . . my failure, really. My terrible failure in all that I set out to achieve. But for a while, a long while . . . I really had been doing so terribly well.

Terence, I am sure, still might feel that I was being cruel to the boy. His word. But he never ever saw, Terence – and nor did Lizzie, Lizzie was exactly the same – just how very much Alexander *thrived* upon it all. I cannot think – this is what I just can't bring myself to think about – how now he must be feeling. Without his mother. Without me there. To love him. But I shall return: and I do believe that in his heart, Alexander will know this. He will understand – because always, we had a mental rapport – and so he will completely understand that here is but a temporary abeyance, a simple pause, no more. For I shall return, refreshed and determined – more determined than ever to secure for Alexander his rightful and towering position in the world. We shall ... abscond, Alexander and I: custody of the child, it will be mine. And then together – the two of us, as ever – we shall conquer, oh ... just everything and everyone, quite as was intended. Because that ... it is, it always has been ... our destiny. And never mind all that Terence very cruelly kept on telling and telling me – yes because it was *he* who was cruel, it was *he*, not I – of course it was never remotely my intention to hurt the boy. Damage him: that's what Terence said – he said I would damage him. And sometimes ... days ago ... could be weeks, because time, it conjures very little substance here ... I used even to wonder whether I had done such a thing. But no: I now see quite clearly that it was all of it very good for him, well of course it was, of course: I am utterly convinced of that. Terence, he had it wrong. He had it all the other way about. For I have given everything, selflessly devoted all that there was of my life to doing all I could to ensure for Alexander a bright and maybe, yes – even dizzying future. And that was wrong, was it? That was a bad thing for a loving mother to do for her only son, is that what you are thinking? Simply to make sure that the world, the whole wide world would know of his brilliance? This is *cruel* ...? This is hurting the boy? *Damaging* him ...? Please. I hardly think so. Because look: I only ever wanted to be nice.